DAN

Eva Stachniak was born in Wroclaw, Poland. She emigrated to Canada in 1981, on scholarship to McGill University in Montreal. In Poland she taught English Literature at the University of Wroclaw. Her first short story appeared in the *Antigonish Review* in 1994. Her acclaimed debut novel, *Necessary Lies*, won the Amazon.com/*Books in Canada* First Novel Award. A communications professor at Sheridan College in Oakville, Ontario, Eva Stachniak lives in Toronto and is working on her third novel.

Visit www.AuthorTracker.co.uk for exclusive information on Eva Stachniak.

By the same author

Necessary Lies

EVA STACHNIAK

Dancing with Kings

HarperCollins*Publishers*
77–85 Fulham Palace Road,
Hammersmith, London W6 8JB

www.harpercollins.co.uk

Published in hardback as *Garden of Venus*
by HarperCollins*Publishers* 2005

This paperback edition published by
HarperCollins*Publishers* 2006
1

A catalogue record for this book
is available from the British Library

ISBN-13 978 0 00 718045 5

For Zbyszek

DANCING WITH KINGS

PART ONE

From Mes amours intimes avec la belle Phanariote

Bursa – where our story so humbly begins – a town spreading at the feet of Moundagnà or Mount Olympus is but a day's journey from Istanbul. Mars, Neptune, and Venus had once been worshipped there, and they could still lay their claims to this land on account of the valiant warriors hailing from the Greek Empire and Byzantium, on account of sailors recruited here, and on account of modern Lais and Phrynes whose presence adorns the cafes and bawdyhouses of Istanbul. The worshippers of the Love goddess, I hasten to add, are of both sexes, for the boys ministering to the desires of the Byzantines are as beautiful here as the girls.

Beholding the multitude of beautiful faces in this mountainous and healthy region, one is tempted to say that, for such delightful fruit to be so plentiful, Aphrodite, sailing in her conch from Cytera to Paphos, must have unloaded in this land some of her precious cargo, her aphros, that essence of pleasure and beauty, the source of our very existence. For this region has always supplied the world with superior talents from the realm of Venus, natural talents capable, with little effort, of conquering the hearts of courtiers and kings. Is this a wonder that, in Istanbul, the terms 'a girl from Moundagnà' and 'a prosperous girl providing fanciful pleasure' have become synonymous?

In this town of Bursa, la belle Phanariote was born in the year of 1760, and very ordinary blood flows in her veins for she is the daughter of a cattle trader and among her relatives are many a ferryman, craftsman, and a shopkeeper. * *Her childhood was spent in the fields and meadows surrounding her native town where she led that free and naïve existence so much praised by some philosophers of yesterday.*

* So much for the rumours of her descent from Pantalis Maurocordato, her kinship with the former rulers of Byzantium!

BERLIN, 1822:

Water

Rosalia

In the end it fell to Rosalia to make sure that the imminent departure of Countess Sophie Potocka (accompanied by her daughter, Countess Olga Potocka, and companion Mademoiselle Rosalia Romanowicz) via Paris to the town of Spa for her prescribed water cure – had been announced three times in the *Petersburg Gazette*. Only then the passports could be collected and the *padrogna* – the permission to hire horses on the way – be signed by the Governor General.

The countess left St Petersburg on 12th July, 1822, (July 1st in the Russian style). 'On Paris, I insist with utmost gravity,' Dr Horn said – his voice raised, as if defending himself and not offering medical advice – 'French surgeons are far superior, even to the English.' Before departure, everyone, including the servants, sat around the breakfast table to pray for a safe journey. They had already been to confession, asked forgiveness for their sins from everyone in the household, and exchanged parting gifts with those who would be left behind, sashes with sweet-smelling lavender, ribbons, holy pictures, and boxes lined with birch bark.

The morning was cold and wet, but, thankfully, the thunderstorm had ended and there was no more talk of omens, in spite of Marusya's dream about her teeth falling out and making a clunking sound as they scattered on the marble floor of the hall. ('Why didn't you stop this foolish talk,' Olga snapped, as if Rosalia could have.)

The kitchen carriage left first, with provisions, cooking utensils and a collapsible table, since the inns en route with their smutty ceilings and walls grown shiny from the rubbings of customers' backs were not to be trusted. Two more carriages were packed with luggage, one carrying a trunk that opened to convert into a bedstead with pillows, so that the countess could rest during the journey.

Rosalia may have come to St Petersburg as the countess's companion, but it wasn't long before the timely administration of compresses and salves became more important than keeping up with the daily correspondence, greeting guests, or reading aloud after dinner. *Which*, as Aunt Antonia triumphantly pointed out in one of her many letters *was not that hard to foresee*.

Aunt Antonia, who liked to remind Rosalia that she was her *only* living relative and, therefore, entitled to such straightforward expressions of concern, might have forgiven Jakub Romanowicz for marrying a penniless Jewess only to die and leave his wife and child on *her* doorstep, but she could not forgive Maria Romanowicz for writing to Countess Potocka and *begging* her to take care of her only child. In Zierniki, the family estate near Poznań, a room was waiting for Rosalia. A room overlooking the orchard, with an iron bed the maids washed with scalding water each spring. A room where her mother's old dresser still stood, its drawers smelling of dried rosemary and mint to keep the mice away.

There had been many times on this long journey when Rosalia pleaded with the countess to stop. The sick needed peace to regain strength and how was she to assure these precious moments of peace with all the packing, unpacking, and constant ordering of vats of boiling water (the grime of the inns had to be washed before the beds could be brought in). She too had her limits, and her nerves were strained to the utmost with this constant migration of coffers, crates, and trunks, the nicks and bruises of carelessness and neglect, futile searches for what should have been there and wasn't. (The embroidered scarves and votive lights for the holy icon of St Nicholas had been left behind three times in a row and a servant on horseback had to be sent back to retrieve them.) Through August and September they had travelled for not more than a few hours daily, usually from four until ten in the morning, to avoid the heat, and then, perhaps, for two more hours in the afternoon. Often, in spite of the hot-water compresses Dr Horn had prescribed for the journey, the countess was in too much pain to travel at all.

It was already the beginning of October when they reached Berlin where Graf Alfred von Haefen put a stop to the nonsense of further travel. The Graf met the countess at the city gates and did not even try to hide his horror at the sight of her. 'I forbid you to spend another hour in this,' he said, pointing at the Potocki's carriage. 'My ears shall remain deaf to all objections. You'll have to submit to a man's judgement. This is the price of friendship.' His Berlin palace would be at their disposal and so would be his own personal physician, Doctor Ignacy Bolecki. Bolecki, one of the best doctors in Berlin, was a Pole but had been trained in Paris. After assuring himself that the drivers understood his directions and would not attempt to take the wrong turn at the first junction – on moonlit nights oil lamps were put out to conserve fuel and that made the sign of Under the Golden Goose tavern where the right turn had to be taken barely visible

– the Graf said to no one in particular that if an operation were truly necessary, a French surgeon would be sent for immediately.

By the time their carriage rolled into Graf von Haefen's courtyard, the party was greatly reduced in numbers. Five servants with the kitchen carriage were sent back to the countess's Ukrainian palace at Uman, leaving Rosalia with only two maids, Olena and Marusya, Agaphya, the cook, and Pietka, the groom. Mademoiselle Collard, the French lady's maid had left in Poznań without as much as giving notice. 'I have to look after myself,' she said to Rosalia before leaving. 'If I don't, who else will?' Always eager to question the refinement of Countess Potocka's tastes, she did not fail to remind Rosalia that the white Utrecht velvet upholstery and green morocco-leather seats of the Potocki carriage had been chosen by Countess Josephine, the Count's previous wife.

'You are my prisoner, *mon ange*,' Graf von Haefen said, opening the carriage door to help the countess step out into the chair that was waiting already, kissing her hand twice and holding it to his heart, 'and there is nothing you can do about it.'

To Rosalia's relief, her mistress did not protest. By the time the countess was resting upstairs, awaiting the final arrangements of her sick room, their journey, she calculated, had lasted three months, three days, and five hours.

Sophie

The heat has abated. It is September, the month of the smallpox. Her time now, *Mana* says. She is old enough and she will not be alone. Six of her cousins will have it too.

'Help yourself so God can help you,' Mana says.

In her hand Sophie is holding her *mati*, a blue stone,

one of her birth presents. It has a black eye in its centre, and – like the red ribbon in Mana's hair – it wards off the evil eye, human malice and the power of jealousy. Every time Maria Glavani hears that her daughter is growing up to be a beauty, she spits three times on the ground.

'My precious Dou-Dou.'

Dou-Dou means a small parrot. A pleasing chirping bird everyone likes, everyone wants to touch and pet. Her true name is Sophie, or Sophitza. It means wisdom.

Mana cooks for three days so that there is enough food for the party: roasts slices of eggplant and marinates them in oil and lemon juice; cooks her best lamb ragout spiced with coriander. The meat will be tender enough to melt even in toothless mouths, and simmering for a long time, it absorbs the fragrance of spices. There is a big pot of soup with lentils and cardamom, pilaf sprinkled with cinnamon. And in the earthenware pot that is rarely used, chunks of feta cheese marinate in the best olive oil Mana can afford. Big jugs of country wine stand in the corner, by the window, like fat dwarfs. Strings of quinces and pomegranates, sage, mint, rosemary and savory hang from the beams. The water in the pitcher that greets the visitors at the front door has been drawn fresh from the well and is still cool. The hens are locked in the chicken coop and the goat is tied to the fence.

'We are not beggars yet,' Mana says. Maria Glavani's daughter is not going to go wanting. There will be four kinds of sweet pastry, and baklava soaked with honey is already laid out on the plate with a yellow rooster in it.

Even the thought of such delicacies is a temptation. Dou-Dou has touched just the rim of the plate, but when she wants to lick the tips of her fingers, to savour even the smallest traces of sweetness, Mana stops her. 'You are not an orphan,' she says. 'You have a mother who has taught you how to eat properly.'

The Glavani smallpox party will be remembered in Bursa for the food and the laughter. And for the singing too.

> Rain, rain, dear Virgin,
> Send snow and waters,
> To moisten our vineyards
> And our gardens. . . .

The old woman who has the smallpox brings it in a nutshell. Her name is Agalia and she smells of soap and dried mint. Her own children have long left the house, but every one of her daughters sent for her when the grandchildren were old enough.

'The best smallpox there is,' Agalia assures the mothers and guests with a serious nod of her head and a smile of satisfaction. 'Fresh as the morning bloom.' There is a murmur of consent in the room, followed by sighs of relief. Maria Glavani has chosen well.

Dou-Dou giggles. Diamandi, most favourite of all her cousins, has poked her ribs, having pointed at Agalia's grey hair. She's so thin that her plait looks like a rat's tail.

'You are a happy one,' Agalia says. 'Good. Laughter is like sunshine. It makes everything grow. It makes people love you.'

The children are asked to present their veins. An ancient custom calls for four openings: on the forehead, on each arm and on the breast to mark the sign of the cross. Point to your thigh, Dou-Dou, Mana instructed her, up here. You don't want a scar on your forehead. You don't want anything to spoil your face.

Her cousins will all have the sign of the cross, but Sophie does as her mother had said. She turns around and points to the inside of her left thigh. Agalia hesitates for a split second. Then she rips the vein open and puts as much venom inside as she can fit on the head of her needle. 'It won't hurt,' she mutters, but it does.

Sophie watches Agalia's hands as the old woman takes an empty shell and places it on the wound. Bony hands with freckles, the skin paper thin. Watches as she binds it carefully with a clean strip of cloth.

One by one the children's veins are opened and the venom is put inside while the mothers and the neighbours watch. Sophie saw a few frowns when she did not present her forehead and her arms to be pierced, but her mother's laughter and the plates she fills with her best stew have lightened the mood. The women eat with delight, praising the softness of the lamb, the fragrance of the sauce. Maria Glavani is an excellent cook.

There will be singing and dancing, and secrets will be whispered in low voices so that the children would not hear them. In the courtyard, under the olive tree, the women will drink the young wine and laugh until their throats are hoarse. Mana will sing for them and they will dance, bodies swooning to the rhythm of the clapping hands.

The children will play together for the rest of the day, play hide and seek, and tag, chase each other until their mothers tell them to stop. Too much running around could upset the bindings. Seven days will pass and nothing will happen. On the eighth they'll all come down with a fever.

'Diamandi is sick already,' Mana whispers. 'And Costa and Attis.'

For two days Sophie stays in bed, like all the other children, her fever rising and falling, her head pounding. Mana, smelling of lemon blossom and laurel oil, wipes her forehead with a wet cloth. Cool and dripping with water which flows down her forehead and sinks into her pillow.

Mana sings to her, funny songs in which goats wish to

become camels and flies envy the eagles in the sky. Mana's cool hand on her forehead is an invitation to sleep. A tiny dab of the balm of Mecca on her finger, she rubs around the smallpox wound. It will keep her Dou-Dou beautiful, she says. Her *epilda*. Her hope for the future. Her only hope.

Thomas

Berlin, Doctor Thomas Lafleur thought, was a grim city, in spite of the profusion of oil lamps swinging on chains, illuminating small circles of the street below. The aftermath of the armies treading through these lands might account for some of this grimness, but Thomas liked to reflect on the universal human capacity for creating misery. He did not assume America would free him from the disgust he felt with the human race, but at least it would give him a chance.

'*Please hurry*,' Ignacy's letter said, '*my dear Thomas. The Art as we have learnt it serving the Great Man is unsurpassed here. I need you badly, and so does my new patient. America can wait. I cannot agree it will be such a Great Deliverance as you are trying to convince me, for Human Nature is the same everywhere. To me it looks more like a Great Escape. Graf von Haefen is sending his fastest carriage, so you can judge for yourself how much you are needed here.*'

The mention of the fee he could charge for the operation, 50 louis d'or (*and more if what I see is any indication* Ignacy wrote), has been enough to make Dr Thomas Lafleur subject his body to the torture of travel. Like his colleagues, he may have saved thousands of lives on the battlefields of Europe, but his rewards had been meagre. A small pension of three thousand francs, a position at la Charité, a few anatomical demonstrations, a few lectures at the Val de Grace.

'Sometimes I think I have dreamt all this,' he had often told Ignacy. 'Borodino, Berezina, Kowno, Waterloo. As if it were nothing but a mirage.'

Anticipating Thomas's wishes, Ignacy had found him simple lodgings in Old Berlin, on Rosenstrasse, two rooms: a bedroom and a small parlour that could easily serve as his study. Frau Schmidt offered services of a maid, breakfast in the morning, and swore that the room would be kept warm if the French doctor were kept longer with his patient. 'Another of your hiding holes,' Ignacy had called it, this friend whose relentless lupine energy in the months of the Russian campaign Thomas had envied.

That the rooms looked poor and bare, with their simple poplar furniture and narrow bed, did not bother Thomas. After being tossed around and jolted in the black box of Graf von Haefen's carriage, he was ready to welcome any place that did not move. Besides he had been an army surgeon long enough not to mind.

Sophie

Diamandi's skin is as smooth as a fresh fig. 'Catch me,' she cries to him and reaches for the first branches of the oak tree at the edge of the meadow where the sheep graze. He is still standing, unsure of what he should do. After all, she is but a girl with scabs on her knees. Thick scabs she likes to tear off, impatient for the new pink skin underneath. She is but a girl, even if she can swim like a fish and steer a *kaiak* better than many boys he could name.

Even if she can outrun him. Make him gasp for breath. Make him pant right behind her like a dog.

'Catch me, Diamandi.'

He makes the first cautious step toward the tree, his tanned hands reach toward the lowest of the branches.

Then there is a snap of a twig. A curse. The sound of a body heaving up, pushing through the leaves. She is halfway up already where the branches are thinner, her hands grabbing, testing their strength. 'Like a squirrel,' Mana has said, in a voice half angry and half approving. A squirrel is agile and cheeky. Digs out bulbs and cuts the stems of flowers. A squirrel mocks the fat tabby who stalks it in hope of a skirmish.

From the top of the tree Bursa looks small and forlorn. Even the big houses of the rich seem insignificant, their gardens but patches of greenery, really no different to her mother's small kitchen garden. The garden where the flowers are only allowed on the edges, for the soil is too valuable for ornaments.

'Come on, Diamandi.'

He is right behind her, and gaining speed. His body is wiry and strong. Stronger than hers, even if not that fast. Her cousin is a ferryman and a shepherd. He is older by seven months, fourteen already, while she is still only thirteen and has not yet bled like a woman.

He wrestles with other boys, pins them to the ground, breathes in their faces until they squirm. His eyes are flashing with victory. He will not let her win that easily. He will hold her down, if he has to.

'Dou-Dou!'

There is pleading in his voice and the promise of tenderness.

'Dou-Dou!'

She stops right before reaching to the thinnest of the top branches that could still sustain her weight. She waits until Diamandi comes right behind her and orders her to climb down. 'Right this minute,' he says and his hand rests on her behind. Just for a moment, for a split second, but enough to make her skin hot and tingly.

'You are crazy. Your mother would scratch my eyes

out if anything happened to you.'

'Then let's see who can climb down first,' she says.

She can feel his eyes on her as she climbs down. A tricky old tree. But she knows which of the branches are rotten through and would not support her. She trusts her strong hands. Her legs can wrap themselves around a branch and hold her. She does not mind the scratches on her skin. The thin trails of blood, the bruises. 'A bit of pain always sweetens the pleasure,' Mana says, laughing, her white teeth even and small. Her father's eyes narrow at such moments. His fingers drum on the edge of the table, a funny rhythm, a staccato of sounds that end as suddenly as they started. There is something heavy in the air, a promise of a storm. She has often heard that her father is a jealous man, and that her mother gets nothing more than what is her due.

'You are not to do it ever again,' Diamandi says. What a voice he has, this boy-man. Pretending to be angry and yet wanting her to defy him. Daring her to shake her head and laugh in his face. Daring her to tell him he is nothing but a boy.

He has jumped off the last branch and is now holding her down. His hands are cool and dry. There is a smell of dried grass around him and of fresh milk. She wriggles away.

To this lithe, olive-skinned boy she is a mystery, the half-wild creature of his dreams. The wind is now cool against her cheeks. 'I'll race you,' she cries and runs until, by the olive grove, he pulls her down onto the soft grass, kisses her lips and pushes his tongue through her teeth. The air is again sweet with blossoms, moist with the sea, and she is shivering.

'I love you more than my own soul,' he whispers, and for now she believes him.

Two tall German grooms who had brought the big empire bed trimmed with white satin asked where Rosalia wanted it. 'By the wall,' she said and pointed to the place far enough from the windows so that the light would not disturb the invalid. The grooms nodded and lifted the bed again. They had already removed the Persian carpets and, once the bed was in place, they would hang a thick curtain of garnet velvet that could be drawn across the room.

Countess Potocka was resting, waiting for the necessary transformations of the grand salon. (The Blue Room suggested by the Graf had proved too draughty.) In the afternoon light, her pallor was turning ashen. Her eyes, wide, liquid and filled with pain, followed Rosalia as she placed a bowl of fresh figs by the makeshift bedside. The countess reached and touched Rosalia's hand.

'*Merci, ma fleur*,' she whispered.

Graf von Haefen had sent basketfuls of delicacies from his Potsdam estate; figs, pineapples, oranges from his greenhouses, fish from his ponds, venison from his forests. 'Which Madame won't even try,' Marusya had said. Rosalia had to admit that flowers would please her mistress better. Roses in particular and orchids.

Only a few days before, at a roadside inn, the countess still had enough strength to make a few long-awaited decisions about Sophievka, her beloved garden right outside Uman. Since Dr Horn's insistence that surgery alone could stop the haemorrhaging, there was no more talk of moving to the Uman palace for the summer (another disappointment that had to be endured). But the countess asked Rosalia to copy the drawings of the mountain ash that she wanted her chief gardener to plant in the spring. *Sturdy and resistant, I am assured it will withstand most severe frosts*, the countess dictated. A bed of purple irises, a symbol of a great orator and a great leader, was to be planted around the marble bust of Prince Joseph Poniatowski. New paths were to be charted. *Make them lead to a vista, or a building. Otherwise a wanderer would turn back in disappointment.* The giant oak by the river was not to be touched. *Don't trim the branches, a human hand has no right to correct such beauty. An oak once wounded, loses its primal force and will always grow slowly.*

'The bed will be ready soon,' Rosalia said, but the countess only managed a slight nod.

Outside, in the courtyard, the hooves of the horses made a hollow noise; carriage wheels clattered and squeaked. Soon, Rosalia thought, Pietka would have to spread a straw carpet on the stones to muffle all noise. And he would have to stop singing, as he was doing now.

In Vinnytsia, on the border,
At the foot of a grave mound, on the bank of the Buh River,
Under the walls of the Kalnytsky charterhouse...

This palace in the heart of Berlin would provide some relief. From what she had seen, Rosalia could tell its workings would be flawless. Since their arrival, the marble floor in the entrance hall had already been washed and wiped dry. After mentioning that charpie would be necessary to dress the wounds and that the French surgeon would likely ask for an old mattress, she was reassured both would be procured without delay. Frau Kohl, the Graf's housekeeper, had also brought a pile of old sheets, well-washed and soft.

Rosalia wiped her mistress's face with a sponge dipped in warm, lavender-scented water, washing away stale sweat and caked powder. Her underclothes were again stained with blood, dark and clotted with what looked like pieces of chopped liver. Mademoiselle Collard used to complain she was a lady's maid not a nurse. 'Neither are you,' she reminded Rosalia. Her family's land may have been sequestered by the Russian Tsar, but Rosalia's father had been a Polish noble and it was her duty to guard her own station in life. It was all too easy to slip down, let herself go. With that Rosalia had to agree, as she retrieved clean undergarments from a travelling trunk and helped the countess change into her lilac dress with little embroidered rosebuds, but then the question remained of who would do it. The maids had their hands full with all the unpacking, mending and ironing. Mademoiselle la Comtesse conveniently managed to vomit every time she caught the whiff of the basin. ('She has her father's constitution, Rosalia. Nature cannot be helped,' the countess said.) Only this morning – having seen the bloodstained undergarments the maids were taking away to be soaked in cold water – she became so agitated that Rosalia had had to give her a double dose of laudanum to calm her down.

'I don't want to see anyone but Graf von Haefen,' the countess whispered, closing her eyes. 'Let my daughter receive all other visitors.'

'The French doctor will be here soon,' Rosalia said. She was trying to foresee what else the surgeon might ask for. If he came from Paris, he would not have assistants. Doctor Bolecki would be of help, but this might not be enough. She wondered if the two grooms were strong enough to hold the countess down. And if they would withstand that much blood and the screaming.

'I'm so tired, Rosalia,' the countess whispered.

The pain was never far away, crouching inside her, but it was letting her breathe. It might let her fall asleep again. 'Mademoiselle Rosalia, you should try to lead her thoughts away from death,' Graf von Haefen had insisted with great firmness, before leaving. 'Talk only of what brings her joy.'

The gardener reported that Sophievka was already covered in snow. He had seen icicles hanging from pine trees and from the gnarled branches of the oak tree by the lake. In the greenhouses roses and orchids were blooming and he wished he could send the countess some blooms the way he used to send them to St Petersburg, in a carriage kept warm with braziers. The nettle tree was doing fine and so was the Turkish filbert from Caucasus. He had planted it in complete shade, as instructed.

'The nettle tree, I was assured,' the countess said, 'would not sink in water.'

When her mistress was dressed, Rosalia combed her hair, grey and so much thinned by her illness. Then, from the red travelling case, she took a black wig, a shapely halo of black locks, trying not to pull as she pinned it to her hair.

'By the summer, you'll be strong enough. We'll go there together.'

The countess gave her the most beautiful of her smiles.

Perhaps, Rosalia thought, happiness could only come from such simple moments. From knowing that the touch of her hands calmed the sick and eased their pain. 'Which is precisely why she would take advantage of you,' Mademoiselle Collard would warn. 'She already has two daughters, you know.' It was in Rosalia's disposition to take unending duties upon herself, feel responsible for the most insignificant of things. Like the lost charcoals, a whole box of cedar of Lebanon: Olena, the maid who had packed the dinner service at the last stop, was sure she put it in the same box with the silver. 'Surely,' Mademoiselle Collard would mock Rosalia's agitation over this trifle if she were here, '*she* can afford to lose a box of charcoals. Isn't *she* rich enough?'

The countess, her eyes closed, looked like a waxen figure. It was only the faint warmth of her skin that told Rosalia her mistress was still alive.

Sophie

Her cheeks still smart from her mother's slaps. One, two, three. A fool. She is a fool. Or a whore. What was she thinking? What was on her mind? Doesn't she understand anything? Anything at all? Hasn't she seen and heard what human tongues can do?

The salty taste of blood inside her mouth frightens her. The memory of happiness, of lightness is gone. Instead, she has to face her mother's fury.

'What did he do?' Mana screams and pushes her on her bed. Another slap, weaker than the one before. Her skirt is lifted, her legs spread. She has been damaged, nibbled at and spat out. Tried and left aside. Who will buy damaged goods now? What man in his right mind would pay for what he can have for free? Who would keep a cow if the milk comes for nothing?

Mana is poking inside her, feeling for the damage. How cruel her fingers can be. How rough.

'Was he hard,' she asks. 'Did he put it in all the way?

'Dou-Dou, I'm talking to you. Answer me, girl.

'Tell me everything. I'm your mother.

'It's for your own good.

'Plenty of dirty pots in the kitchen that need to be scrubbed. The maid can be let go, the scruffy thing she is, and dirty too. You want dirt? You can scrub the pots with ashes. See how your hands redden from scalding. See how your knuckles grow and crack open. See how they bleed.

'Is that what you want, girl? Is that what I gave you your life for? Is that why I screamed with pain for the twelve hours you took to be born? Tearing me apart, almost killing me?

'And for what? A poke from this runt? This good-for-nothing? This high-and-mighty cavalier whose tongue is stronger than his dick. Who now walks around the town in his glory, telling everyone what you let him do.'

In the end Mana's tears are harder to bear than her anger. Seeing her hide her face in her hands in shame. Hearing her sobs.

'All I ever wanted for you is now lost.'

Dou-Dou wants to scream that this is not true. Isn't she still her mother's beloved daughter as she was a day ago? But her mother only looks at her with unseeing eyes.

'You do not know the power of the human tongue.'

The sun is caught in Mana's raven black hair. If angels have faces, that's how they must look. The shape of the brows enlarging the eyes, the cheeks full and smooth. The lips like cherries, glistening from the tears that have rolled down her cheeks.

'Is that what you want girl? Is that what I gave you your life for? Is that why I screamed from pain for the twelve hours you took to be born? Tearing me apart so badly that I could have no more children?

'I've always wanted my daughter to do better than I've done. Not to waste what God has given her. Not to throw it away. Was it too much to hope for?'

Konstantin Glavani comes back from the tavern. Even from his steps, Dou-Dou can tell that he knows. From the force with which his heels hit the ground. From the way his fist lands on the table. With a thump. With choking anger. Something falls off, rolls, smashing on the floor.

There is a slap, then another one, and a scream. 'Like

mother, like daughter,' he yells. 'Is that what you teach her? To spread her legs for every loser in Bursa?

'To be the talk of the town?'

The door opens and Sophie's body softens like a kitten readying itself for a fall. She is lying on her stomach, sobbing into a pillow and her father is standing beside the bed. His breath is all she hears. In and out, in and out. In his big hand she can see the handle of the whip Konstantin Glavani uses to corral the sheep.

This silence frightens her more than Mana's screams.

He lifts her skirt, her shift, and exposes her buttocks. If she doesn't tense them, it will hurt less. The swish of leather through the air comes first, before the spasm, before the warmth of her pee dissolving into the mattress. When the strap touches her skin, she feels another spasm. And another until there is nothing but burning pain.

She doesn't scream. Her face is buried in the pillow. Tears soak into the embroidered fabric. Mana had stitched these birds singing on branches, their beaks open wide. And the tall cypresses that sway in the wind. She did it in another time when Sophie was but a child and wanted to know about everything. How to make such a bird look real. How to make a thread go through the eye of the needle.

Her father stops and turns her over. 'Look at me,' he says. 'See the man who can't look his friends in the eye. Who has to listen in silence as his daughter's name is dragged in filth. The man whose daughter is a whore.'

She looks at him. He is standing above her, big body swaying, his breath smelling of wine and roasted lamb. Red blotches have sprung up on his neck, his mouth is twisted into a grimace of disgust. She remembers that his fingers can bend a horseshoe. He will not be made the laughing-stock of Bursa. He will not allow his daughter to disgrace his name. He will kill her first, and then kill himself.

'A brood mare.'

He lifts his hand in the air. A big hand, calloused and reddened, with chapped skin on the knuckles. Will her neck snap with a crack, like that of a chicken?

She fixes her eyes on him. Everything can happen now. Everything is nestled in such moments, the malice, the revenge, the pain. The hand falls down slowly, limp, alongside his body. It clenches into a fist and then relaxes, defeated.

How does one escape the power of human tongues?

She has heard of a man slashing his daughter's face with a razor. Of burning her cheeks with hot coals to scar her beauty. Her father keeps looking at her, forcing himself to keep looking, until, in an instant, he turns on his heel, and walks away. The door slams after him, and she wipes the tears from her eyes and cheeks. There is a pitcher of water and a basin her mother has left for her, and she splashes cold water on her face. Then she squats over the basin and washes the place between her legs, still wet from her pee. Where the strap hit her, she can feel needles of pain in a web of punishment, the memory of her defeat.

Konstantin Glavani announces that they are leaving Bursa.

She watches his quick, determined steps, listens to the stomping of his heels on the floor. Outside, the earth smells of camomile, lemon blossom, and laurel. Her friends are in the fields, running or riding horses. Or making bonfires on the edge of the river. Diamandi is there too, but she won't see him. She is not allowed to leave the house of shame.

The stories flow, thicker and more poisonous each day. The stories men whisper in low, lusty whispers. The stories women repeat with gasps of disbelief. There will be no end to them now, no end to the malice of lashing tongues. The torrent of gossip will follow her until the day God pleases to call her to His presence and account for her sins. An egg once broken cannot be made whole again.

Konstantin Glavani is pacing the room. He has been punished for the sins of the flesh, for marrying beneath himself. For being a fool and closing his ears to the words of the wise. Slash her throat, people tell him. Make her kneel in the dust and cut your daughter's throat. Make her bellow like a heifer when she sees a knife raised above her head.

What a fool he has been for thinking that God has blessed him when his daughter was born. For thinking his little Dou-Dou would be the light of his soul, the blessing of his old age. For thinking that he, a father of but one child, would sit in her garden one day and rock his grandchildren on his knees.

This is not what God in His wisdom has prepared for him. The sins of women are bred in the bone, working their silent way from the day a woman is born until the day she dies. He should have known that this daughter of his would be his Gehenna. The day she was born he should have sprinkled ashes on his head.

Women are like bitches in heat, bringing nothing but trouble, but Diamandi is no better. Diamandi is a traitor. A man of no honour, no family loyalty. For what he has done to his own cousin, for bragging to his friends about it, he should be hung from the tree. Or branded on his forehead like the liar he is. But Konstantin Glavani is not a murderer. He is not a Turk. He is a Christian man. A Greek. A man of honour. If he were a lesser man, he could have dug out some dirt too. Everyone knows what Diamandi's elder brother is doing. A barber, his father says. Working for a Turk, a man from Istanbul who calls himself a philosopher. A worshipper of Sodom who carries his lovers' powdered filth in the box around his neck.

'Let him who is without sin cast the first stone,' he says.

Has he forgiven her?

Mana is listening, too, her silence dark, furtive. There is a black bruise around her left eye and her neck has red blotches on it. Her eyes rest on Sophie, tell her to keep quiet, to wait it all through.

Yes, this daughter of his is his burden, but Konstantin Glavani will not refuse it.

He has already sold all his cattle. For a song. For a quarter of what the herd is worth, but such is the ruthlessness of those who know he cannot afford to wait. The house will be rented to a distant cousin. An honest man, even if a bit slow in the head. They are going to Jerusalem, to the Holy Grave. The three of them, together. To beg God Almighty for forgiveness.

When their journey is over, they will not come back here. They will go to Istanbul where no one knows them. Where, with the money he got for his cattle, Konstantin Glavani will buy a position with the Istanbul police. He will be in charge of Christian butchers in the district of Pera, and there no one will dare spit after him when he walks the streets.

Rosalia

In the room Frau Kohl has chosen for her, on account of its closeness to the grand salon, Rosalia took out her dresses from the travelling trunk, gave each a vigorous shake, and put them in the wardrobe which smelled of varnish. That's also where she placed her dark grey overcoat, but even then the wardrobe was only half filled. The three hats and two bonnets went on the top shelf. Her petticoats and chemises filled only one of the five drawers.

'An operation,' the countess had said, 'cannot be on a Tuesday.'

'*If* there is an operation,' Dr Bolecki had said. The examination had been a short one, the smile on his face forced.

From the bottom of the trunk Rosalia took out the miniatures of her parents, Jakub and Maria Romanowicz, and placed them on the small table beside her bed. The silver-framed miniatures had been painted right before the Kościuszko Insurrection of 1794 and the final defeat, before the day the word *Poland* had been erased from the map of Europe. The painter was not skilled. The expression of the two pairs of eyes were identical, as if mere copies of each other. Both her parents were looking ahead with melancholy, as if they could already see the future.

'It is that Tuesday is a bad day,' the countess had said.

'Will it hurt much,' Olga asked. The way she bit her lower lip touched Rosalia more than the sobs she sometimes heard at night; a sign that Olga too feared the worst. Perhaps because the sobbing *was* invisible.

In the miniature her father was in the Kościuszko uniform, a white peasant *sukmana,* a cravat tied in a bow under his chin, a symbol of Equality and Freedom for all Poles. His face was clean-shaven and, like Kościuszko, he was not wearing a wig. Her mother's black hair was parted in the middle. It encircled her white, porcelain face and dissolved into the background. A string of pearls was woven in her hair and she was holding a fan with which she covered her chest. Rosalia remembered that fan. When it was flicked open, Artemis appeared. The goddess with a leopard's skin on her shoulders, its limp paws hanging behind her like a train. Where was it now? Lost in one of their many moves, forgotten perhaps in one of the trunks Aunt Antonia was keeping for her in the dusty attic in Zierniki.

You have already turned twenty-six, Rosalia, and I shall never believe you are foolish enough to trust your mother's misguided hopes. Did she really think that being Count Potocki's godchild would give her some special rights? That it would make the count's wife take special care of her orphan? Sometimes I think it best your dear father had not lived to see this.

Two years before, on such an October night as this one, Rosalia had listened as her mother moved about her bedroom. Drawers opened and closed; the floorboards creaked. The smell of burning paper wafted through the doors. For a moment it seemed that she could hear sobs but, when she rose from her bed and listened, what she took for crying turned out to be the sound of wind in the chimney.

'The matter has to be treated most seriously, Madame Romanowicz,' the surgeon said. He looked pale in his black suit and drops of perspiration appeared on his forehead. He wiped them off with a chequered handkerchief. 'Most seriously, Madame,' he repeated. Her mother's eyes had a vacant look Rosalia didn't like. The examination had been short. The breast was swollen, the tumour had grown to the size of a plum. Time had already been lost, too much time. The surgeon spoke of women who withdrew from the world suffering only a trusted nurse to come and wash the fetid running sores as their breasts were eaten away, drowning in filth.

He would not reveal the date of the operation. He never did. All he could do was to offer a warning of two hours at the most, for anything longer would only be the source of undue agitation. He would need old linen, charpie, old undergarments freshly laundered. Soft. An old armchair. No carpet. Nothing that could be splattered with blood and would be hard to wash. 'But first, Madame

Romanowicz will have to sign a permission. This is of utmost importance. Without it I cannot proceed.'

The note from the surgeon came as they were sitting down to breakfast. *Today at ten o'clock*. The maid brought it on a tray, perched against the coffee pot.

'I've made my peace with God. There is nothing else for you to do,' Maman said. She had been to confession, she took communion and asked for extreme unction. Seeing the alarm in Rosalia's eyes, she assured her that the last rites had been known to heal the sick.

She won't die, Rosalia repeated to herself, registering the progress of fear. In Zierniki, in winter, she had seen ducks imprisoned by ice in the pond. At first they were still able to move, until the ice thickened and refused to crack. Then to free them, the grooms had to hack at the ice with an axe and take the birds to the warm kitchen to thaw.

I won't let her, she repeated over and over again. I won't.

When the doctor arrived with three assistants, all dressed in black, Maman emerged from her room in a light batiste nightdress. If she were afraid, Rosalia could not see it. Her voice was steady and her eyes dry.

'I want all the women to leave,' the surgeon said. The maid scurried in the direction of the kitchen and closed the door. Her muffled sobs reached them a moment later.

'I'm a soldier's daughter,' Rosalia said. 'Let me stay.'

The surgeon glared at her as if she were creating difficulties, but she met his eyes without flinching.

'If you faint, no one will have the time to attend you,' he said sharply.

'I won't faint,' she replied. Maman looked at her with relief.

Bare of furniture, with just the armchair in the middle covered with three white, freshly laundered sheets, the parlour looked bigger and far too bright. The wallpaper was darker where the picture and the oval mirror had hung. The ceiling, Rosalia saw, needed a fresh coat of paint. Her mother's hand when she held it was cold and dry but then, without warning, perspiration broke out.

'When you were giving birth, Madame,' the surgeon asked. 'Did you scream?'

'Yes.'

'Good. Then I want you to scream – scream as much as you can.'

The operation was performed in absolute silence. The doctor seated Maman in the armchair, gave her a glass of wine cordial to drink, and covered her face with a cambric handkerchief. Then he motioned to the tallest assistant who placed a pillow under her head and positioned himself behind. The other two assistants silently came to stand on each side of the armchair, holding her arms. Her mother motioned to them that it was not necessary, but when, through the fine mesh of the handkerchief, she saw the glitter of steel she tried to stand up. The men held her so fast that she flinched.

Nothing, no past memory of love would ever equal this moment when Rosalia could feel her mother's fingers clutch hers like clamps and saw her knuckles becoming white. It did not seem odd that her own body registered her mother's pain. That this pain united them, sealed them to each other. That together, she with a clear eye and her mother through the mesh of her handkerchief, they watched as the surgeon made the sign of incision in the air, with a straight line from top to bottom of the breast, a cross and a circle. That they shuddered together when the blade cut horizontally, nearly in the direction of the rib, a little below the nipple. That the scream that came, came from them both.

The two assistants on either side pressed their fingers

on the arteries, and the surgeon began the cleaning, his hand separating the tumour from the skin and muscles, cutting off the cancerous tissue. Blood splattered his hands and arms. There were a few drops of it on his face. When Rosalia heard the blade scraping the breast bone, she could feel her mother's hand loosening her grip. Maman had fainted and for a moment something close to panic overtook her until she reminded herself that, unconscious, her mother was free from pain.

The procedure took twenty minutes. There were operations that could be performed well and fast, but this was not one of them. The whole of the diseased structure had to be removed, the surgeon said afterwards, and he could not afford to miss anything. 'I can amputate in under two minutes,' he said. 'But with this, no half measures will do. If the reoccurrence of the mischief is to be prevented. . .'

Rosalia was so hopeful then. The surgeon assured her that the operation had gone well and showed her how to dress the wound, applying a large, thick compress of charpie to the sutures and binding it on with a flannel roller. It didn't take long for blood to appear through all the bandages. Maman's face had lost all its colour and her limbs all life. The assistants carried her to her bed, and Rosalia was told to change her dressings every two hours and watch for signs of infection, for the weakening of the body.

At midnight her mother opened her eyes, but she did not seem to know where she was.

'He is standing by the window,' she kept saying.

'Who is?' Rosalia asked. All she wanted was to throw herself into her mother's arms, to hide her face in her breasts the way she did when she was a child. Instead she could still hear the knife scraping against the bones.

'He is pointing at his heart.'

Her lips were parched and she drank a few sips of water. 'I am going with him,' she said. 'I have to.'

Rosalia tried to quiet her. The surgeon had assured her the operation was a success. The cancer was removed, all of it. 'You must be strong, Maman,' she pleaded. 'You cannot leave me alone. You cannot leave your only child.'

'I have to go,' her mother whispered and closed her eyes. 'He is waiting for me. He will take me away.'

Seeing that the blood had penetrated the dressing again, Rosalia replaced it with a fresh one. Maman did not open her eyes, but she no longer seemed in pain. Perhaps, Rosalia thought, the crisis had passed. She promised herself not to fall asleep, but the silence and her mother's calm, soft breaths proved too much. When she woke up, startled, it was still dark. The windowpanes were covered with the white, intricate patterns she loved to watch in Zierniki where the windows froze for most of the winter. Beautiful white ferns, branches of trees with spiked leaves, flowers of tiny petals that reminded her of figures her father drew to amuse her: pentagons, hexagons, octagons.

The room was silent and still. Death she thought was like that. A moment of loss too profound to comprehend. A moment in which love fuses with pain. A moment from which there is no now and no future. Nothing but memories of the past, crumbling and fading with time.

She didn't have to touch Maman's face to know she was dead.

Just as she did on winter days in Zierniki, Rosalia breathed at the windowpane. When the ice petals melted, she peered through the hole and saw a boy pass by. He was carrying a lantern carved out of a turnip, slits in its side let out enough light for him to see where he was going.

There were a few other objects in Rosalia's travelling chest but these would remain unpacked, a testimony to the temporary nature of her stay in this Berlin palace: a small wooden star she had found among her mother's things; her father's snuffbox with the Rights of Man engraved on the lid; a black silhouette of Kościuszko's profile and three sketches of Napoleon in a wreath of oak leaves – her father's heroes.

These treasures Rosalia kept locked in a mahogany box, underneath her clothes in the trunk. It was a flimsy hiding place. Any of the servant girls might want to go through her things, try on her dresses or petticoats. Smell her rosewater or jasmine oil and dab a few drops on her brow. In St Petersburg handkerchiefs and sheets of paper disappeared routinely. The paper was what the cook used to curl her hair with. 'If it wasn't meant to be taken, it wouldn't be lying around,' Rosalia had heard Marusya mutter.

Her back hurt from lifting sacks of clothes, from helping the countess stand up. Taking off her shoes and her stockings, she walked about the room, until her aching feet were consoled by the smoothness of the carpet. If only Olga cared to help more, but some people were born to luxury and some were not. 'It's your own mother,' Rosalia was often tempted to say, but never did.

Her most excellent bed, as Frau Kohl – the Graf's housekeeper – had described it, did not help. It felt too big, too cold. Rosalia turned and tossed around, trying to warm up the clammy sheet, wondering if she should call for another eiderdown. There were noises outside her room; German words exchanged by the footmen; the sounds of doors opening and closing – the life of this palace, temporarily interrupted by their arrival. She recalled Marusya's talking about strange noises in the maid's room, like someone's knocking on the windowpane, and complaining that the room smelled of mice. 'Perhaps the Count has come for the Mistress,' the cook had said.

Sophie

She opens the gate. The fence of their Istanbul house is made of staves of wood fastened with wire. The wind pushes her back, and the first rain drops fall on her face. She is thinking of the smooth feel of velvet on her cheek.

'Quick,' Mana screams. 'Upstairs. To your room.'

The front door is hanging open. A doctor is in her parents' bedroom, bending over her father. Or someone who looks like her father, in spite of the swollen red face, an eyeless face locked in a scowl.

'Go,' Mana screams.

Upstairs, in her small room, Sophie throws herself on her bed and listens. The doctor's voice is harsh and commanding. He is calling for water, and he is pounding something. Pounding hard and shouting at Mana who rushes outside and then comes back.

She can smell her own body. A slightly sour smell she breathes in and out. For a moment she feels that she is growing large, her feet are endless and wide, stretching to the edge of the world, but then she moves and the feeling is gone.

She remembers the time when he was proud of her. When he told Mana to dress his daughter in her best dress and to plait her hair with ribbons so that her father could take her with him to the garden where, under the deep shade of almond blossoms, his friends gathered for their evening coffee and sweetmeats.

Her father stood her on the carpet and clapped his hands. She bowed and smiled, eyes stealing swiftly across the faces of the men and back again to her father. From the overgrown lake, right beside them, came a rotting smell of reeds.

Her father took a garland of flowers and put it around

her neck. A beautiful garland of reds and yellows, of roses and wild daffodils. She sniffed at the flowers and their scent made her sneeze. 'A sign,' her father said. Someone was talking about her now. Right this minute someone was saying her name.

The thought pleased her. The waves of whispers, the eyes of strangers following her.

'Pray to the Lord,' her father said, 'that what they say is always good. Once soiled, a good name is lost forever.'

The men laughed and clapped their hands.

This is what she wants to remember: the wine glasses raised to the sky, toasting her health and her good luck. Toasting her beautiful voice breaking into a song of love. A song sad and sweet. A song she has heard shepherds sing in the fields.

A child thrice blessed. A child kissed by an angel.

Her father carried her home that evening, and she remembers his breath, in which wine and coffee mingled. He carried her in his arms like a princess so that her embroidered slippers would not, Heaven forbid, be soiled. The soft slippers Mana had made out of an old dress she had stopped wearing.

Downstairs the pounding stops and there is silence. She crosses herself three times. She is sorry for all the times she has been angry at him.

In Jerusalem, in the Temple, she cried as the friars lifted up the cross and led the pilgrims to the place where Our Lord suffered and died. She was holding a candle and the wax, melting, scorched her skin, but she did not feel pain. When they reached the Mount of Calvary she fell to her knees, recalling the suffering of Our Lord and those who were with him in these dark moments of pain and despair. Recalling Mary Magdalene, forgiven for her sins, taken back into the heart of the Lord. And then her own heart filled with love and compassion for all human suffering, and she could not think of anything she wanted so much as to lie there, on the holy ground and let her tears soak into the earth.

Mana is standing at the door, her hands hanging loose, her lips moving. There is a drop of sweat rolling down her forehead.

'It's Tuesday,' she hears.

Tuesday is a bad, unlucky day. On a Tuesday, Constantinople, the heart of the Byzantine Empire, fell to the Turks and would from now on be called Istanbul. On a Tuesday the Emperor Constantine turned into marble. Just before he was to be struck down by the Turks, Byzantium's last Emperor was seized by an angel. The angel, his golden wings shining in the rays of the sun, carried him to a cave near the Golden Gate and turned him into a statue. 'You will wait here,' he said, 'for the time when God our Lord is ready to restore freedom to the Greeks.'

'Cry, Dou-Dou,' she says, 'cry for your father. We are all alone in the world.'

But her own eyes are dry.

In the Istanbul port, where the straits merge with the sea, opaque patterns glide over the water and flocks of shearwaters skim low over the surface, never to rest. The Turks say they are the souls of the damned.

Mana says these tiny birds are the souls of the odalisques the Sultan sent to their deaths. Drowned in the Bosphorus, in brown burlap sacks, their hands tied, their mouths gagged. In this world it is better to be a dog than a woman, Mana says, for she has seen carriages stop for a dog lying in the sun. She has seen servants get out, lift the dog up, and carry it out of the way.

The fishermen come back from the sea with swordfish,

red and grey mullet, sea bass, lobsters and mussels. Sprats are caught with a lantern. The light reflected in the water makes the fish blind, she has heard, and they do not see the net.

'Sing for us, gorgeous,' the sailors ask.

In the market her mother has shown her how to watch out for bad fish. The stink of decay can be rubbed away with pine tar; dull skin buffed with a piece of rag until it shines. Air can be blown inside the belly to make a catch look bigger and more succulent.

Watch out, Mana says. You have already bled like a woman. Men can pick that scent. Men can tell.

She likes the sight of them. The young men with olive skin, shirts stained with grease, open at the chest. Their muscles tense as they pull on the ropes.

'I won't,' she laughs and hurries away.

For a Christian woman the streets of Istanbul are fraught with danger. Even if she casts her eyes down and follows her mother, quickly, without looking. Even if she promises herself not to stare at the rich, handsome cavaliers who come to the district of Phanar where the Greek merchants' wives lounge on their verandas, attended by servant girls. Men whose steps are light and sprightly. Whose embroidered belts are fastened with broad golden clasps. Whose horses prance and neigh, impatient with restraint imposed on them by their riders' hands. Men whose eyes are on the prowl.

She has seen the Janissaries with white feathers on their heads, and the royal gardeners dressed in their habits of different colours so that from afar they looked like flowers themselves. She has seen the Aga of the Janissaries in a robe of purple velvet lined with silver tissue. His horse was led by two slaves. Next to him was the Kilar Aga, the chief eunuch of the Seraglio in a deep yellow cloth lined with sable. The Sultan was mounted on a horse whose saddle was studded with jewels.

She often thinks of fate. Fate that can push her any which way, make her a slave or a queen, a lady or a whore. Lady Fate whose breath she feels right behind her, tickling the skin on her neck. Lady Fate, blind, fickle and full of spite.

Or is it benevolence.

Help yourself so God can help you, Mana says.

'Look at yourself, Dou-Dou.'

This is her aunt who says she could be her sister. Whose dresses are made of Genoan damask and silk. Whose rings catch the rays of the sun and reflect them back with a rainbow of colours. 'These, my little Dou-Dou, are real diamonds.'

Aunt Helena, Mana's younger sister, hardly hides her annoyance at their hungry eyes trailing after her clothes, after the food on the table, after the trinkets with which she adorns herself. Aunt Helena with her sweet voice and the scent of roses around her, with hands soft and white.

'Look at yourself,' Sophie hears and watches how her cheap, coarse dress drops down, how her aunt's fingers gently release the hooks of her petticoats, the folds of her chemise. How nothing obstructs the sight of her body. The shapely breasts, the belly button, the mound of black curls below. 'Move your hips, Dou-Dou,' Aunt Helena whispers into her ear, the hot air of her breath tickling. 'Slowly, slowly. Don't shake too much.'

She sways her hips, shy at first, cautious. But she likes what she sees, she likes this nymph, this slender, beautiful girl framed by the gilded mirror. Standing beside this aunt of hers, her mother's sister who now braids a string of pearls into her long hair. Is this the way Eve felt in the

Garden of Eden when she saw her own reflection in the mirror of still water?

'You are so beautiful, Dou-Dou. You can have everything you want. Don't let anyone tell you otherwise, girl.'

She turns her back to the mirror and looks over her shoulder. Her back is smooth and flexible. She can bend as easily as she climbed the branches of the oak tree in Bursa. She can kneel on the floor and let her body fall backwards, into a graceful curve, and then come back, slowly, her eyes locked on her own image.

'You are worthy of a king's bed.'

The longing in her is like an ill wind that makes the air clammy with heat, filled with dust, unbearable. There has to be a release to all this want that has gathered in her. In the mirror her own eyes stare back at her. Two black coals of desire.

She lowers her eyes, as if she were ashamed of her own beauty, and her aunt claps her hands and laughs. 'Perhaps, I don't need to teach you that much after all,' she says.

From the big mahogany chest of drawers, Aunt Helena takes out her best cashmere shawl, the one on which there is a flower on a stem, its roots dangling in the air. Long tendrils, clean of soil, no longer hidden in the earth. Such is the taste of the true ladies, her aunt says. They like botanicals. *Botanicals*, the word itself sounds different, more worldly than mere *plants* or *flowers*.

Soft and silky to the touch, the shawl envelops her with misty warmth, a promise of a caress.

'For a woman, nothing, my little Dou-Dou, works better than a bit of mystery.'

A length of gauze replaces the cashmere shawl. Her aunt drapes it over her hair, around her waist. There is something flowery about the girl in the mirror now. A promise of lightness and fragrance of petals.

Sophie laughs. She preens and coos, and kneels in front

of the mirror. She bows her head in a sweet gesture of submission her eyes deny. For the girl in the mirror is no longer a girl; she is a young, beautiful woman. A woman who likes her own boldness. A woman who likes the brightness of her own eyes; the flash of her beautiful white teeth; the dimple in her cheeks, and the pink nipple peeking from underneath the white gauze.

'I'll teach you to dance,' her aunt whispers into her ear. 'The Oriental dance.'

Thomas

Right after his arrival in Berlin, Thomas took a brisk walk, past an old church with twin spires and a red roof. Rosenstrasse was a narrow street, lit only by the light coming through the windows. A night watchman with a horn under his belt gave him a quick, cautious look, his sabre catching the reflection of the light. The insides of the houses were hidden behind curtains, lace, muslin, silk screens that kept secrets well. Sometimes Thomas could get a glimpse of someone moving inside, like a figure in a shadow play or magic lantern.

In his letter Ignacy had mentioned the patient was a rich Polish countess who had just arrived from St Petersburg. *Countess Potocka, once the most beautiful belle of Europe, in search of a healer. She is unable to travel to Paris, so Paris will have to come to her. After all, my friend, you too will profit from a change of place and a good dose of forgetting.*

'Please, the best of friends,' Thomas muttered in response. 'Don't.'

In spite of his fur-lined cape and high boots, the leather soles squeaking as he walked, he could not warm up. The air was clammy. The whiff of the sewers made him cringe. As he almost stepped onto gobbets of horses' dung, he heard a woman and a man quarrelling behind one of the impenetrable windows. The woman's voice was whiny, drowning the man's complaints in a barrage of reproaches. Then the doors of the house opened and the man stepped out. Tall, lanky, tattered leather jacket on his back. The door slammed. '*Du blöde Hure*,' the man yelled at the closed windows and walked away.

Thomas followed the man from a distance, hoping he would lead him to a neighbourhood tavern where he could have a beer and drown the constant stutter of the carriage wheels in his head, but when the man walked into a dim alley Thomas decided to turn back. This time he took a different direction and in one of the windows, its curtains parted to allow for a glimpse inside, he saw the glow of red and blue lanterns, golden tassels, scarlet ottomans. Two young women in low-cut gowns sat at a small table staring at cards, laid out in a cross. Beside them stood two glasses of clear yellow liqueur.

Sex was the need of a body. A fundamental need, Thomas stressed when he lectured to his students at Val de Grâce, that kept the disintegration of life at bay. He was not entirely convinced by Dr Brown's theory that the flow of life needed to be controlled, boosted or dampened according to need. 'The word *need*,' he liked to warn his students, 'is the problem. How would one know one's true needs?' Such doubts, of course, did not trouble Dr Brown. In London he was known to lecture with a glass of whisky in one hand and a bottle of laudanum in another, taking sips from one or the other.

For Thomas, the sight of the corpse stretched on the metal table was enough to renounce vain discussions and hypotheses. Life and death, he told his students, should be observed and examined without preconceived notions. *Ars medica tota in observationibus*, as Laennec had repeated *ad nauseam*. There was always something theatrical about that first incision. A moment pregnant with revelation, best approached in expectant silence. 'Gentlemen, watch and take note. Refraining, if you can, from idle speculations.' Ignoring the flicker of impatience in some of the eyes set on him, Thomas would perform his magic. His arm slightly raised, aware of the glitter of steel, he would wordlessly bend over the corpse and cut the skin without further declarations, defeated by the eagerness of youth.

One of the women in the window must have noticed him, for her hand slid down her neck in a well rehearsed gesture, inside her frilled décolletage, revealing full breasts. It was only then that Thomas realised with embarrassment that he was staring at her, the mute cause of her performance to which a smile was now added, tongue lingering over the bottom lip. Quickly he wrapped his cloak around him and turned away, walking down the dark alley as if pursued, though he could hear nothing but the pounding of his own heels on the pavement.

In Paris, in Rue de Clairmont, Minou expected him on Fridays. Dressed in black lace, with her smooth breasts pushed up by her corset, she smiled gently and poured a glass of red wine for him the moment he walked in. There was a pleasant smell of lavender and he liked her room, in spite of its garish combination of red and black, the lowered blinds and the smoky lamp. Minou didn't try to talk or pretend he was anything but a paying client. She washed in front of him and made love with a pleasant efficiency that both excited and released him from desire. He paid her well, and his demands were simple. When the lovemaking was over, he liked to watch her comb her long, reddish hair. Thomas suspected she dyed it with henna. Redheads made more money, he had heard. She came from St-Malo; her father and her two brothers were sailors.

'A sailor,' Ignacy once said to him in response to a statement long forgotten. 'You know what they say of sailors' wives? *Femme de marin-femme de chagrin.*'

It was ten o'clock by the time Thomas returned to his lodgings. His landlady was in the living room with her embroidery hoop. In her heavy dress, plaited hair arranged into a tight bun, she looked the embodiment of domesticity. She offered him tea, but he made a lame excuse and rushed up the stairs to his rooms.

Upstairs, he poured cold water from the jug into a porcelain basin, took off his jacket and rolled up his shirt sleeves. He didn't think of himself as handsome or well-built, in spite of Minou's protestations to the contrary. She liked his ruddy skin and brown eyes, and, with an air of fake ease, swore that his nose was 'aquiline'. Where did she get a word like this, he wondered. In the mirror he could see that his hair was thinning already. He was not as tall as Ignacy and far thinner, but his body had the sturdiness of generations of peasants, and could carry him in the saddle for hours.

He lay down on the hard, narrow bed and closed his eyes. He thought of a young woman, a girl he healed once, at la Charité. She was not older than fifteen, with red, lush curls and little freckles all over her face. She was writhing in pain, her lips livid and bleeding from the pressure of her crooked teeth biting into flesh. He had ascertained that the patient was brought by a young man who had left as soon as he could, without leaving his name or address. When he examined the girl, he found a pig's tail pushed into her anus. The nun who had helped him undress her, averted her eyes. Someone had tried to remove it, but the hair on the tail had got stuck in her flesh. The girl was bleeding and her anus was filled with pus.

Thomas inserted a small tube around the tail and extracted it. He didn't take the girl's money. He didn't warn her against continuing her trade. He didn't tell her how often he saw women with their private parts torn, with broken glass stuck in their vaginas. He figured she knew all that. She cried and thanked him in her thick, Breton accent. He kept her at la Charité for a few days until her wound began to show the signs of healing. Then he let her go.

Sophie

The plague is stalking the streets of Istanbul, this city of golden towers, of mosques and minarets, of crescents, kiosks, palaces and bazaars. At street corners bodies of the diseased are being burnt, together with all their possessions. The smoke has already filled the air, spilled into every street, lodged deep into the fibres of everyone's clothes. Whole sections of Istanbul have been cordoned off, though people say that well-placed *bakshish* can do wonders. Announcements in Turkish and in Greek forbid all contacts with foreigners, especially visits to the foreign missions. Any Greek woman caught with a foreigner would be beaten in public. Forty lashes to the heels of her feet.

Maria Glavani is carrying cloves of garlic in a sash around her neck and blue beads to ward off the evil eye. She never leaves the house without the holy picture of St Nicholas to whom she prays until her knees turn red and sore. In the mornings, when she comes back home smelling of liquor and men, she washes her hands and face with water to which she adds a few spoonfuls of vinegar.

'You stay inside!'

Mana's voice is harsh, impatient. The lines on her face are deepening, no matter how diligently she massages them every day. Sophie does not like these frenzied preparations, the ironing of dresses, the pinning of hair. The slaps when she is too slow or clumsy; when a hem is ripped; a pin misplaced; a line of kohl smudged. But after Mana leaves, the silence of their small house chokes Sophie. In her empty bed she hugs herself. What comes back to her is the smell of smoke and vinegar mixed with her own sweat. Everything that has happened in her life so far seems to have curled up in her, poised and waiting for release.

Death does not frighten her. In the street she does not turn her eyes away from the burning bodies. This is not the way she will die. She knows that. A fortune-teller told her once that she would die after a long life, without pain. Far away from home, but among those who loved her.

Mana's black crêpe mourning dress is folded at the bottom of her coffer. In Bursa Maria Glavani would have been the talk of the town. Here, no one remembers Konstantin, the unlucky Greek with greying hair, or his widow. If only she knew what life had in store when she looked into his black eyes for that first time. If only she listened to her own mother who pointed out the threadbare clothes and the chaffed shoes of this man who talked incessantly of diamonds big as walnuts, of herds of cattle, of silk and gold lace. Such is the fault of love. Love that brings a woman down and leaves her at the mercy of strangers.

Mana no longer talks of Christian duties, of sin and honour and the good name. They are eating meat again, and fresh fruit Mana buys at the market herself. The days are still cool. To keep warm, they put hot ashes into the *tandir* and sit with their feet on it. The warmth stays in their bodies for a long time. They need to be strong and round off their hips. By the time a fat man gets thin, a thin man dies.

'I want the best for you,' Mana says, and Sophie believes that. Her thoughts fold and refold around the promises of the future. She knows her mother has been making enquiries. Do any of the foreign diplomats in Istanbul show the first signs of boredom with their current mistresses? A Frank, rich and powerful, and refined. A man who would not slap her daughter around and then leave her without means to lead an honest life. The girl, she hears her mother's whisper, is an unspoiled virgin, worthy of a king's bed.

When she hears this, Sophie thinks of Diamandi's hand on her breasts, his body crushing her to the ground, his hot tongue parting her teeth, its earthy, lingering taste. She thinks of his strong, smooth legs, the man's hair on the boy's chest. The sharp pain of his love, and the blood on her legs.

An innocent girl, her mother says, with a good heart who could be grateful, who would be so grateful for a nice home, a carriage, beautiful dresses that would show off her skin and her hair. Dresses that would add glitter to these beautiful black eyes in which some have already seen the moon and the stars.

Dou-Dou. A virgin. Unspoiled. Innocent. Naïve to the highest degree, and with a good heart.

Yes, Dou-Dou can be grateful and funny and good at pleasing. Skilful, too, in the art of massage. Her touch is light, her skin is warm and dry. The girl is no weakling, she can press what needs to be pressed, knead what needs to be kneaded.

A foreign diplomat, her mother whispers, would leave one day. But, as any honest man would do in such a situation, he would provide a dowry for his girl. Sweeten the nibbled goods for his successor, a merchant or a shopkeeper. Someone solid, honest. Someone who would want children and a beautiful wife with a handsome dowry, even if he had to close his eyes and take a jewel from the second floor.

Why is Mana hiding all these schemes from me, Sophie thinks. Why the charades, the pretence, the games. I'm no longer a child. I know no one will marry me without a dowry. In bed at night she lets her fingers run down her neck, over her breasts, down to her belly. There is a moment in which a touch turns into a caress. A sweet moment of pleasure. She likes the thought of a rich man of the world who would tell her what lies behind Istanbul and Bursa. A man who would teach her the dances of the Frank courts, tell her what the ladies do to hold their hair so high. A man who would teach her to speak French. She is quick with languages, has always been. Greek, Turkish and Armenian come to her naturally like breath. She has already picked quite a few French words from her aunt, and some Russian ones too: *Bonjour mon cherie. Spassiba. Slichnotka.*

Aunt Helena, a frequent guest at the Russian mission's balls and soirees, has promised to keep her eyes open. She has always liked the Russians whom she calls 'the fair race from the North', and 'the people who know the meaning of pleasure'. She has always liked their caviar from Astrakhan, their clear vodka that goes right to your veins. Liked their dances until dawn, as if there were no tomorrow, as if the world would end that very day. Glasses, she tells her niece, get smashed against the wall so that they could not hold another drink at an inferior time. There is one more thing that pleases Aunt Helena. The Russian victories over the Turks. 'The black camel of death will soon kneel at *his* doors,' she says, pointing in the direction of the Sultan's palace.

Yes, a Russian diplomat would be best for Dou-Dou.

All talk, Mana says with bitterness. Liars are branded in this country for a reason. Her sister, may dear Lord forgive a widow's bitterness, has always been fickle and not above jealousy. Just because she lives in the district of Phanar does not make her rich and powerful. And all these stories she comes with are nothing more than accounts of her own goodness. Fanciful accounts given to them like scraps from her own table. Maria Glavani knows such talk when she hears it. Didn't she have a good teacher? Konstantin too never stopped weaving his schemes until the day of his death.

So Aunt Helena's words are listened to but not believed. For there is always a little mishap in her stories, a small obstacle that would have to be waited through, ironed out, removed. The undersecretary who kept asking to see Dou-Dou before he would recommend her to his superiors was a known libertine and his request to meet Sophie had to be dismissed. We don't want to cheapen her, Maria, her aunt has said. No touching if they are not buying.

The plague is what makes Sophie's situation worse. The plague cools many a heart. In the presence of death, *amour* wilts and shrivels. Besides, even a foreign diplomat caught with a Greek woman would have to face the Ottoman justice. Not everyone wants to risk that much. Not even for such a beautiful pair of eyes.

In the Russian Mission, Monsieur Stachiev's wife is so terrified of the plague that she has locked herself and her children in an upstairs bedroom and refuses to see or meet anyone. This, in itself, is not such a bad thing, for it leaves Monsieur Stachiev free to pursue his own merry interests. But it doesn't help to have people talk that she has sent her surgeon away for wanting to bleed her. That she screams at the top of her voice. 'We'll all die here in this infidel country. We'll all be punished.' She has already cursed her husband. 'Your sons will pay for your fornication,' she said. 'You will kneel at their coffins and then where will your whores be?' She will call the Janissaries, if she but spots a Greek woman entering the mission building.

* * *

'Dou-Dou, you are slowing me down,' Mana says. They are coming back from the market, their baskets heavy with meat and fruit. As always, people stare at them as they pass. The men look at them with longing and often stop them, asking for directions or pretending they have mistaken them for someone else. Women's eyes are curious, assessing their beauty as if it were a threat, a challenge.

'Come on, girl, we don't have all day.'

A black man who stops them is a eunuch. Not an ordinary eunuch either, but a eunuch from the Sultan's court. His robes are woven with gold and silver and mazanne blue. The face under the burgundy fez is smooth, layers of fat testifying to the richness of his table. His voice is soft and warm. Having lived his life among women, he knows how to calm their fears.

'Beautiful ladies,' he says and smiles, flashing his teeth. As white as hers, Sophie thinks.

The Ottoman Princess, the Sultan's daughter, has ordered him to stop them. He was summoned by his mistress, told to drop all he was doing, and go after them. Go after two Christian women who have caught the Princess's eye.

Sophie's eyes travel upwards, toward the palace windows. She cannot see anyone there. Perhaps it is the Sultan himself who has seen her. Perhaps, with one look of His eyes, her life has changed forever.

'Follow me. We mustn't make the Princess wait.'

'Are you sure you are not taking us for someone else,' Mana asks the eunuch, but the black man laughs. His mistress's mind is an open book to him. They should not doubt their luck. The heavy baskets can be left with the servants who can take them to their home. 'Just tell me where you live,' he says.

'We'll take them on our way back,' Mana says sharply. 'Ourselves!'

Is there is a note of fear in Mana's voice? Unease? Anger as she clasps her daughter's hand in a firm grip as if she wanted them to turn away and run? But how can a Christian woman refuse an Ottoman princess? How can a Greek say *no* to a Turkish master?

Dou-Dou does not want to notice Mana's fear. Her mind flutters with delicious visions of glittering jewels, gauzy dresses and garden paths bathing in sweet, dappled shade. She can feel the harsh impatience of her mother's hand, the reluctance of her steps. She wants to laugh and assure her Mana there is nothing to worry about. She is ready. When her chance comes, she will know what to do.

They follow the black eunuch past the palace gate, past the first courtyard filled with cool shade, fragrant with the jessamines and honeysuckles that coil around tree trunks, past the giant clay vases filled with blooming roses. The big courtyard is bustling with life. Two tall grooms hold Arabian horses, snow white, with the legs of dancers. A short, fat man in a leather apron is rolling a big wooden barrel. A young man is whistling a merry tune, trailing Dou-Dou with his eyes until the eunuch's look stops him.

Inside the Seraglio the sweet perfume of the jessamines penetrates the gilded sashes easily. A white marble fountain releases the stream of water that falls into four basins below. The sound is pleasing. By this fountain, the eunuch leaves them. 'The Princess shall send for you,' he says, lifting Dou-Dou's head with his index finger and looking straight into her eyes.

'Beautiful,' he murmurs. 'These eyes will shame the light of the moon.'

When they are left alone, Sophie looks around. The tiles on the floor are cool to the touch. She would have liked to take her shoes off and step on them with bare feet, but Mana's eyes stop her. The walls are covered with tiles of different patterns. Most of them have blue, and gold in them, and the colours mingle in her eyes and shimmer. The thick stained glass windows dim the rays of the sun, make them dance with colours of amber and silvery dust. There are no chairs, but a few big cushions on a raised sofa covered with Persian carpets. The scent of honeysuckle joins the jessamine, the scent that penetrates her hair, her dress, clings to her skin.

Is this how the Sultan smells, she wonders. Is his skin as soft as she imagines? As cool as the tiles?

'Don't say anything until you are asked,' her mother whispers. Her face is pale and her eyes dart around the room. What is it that she wants to find?

'Don't look at the Princess. Keep your eyes down.'

Mana has removed her own kerchief and wraps another layer of cloth over her daughter's hair.

What if the Sultan will not care for her? What if he takes one look at her and sends her back?

But these are thoughts easily laughed away. In her heart of hearts she trusts her joy. A woman the Sultan summons becomes a *quadin,* a chosen one.

'Someone must have seen you,' Mana hisses, her voice rough with anger. 'Didn't I tell you not to wander alone.'

The servant woman who enters the antechamber is wearing a pink kaftan over blue drawers, her hand touching her heart and lips in greeting. Silent, she beckons with her right hand and they follow, their heels clicking on the tiles. They walk through long winding corridors of closed doors, past a big room where women sit on big satin cushions, smoking *nargila*, working on their embroidery. One of them with diamonds in her turban, sitting on a lap of a Negress throws herself into her arms as if to hide in them. In another room a woman in a red dress is bending over a big loom, absorbed in the invisible patterns. To Sophie these images seem like pieces of a puzzle, a mystery she alone would be allowed to solve. This is making her deaf to Mana's sighs.

The Princess is wearing a vest of purple cloth, set with pearls on each side down to her feet and round her sleeves. It is tied at the waist with two large tassels embroidered with diamonds. Her shift is fastened with an emerald as big as a turkey egg. In the middle of her headdress two roses glitter, each made of a large ruby surrounded with clean diamonds. She is seated on a big silk-covered cushion, like an enormous animal at rest, its belly still full, but its eyes already on the lookout for the next meal. Her arms are strong and muscular, her skin smooth. Her black eyes, lined with kohl, are short-sighted for she leans forward as she speaks.

'You have come,' she says, as if their obedience surprised her. 'Welcome to my home.'

Perhaps, Sophie thinks, the Princess has been sent to appraise her, to see if she is worthy of the Sultan's time. The Ottoman Princess, blessed with the riches of her father, her body cared for by her army of slaves, scraped, massaged and perfumed with the most precious of scents. Her hands are too big though, in spite of all the beautiful rings. Five on her right hand only. Two have diamonds bigger than hazelnuts.

'Your Highness,' she says, with her loveliest smile. 'Is too kind.'

The Princess gives a sign and servants enter with wooden trays, carrying sweets and strong Turkish coffee, its aroma filling the air. There are dried apricots, figs, raisins and dates from Basra, the sweetest that there are. Nuts in a gilded bowl. Fresh figs too, black and green. A jug of sherbet to drink. A sherbet for which, Sophie is told, snow has been fetched all the way from the highest mountains of India.

'I love figs,' Sophie says brightly and clasps her hands in delight.

It's too late for Mana's look of warning. The Princess laughs too and promises that such a sweet child, such a beautiful girl could have all the figs in the Ottoman Kingdom. And apricots, and raisins. And pistachio nuts and sweet dark coffee that races in the veins and brings flashes of colour to the cheeks.

She can have everything she wants. Beautiful dresses. Shawls. Velvet and damask and silk that the merchants bring all the way from China. The most exquisite patterns. A girl so beautiful should be wearing lots of gold to set off her raven hair and her olive skin. And soft, soft leather for her feet.

'This child deserves the best,' she says, her eyes leaving Sophie for a moment and resting on Mana, as if she were responsible for her daughter's poverty. 'Not the rags that she is wearing now.'

Mana wriggles on her cushion.

'Most illustrious of Princesses,' she begins. 'Your Imperial Highness. The light of my eyes.'

She begs the Princess to think of her. A widowed mother of an only daughter. A beloved daughter she cannot think of parting with.

'But she would live with me, in the palace, you silly woman. Have everything she could ever need. Can't you see that? Does every Greek have to be so dense, so infernally stupid?'

Seeing a frown on Sophie's forehead, she changes her tone, quickly. Too quickly.

Surely a mother cannot deny her child's fate. Fight the fortune God offers her. The good life of opulence and comfort. Look at her hands, the Princess says, still accusing. Cracked and reddened like those of a scullery maid. Is that what you want for this angel? Is she to be your maid? Scrubbing pots? Ruining the gifts Allah has bestowed on her?

'My God,' Mana says, 'forbids a mother to leave her child among strangers.'

'My God,' she says, looking straight into the Princess's eyes, 'does not allow some kinds of love.'

The Princess laughs. 'I know your God, woman,' she says. 'All your God wants is a good price for her. Here. Take this!'

A purse filled with cekins lands in Mana's lap with a thud. It is heavy. A bounty, a treasure. Money that could last them a few months. Pay the debts, buy new dresses, good tender lamb and fresh fruit. Pay for dangling earrings that would set off Dou-Dou's shapely lobes, the graceful turn of her neck.

A purse filled with gold.

This is a fair price for a poor Greek girl, isn't it? This and a promise of a good life, a full stomach, and hands that would not have to touch dirt ever again.

'With me she will want for nothing.'

Sophie looks at her mother. There is nothing I can do, Mana's body tells her. I can refuse the gold or take it, this won't make any difference. But I cannot tell her I do not allow you to stay here.

'She'll be like a daughter to me,' the Princess coos. She has moved closer and the heat radiating from her touches Sophie's arms.

'She will sleep in my bed. She will go everywhere with me. I'll buy her everything she wants.'

Fear signals its beginning with a spasm in her stomach, then another, closer to Sophie's heart. The soles of her feet are cold, her hands begin to tremble. In Bursa she has seen men show a bloodied leg of a fox, all that has remained in the snare they have set. The beast has chewed off its own hind leg and escaped.

'I have never even asked your name,' the Princess says.

Sophie hesitates. She doesn't really like the Princess at all. She doesn't like the way her strong hand rests on her knee and squeezes it, as if the two of them had to stand together against Mana. She doesn't like the hint of rot in her mouth. The tooth in front is black with decay. The visions of the Sultan's favour have receded and suddenly she sees herself as a servant in this palace, carrying trays with raisins and nuts, making coffee somewhere in the kitchen. Perhaps scraping hair from the Princess's legs and arms, holding a towel for her in *hammam* as her big body breaks out with sweat.

How do you say *no* to an Ottoman Princess whose whims are their orders? Who could, with one word, send them to their deaths, the way the Sultan is said to dispose of unfaithful concubines: wrapped in a burlap bag, and thrown into the waters of the Bosphorus; or left naked in the street of Istanbul, unknown to anyone, a corpse with raven hair and skin white as milk, chest pierced with a dagger.

'Don't be shy, my precious,' the Princess says.

Sophie raises her eyes. There is a flash of defiance, though she is trying to disguise it.

'My name is Sophie,' she says. 'It means wisdom.'

She watches how, with one gesture of dismissal, her mother is made to leave the room, the purse of gold cekins in her hands. How she takes one more look at her daughter, a look of such pain and despair that Sophie wants to run toward her and throw her hands around her neck. 'I've failed you after all,' Mana's eyes say. 'I have not kept you from danger. Forgive me.'

The doors close after her, silently, like the doors of a tomb.

Rosalia

Only a week had passed, even if the memory of the journey seemed already faded and oddly remote, as if whole weeks separated them from the grimy inns and the jostling carriage.

In the first days of October, morning took a long time to arrive. With curtains drawn, the only light in the grand salon was a votive lamp underneath the icon of St Nicholas. In the twilight, the red reflections on the Saint's bearded face made the holy image waver and float.

The countess was awake already. She tried to lift herself up, but the task was too strenuous and she fell back on the pillow.

'Don't look at me, Rosalia,' she said. 'I don't want you to remember me like that.'

Blood stained her clothes, seeped through the sheets, the blankets. They should be soaked in cold water right away. The mattress would have to be burned. The maids have to stop gossiping in the kitchen and clean more carefully. Rosalia could see the patches missed by the duster, the trails of neglect. *One cannot rejoice at this constant lowering of your station in life*, Aunt Antonia had written, hinting once again at the *disastrous but perhaps foreseeable consequences* of her father's Jacobin dreams, the true cause of all her misfortunes. She herself was far from supporting tyranny or injustice, but all this talk of freeing the serfs or making Poland a republic frightened her. Like everything else in life, equality too had its limits. *Your place is here*, her letters to Rosalia invariably ended, *at my side*.

An operation would take place right in this room. A mattress could go on a table. She did warn Frau Kohl that one might be needed at short notice. A fairly big one, with sturdy legs.

Since their arrival in Berlin, breakfast meant a few

morsels of bread dipped in red wine to strengthen blood and on a better morning a few sips of consommé the cook prepared fresh every day. Dr Bolecki always came around ten o'clock and, after a short examination of the countess, insisted that Rosalia escorted him downstairs. This was the only time, he said, they could exchange their observations about the patient, only they never did.

On the first day Dr Bolecki told her that his father had fought in the Kościuszko Insurrection; that he, Dr Bolecki, trained in Paris, thanks to Napoleon's insatiable need for army surgeons; and that the French doctor who was coming from Paris could amputate a limb in under two minutes. On the following day she learned that Dr Bolecki's beloved wife died of consumption and his only daughter was a Carmelite nun, in Rome. He had to take her there himself, in January last year. On a day so cold that he couldn't stop thinking of Napoleon's Russian campaign. 'Was it really that terrible?' Rosalia asked, out of politeness. 'I mean the campaign,' she added quickly lest he thought she was prying into his life. He hesitated for a moment, and said that the most eerie was the silence before the Moscow fires started. 'A void,' he said, 'awaiting human screams.' Of the march back he refused to speak at all. 'It's better for you not to know,' he said. But then, even though Rosalia did not insist on returning to the subject, he added that death from cold was kind. 'The worst,' he said, 'always comes from a human hand.'

'I think him very pleasant,' Rosalia said when the countess asked how she liked Dr Bolecki. She meant 'reliable', but 'pleasant' seemed a safer word to use. Olga had complained, on two occasions, that Rosalia was putting on airs. 'As if *she* were a doctor here,' were Olga's words.

Today, as the examination followed its usual route – pulse, signs of fever, the usual questions about appetite, bleeding, and acuteness of pain – a lock of grey hair kept falling over Doctor Bolecki's left eye. This, Rosalia thought, might be responsible for his air of restlessness. The countess suffered these ministrations without a sign of impatience, but let Rosalia answer all the questions. Only Dr Bolecki's assurance that he would bring the French surgeon the next day, restored some alertness to her face. 'As soon as possible,' he kept saying. He kept looking at her too, Rosalia noted, as if something managed to change about her since the day before. Her nursing skills, he said, were most impressive. Not every patient was thus blessed. 'I trust you, Mademoiselle, completely.' This he repeated three times in a row, adding that he was sure his high regard would be shared by Doctor Lafleur.

There was a sound of footsteps outside the grand salon, then silence. The door opened and Marusya appeared, balancing a tray with letters and a pot of coffee with some difficulty. It was one of the countess's whims, a pot of freshly brewed coffee at her bedside. The smell of it, she said, was enough. She could not drink any of it, but that shouldn't stop Rosalia from having some. The maid put the tray on the table. Her eyes were fixed on the tray and her chore, as if any distraction could cause her to lose control. The tray wobbled and Rosalia half expected to hear the crash of china falling to the floor, but this did not happen.

'Your son has written, just as he has promised,' she said, spotting Bobiche's handwriting on one of the letters. The countess's youngest son had managed to write two whole pages instead of his usual one. L'abbé Chalenton was making progress.

> When are you coming back, Maman? We have had terrible history with dogs. Fidelle bit a Postillion and Basilkien declared that she must be mad. But she continued to drink water and came when was called, so we thought she would be all right. Then she bit

Basilkien's finger and ran wildly in the yard and bit a pig. A week later, Basilkien showed symptoms of madness and the doctor made a cut on his finger to obtain a few drops of blood. Then he mixed the blood with milk and gave it to Basilkien to drink. He is much better as I write this and has stopped complaining! The Postillion, is also well, but the Doctor said Fidelle had to be killed, for there was no way of telling what will become of her, and so she is no more.
Everyone misses you very much. Tell Olena I'll take her for a ride in my new carriage when she comes home.

Nothing, yet, from Odessa, from the countess's elder daughter, Madame Kisielev. As soon as the news of her safe delivery reached them, Rosalia insisted that Madame Kisielev should be told the truth. The baby would no longer be affected by the mother's agitation. Besides what daughter would want to be away from her mother in her time of need.

And so, in her last letter, the countess asked her daughter to come to Berlin. *Please hurry, my dear Sophie*, she wrote, *if you want to see your mother alive*. Enclosed with that letter was a bank order for 50,000 roubles. Madame Kisielev could well be on her way.

Sophie

That night, the silent servant with an unsmiling face takes Sophie to her bath. Her body is scrubbed and scraped clean with a sharp end of a seashell dabbed with precious drops of perfume. The dress that touches her skin is light as gossamer, soft like the skin of a newborn baby.

When her nail snags the soft fabric, the servant clucks

her tongue. She is shaking her head, mouth twisted in a grimace. Without a veil, she is no longer mysterious. A woman with crooked teeth and nose too big for her face who pinches Sophie with impatience reserved for those whose position is not yet established. Reserved for a Greek slave girl with uncertain future who might not please the Princess after all.

'Her Highness is waiting,' the servant whispers. 'Hurry up, girl.'

The Princess has her own apartments in the Harem. There is a tiled fireplace in her bedroom for nights cooler than this one. The walls are wainscoted with mother of pearl, ivory and olive wood, more beautiful than the lid of the best jewellery box in Aunt Helena's home. The carpet on the floor is soft and thick. On the bed a golden throw glitters in the candlelight.

'Come on, my sweet wisdom,' the Princess says and pats the spot beside her. She is not wearing her pantaloons, but a loose dress. Through the slit of the dress Sophie can see her leg. White, smooth skin that she does not want to touch.

The Princess removes the smallest of her rings and extends her hand. 'Take it,' she says. 'I want you to wear it.'

The ring is too big. It will have to be resized. The jeweller will be summoned first thing in the morning. For now, Sophie can wear the ring on a string around her neck.

Sophie casts her eyes down. Thoughts abandon her. Her body shudders, each movement is an effort.

'Lean on me, my child. I want to feel your warmth.'

It is not cold, she wants to say but doesn't. On her way here the silent servant ushered her into a latticed room and opened a large coffer. Inside there was nothing but a silk belt. The servant gave her a curious look and mimed strangling her own throat.

Sophie closes her eyes when the Princess's hand caresses

her cheek, her neck, her breasts. A hot, heavy hand, burrowing its way into her body. Is this what Mana knew would happen to her?

What a fool she was to dream of the Sultan's love.

Someone walks by the Princess's chamber, something rustles, something falls to the floor with a thud. The hand that touches her freezes, but only for a moment.

In this moment Sophie closes her eyes and tries to imagine this is the hand of a rich foreign diplomat, the man of the world who will teach her to dance and tell her stories of foreign lands. Stories in which women have carriages and beautiful jewels. Where their hair is piled up and adorned with flowers and birds and strings of pearls. Where men whisper sweet words into the women's ears.

'How soft your skin is, my sweet wisdom.'

'Come closer. You are not afraid of me, are you?'

Is this what fear does? Freezes the heart? Stops the mind from dreaming?

She lets the Princess hold her hand. Mana has taught her how to give pleasure. Each body has its own desires. She knows how to press a muscle, gently first, then harder, and harder, until the pressure inside it is released. She knows how to dissolve the knots of tension, to bring relief.

A smile is pasted to her lips, a contortion of flesh. It makes her mouth quiver. The Princess calls her an angel, a sweet, beautiful child. A temptress. Sophie will lack for nothing. Ever. Sophie will be like a queen.

'Kiss me,' the Princess says, pointing at her lips.

'Not like this. Harder.'

There are bruises on her thighs and arms, but she has not felt pain. Her own body feels as if it belongs to someone else, to another woman she can see from above. A woman whose face is covered with kisses, whose body is pinned to the bed. Whose clothes are prised away from her and whose hands clutch to her naked breasts. This other woman has stopped fighting her fate. She is lying motionless in the soft bed, with her eyes closed. She is trying to sink so deep that no one would find her. She is trying to close herself to the touch that yanks her from her dreamlike state. Nothing is happening, she repeats to herself. This is nothing. Nothing.

'What is done once,' the Princess whispers, 'cannot be undone. What is felt once, will never be forgotten. You are mine, now,' she whispers. 'My own little wisdom.'

In the darkness Sophie prays for time to hurry, to go faster. Her lips are sore where the Princess has bitten them.

'I am making you happy. You cannot hide your own pleasure from me.'

'Say it!'

'You are making me happy. I cannot hide my own pleasure from you.'

'I am your mistress. There is no one else but me.'

'You are my mistress. There is no one else but you.'

'Ever.'

'Ever.'

The bed is crumpled and moist with sweat; pillows have fallen off, to the floor. Silk-covered pillows, soft and smooth. The Princess is still holding her arm, making her lie there. There are other kinds of wisdom, she says. Many crave it, but few are chosen. Only to the few it shall be revealed. Wisdom that speaks of the true delights of love, of secrets common women are not meant to know.

'Listen, my little wisdom. With me you will know it all.'

These stories speak of mysterious journeys across parched deserts; of abandoned inns where, in spite of the worst fears, sumptuous meals await an exhausted traveller; of crossroads where the hanged long for the mercy of the burial; of old hermits who know the way. It is enough to close her eyes to see the deep dungeons where hatred and envy rule and the fragrant gardens where beauty and love meet in secret. In search of their fate, the travellers of those tales fight hunger and thirst, battle false desires – the phantoms that drive the soul away from its dream.

'Such are the stories of the night,' the Sultana whispers. 'They are all for you, my sweet wisdom.'

For there are more stories. Stories wrenched away from the possessed. Stories from forbidden books, stories of women who know as much as the men, but who guard their secret knowledge with their lives.

'I know them all, my sweet wisdom,' the Sultana says. 'And soon, you too will know them.'

But then, a moment later, she is snoring, her arm heavy on Sophie's shoulder. For a long while Sophie tries to wriggle out from under this arm. To stand up, gasp for breath. Her stomach churns and the coffee she has drunk rises up her throat. For a brief moment of despair she considers standing on the edge of the window and throwing herself down, into the paved courtyard underneath, but she doesn't want to die.

She lets the tears flow, silently, until sleep comes. In the morning, she will think of something. Luck will not abandon her like that. Without warning, without giving her another chance. Luck may have played a mean trick on her, but Sophie has not lost her faith.

'I'm worthy of a king's bed,' she thinks, just before sleep comforts her, just before she remembers the smell of jessamine and honeysuckle; just before she forgets the silk belt in the black ebony coffer and the cold anger in the servant's voice.

* * *

The Greeks are but our slaves, she hears, their race a perfect example of what happens when the men are not separated from the women. No work ever gets done, because with all these women running in the streets men only want to have fun. Idleness and lies rule them. And deceit.

But the Russians, she says in protest, do not separate the women. Or the French. Or the English. No one heeds her words. What does she know, a plaything that has caught the Princess's fancy. Clanging bells on her arms so that her arrival does not go unnoticed.

The Harem, she hears, is a woman's blessing. Without it, a woman would be exposed to curious glances in the streets. To prying eyes, to jeerings from the passersby. Here, a woman has everything she may ever want. Why would she want to venture outside? What is it that she lacks?

When she laughs, the women say: 'Don't laugh too much or you'll cry soon.'

It is in the small courtyard, by the fountain, that the women gather: odalisques, servants, and slaves. On low tables the slaves have laid clays, dried pomegranate peel, nut bark, saffron, dried roses, myrtle, orange flowers. There are fresh eggs the whites of which will be rubbed with *shebba* to make the thick lumpy mass that will cleanse the skin. For it is with the skin, they say, that you touch the world.

The women, their faces covered with gooey masks, sit patiently and talk. Things have to be done right, the way they were done before. Only the conceited believe one could discover a better way than the one practised for generations. A better way of embroidering or preparing a face mask. A better way of dancing or making coffee. A better way to live.

But there is other talk too. Of slaves whose beauty caught the eye of the Master, of these moments for which one prepares one's whole life. A moment in which a man's eye can change the woman's fate; when a slave can become an odalisque; and then, if Allah wills that, maybe even a mother of a Sultan's child. Unless, of course, one day, in the *hammam*, such a woman finds the doors locked, and the heat and the steam take her breath away.

Why?

The women shrug their shoulders. Doesn't she know how easy it is to cause envy? To make a false step, say one word too many. Doesn't she know anything?

Every night it seems to Sophie that she can hear the locking of many doors. There is a restlessness in her. A force sets upon her as soon as she opens her eyes and does not leave her until she falls asleep under the heavy arm of her mistress. The same restlessness that makes a fox caught in a snare chew off its leg.

To stop it Sophie thinks of the black eunuch. His black skin has a warm tone, and he smells of sandalwood. *Hadim Effendi*, a learned one, the Princess sometimes calls him, laughing. He was but a boy when he was first brought to the Palace. A boy who cried and cried until one of the slave women had the presence of mind to sing to him. Now he is *kislar aghasi*, master of the maidens. Unlike the white eunuchs who guard the gates of the Seraglio, he is allowed to enter the chamber of the women. He is fond of bright embroidered patterns, of jackets trimmed with gold.

Hadim Effendi likes her. She has discovered that on one of the restless nights when her mistress sent her for a pearl necklace, and she got lost in the corridors of the Seraglio. To silence the clanking bells, she stopped by the latticed window and looked outside. A beautiful moon, milky white, illuminated the sleeping city. It was difficult to believe that people lived there, in these dimly lit streets. That they loved, worked, slept, died there. That there was anyone else there besides *Bekjih*, the night watchman, his feet tapping on the cobbled stones as if he came from the kingdom of the dead.

'Do you know the rules?' Hadim asked, startling her with his presence.

'Yes,' she said, emboldened by the moon. 'The rules do not allow holding any woman in the Palace against her will.'

'The same rules also allow for killing anyone who has left. You should remember that.'

He was looking at her. There was much softness in his eyes, beside the sadness she had noticed before. She smiled.

'The secrets of the Palace may not be shared among the living.'

Slowly, as if she were asleep, she opened her shirt and bared her breasts. He did not stop her. He did not touch her either, but stood there looking at her for a long time. She didn't move.

She removes the clanking bells from her arms and knocks on the door to his room.

'Come in,' the master of the maidens says, lifting his eyes from a thick leather-bound volume.

'I'll die here if you don't help me,' she says and holds her breath. With one word he could have her flogged. With one word he could have her begging for her life.

He closes the book and motions to her to come closer.

'You won't die,' he says. 'Your eyes have nothing but life in them.'

He hands her a cup of coffee and motions to her to drink. She takes a sip, then another, but he shakes his head. 'Drink it all up,' he says.

In her coffee grounds he reads her future. He doesn't talk of death without pain. He sees five dogs that bring her gifts. He sees three camels with more gifts and light shining in her way and a great door opening up. There is a tree too, its branches touching the sky. A tree with thick foliage, its branches laden with fruit.

'Please,' she whispers. 'Tell me what to do.'

The master of the maidens stares at her coffee grounds. 'You will travel far and wide,' he says, smiling at her. 'There is no cage in this world that will hold you.'

'Will I be rich,' she asks, pleased by what she takes as a promise of a merchant husband who might take her with him on his journeys.

'Yes,' he says. 'Richer than you can imagine.'

'Happy?' she asks.

He puts her hand down and shakes his head. 'This,' he says, 'your coffee grounds do not reveal.'

There is a long moment of silence. She moves her fingers to her blouse, wanting to open it as she did before, but he extends his hand and stops her. It is a warm, chocolate colour against the whiteness of hers. When his fingers touch her lips, she kisses them.

'Tell me what to do,' she asks. 'Please.'

'I'll never have children, but this does not bar me from having pleasure,' he says.

She closes her eyes and feels his hand caress her neck.

She is to wait for the time of great commotion. When she sees the camels in the courtyard, she has to be ready. She will have to climb down the vine to the courtyard, wrapped in a servant's yashmak. It is high time for the Princess might well have noticed the change in her. She has become careless, impatient. The other day, she turned so abruptly that one of the slaves dropped the tray of coffee cups and smashed them all.

'Will you be there?' she has asked, but the master of the maidens shook his head. No one should see them together. But under the jasmine bush, she will find a basket she will carry right outside the gates.

On the fourth day, at dawn, she hears a soft tap on the door. The Princess is fast asleep, and Sophie dresses quickly, in the dark. Pantaloons, a kaftan. The plainest yashmak she can find. The bells she stuffs under the big cushion in the corner.

There is no one in the hall when she opens the window. Outside, she holds on to the thickest of the vine, and doesn't look down. For a moment she is the child in Bursa again, Dou-Dou who can outrun every boy and climb the tallest trees. Her hands tell her that the vine is old and sturdy.

On the ground, under the jasmine bush, she finds the basket..Inside there is a gift. *Nazar Bonjuk*, a blue glass eye to guard her against the evil look. She pins it to her kaftan and waits for what seems a long time, until the gates open and the caravan arrives. As soon as the first camel enters, she leaves her hiding place and heads to the gate. A servant on her master's errand. When the time comes, the master of the maidens said, eyes will be averted, swords will stay in their sheaths, and no one will be sent after her.

The guard takes one look at her basket and waves her through.

Thomas

At Graf von Haefen's palace, their arrival was anticipated with visible impatience. As Ignacy's carriage approached the front courtyard, Thomas saw that one of the Graf's Swiss guards was standing on tiptoe, shouting in the direction of the carriage house, summoning a groom to hold their horses. A tall footman who had been waiting in the open doors disappeared as soon as he saw the carriage roll in.

'Gossip I take to be not unlike cancer,' Ignacy said,

oblivious to the signs of impatience they were the source of, concluding the monologue of the last ten minutes. 'Insidious. Surfacing when we think it conquered.' He hadn't changed at all, Thomas thought, if one overlooked the grey in his hair.

Thomas was not paying as much attention as he perhaps should have. But why really? The countess, like most women of her class, had had many lovers so did it really matter if this German Graf had been one of these *liaisons amoureuses*? He could see why Ignacy was so keen on her *unprecedented* influence in St Petersburg. ('After all, the Tsar, Thomas, *is* her close friend and, I take it, quite ready to listen.') Why was it 'unprecedented', Thomas could not tell, but it had to have something to do with the late Count Potocki's position at the Russian court. Or with the perennial Polish hopes, doomed fights for the lost independence. Yes, the Poles had been dealt a rotten hand. No other country had been eaten alive in the middle of the Enlightened Europe and told it was for her own good. But wasn't it all part of what old Europe had always been? A whore siding with the strong and the mighty. Preening herself for the favours of the rich?

'Only one does not die from being talked about, Ignacy,' he said.

Graf von Haefen's palace was a two-storey sand-coloured edifice in the Renaissance style. On the entrance gate of wrought iron two plump-looking angels were clinging to their posts. The footman, still panting from a rushed run upstairs and back, the gold trim of his crimson livery slightly dull at the edges, led them into a small vestibule whose tapestry of nymphs, monkeys, and flowers was reflected back in giant gilded mirrors. A few moments later, a thin, young woman appeared, black hair coiled around her head. The diamond on her neck, Thomas thought, could have paid for a good pair of horses. She extended her hand to be kissed. Ignacy took it first, in both hands. Then Thomas bowed over it, awkwardly, merely brushing it with his lips.

'Mademoiselle la Comtesse! How is your dear Maman? Has she slept well? Has the pain lessened?'

'You've arrived at last, Doctor,' Mademoiselle la Comtesse said, ignoring Ignacy's questions. Her eyes were bloodshot, her hands trembled slightly, but her voice was calm and composed. 'Maman has been waiting all morning.'

The countess's daughter was wearing a simple morning dress, and, Thomas noted with some bemusement, her right cuff was stained brown. Youth made her attractive in a coltish sort of way, but she could do with some fresh air and less coffee. There was a gauntness to her face he did not quite like.

'Doctor Lafleur I spoke to Graf von Haefen about,' Ignacy said, pointing at Thomas who bowed slightly, 'straight from Paris. Heartily recommended by Baron Larrey.'

Larrey's name made no visible impression on young Countess Potocka who led them upstairs and into a grand salon that had been turned into the sick room. The enormous empire bed, by the wall, was covered by a golden throw. A day bed and an armchair had been placed beside it. An Oriental screen hid the paraphernalia of illness, the medicine bottles, the chamber pot. The air was thick with the smells of almond milk, camomile, and mint. The underlying whiff of ammonia made Thomas clear his throat.

The countess was fully dressed, reclining on the bed, her eyes closed, black eyelashes evenly set in her white lids. She was breathing slowly, as if asleep. One look was enough to make Thomas see that the illness had melted the skin on her bones. She was deathly pale.

She doesn't need a doctor, he thought, she needs a miracle.

His eyes lingered over two women standing by their mistress. One was obviously a maid, of rosy plumpness, flaxen braids wound around her head like a crown. The other, in her pale yellow dress, a cameo brooch pinned to a lace collar around her neck, he decided, was the nurse. Mademoiselle Rosalia Romanowicz. Perhaps he should have paid more attention to Ignacy's words. He vaguely recalled the praises of her nursing and her devotion to her mistress. *A daughter of a Polish hero and a Jewess from Uman.* Or was that someone else entirely? He noted the thick auburn hair, pulled back and held tight by a barrette, in the shape of folded hands.

'Good morning, Doctor Bolecki,' the countess said, turning to Ignacy. The back of her head rested on the day bed. 'I've been waiting for you all this time.'

This was a reproach.

'I came as soon as I could, Madame,' Ignacy replied in what Thomas thought was too much of an eager schoolboy's tone.

Thomas made a step toward the bed, but stopped, unsure if the examination should begin that abruptly. The countess's eyes were clearly her most striking feature. Large, black and luminous eyes that lit up her face. Fixed on him, now, probing. Suddenly he became aware of how baggy his trousers had become and wished he had ordered a new pair.

'Doctor Lafleur, great surgeon, Madame la Comtesse,' Ignacy continued what to Thomas sounded like a mountebank's pitch for snake oil and the elixir of youth. 'The only one, Your Highness, I would trust with my own life.' He mentioned the years spent at la Charité, lectures at Val de Grâce, and once again flaunted Baron Larrey's personal recommendation.

'Please, my dear Doctor,' the countess said, lifting her hand to her lips, and Ignacy stopped. Her eyes did not leave Thomas for a second, taking in the aquiline nose, his reddened hands, and baggy trousers shiny at the knees.

To steady himself, Thomas thought of his father who had been beaten by his mistress for being inadvertently in her way. He recalled wounds masters had inflicted on other servants: burns on the hands and legs, cuts, lashes. In Russia, he reminded himself, serfs were called 'slaves' for a good reason. Once, in Vilna, he had been asked to treat a man whose back had been broken by the lashes his master commanded. When the man died a few hours later, his master promptly ordered another serf to marry the widow.

'What are you thinking of, Doctor Lafleur?' the countess asked in a low, raspy voice that held a note of irony as if she had guessed his thoughts and already found fault with his reasoning.

'You should not exert yourself, Madame la Comtesse,' Thomas replied and he approached the bed. He tried not to look at her eyes but to observe. The shade of her skin, the spots on the pillowcase were all hints as to what her body was harbouring inside.

'Yes, Doctor,' she said, tilting her head slightly. 'From now on, your words will be my commands.'

The smile she gave him lit up her face making him think of a child offered a rare treat, a reward long lost, despaired over, but never forgotten. In the morning light that swept over her, Thomas thought he had seen the secret of her attraction, the way she must have appeared to all those men Ignacy spoke about. Men who had loved her over other women. Yes, he had seen through her pale, luminous skin no longer fresh and supple; through her parched lips folding as if ready to grant him secrets revealed to no one else. You will be my saviour, her eyes said. There will be no one else, but you and me. You have all my attention, all my loyalty. Nothing and nobody else matters.

'I've dismissed Doctor Horn, my Russian doctor. He was not helping me at all.'

'Are you in much pain?' Thomas asked, piqued by the casual reference to a hapless man who had, undoubtedly, tried his best.

The countess stopped smiling. Her beautiful eyes were dry.

'They say that my womb is rotting, Doctor, and it hurts. Is that what you want me to describe to you?'

'But Madame la Comtesse,' Ignacy protested. 'Courage! You are in the best of hands.'

'Let Doctor Lafleur decide,' the countess said.

The nurse stepped forward, placing her hand on the patient's arm with a gesture of appropriation. A firm, steady gesture meant as a warning.

'*Madame* slept well last night,' she said. Her voice was pleasant, her French just slightly foreign. Foreign, Thomas would reflect later only because, in spite of its flawlessness, he could attach it to no specific region or city. 'But today she complained of pain in her back. On both sides.'

A bit over twenty, the thought flashed through his mind, still considering the possibility (however slight) of an operation. Good solid constitution. There was no frailty about her, no threat of fainting spells. She would not be a nuisance.

'Rosalia, my dear,' the countess said. 'Send everyone away. Let the doctor examine me.'

'Everyone,' she added, seeing how her daughter hesitated. 'Only Rosalia and Dr Lafleur will stay. No one else.'

The countess was, indeed, in the last stages of the disease that had been ravaging her for years: her face a wax mask over the skull; her arms, hands transparent. Thomas could almost see the tendons clinging to her bones. She had prepared herself carefully for this visit. Her clothes were of embroidered velvet, the kind maids were told to be careful with for their wages would never pay for the damage carelessness might inflict on the fabric. He had noted that the dress had been hastily altered to fit a thinning body. The lingering smell of musk and wild roses told him that she had bathed and oiled her body for this encounter.

As she stood up, she tried to hold herself straight, but the effort it required was obvious. Even in her slippers, flat and soft, she rested her arm on the day bed, to steady herself. The nurse jumped forward to hold her, but the countess shook her head.

Her eyes were now following his every move. She was, he decided, studying him very carefully: the way he stood, sat down, opened his bag, assembled his stethoscope.

He began to establish her medical history, the way he had been examining his patients at la Charité. She said she was fifty, but even though traces of obvious beauty were still visible, he could see she was not telling the truth. Closer to sixty, he would say.

'How many children have you had, Madame?'

'Ten.'

'How many are still alive?'

'Six.'

'How old were you when your first child was born?'

'Is it important?'

'Yes,' he said. 'Your medical history is important.'

'I was seventeen.'

'Were there any complications?'

'No, my children came easily to this world. They didn't cause me trouble then.'

He asked if she remembered her childhood diseases, and she laughed. 'In my childhood, Doctor, there were two kinds of diseases: those you survived and those you did not.'

'How many of them did you survive?'

'My mother told me of two times I was near death with fever. She prayed for me and the fever went away. I also had measles.'

He proceeded to ask her about her diet, her sleeping patterns, the ease of her bodily functions. She was frank and unembarrassed by his questions, a fact he noted with some pleasure for many female patients shied away from telling him about their bowel movements and gas. Many times it was their relatives who had to provide the information he needed for diagnosis. Countess Potocka said she ate very little, having lost her appetite quite some time ago. She was thirsty most of the time but couldn't drink more than a few sips of water and found the simplest tasks tiring. The nurse was smoothing the folds of her patient's dress, nodding as if to confirm her words.

'When did you begin feeling the first symptoms?'

'Five years ago,' she said, 'I was losing weight, but I didn't think much of it. And blood.'

Blood stained her undergarments, but the Russian doctor maintained that this was normal for a woman of her age, clearly not a point of concern. It was as if her menses returned, she continued, and she felt a slight pain in her belly. At that time it was more of a thought rather than a feeling.

But this pain began bothering her. That mere thought, uneasiness, soon became a constant companion. She woke up aware of it, and it was with her until the time she fell asleep. This pain began interfering with her days, forcing her to come home earlier from a ball, a soirée, or even stay in bed for a day.

'I'm so tired, Doctor,' she said. 'I cannot stand up without feeling faint.'

Thomas ascertained that the first haemorrhage had been almost five years before. The treatments did not work.

The dismissed Russian doctor bled her for five consecutive days, told her she had too much heat in her and that she needed cold baths. She was advised to take a water cure in Carlsbad, which she did. The haemorrhaging did not stop.

Thomas turned away as the nurse helped the countess take off her heavy velvet dress.

'I'm ready,' she said and when he turned back she was wearing nothing but a light, batiste nightgown. He asked her to lie down on the bed.

All there was to know, the evidence of her life was here, written on her body. He could see stretchmarks from pregnancies, dry patches of skin on her thighs and breasts. In her youth she must have been agile; the muscles, even in their deterioration, still preserved a shadow of their strength.

Her breasts were still relatively full and smooth. Obviously she did not breastfeed her ten children. On her thin thighs there were scars. A series of cuts on one, three burnt patches on the other. Two scars on the inside of her knees clearly were smallpox inoculations – round hollow pockmarks, whiter than the skin around them. He could also see scars on her back, long, white traces of something sharp slashing the skin. She closed her eyes often as he was examining her and breathed with difficulty.

Her disfigured, chafed belly was hardened by the mass growing over her uterus. Fixed. That realization alone was the death sentence. If it were mobile, he might have attempted an operation, but he would never operate on a fixed tumour. He agreed with Le Dran that cancer had commenced locally and was later spread by the lymphatic vessels to the lymph nodes and then into the general circulation. That's why when he performed mastectomies, Thomas made sure that he dissected the associated lymph nodes in the axilla.

He put no faith whatsoever in various remedies that promised to dissolve the tumour. He had also seen disastrous effects of caustic pastes. As far as research into cancer was concerned he hadn't seen much of value. Bernard Peyrilhe extracted fluid from a breast cancer and then injected it into a dog. But all he achieved was that the animal howled so much that his housekeeper objected and the dog had to be drowned.

'The pain,' the countess whispered. 'It's keeping me awake at night.'

He placed the stethoscope to her chest. Her lungs, he could tell, were clear. The difficulty with breathing was a sign of the general weakness of the body. Her pulse was fast and weak.

'The bleeding,' the nurse interrupted, 'has never stopped.' The pad she removed quickly from between the countess's legs was stained with dark blood. He asked to see it and noted that the discharge was caked, clotted thick.

The children who died in infancy, Thomas ascertained, had no abnormalities. The countess had had the mercury cure a few times, but he could see no other evidence of syphilis than her weakened heart. When he pressed a fingernail on her index finger, he could see a pulsating vein, a sign of dilated aorta. This, however, was not what was killing her.

'The pain,' the countess repeated.

It was this pain that had made the journey impossible to continue and had forced them to stop here, in this Berlin palace so kindly offered by an old family friend. This pain took up all her thoughts, made travelling impossible.

'It's in my bones, Doctor. It is in my womb. I cannot move without crying.'

Carefully he disassembled his stethoscope, and put it

back inside its leather case. He wished Ignacy had not been ordered out of the room with the others, leaving him alone to pronounce his diagnosis. The nurse, no matter how capable, would not be of much help at the moment of truth. He expected a fainting spell, a fit of screaming. This was the time to talk of God, of afterlife, of grace and repentance. Of fate and resignation. Not his kind of talk.

'Please, Doctor,' the countess said. 'I want to know.'

Ignacy would not agree with me, Thomas thought. What right do we have to take hope away, he would ask. Why cut off the flow of the vital force? Deprive the body of its only defence. But hope, as far as Thomas was concerned, was a fickle notion. He had come to value facts over feelings and so far, he had had little reason to doubt the wisdom of such an approach.

'I cannot offer you any hope, Madame la Comtesse,' he said, finally, defying Ignacy's voice in his head. 'The tumour emerges out of the womb. It feeds on your body. It is fixed. I cannot operate.'

She was silent. Her eyes followed the movement of his lips. The nurse, he had noticed, grasped the countess's hand in hers. Two hands, one strong and smooth, the other like a claw of some starving bird.

'Cancer is like an invasion,' he went on. 'Your body has fought bravely, but the battle has been lost.' Encouraged by her calmness he told her that before death came she could expect a few better days. She would have more energy, not enough to walk, but clearly enough to take an account of her life and prepare herself for the end. He did not avoid her eyes as he said all this. Their beauty urged him on.

'Thank you, Doctor Lafleur,' she said when he put the rest of his instruments back into his leather coffer. 'For telling me the truth.'

'I'm truly sorry. All I can do is to try to diminish the pain.'

The countess closed her eyes.

'I want to be alone now,' she said.

Sophie

She is standing behind Mana, waiting for Monsieur Charles Boscamp, the internuncio of the Polish mission in Istanbul. The study in the mission building is a big, bright room with an enormous gilded desk in the centre. The portrait of the Polish King hangs above it. In it, the King is holding a map and is looking at an hourglass. As if he didn't have time for all he wanted to do, for his face is sad and withdrawn. There are wrinkles of sorrow on his forehead. In his eyes she sees an uncertainty that makes her wonder what has he seen in his life to doubt like that.

Don't touch anything, Carlo has warned her. It is for him that Mana reddens her lips with carmine, and makes them shiny with walnut leaves. It is hard to tell if he is a guard, a valet, or a butler in this house, for he is vague describing his duties; but sometimes he makes it sound as if the internuncio could not take a step without consulting him. For weeks Carlo has been a frequent visitor to their house, growing more and more alarmed by Sophie's presence. The Sultana has been making inquiries, sending her spies to find out where her little ungrateful wisdom lived. No house in Istanbul would be safe for long.

'Don't show your face to anyone,' Carlo has warned her every time, bringing his gifts of food and wine. Right from my master's pantry, he always says, drawing their attention to the internuncio's fine tastes. What *he* doesn't see, *he* doesn't miss, he also says. It is this master who will be Sophie's salvation, her escape. Carlo has told him a story of a beautiful girl from Phanar who has to be saved from the ardour of a young, penniless *pasha*. It is Aunt Helena who lives in Phanar not them, but a little stretching of the truth never hurt anyone. A daughter of a friend of his, an honest Greek widow who wishes only for her daughter's well-being. 'A girl,' he said, 'worthy of a king's bed.'

The internuncio is still not ready to see them, even if it is long past midday. The annual mission party to celebrate the King's name day ended at dawn. Everyone had been there. The Russians, the French, the English. Diplomats and men of stature and importance. The whole house still smells of roasted meat and melted wax. Over a hundred candles, Carlo has said, all burnt to the very end.

Mana has placed a shawl over Sophie's head. 'We won't let him see you right away,' she whispers in her daughter's ears. 'Stand straight, but don't look at him. Keep your eyes down.'

But Sophie cannot stop herself from looking. After the Harem, this is the most beautiful room she has ever seen. The walls are painted the blue of the sea and have its luminous shine. The glass in the window sparkles. On the shelves, there are rows of books bound in leather. Has the internuncio read them all? What sort of things are in them? Tales of other worlds, of ships sailing through seas and oceans? The maps on the desk are spread wide, their ends kept from rolling up by two white rocks, studded with white crystals.

She doesn't even know the names of the lands drawn so beautifully on these maps. Her own ignorance angers her, for she can imagine another woman, a woman who can walk through such rooms with ease, who can talk about the books she has read and journeys she has taken.

'Look down,' Mana whispers, pinching her elbow.

The internuncio is not as she imagined him. She thought he would be big, with strong hands, ramrod straight. Instead he is small and sinewy with rouged, wrinkled cheeks. Like an apple stored for the winter. She doesn't like his stained and crooked teeth either.

His name may be Charles Boscamp, but, even in her mind, she cannot bring herself to call him anything but *the internuncio.*

'Better be right,' the internuncio says to Carlo who towers over his master. There is no anger in this voice though. No tension. No, he is not *quite* as she imagined him, but his clothes are rich. A green velvet dressing-gown embroidered with gold, white stockings and silver clasps on his shoes. The powder from the wig has spilled over on his vest. His valet should be told to be more careful. She is trying to keep her eyes down, the way her mother told her to, but cannot stop watching him.

There is an air of importance around the internuncio, in the force of his steps, the upward curve of his spine. In the way he wrings his hands, which are the white perfumed hands of a noble. She can imagine him riding, his legs spurring a horse on to greater effort. She can imagine him touching her.

She likes that thought.

Mana is talking fast, assuring the internuncio of her beloved daughter's meek nature and good humour. Dou-Dou will not be a burden to a gentleman. There is not a trace of moodiness in her, or anger. She is sweetness itself. She is love and devotion and purity, so unlike these French ladies she hears so much about, brought up to speak their minds and put their wants ahead of anyone else's. Dou-Dou's heart is filled with nothing but the desire to please. She knows how to be grateful.

'She is my daughter,' Mana says. 'My beloved Sophie. You will not be sorry.'

The internuncio looks at her sharply, as if doubting all these words. She keeps her eyes down, fixed on the clasps of his brown leather shoes. She crosses her arms across her chest and trembles.

'Is that what you really want, child,' the internuncio asks. He has lifted her chin up. His finger is soft and warm. Dry like a handful of sand. His eyes are blue, like the sky over Bursa, the whites reddened by last night's excitement. Can she really make these eyes see nothing but her?

She doesn't say anything. Her chin rests heavily on his finger. Her hands clutch at the shawl that covers her breasts.

His lips are thin and pale, but there is a smile on them. A smile of pleasure.

He touches her lips, slowly, lingering over their shape. He parts them gently with his finger and touches her teeth. There is a taste to his skin, bitter, pungent but not unpleasant.

'Leave her then,' the internuncio sighs. He is so close to her that she catches a sour whiff penetrating his shield of musk and snuff.

'Not now, My Illustrious Lord. Not yet,' Mana says. 'The girl is suffering from her menses and our Lord forbids a woman to lie with a man at a time like that. Wait a few days and I'll bring her back to you, clean and scrubbed.'

Her mother is not leaving anything to chance. There will be a deposit of 1500 piastrs made with Kosta Lemoni in Phanar, the spice merchant who will keep the money in trust for Sophie, her daughter's dowry to be paid to her on the day she stands at the altar beside her groom. There will be assurances for the rides in a carriage, and the new dresses, and shawls Dou-Dou likes so much. She could keep all the gifts he might give her: the dresses, the rings, the pendants.

'Do you want my soul too, woman,' the internuncio laughs, but Sophie can tell he is not angered by her mother's shrewdness. He is a man of honour, he assures Mana. He will do what is right.

'If she pleases me though,' he says, his finger raised in the air as if he were warning her that not all is settled yet.

'A virgin,' Mana answers boldly, 'needs a good teacher. Then she will learn how to please.'

He likes that. His laughter rings out, shaking his belly up and down, bringing moisture to his eyes.

He takes a small ring from his finger and slips it into Mana's hand. They examine it later, carefully. Note the thickness of gold, and the shine of the small sapphire. The colour, Mana would tell her later as if Sophie hadn't noticed it herself, of his eyes.

The crimson robe is wrapped tightly around him. Crimson, he will tell her later, is the colour of the Polish nobles.

The internuncio is sitting in a gilded armchair, a glass of wine in hand, legs spread. 'Come,' he says and she walks slowly, her eyes cast down. Slowly, holding her legs together, just the way Mana has shown her. Inside her, her mother's fingers have slid a pessary made from a lamb's bladder. She is not to upset it by too sudden a movement. A vial of dove's blood is hidden in a secret pocket in the fold of her shift. When he is asleep beside her, she is to quietly spill the blood on the sheets. She takes small steps, her hips swaying gently.

'Closer,' he says. Her feet are bare, the skin tingling at the smoothness and richness of the carpet.

Her head is spinning with her mother's words. Don't look him in the eye. Hold your head down. Smile, don't laugh. There will be time for laughter later. There will be time for dancing and for rejoicing when your future is assured. Not now, not yet.

'He is a libertine,' Aunt Helena has said. 'For such a man there is nothing sweeter than corrupting innocence.'

Now her shift is lying on the floor. Her naked body is covered with a sheet, so white that it shines. Her hair has been beautifully braided and pinned high, revealing the nape of her neck. Her eyes have been kohled, lips reddened. At the *hammam* her mother has helped her scrape the hair off her legs and made a special nourishing face mask from an egg yolk and honey. Her skin when she touches it is smooth.

'Closer. You are not afraid, are you?' he asks, rising from the chair, putting his glass aside. There is another glass of wine on the side table, filled to the brim. It's for her. She is to drink it with him. To pleasure. To love. To the good times.

'Life is so short, Dou-Dou, so fleeting. Shouldn't we suck the pleasure out of each moment?'

Nodding, she takes one more step toward him. She takes the glass in her hand and sips the wine slowly, avoiding his eyes. One small sip after another. The wine smells of oak and berries. It is heavy, with a tinge of sweetness.

'Is it good?' he asks.

She nods. She can hardly stop her eyes from darting to the sides. The internuncio's bed is big. The four posts rise almost to the ceiling. Underneath she can see a white chamber pot, covered with a lid.

The wine dizzies her. She giggles and puts the empty glass back on the table. The room is hot and she feels drops of sweat gather and roll slowly down her back. The internuncio fills the glass again, but he is not asking her to drink, so she doesn't reach for it.

She closes her eyes, just like Mana told her to do, when he parts the edges of the sheet and stares at her for a long, long time. He is muttering something in a language she doesn't understand. He sniffs her like a dog might, nose close to her skin, tickling her. There is a grimace of displeasure on his face.

'Your odour,' he says. 'Too strong for my taste.'

She reaches for the second glass of wine and drinks it fast. Then, standing straight, she lets the sheet fall down from her body. It's her beauty that needs to speak now. The shine in her eyes, their brightness. The purity of her skin. She takes his hand in hers and kisses it. Kisses it again and again.

His hand caresses her breasts, her belly. Then it slides down, touches the mound of Venus. She shivers.

The internuncio calls it *Mon Plaisir*.

The robe unwraps. He is naked, his belly protruding, over a patch of grey curly hair. He turns his back to her and makes a few steps to lie on his bed. His bottom is sagging. 'Turn your eyes away,' Mana has said. 'Tell him you are afraid. Tell him he is too big for you. That he will break you inside and make you scream.'

But she has no time to say anything for he sits on the edge of the bed and motions to her to come to him. He is smiling, his eyes narrow, like folds of fabric. The vein on his temple has thickened and darkened.

She sits beside him on the bed and waits.

'Come on, girl,' he says. 'Hasn't your mother taught you what to do? Should I have taken her instead?'

She shakes her head and crosses her arms, as if to cover her breasts. In his voice there is a note of anger, but perhaps she only thinks it is.

'Do what I tell you then,' he says.

She is thinking of the pessary inside her. What if it slips out. What if he puts his own hand there and retrieves it, calling her a liar. Sending her back to her mother. The orders are a relief, for at least she knows what to do to please him.

'Lie down.'

He is a traveller in the land of Venus, he tells her, a true Explorer, for whom the sight of a Foreign Land is always welcome. A Land with all its Harbours, Bays, Rocks, Beacons and Caverns. Especially a Land not Ploughed before. A Land for which Directions have to be established. A Harbour which has to be thoroughly assessed to assure the safety of his precious cargo. Its Waters explored with Proper Instruments that will measure its width and depths.

Just do what he wants you to do, Mana has said. Make him happy.

The candles in the room make the shadows dance on the ceiling. She tries not to look at his sagging skin. *His Instrument* and his *precious Stones* are of excellent order, he assures her. She should thank her lucky stars.

She thinks of Diamandi's smooth olive skin and the strength of his boyish arms. She thinks of their run across the fields, their mad run of desire.

She can smell the wine on his breath, or is it hers. Somewhere in the back of her mind questions hammer. What if she is not pleasing him? What if she is not what he has expected? What if she doesn't know what a man wants?

He is grunting, crushing her with the weight of his body. He has pushed himself into her, as if he were squeezing in something soft and lifeless. His hands rest upon her breasts, pinching her nipples.

Her scream pleases him.

But it is only when he wakes up in the morning, when he pats her buttocks and tells her that the Fortifications were not very strong after all, not a match for his Vigorous Attack, and when he sees the blood on the sheets that she knows she has not disappointed him at all. He will not send her back to her mother.

Outside, in the small vestibule decorated with panels of pale green marble and white Grecian urns, Mademoiselle Rosalia stopped him.

'Please,' she said. 'Just a few words.' Her hazel eyes were bloodshot and the dark circles under her eyes spoke of sleepless nights. *A daughter of a Polish hero and a Jewess from Uman.* He knew what she would ask before he heard the words.

'Is there really no hope, Doctor?'

'None.'

'I thought so too,' she said, which killed the note of irritation in his voice. 'But both Dr Bolecki and Dr Horn before him sounded so sure that an operation could save her.'

Rosalia, for this was how Thomas began thinking of her from that moment on, insisted on reporting the details of Dr Horn's last treatments. It would be important for him to know, wouldn't it. She had been taking detailed notes, if he only cared to take a look: purgings with senna and salts; thirty leeches, every two hours to restore the body's internal harmony; no solid food.

'Doctor Horn said that cancer always starts in the stomach,' she said, swallowing hard. 'Is that what you also believe?'

'I haven't seen much evidence to support this theory.'

'What is it that you believe then?'

'Nothing I cannot prove. Not much I'm afraid.'

She gave him a quizzical look, but did not ask anything else.

Dr Horn, with whom Thomas had less and less sympathy, clearly was an ardent follower of Brossais's methods. It was his caustic salves that had irritated the stomach area. He scribbled a note for the pharmacist for a lotion that would calm down the skin.

'For now,' he said, 'I would double the dose of laudanum. Then switch to pure opium to dull the pain.'

She took the note from him. 'I'll send the maid for it right away.'

'I'm sorry,' he said. 'You must think me cruel.'

'No,' she shook her head in protest. 'Madame la Comtesse wanted the truth. You were right not to lie to her.'

'I'm sorry,' he repeated. 'I don't know what else to say.'

Olga Potocka, Mademoiselle la Comtesse, called him a complete fool. She bit her lip and said she insisted on a second opinion. 'Doctor Bolecki assured me that a skilled surgeon would be able to remove the tumour,' she said.

'Of course, by all means, you should consult another doctor,' Thomas said. 'I'm not God.'

'But Thomas,' Ignacy's face was red, either with exertion or embarrassment, he couldn't tell. 'Are you that sure?'

From the corner of his eye he could see Rosalia lean forward as if she wanted to defend him. A thought flashed through his mind: I wonder why she is not married.

'Yes,' Thomas said. 'I'm that sure.'

He had to repeat the same words a few minutes later when the Potocki coachman drove them through the Berlin streets, swearing at the horses in either Russian or Ukrainian, Thomas couldn't tell.

'I'm not saying you should have operated, Thomas, but you should've given her hope,' Ignacy said with an impatient gesture.

'I didn't think she wanted false hope. And I don't believe in lying.'

'This is but one way of looking at it, my truth-loving friend,' Ignacy said, obviously vexed. He was breathing with difficulty. 'Now, she will let some charlatan take advantage of her.'

‘That I cannot stop,’ Thomas said, preparing for a long tirade, but nothing else followed.

They kept silent until the carriage reached Ignacy’s home. Ignacy alighted but did not continue his reproaches. He didn’t wish him good day either. Thomas watched until his friend’s ample figure disappeared behind the front door. Disappointed. There would be no influence in the Russian court for him now, Thomas thought not without some malice.

As the Potocki’s carriage rolled on the cobblestones toward Rosenstrasse, Thomas tried to talk to the coachman and find out where he was from, a task rendered difficult by the fact that they only had a few French and German words in common. His name was Pietka and he was a Cossack.

‘Zaporozhian,’ he said with pride. The skin encircling his eyes had a sallow tint. ‘Here,’ he said, pointing to the street. ‘No good. No life.’

Thomas would have liked to learn what a Cossack considered life, but Pietka’s French ended there. As he spat onto the ground, his teeth, Thomas noticed, were black with decay.

‘Uman,’ Pietka said. ‘Beautiful. Doctor know where?’

‘Poland,’ Thomas asked. ‘Russia?’ He was trying to recall what Ignacy had explained so often. The shifting borders of the east. The changing of hands, loyalties, the trajectories of hope and despair. Ukraine, once the easternmost Polish province, now part of the Russian Empire. Poland no longer on the map of Europe, partitioned by her neighbours. Who did this Cossack side with?

‘Ukraine?’ he said now. The name caused a vigorous nod of Pietka’s head and a torrent of words, fleeting, like a melody. He must have touched on something he was not aware of. He did not know what to say next.

When Thomas made his first step toward Frau Schmidt’s

pension, the Cossack turned to him and said, 'People here. No heart!' He cracked his whip and was gone.

Sophie

You have to make him jealous, Mana has said. That's why a man would want to keep you; to stop others from having you.

She tells her internuncio of a man who lives across the street and who stares at her every day. An Armenian banker, millionaire and the director of the Padishah's mint. He clicks his tongue at her. He has sent his servant to her three times already. If she agrees to come to him, he would give her a purse filled with cekins.

'What did you say to that,' he asks.

'That my master takes good care of me.'

But the man is insistent. Every time he catches her eye, he shows her something new to tempt her. A ruby as big as a nut. A diamond that glitters in the sun like the stars in heaven.

'And you didn't take it?' the internuncio asks.

She shakes her head and says that nothing on this earth, no diamond, no ruby, no sapphire would ever make her turn away from her beloved master.

'You shameless liar,' the internuncio says and pinches her cheeks. 'Confess right away. You are waiting for me to leave.'

'Yesterday,' she says, 'he has parted the folds of his *anteri* and pulled out his own jewel.'

'How big was it,' the internuncio asks, and she whispers right into his ear that it was big enough to bring Saint Mary Magdalene to fall again.

His ensembles are embroidered with silver or gold threads. She likes the feel of velvet, the thin cambric of his shirts.

He wants her to walk around the room barefoot. Sometimes he asks her to put her feet on a pillow for he likes to touch her toes.

He tells her strange and wonderful things. Tells her of that other Greece, the Greece he calls the land of wisdom and true culture. In that other Greece, men possessed true nobility of spirit. They were heroes and valiant warriors, their bodies as perfect as their minds and hearts. He also tells her about the women he calls *haetteras*, women so wise that the famous philosophers thronged to see them.

'It is the art of conversation, my Dou-Dou, that distinguishes common souls from people of quality. Every woman knows how to spread her legs, but not everyone has learnt how not to bore.'

She listens to his every word.

The Greek women of today, he tells her, are but pale replicas of these other women, Lais and Phryne, women of quick minds and beauty seasoned with wisdom and refinement. He tells her that his heart bleeds when he thinks of modern Greeks; slaves, their hearts cowardly, unworthy of the glory of their ancestors.

How, he asks her, can a handful of lazy Turks keep with pistols and daggers the descendants of the ancient race who bore Homer and Scio in submission?

How could the descendants of such a noble race have sunk to the level of thieves and whores? He has been to miserable Greek villages littered with fragments of ancient pillars that once adorned an ancient temple. The peasants shamefully hide these traces of the past glory, as relics of pagan rites they wish no part of. In one of these villages, he tells her, he once saw a piece of white marble that bore the inscription: C. MARCIVS. MARSVS/V. F. SIBI. ET. SVIS. Covered with mud and manure it paved an ignorant peasant's barn.

Had he not been taught to admire Grecian courage,

wisdom, and talents, he might look upon the meanness of her race with less emotion. The victors from Marathon, Salamis, Platea, he says in an accusing voice, while his hand pats her buttocks, cringe at the feet of their Turkish masters. He tells her how, at the Isthmean Games, Titus Quinctius announced to the Greeks that they were free, but that was nothing but a ruse – a trap into which they all fell when they began shouting for joy. For the true freeman needs no trumpet to declare that he is free. His looks, his expression are the heralds of his own independence.

'Does your little head understand any of this, Dou-Dou?'

He tells her that when beautiful Lais moved from her native Sicily to Greece, princes, lords, speakers, philosophers, all rushed to see and admire her. But then a few common women, jealous of her beauty, murdered her in the temple of Aphrodite, forty years before the birth of Christ.

She thinks about it for a while. About jealousy that can kill. About a knife plunged into a woman's heart.

'The art of conversation,' he says, 'is the most powerful of arts. It alone can open the doors of palaces.'

'What did they talk about, these ancient *haetteras*.'

'Philosophy, art, literature. They enjoyed exchanging arguments, civilised dispute. Things, my little Dou-Dou, you have no idea of and never will. Things far too complicated for you.'

'Tell me,' she asks.

'Tell you what,' he laughs at her eagerness, but he is not displeased. Clearing his throat he says: 'La Mettrie contends that all we imagine comes from our senses: no senses, no thoughts; a few sensations of the body – a few notions in the mind. Do you understand?'

She thinks she does, but shakes her head. He laughs again.

'If there is no soul, and if the essence of life can only be found in separate parts of the body, where would most of you be, Dou-Dou.'

She smiles and waits for what might follow, but he gets tired of his own game.

'You have to learn French,' he declares. 'One cannot have an intelligent conversation in any other language. French is the language of polite company, the language of the courts and salons.'

'Teach me,' she asks.

'*La chambre, la cocotte, meux beaux oeils.*'

He likes when she pours oil on his skin and massages it the way Mana has taught her. Gently at first, then deeper and deeper until she reaches the knots and dissolves them under her fingers. She is proud when he groans with pleasure.

Sans Vous je ne peux pas vivre.

Je suis Votre esclave.

In the Sultan's palace, she tells him, beautiful slave women serve the Princess on their knees. Their breaths are sweet and their eyes deep and soft. The Sultan's every order is obeyed instantly, for punishment is swift. She has seen a room where whips of black leather hang on the wall. A whole row of them, with knots and little hooks tied to their ends. She has seen burlap sacks filled with stones, ready for the death by drowning.

He is listening.

'At the Seraglio, dinners are long. They can last for hours. Dishes are brought one by one.'

'Everyone knows that,' he says yawning.

'Does everyone know the eunuchs make sure that all cucumbers are served sliced?'

His belly shakes when he laughs. One of his front teeth is longer than the other. It gives him a slightly lopsided look. His brows are thick, bushy, forming a straight line over his nose. Such brows, Mana has said, are a good sign in a man. This and a hairy chest.

He wants to know about the Princess. Is she really as ugly as Dou-Dou swears she is? With pimply skin and black fuzz on her upper lip? Or perhaps this is just another lie? Perhaps there *was* something about the Sultana's strength that wasn't all together unpleasant? Is she indeed what the Turks call a *čibukli*, well equipped to play the role of both sexes? Are the women in the *hammam* at the Seraglio really not allowed to touch one another?

But most of all he wants the stories of punishment. Of whips and satin belts. Of deep dungeons from which only groans are heard. Of purple bruises on milky white skin. Stories that grow as she tells them, twist in new directions, each measured by the intensity of his attention. Stories that astonish even her.

'These,' she whispers to him, 'are the secrets of the Palace for which I was to pay with my life, had I not managed to escape. You may be the only Frank to know them.'

The girl from Galata, her predecessor, has sent words of venom. *You viper, you dirty whore*, she had scribbled on a piece of paper. *I'll scratch your eyes out. I'll make you lick the floor of the room that used to be mine.*

'I didn't even know the frumpy creature could write,' the internuncio says, reading it, crumpling the paper into a ball and tossing it into the fire. 'Now, I know what to do if you do not please me the way I want it.'

She doesn't like it when he says things like that. The girl from Galata is younger than she is and was sent back to her mother without warning, just because Carlo brought her round, a new toy, a new distraction.

There are days when her internuncio does not come at all. The walls of the apartment he has rented for her seem to close on her. She dresses herself in her new clothes; pins up her hair; forces the maid to clean her room once again; arranges fresh flowers beside the mirror, so that the blooms are reflected in it. Fusses with the throw on the bed, the pillows, until everything is pleasing to the eye. Then she waits and waits, watching through the window how other people, free, walk in the streets. She envies them sometimes. Even the servants carrying big baskets of fish, or leading donkeys. She envies the dogs that roam the streets in packs, or lie basking in the sun knowing no one will disturb them.

His life at the Polish mission is busy, the internuncio tells her. He has important duties to attend to. A delicate position to maintain. 'The art of observation, my little Dou-Dou,' he tells her. 'Of knowing what you are not supposed to know.'

A very useful art. Indispensable in politics, for politics is the art of knowing. Of predicting. Of turning your enemies against each other and making sure your friends stay loyal out of self-interest. An art Charles Boscamp, Esquire, excels at.

As soon as he comes in, she helps him remove his coat and his shoes. In her company, he is emptying himself, clearing his mind, softening himself for pleasure. She should be like the sound of a waterfall, the soothing distraction. Like a garden where he can find respite.

'I would like politics,' she says.

'I'm sure you would.' He laughs when he says that, pinching her cheeks. He likes when he senses the want in her, the desire for his world. Sometimes she thinks that he doesn't really want anything any more, that in his mouth sweetness is not as vivid as in hers. That his pleasure is not real until he sees it in her first.

'*Divide et impera*,' he says, wiping his hands on a towel she is holding for him. 'The Sultan's counsels are vying for power. There is no consistency in the Porte.'

His caresses are short and fleeting; his hands touch her as if she were a pillow or a thick blanket meant for comfort. He likes when she kneels in front of him. He never stops talking when he pushes her head down between his legs. 'My jewel,' he has taught her to say. She has learnt that release comes quickly, and she is grateful for it. Sometimes she thinks he prefers a massage to the act itself, for then he can close his eyes and forget about her altogether. His presence leaves her hungry, filled with longings. She has taken to touching herself when he leaves, imagining that it is his hand that slowly rubs the sweet spot between her legs.

The internuncio likes to talk. He has met the Emperor of Prussia and the King of Poland. He tells her that the Polish King became king only because the Russian Empress wanted it. She has sent her troops to Warsaw, to the election field. Some people say that she ordered her own husband murdered. Suffocated with his pillow.

Men tremble at the sight of her, he says. Handsome Russian boys are groomed to catch the eye of the Empress, coached by their mothers in ways to please a woman, the whole family making plans for its illustrious future. His wise friend, Count Vronsky, always bows to all handsome *valets de chambre* and calls them *brother*. He knows that a day may come when one of them would be elevated above him by the whim of his Empress.

'This is not natural,' the internuncio says. 'Not right. It is against the order of things.'

She closes her eyes and imagines the Russian Empress pointing at a young handsome man. She imagines sending her troops to Poland to make her lover a king. Bending over her gilded desk and signing important papers. Stamping her foot to make her courtiers hurry.

'The Ottoman Porte,' the internuncio says, 'is crucial for the Russian Empress, and therefore, my position here is of a delicate nature. The Russians do not like that the Poles are courting the Sultan's support.'

He has been warned a few times; questioned at the Russian mission. He smiles in a way that tells her he is not concerned.

She pours oil onto her hands and warms them with her breath. Slowly she begins pressing his shoulders, kneading away the tension. She loves when he talks of such important matters. Of people rich and powerful and yet how very much similar to the *signoras* and *signores* of Phanar.

Once she tells him that. Tells him how people seem to be the same everywhere, how the powerful are not as different from those who are beneath them. How men are really not that different from women, either.

'Phanar,' the internuncio says, 'is the kingdom of busybodies, of chatterboxes feeding on any hint of scandal – the kingdom of calumny and hypocrisy.'

There is anger in his voice, impatience.

'The world,' he says, 'is not what you imagine.'

Rosalia

She was born in exile, her father always said. Better than born in chains, for 1796, the year of her birth, was the first year there was no Poland on the map of Europe.

'You saved your father's life,' her mother said. 'Before you were born he spoke of nothing but death.'

In her father's study, there was an engraving of Poland led to her grave. Polonia was a young woman in white, her hands chained. The grave was a square hole in the ground, and three men, Russia, Prussia, and Austria, were already holding the stone lid that would intern her. 'But not forever,' her father always said.

In 1795, at Maciejowice, defeated by the Russians in the last battle of the Insurrection, Tadeusz Kościuszko, thinking himself dying, said: '*Finis Poloniae.*'

'This is what we all feared then, Rosalia,' her father continued. 'But we were wrong.' The soldiers in Napoleon's Polish Legion had a reply to these words spoken in that black hour of defeat:

Jeszcze Polska nie umarła póki my żyjemy
Co nam obca moc wydarła szablą odbierzemy
Poland is not dead as long as we are alive
What the foreign powers took away from us we
shall regain by the sword

It was Napoleon Bonaparte, a man of iron will and a god of war, who had taught the Poles how to win. A god of war who had gathered the defeated Polish soldiers under his wing and gave them the chance to fight the enemies of their country. Bonaparte who would soon smash the might of the Russians and lead Poland out of her grave. Then there would be no more exile, no more rented rooms, no more packing and unpacking of trunks and crates. They would go back to Poland, to their manor house confiscated by the Russian Tsar because Jakub Romanowicz had refused to stop fighting for Poland's freedom, had refused to live in slavery.

Rosalia loved when her father said that. She loved the way he smelled of snuff, the way his prickly cheeks chafed her lips.

'Where is Poland now, Papa?' she liked to ask, sitting down to a familiar ritual. Wherever they were – Paris, Rome, Livorno – his response was always the same. He would take her hand in his and place it on her chest.

'Can you feel it?' he would ask as her hand registered the rhythm of her heartbeat.

'Yes,' she would say, in her solemn, serious voice, waiting for what was coming.

'This, Rosalia, is Poland.'

She believed him. She believed that Poland, this beautiful maiden entombed alive by Russia, Prussia and Austria would one day be resurrected. Like Jesus Christ, the Saviour, she would rise from the dead and lead the nations of Europe to a new world order. A just, wonderful world without wars, hatred and slaves. A world where it would not matter if you were a Pole, Jew, or a Cossack, a noble or a peasant, a merchant or a pauper for Poland, like a good mother would make room for them all.

'I may not see it, Rosalia. You may not see it. But your children, or your children's children will.' Her father's voice shimmered like pebbles in the stream. She imagined them, these faint generations yet unborn. Shadows waiting to come to being. Waiting for their time.

Sophie

The girl from Galata must have bribed the Janissary the internuncio has placed at the entrance of the building, for three Greek furies – the girl and her two cousins – enter her bedroom when she is alone. They throw themselves upon her. They tear out clumps of her hair; scratch her face. She tries to defend herself, but the three of them are bigger and stronger. At one moment she almost manages to escape, but she trips over her own shoe and falls flat on the floor. With that same shoe her enemies beat her, leaving bruises all over her body. 'He will turn away from you as he has turned away from me,' the girl from Galata screams. 'He will see how pretty you are with a black eye and scratches on your cheeks.'

They slash her dresses with razors. They smash the glass she keeps near her bed. They spit on her, on her bed, on the sheets folded neatly in the closet and smear it with something foul. Then they leave as suddenly as they have come. She hears their footsteps on the stairs, their braying laughter, their whistles of triumph. She gathers herself up, wipes the blood from her face, wraps herself in a blanket, and runs away to her mother.

The internuncio is shocked and very sorry. This is what his note says. He sends his own doctor to bleed her and clean the wounds. She has a fever and her body is rattled with shivers. 'Tell my master,' she says in a low whisper, 'that I'll die thinking of him.'

The doctor says she won't die. 'No one has ever died from a few scratches. Your bones are intact. You've just had a bad fright. Nothing more.'

Mana is sobbing in the corner, cursing her fate and her daughter's misfortune. She doesn't want to accuse anyone, but wouldn't her daughter be safer within the Mission's compound. Where she is now, anyone can find her. Only the other day someone came asking about a Greek girl called Sophie. A man with a red beard and shifty eyes. A sign that the Sultana has not forgotten.

By the time the internuncio comes to see her, it is already dark. The invalid is washed and bandaged, her breath is uneven, her forehead hot. 'If she dies,' Mana says, 'I'll never forgive myself.'

The internuncio is uneasy. He touches her forehead as a father might, checking how his daughter is feeling.

'I thought I could trust you with my only child.'

'Poor Dou-Dou,' he says. In his voice there is something she could take for concern. When he raises the covers to check the bruises on her body, he is really looking at her.

He calls the doctor and takes him to another room. She can hear their raised voices, a barrage of questions followed by long explanations. When the two men emerge from the room, the internuncio smiles. To Mana he says that he will make sure Sophie gets the best of care. Two of his own servants will be at her disposal, day and night. She will have meals brought from his own kitchen.

'Am I like Lais?' she asks.

'Only you won't die,' he tells her, holding her hand. 'The doctor tells me you have a strong constitution. That it would take much more to kill *you*.'

She asks him to tell her about Poland.

He tells her of palaces with green lawns and hundreds of servants, hurrying around. Of carriages speeding through the streets, of balls where women of quality dance *polonaises* and *mazurkas*. Of *tableaux vivants* in which the court's most beautiful ladies appear in the costumes of nymphs or muses.

What do they do?

Nothing. They pose as if a painter painted them. Let everyone admire their beauty. The themes of these tableaux often illustrate a saying or a proverb. Or an old story. Amor bending his golden locks over sleeping Psyche, Danae showered with golden rain.

She asks about the King. Do men tremble when they see him?

He laughs. In Poland, kings are elected and therefore weak. Their powers are limited by the golden freedom of the nobles. *Liberum veto*, he tells her. Remember that. It means that one Polish noble can stop the law, one Polish noble can break the *Sejm* for his own private reason. One Polish noble can oppose the king's wish.

'Eat, drink, and loosen your belt,' he says, 'that's what the Poles care about.'

She listens.

He is not Polish by birth. His is a complicated story,

he warns as if she were unable to understand anything of importance. He was born in Holland but his parents were French Huguenots. That of course would not mean anything to her, would it, but as any intelligent person would know, they had had to flee France to keep their heads on their shoulders. Having lost their estate, his parents could give him little more than his education. This he put to a good use, serving the Prussian King for seven years, and then moving on, to Poland, where the Polish King, then newly elected, recognized his outstanding qualities.

'That's why I became Polish, my little Dou-Dou. I thought it far superior to becoming Prussian.'

She doesn't know when he jokes and when he is telling the truth. The Prussian court, he likes to say, is so enamoured with thrift that guests leave the table hungry and grey stuffing sticks out from the cushions of gilded chairs.

'Can one just become Polish?'

He laughs. Not 'just'. Not everyone. A foreign man has to prove his worth, document his belonging to the gentry class. It takes years of patient pleading, of favours bestowed on those with influence. But he has done all this. He even has a new Polish name now, Lasopolski, which means 'coming from a Polish forest'.

She looks at him with pride.

A foreign woman, he says, reading the question in her eyes, has an easier path before her. All she has to do is marry a Polish noble.

He pinches her cheek as he says it, laughing at the thought. 'Let this not turn your pretty head,' he warns her. 'Your father was a cattle trader. You should be happy with what you've got.'

She gives him a mischievous smile and nods.

In her dreams Poland is very close by, a place she stumbles upon almost by chance. She knows it is Poland for everyone speaks in a strange language she doesn't understand, and she bows and asks to be taken to the King. 'He will know who I am,' she repeats. 'The King,' she says slowly, and makes the sign of a crown over her head. The people stare at her for a long time, nodding, but not moving at all.

The dream always ends before she can see the King, for when she starts running toward him, the distance between them never diminishes, as if she were running, on soft legs that sink into the ground.

When she is alone in the Polish mission she goes to the internuncio's study to look at the King's portrait. In His presence she practises her curtsying and gentle bows of the head. She looks into his blue eyes and says things like, 'My soul thirsts for you, Sire.' Or 'The light of your eyes is too bright for your humble servant, My Lord.' She says it in her new voice, which is sweet and lingering, thick like honey dripping from a spoon.

One day as she is practising what she thinks of as her manners the internuncio surprises her. Having hidden himself behind the door, he cracks with laughter and tells her that she is ludicrous, a true spectacle.

His hand is pinching her bottom as he says that. 'Aren't you getting ahead of yourself, Dou-Dou?' he asks. 'Forgetting your place? Your god-given station in life?'

'The King,' the internuncio says, 'is in need of a bath attendant *à la Turque*.'

When she enters his study he is sprinkling sand over the letter he has just finished writing. He motions to her to sit and begins to read it out.

> Massages given by men resembles torture so that one has to be a Turk or a devil to enjoy them. Those who had experienced such baths here say similar

things one hears in Warsaw about male and female cooks, i.e. that the latter are cleaner and it is better to be served by them when it comes to the main dish. It is only in the company of a pleasant woman who can bathe, massage, and dry the body of her companion in so many ways, that one can imagine the delights promised by Muhammad to his faithful Muslims. I know of a girl from Phanar, sixteen years of age, who would please Your Majesty highly. I could arrange for her to travel to Warsaw as soon as I received word from Your Majesty.

Without thinking she rises and throws her arms around his neck. She covers his face with kisses. She jumps up and down with joy.

The internuncio likes being able to speak French to her. The true language of the salons, he says, of intelligent conversations. She will now take French lessons. Every day for three hours. If she doesn't make progress, he will whip her.

'I'll take any punishment,' she says meeting his eye, 'if it comes from my master.'

'What an eager girl you are?' he murmurs, but she can hear from his voice that her exuberance pleases him. 'Perhaps I should be a bit jealous?'

Jealousy, Mana says, is a good sign.

That day – when she prepares to give him his daily release – he pulls her toward him and places a kiss on her lips. A long, lingering kiss that she will remember for a long time for it tells her that – perhaps – she is not as worthless to him as he wants her to believe.

In the weeks that follow she can't hide her excitement. When she is alone she likes to imagine herself in Warsaw, this city filled with palaces and green lawns. In her dream, the King is brought to the *hammam* by his attendants, but he waves them away and enters it alone. He is naked but for a thick towel wrapped around his body, a towel she will peel off. His skin is soft and perfumed, his hands slender. A bath pavilion she imagines covered with tiles. Musicians are cleverly hidden in tunnels, and they fill the royal bath chamber with delightful music. Warmed by the fire, her hands are soothing and strong. Around her she imagines jars with the scents of jasmine and musk. The King is tired after the long day of ruling. He talks to her, his only real friend. He tells her of all the people who want something from him, who make his life a misery. With each motion of her hands, she melts his tensions and soothes his sadness. She alone is different, the King says. She alone understands him, makes him laugh. She alone brings life back into his heart.

There are many such reveries. In some she is no longer at the royal *hammam*, but has her own little palace in Warsaw, a carriage with six white horses, a valet and a whole army of servants. She is the King's mistress, a lady of distinction. Monsieur Boscamp has to wait in the antechamber until she deigns to see him. When she admits him into her boudoir, he falls to his knees and tells her that her word, whispered at the right moment, could change his fate.

'I'll see what I can do,' she says, fanning her cheeks. The fan is trimmed with purple feathers. Then she turns away from him. In her mirror she can see his face, lost and unsure.

He'll want to remind her of Istanbul, but the King's displeasure is too dangerous to risk. The King's grace is too precious to squander.

There is a note of triumph in the internuncio's voice when he tells her that the King has changed his mind and no longer needs a bath attendant. He tells her that, in passing, when he is leaving her room in the morning, just before closing the door. As if it were not terribly important. He doesn't tell her reasons for the King's decision. It simply won't happen, that's all.

'There might be other opportunities,' he says, stressing the word *might*. 'Count Humeniecki is asking for a Greek girl for his sister's *frauzimmer*. A pretty girl with good breasts.'

She is pretty enough, he tells her, but her breasts are withered, shapeless and quite inflexible. They hang like pears on her belly and would disappoint any man with discerning tastes.

Rosalia

The German staff of von Haefen's palace – a skeleton staff as Frau Kohl put it, but more than adequate under the present circumstances – kept to themselves. The German maids could be seen dusting the portraits, polishing silver. The footmen quietly moved furniture from the east wing. A decorator hired to give the front rooms a new look, much admired in Berlin, had already been told that the renovations would have to be postponed. Rosalia saw his painting of the new décor: big slabs of beige marble on the walls, narrow blue curtains, white vases at both ends of the salon. Clean, sparse lines, almost embarrassing in their simplicity, were to replace plump putti and crimson silk-covered walls.

'You have an exceptional nurse,' she had overheard Dr Bolecki say to the countess. 'A treasure most rare these days when greed and selfishness rule the world.'

'I've always been lucky, dear Doctor.'

'I have to protest. Such luck is always earned, Madame la Comtesse.'

Unpinned, Rosalia's hair spilled over her shoulders. She

was aware of the growing pressure in her temples, a pressure that, if unchecked by laudanum, would soon turn into a headache. Doctor Bolecki was right to insist she had her own supply, right in her room. She poured five drops into a shot of water and swallowed before the bitterness spread inside her mouth.

'Despondency is a sort of treason,' Dr Bolecki had also said to her. 'It is true of politics, and it is true of life.'

The hurry with which he spoke, waving hands in agitation had something boyish about it, something reassuring. 'Please do not misunderstand me. I do not mean to question Dr Lafleur's diagnosis. Or his decisions. But how can life proceed otherwise? The fate of nations or individuals is quite similar after all. Death has to be fought until the last breath and beyond. Fought with hope that is stronger than despair.'

'My father would have agreed with you,' she had said.

'How honoured I would be.'

She was aware of the hissing fire, the waves of warmth reaching her feet, the hooves of horses rushing through the streets, and the pressure at her temples relenting. Beyond this half-empty palace there was a city, teeming with life. The whole world filled with life and death, hope and despair.

The chair screeched on the floor as she sat down at her writing desk and took out her diary. Each entry was carefully separated with a thick, even line. The inkwell was of rare beauty, amber in colour, with silver top. One of the German maids had brought the sander she requested on a silver tray and placed it, silently, on the writing table.

Since her arrival in St Petersburg, in October last year, Rosalia had kept notes trying to record the details of what her mistress called her 'little indispositions'. She did not like the word 'little'. After her mother's funeral she ran into her mother's surgeon in the street. 'Grave illnesses, Mademoiselle Romanowicz', he said then, 'come from small symptoms ignored. Neglect of what seems of little importance at the beginning is what kills us.'

It was all there, in her brown leather-bound notebook. Even in the first week, with all the talk of her duties and accommodations, the dresses, the visiting hours, the procedures to be followed with calling cards, the countess had complained five times of exhaustion and lack of energy. Of having to come home earlier from soirées and having missed Countess Naryshkin's autumn ball.

After the fainting spell at the Winter Palace, the Tsar wrote to inquire about Madame's health and sent a bouquet of white orchids. The letter from the Tsar is to be placed on the small table at the entrance to the salon. No other letter is to cover it. 'Make sure Countess Naryshkin sees it, when she calls,' Madame la Comtesse said and smiled as if it were the best of pranks. There was blood on the undergarments in the evening, again, but it was not the return of 'dame Thérèse'.

'Hasn't the fate of our families been linked before,' she has asked me when I tried to thank her for taking me into her home after Maman's death. The countess assured me with great force she was doing nothing less than her late husband would expect, taking care of a child of the Uman orphans. Hadn't the late Count stood godfather to my dear mother the day she was baptised and married my father? All the countess wanted in return is that I pray for her in her time of trouble. That I promised, of course.

Gifts: pins with black pearls for the countess's sons.

Each pin is set in a gold wreath of tiny oak leaves. (Also two dozens of white gloves.) The daughters will receive a diamond pendant. In her last letter Madame Kisielev described a bad dream she had. A wave from the Black Sea rose and washed away her house. All that was left were a few timbers, smashed and floating on the waves. The countess is very upset on account of her daughter's pregnancy. She has sent Madame Kisielev an icon of the Virgin Mary and a special prayer to say every morning and evening. 'It will protect you,' she asked me to write. 'As it protected me when you were in my womb, waiting to come to this world.'

Order: quilts filled with eider down, one for each of the countess's children.

Count Jeroslav is in St Petersburg, trying to get the Tsar's attention, on behalf of his brothers and sisters. 'I presume he will never stop,' the countess said. I could see her hands were trembling and she had to hold on to a chair to steady herself. 'My step-children would drown me in a spoonful of water if they could.' There had been talk of some vicious letters copied and circulated in St Petersburg. I didn't want to ask, but the countess told me herself: 'My step-children accuse me of killing their father and stealing the Potocki fortune. Luckily their motives are too obvious to His Majesty and they'll achieve nothing.'

Today the Tsar sent another bouquet of orchids and Madame là Comtesse felt strong enough to spend a day at Tsarskye Siolo. I expected her back around nine, but she stayed well past midnight and returned in a good mood. 'Appearing at balls,' she said, 'is to make sure the world does not forget us. As soon as your mourning is over, I expect you to accompany me.' That evening she opened a secret drawer in her escritoire and showed me three miniatures of two boys and a baby girl. Kotula, Nicolai and Helena – all three died within days of each other and were buried in her Sophievka gardens. On consecrated ground, she said. Each spring the gardener sends her the first flowers that bloom on the graves.

A gypsy came to read the countess's cards. 'You will see your grandchildren grow,' she said. 'The great pain will come and go. There will be a long journey.' The countess gave me her green satin dress, to wear when the mourning is over. She said that green will go well with the colour of my hair. The dress is too big for her for she has lost weight again.

I washed the skin on the countess's stomach with soap and water, then again with water alone. The leeches were of superior quality, from Bordeaux. Dr Horn let them creep over a dry cloth first, to make them thirsty. He started with two leeches, but they did not attach themselves, so he asked for sweetened cream and spread it on the skin. When this failed, he punctured the skin with a lancet.

Dr Horn gave me a lotion (an ounce and a half of the tincture of muriate of iron, with several ounces of distilled water) for calming down the skin. He said it was much better than the pulp from boiled carrots I had been using before. Allowed food: camomile tea and a cup of broth followed by a glass of strong red wine.

For rheumatic pains: purgings with senna and salts, massage followed by nettle pulp for the joints and nettle tea to drink. The pain in the womb is growing and so are the haemorrhages. Dr Horn continues with daily bleedings, to restore the body's internal harmony. Her arms and legs are bruised and sore from the lancet. The countess is very strong, but I can see she is getting tired. 'Does he think he is paid for every quart of blood he drains from me?' she asked me in the morning.

Dr Horn wants to stimulate the vital functions of the body, and then to dissolve the growth with medications. His explanation: diseases are the direct result of the over-stimulation of organs that cause lesions. The irritants are cold air, food, drugs, miasmata in the air, and the percepta, moral influences on the nervous system. All of the stimuli produce contractions in different organs. Disease begins as a change of function of the irritated organ which, through sympathy, soon spreads to other parts of the body. Cancer is the aftermath of inflammation. In the countess's case the womb is a secondary symptom. The stomach is the seat of disease, for this is where the over-stimulation always appears first. The only way to cure the womb is to reduce this irritation. Then the tumour will dissolve and the illness will retreat.

The countess called me to her bed and gave me a turquoise ring and a necklace; the stones are arranged in such a way as to resemble forget-me-nots.

The entries she made on the journey were short. The list of inns and distances covered, the objects lost and misplaced. The moments when strength and hope were seeping away.

Today we covered merely 3 versts before the morning heat.

Lost: red scarf, two cambric chemises, a new box with toothpowder that has only just arrived from Freiberg, a bottle of Schweizer-oel, a box of whalebone buttons. The saddest loss: a watercolour of the Uman palace made by the countess's eldest son. Olga insisted it was because of my negligence, painful words that made me cry.

Under the Golden Goose – the third inn of that name in the last five days! The White Eagle. Under the Golden Horseshoe. The Lone Heron. Under the Wild Boar.

Broken: the china cup with the panorama of St Petersburg and the second ivory comb this week.

Before we left St Petersburg, the countess spent two whole evenings with her lawyer, and then she wrote farewell letters to all her children, except Count Mieczysław with whom she had fallen out. 'Because of him, my foot will never cross the threshold of the Tulchin palace,' she had said. The letters are in my care, sealed, addressed in her own handwriting. I am to make sure they are delivered to her children, if she does not survive the operation.

Berlin: 'I have seen patients recover from bigger tumours,' Doctor Bolecki assured the countess. 'Patients who lacked your strength and courage, Madame la

Comtesse.' In the morning the priest came and the countess received extreme unction. 'To give health and strength to the soul,' the priest said. The countess called Olga and me to her side and asked us to kneel in front of St Nicholas and thank him for this day of hope.

The countess asked for the fresh figs Graf von Haefen sent her, but only held one in her hands and smelled it. Then she asked me to place it on her night table. She said that when she was little, she climbed trees to get them. 'Have you ever climbed a tree, Rosalia,' she asked. When I said I had, she smiled. 'Alone?' she asked. 'No, with my cousin. It was quite a big tree,' I said. 'And you did not fall down,' she asked. 'No,' I said. A conversation even that short tires her.

I put compresses of camomile tea on her eyelids, for she constantly complains of redness and eyestrain. I have also tried eyebright with excellent effects.

The French doctor, recommended so highly by Dr Bolecki, has arrived. There is in him the complete absence of servitude my father always noted and praised. He is tall and rather thin and there is a certain carelessness about him, a touch of absent-minded neglect, a cuff button undone, a scarf needing retying but I have found him most capable. He agreed that Dr Horn's bleedings were excessive and caused too much weakness. He has no trust in the water cure.

There will be no operation. The French doctor says it is too late.

'Nature creates redundancy,' the internuncio tells her. They are taking a walk in the Mission garden, a neglected garden of few trees and unruly bushes. He points out the seedlings hopefully pushing through the spring soil round an old oak.

'See how many of them have high hopes,' he asks. 'How many, do you think will be allowed to grow.'

'One,' she says. 'Perhaps.' Some of the seedlings are trampled already, others are growing too close to the tree. The gardener will mow the rest with his scythe. All she can hear now is the clanking of metal on the whetting stone and the swish of the blade.

'Perhaps. If it is of use.'

'Beauty is cheap,' he tells her, and she knows he is right. Mana repeats this too, over and over again. 'Being of use is not.'

With Mana she can still quarrel. She can say that the internuncio likes her more than he lets on. That her company pleases him and pleasure is good. She can make him laugh, and he likes that too. When they eat together, he teaches her how to hold the fork, the spoon. How to lift a cup of coffee so that people would not stare at her in polite society. Doesn't that mean that he has plans for her?

He is a curious man, impenetrable. When she asks him about his past life, he shrugs his shoulders and talks of something else. He has asked her to dress as a page so many times that she begins thinking he might be tired of women. When, prompted by her mother, she suggested bringing a young boy to him, he agreed. But then he sent the boy home without touching him and said he was just testing her. 'Testing your willingness to sacrifice,' he said.

Mana likes to remind her that the internuncio is leaving in a few months, and that she will never see him again. Yes, she says, but . . . and there is a whole world in this *but*. A whole world of promises. I'll miss you, he has said. In Warsaw, I could do with a little bit of cheerful company.

He will send for me, she tells her mother. When the moon turns blue, Mana replies. Men are all alike, Dou-Dou. Don't trust them. Look out for yourself, for no one else will.

'Are you listening to me, Dou-Dou?' the internuncio says sharply.

'Yes,' she says.

'Beauty is cheap,' he repeats as if she hasn't heard him say it before.

She nods.

He tells her that the universe is made of two kinds of matter, active and passive, and these two kinds of matter attract each other. The dance of the universe, he calls it, the essence of life itself, the only force able to defy decay and rot. In the universe everything, every material is either male or female, and the function of the male essence is to penetrate the female, and infuse it with life. The sun is like a man, while the planets that circle around him are female. The rays of the sun fertilise the earth that contains matrices of an infinite variety of life forms. Without it there is nothing but death.

Only God, he says, is above this universal struggle. Only God, in whom all things are contained, is neither He nor She.

'Listen to me, Dou-Dou,' the internuncio says.

A beautiful woman has been put on this earth with special duties to perform. In her, like in no one else, the passive principle is at work. To release the best in the male spirit, to stimulate the essence of humanity is her duty, her destiny. To use the power she has been given for the force of life.

'Tonight you will do something for me,' he says. He is taking her with him to a private party given by Monsieur

Stachiev of the Russian mission. He trusts she is smart enough to know which side her bread is buttered on. Unlike on other occasions she will not be dressed as a page.

Her new dress has just arrived. The clean blue of the sky, festooned with tulle and tied with three bows down the bodice.

'It will make you look tasty,' the internuncio says and makes a gesture in the air, as if he were opening her up like a box of sweetmeats.

You will be wise to keep your eyes open, Mana has said. Benefactors have disappeared before, leaving behind nothing but debts.

'It'll make them all green with envy,' the internuncio says.

Monsieur Stachiev has asked for her three times, he informs her, in the flippant voice he assumes when he speaks French. She can understand enough already to make him abandon Greek altogether. If she tries to answer in Greek, he tells her, *Français, s'il te plait*. In French her thoughts come out unsure, hesitant. Words elude her, trick her into using them, only to prove something other than she intended. In French she apologises a lot, and is much more quiet. Every time she makes a mistake, he corrects her with an air of uncontested superiority. Is language part of the male essence too, she wonders. Or are some languages male and others female?

Tonight he wants her to be especially nice to Monsieur Stachiev.

'Someone has been pressing the Sultan not to receive me. I need to know who.'

How *nice* should I be, she wants to ask, but doesn't. 'What if he tells me, but I don't understand what he is talking about,' she asks instead.

He stops in mid-step to take a look at her and laugh. 'It is capital,' he says, 'to discover over and over again how highly you think of yourself.'

The internuncio doesn't expect Monsieur Stachiev, the Russian ambassador to the Sublime Porte, to tell her anything of value. Why would he? But if she is nice to him and Monsieur Stachiev loses his head, being the fool he is, then he might have to give up something for the privilege of a sweet little visit to *Mon Plaisir*.

'You want me to go to him,' she asks. Her throat is dry, but her voice comes out steady. Her mother would be proud of her composure.

'If he cooperates,' the internuncio says. 'Only then, and not before. Only when I tell you. Tonight, give him a taste, but don't let him try too much. I don't have to teach you how, do I?'

She is thinking of the seedlings growing in the shadow of the oak tree; of the silk belt in a coffer at the Seraglio; of the nights when her mother's body is racked by fever and when sores open on her skin. Sores on which she smears foul-smelling salves knowing they will not heal.

Rosalia

'Tell me about your parents,' the countess asked.

Their story began on that fateful June day, in 1768, when Ukraine was still the easternmost Polish province. The scorching hot June day in Uman, the Potocki's town, the jewel of the Ukrainian steppes, its cellars filled with gold and wine, its only well empty of water. Her parents remembered that empty well, the way they remembered the dried bones in the steppes, skeletons of man and beast cleaned of all flesh by the crows, bleached white by the sun. The way they remembered tussocks of grass, high enough for outlaws, *haidamaks* on horseback to hide among so well that a traveller would not spot them until their cold blades touched his throat.

Ukraine, the province of Polish lords, Jewish merchants,

and Ukrainian peasants. The land of vast estates where a lord ruled like a king and of wild fields where the only true master was a man with a sharp knife and a fast horse. A peasant was a chattel, bound to till his lord's land and to obey his owner. But who would find him if he refused? Who would find him if he took to the steppes, become a *haidamak*? Or a free Zaporogian Cossack if a Cossack unit took him in and let him live in the Sich, the Cossack haven, the lands on the left bank of the Dnieper river where neither the power of the Polish King nor the Russian Tsar meant much, where the Cossack warriors could dream of a free Ukraine, empty of Poles, Russians and Jews.

Their story began with fires at the edge of the forest, rumours of hangings and plunder. Rumours of men in bast shoes turning village trees into gallows. Of throats slashed, gifts refused. Polish lords and their Jewish lackeys. *Lach, Zyd i sobaka, vse vira odnaka*: Pole, Jew and a hound, all by the same faith bound.

The story of hatred and revenge.

The story of fear.

The story of a Jewish girl and a Polish boy orphaned on the same day when churches and synagogues of Uman went up in flames.

'Why?'

Rosalia had often asked her father that. Why did the *haidamaks* leave their homes and fields to ride through the Ukrainian steppes, to kill and burn?

'When men live in slavery, their hearts breed hatred and sin. When men turn away from nature, Rosalia, they turn away from reason.'

'So your father was a Jacobin?'

Her father believed that all men were created equal, that no one should be deprived of freedom. Did that make him a Jacobin?

From her Ukrainian manor, Helena Romanowicz, Rosalia's grandmother, sent to Paris for her copy of Jean-Jacques Rousseau's *Emile* the way other women of her station sent for ballgowns or lingerie. She had nursed her son herself, and bathed him in cold water, summer or winter. She forbade swaddling and in his nursery, in loose flannel flaps he was left free to wander and explore. He was fed when hungry, and left alone in the dark so that he would not grow up to fear it. Jean Jacques. Jan Jakub.

'Nothing in nature, Jakub, is disgusting. Evil and shame are bred by servitude and restraint. Only when a man turns away from nature, the world goes all wrong.'

He thought about it on the evenings he heard his father's bellowing, his curses bestowed on the whole world: the King put on the Polish throne by his Russian whore, chosen over a true-blood prince from Saxony; priests with big bellies and even bigger collection boxes; dirty Jews sucking out the blood of the Christian nation; stupid serfs who were ruining him with their cunning indolence.

His mother was his real teacher. *Pan* Jankowski, the tutor hired by his father preferred to spend his days shooting swallows and was satisfied if Jakub recited his daily pages of Alvarez, his grammar book. His mother taught him French and geography, and she told him stories of the past. History excited her, but unlike his father, she didn't care much for military glory. Her hero was Kazimierz Wielki of whom she said that he found Poland 'made of wood' and left her 'made of stone'. She told Jakub of Queen Jadwiga who founded the Jagiellonian university; of Copernicus who proved that the Earth moved around the sun. But most of her tales were cautionary stories of lost opportunities, of dissipation and betrayal. She told of the magnates – richer than the King – growing in power, believing in nothing but their golden freedom; of Prince Radziwiłł's trips to Paris, his horses shedding golden shoes, Polish largesse to the Parisian mob at the time when public coffers were empty at home; of the mighty Potockis, unsatisfied with their vast Ukrainian estates, dreaming of the Polish crown; of *liberum veto*, the law once meant to protect the dissenting voices and foster debate, which was now like rust eating up iron, allowing one man to break the *Sejm* for some private reason. She mourned the long rule of the Sas kings, electors of Saxony and kings of Poland, whom she blamed for the dissolution of the Polish virtues. King Augustus III, she said, had made himself invisible. In Warsaw, the Russians did what they pleased. Indifference and greed were choking the once mighty country to death, breeding hatred in the hearts of the peasants. 'Eat, drink, and loosen your belt,' she said, 'that's all the Poles care about.'

'And your mother, Rosalia?'

A pang of pain, still so fresh, so raw.

Her mother's name was Miriam, that of Moses' older sister who hid in the rushes to watch her brother float away to safety; who rejoiced at the sight of the pharaoh's daughter, kissing the baby's head, pledging to protect him from all evil; who asked, *Shall I go and call to thee a nurse of the Hebrew women, so that she might nurse the child for thee?*

Miriam, was the daughter of Avram Davidowich a wine merchant from Uman and his wife Rachela who always hid a splinter from the Uman gate in her husband's travelling trunk so that – on his long journeys – he would not forget his home and people. When she saw the first fires outside the gates of Uman, Rachela hurried to the Uman cemetery, to make the candles for the living and the dead, to awaken the forebears of Israel, the matriarchs and patriarchs, Adam and Eve. To plead for the purity of her soul, the resurrection of the dead, the deliverance from exile, and the restoration of the Temple. To plead for the enemies to be turned away from the gates of Uman. To beg the dead to help her save the life of her child.

But neither reason nor faith were of much help on that day of blood and hatred.

'Tell me about love, Rosalia.'

Love was waiting for her in the lilac bush, thick and covered with white clusters of fragrant flowers. The lilac bush into which Rachela pushed her little Miriam and told her to hide.

Miriam had to close her eyes for the lilac twigs were smacking her cheeks. Rachela's voice was urging her not to turn back, but she would have, if Jakub did not stop her. Jakub Romanowicz, a boy in brown breeches, with curly blond hair and eyes the colour of the sky. A *goyim* boy staring at her in silence, who then, slowly, took her hand in his.

'How do they call you?' he whispered, and she said, 'Miriam,' trusting him already. She let him pull her toward him, to make a spot for her, away from the moist earth that might dirty her dress. She let him tell her how they should stay here, in this hiding place, for a while.

This is how amidst the blood and the screams of the murdered, the two children who would one day become her parents fell in love, and everything that happened later was but a consequence of that dive into the lilac bush in Uman. That day Jakub covered Miriam's ears to drown the screams of the murdered, whispering stories into her ears. Stories of fairies and silly devils tricked by smart girls who kept their wits about them. Of a Polish king whom his own mother called a Piast, for unlike other kings he did not come from foreign lands and had no other kingdoms to worry about but Poland,

and who would come to Uman, to save them all.

'From the Cossacks?' she had asked.

'From the Cossacks and from the *haidamaks*,' he had promised.

In the hours that followed, men walked past their hiding place, and a small dog came, too, and sniffed for a while but then it went away, limping. All this time Jakub held Miriam in his arms, wiping the tears from her eyes and cheeks. He covered her ears and watched her fall into a shallow sleep, eyeballs moving under her eyelids. He wished to see what she saw then, now unable to stop himself from brushing her hair with his lips. He tried not to move even though his shoulder had gone stiff and he desperately wanted to stretch it. He must have slept, too, but his was a feverish sleep in which he saw the eyes of dead foxes staring at him, and heard his mother's screams.

The lilac bush that had harboured them, gave away its secret in the end. The branches fell under the sabre, revealing the face of a Cossack who had cut it down, his yellow *żupan* stained with blood.

Six pairs of eyes staring at each other. A moment when all is decided for reasons never revealed. Miriam's hand clutched on Jakub's, her fingernails digging into his skin. It seemed to Jakub that his heart had stopped. He saw every line on the Cossack's face, every smudge of blood and soot. Every hair in his long curly moustache, the colour of dirty straw.

'*Ne lekayte se. Boh z vami*,' the Cossack said. Don't be afraid. The Lord is with you.

'*Budes zyty*,' he added when they followed him. You will live. Their eyes were blinking at the daylight. Miriam never let go of Jakub's hand. She had wet her skirt and the fabric clung to her legs as she walked. Jakub tried not to look at the human limbs lying in the dirt, tried not hear the moaning of the maimed, begging to be killed.

They followed the Cossack through the streets littered with black burnt-out wood. Before that June day in Uman, Jakub had never seen a house burn. He had not seen the wall of flames, the fiery boulders crashing to the ground, the smoke now gathering into black clouds, now soaring up with the glitter of sparks, filling up the streets. He never knew how bright the flames could be when they licked the dry wood, how hot the air that made its way to his lungs.

They walked quickly, behind their Cossack captor, past the piles of rubble, books with pages torn out, quilts emptied of feathers. Feathers covered the streets like snow, drifting in the wind. Floorboards torn out in search of buried treasures. A shoe, a yellow satin shoe with a bow, crushed and stained with blood.

'I want to go home,' Miriam whispered to him.

Yes, her father had been a Jacobin. For him it meant that there was a reason for everything, that there were lessons in betrayal and revenge. Nothing happened to one human being without affecting the lives of others, touching them in most unexpected ways. The progress of the human race may be rigged with pain, but it must take place.

The Polish troops did not come in time to save anyone. It was the Russian units who arrived first, coaxing the Ukrainian rebels to lay down their arms. 'We are your brothers,' they said, 'bound by the same faith. You can trust us. Let's celebrate your victory over the Poles. Let's celebrate your newly won freedom.' And so the Ukrainian leaders joined a feast prepared by their Russian brothers, a feast from which they woke up in chains, to be delivered into the hands of their Polish masters.

This, they heard, was the time of revenge.

Miriam and Jakub. This was the way Rosalia saw them, two children walking through the burnt-out streets of Uman. She knew that her father had covered her mother's eyes so that she wouldn't see the corpses with outstretched hands and gaping eyes. That he whispered into her ear, 'I would not go anywhere without you.' She knew that, before Miriam's uncle came to take her away so that a Jewish orphan could grow up among her own people, they stayed together in the charred remnants of her father's ancestral house and that Miriam would let no one but Jakub put her to sleep.

True love, her father used to tell her, never died. Once joined, some souls would never part, no matter how hard they were prised apart.

Ten years passed before Miriam was to see Jakub again. Ten long years when only memories sustained them, when love could only be imagined. Ten long years of longing and dreams.

Jakub had just arrived from Warsaw, a captain in the Polish army, and he waited for Miriam, in the dark like a thief. He waited for her outside the Uman tavern where she had helped out since the day she turned fourteen. There would be a wedding soon, her hand was promised to a rabbi's youngest son. 'A good Jewish boy,' she heard. 'Who would make us all proud.'

Miriam wished there was no such thing as marriage. She wished she were old and grey and ugly or that she could run away and hide in the forest. Hide in a hole, a burrow, a den where no one would find her. Where they would all leave her alone. To a Jewish girl, a Polish man was danger, he was trouble. He was a dream better forgotten.

Lit by the moon, Jakub's face seemed pale to her, haggard and yet so handsome and strangely familiar. He had a narrow nose and a mop of thick hair, tied in the back with a black ribbon. The light stopped on it, as if broken in half. His clothes were so fine – she thought, with a shot of shame at her own homespun dress – a cambric shirt, leather breeches, silver clasps on his shoes.

'Miriam,' she heard. 'Sweet little Miriam.'

She wanted to cry with shame. Shame at the smells of the inn, the sauerkraut and pickles she had put back into the barrels only a few minutes before. Shame at the coarseness of her hands.

She ran away that first evening of his return.

But Miriam did not run fast enough. The next evening she stopped to hear when Jakub spoke of the years of longing. Of his mind, wherever he was, always taking him to the streets of Uman in search of her. Of knowing that she too thought of him, of hearing her voice calling him through the steppes. A Polish and a Jewish child united by common fate, united by love stronger than everything that tried to pull them apart.

'Will you let this love be our teacher,' he asked, 'make us better and wiser?'

For Captain Jakub Romanowicz had already asked Count Potocki for a permission to marry a Jewess from his town, and the Count promised to be her godfather at baptism.

It was still dark on that day when Miriam slipped away from her uncle's house, and climbed into Jakub's carriage, taking nothing with her but the small wooden star her uncle, a carpenter, once made for her. Her travelling cape covered the grey, homespun dress but not her shoes, rubbed at the sides.

This was how Rosalia would always see it. The carriage speeding toward Warsaw, past the ripening fields and the villages waking up. The wooden huts with whitewashed walls, thatches crowned with rows of crossed sticks. Barns, chicken coops, churches with onion domes and dark cedar shingles like scales of a giant fish. The small orchards fenced off with willow boughs where apples and cherries ripened. The gardens where beans and cucumbers and cabbage grew. Where barefoot children wiped sleep from their eyes, herding the cows and geese. Where the women came out to the wooden porches and stretched their bodies for a short blissful moment before diving back inside.

Miriam and Jakub.

Ego, Andrzej Jankowski, baptisavi judeum, conversum ex infedilitate judaica cui imposui nomen Maria.

This love, her father always said, was far greater than hatred and pain, greater than death.

Her mother was silent. 'There is nothing to tell,' she repeated when Rosalia asked about her grandparents, the aunt and uncle who raised her. About these years in Uman when she only imagined Jakub, somewhere in the world beyond the steppes. 'I don't remember,' she repeated, pointing out something that needed doing: a button hanging on the last thread, an unfinished chore. She knew how to make herself invisible every time the Jewish factor came to the Zierniki manor, or black-clad men with side locks passed them by.

Przechrzta.

A Jewess turned Catholic will always remain a Jewess.

It was this silence that would outlive her father's words.

Sophie

The private party is held in a rented house. It is a Turkish house. She can tell that from the brightly coloured pom-pom hanging over the portal, twirling in the wind, meant to catch the evil eye, divert its power from the house back to the Christian eyes that are carrying it.

In the room the internuncio leads her to, men sit on the floor Turkish style. The tablecloth is spread on the carpet, covered with bowls and platters. There are the partridges she likes so much, and slices of roasted lamb, pink inside; roasted aubergine and slices of red pepper;

plates of red caviar and slices of pineapple; oysters too – a whole platter of oysters, glistening in candlelight.

She tightens her grip on his arm.

'Odalisque,' someone says. One of the men bends forward as if to get a glimpse of her, but when she smiles at him, he makes a comic face and clutches at his heart as if pierced by an arrow. Her time will come, there is no reason to rush pleasure. She won't go away, will she? For now the conversation can turn to far more interesting matters.

Turkish horses are praised for their gentle nature, their respect for their master. The Ottoman training of discipline and obedience. If their master lets a staff fall on the road, a Turkish horse will fetch it with its teeth and hold it up to him.

The internuncio laughs at that, though Sophie fails to see what is so funny about an obedient horse.

Turkish horses are beautiful, too, with long black manes, the immense, flaming eyes. Sweet and intelligent. In the darkness and solitude of the European stables, their very beauty and sweetness would be lost forever.

She watches them, men warmed with wine, their bodies stretched out on the carpet, propped against cushions: Franks, visitors, travellers in search of what they have imagined would entice them.

The talk turns to other matters: the Turks spying on the foreigners on the Sultan's orders; the friends at home making too many requests. Balm of Mecca is coveted more than anything else, as if it were to be obtained for nothing in Istanbul. French women are declared far too bold and arrogant. Even the shortest trip to Paris makes one think that women rule France, and everybody knows what happens to countries governed by the weaker sex. 'Monsieur Stachiev,' the internuncio whispers in her ear, pointing at the man who has just come in, a stocky man in a lopsided wig. Russian ambassador. His eyes dart across the room until they spot her. She can feel the internuncio's hand pushing her toward him. 'He likes his women face down. Nice and easy.'

The Russian ambassador's face is pox marked and red. She sits beside him and folds her hands the way the internuncio has taught, on her lap. Monsieur Stachiev stares at her face openly, eyes blinking, as if she were not a woman but an apparition.

'It is too warm here, don't you think?'

'Yes. I wish we could go riding,' she answers. 'Just to feel the breeze on my cheeks.'

Encouraged by her attention, he paints pictures for her, of St Petersburg, of Empress Catherine, of the beauty of mighty Russia, his motherland, which he misses greatly, even the dead cold of winter. A Russian heart is not happy among strangers, he tells her.

'Friends, Monsieur,' she says, leaning toward him. 'Friends who would do everything to bring you happiness.'

The servants bring in glasses of vodka. She only takes small sips herself, but Monsieur Stachiev does not miss his turns. Soon he is leaning on her shoulder, his pungent breath over her face. His hand is on her lap, digging into the folds of her dress. She lifts it up and places it on the table.

'Monsieur Boscamp is watching,' she says. 'Please, sir, do not get me in trouble.'

'Monsieur Boscamp is a lucky man. With a knack to find jewels where other men would not even look.'

She half listens to what he says, aware that the men are stealing looks at her all the time. They look away when she turns in their direction, but they are all clearly watching her. As if she were a cricket in a wooden cage. Or a bird.

They send old women to the crossroads,
And they bring men into the harems,
And the bribed eunuch sleeps.

It is the internuncio's voice. His is a pleasant baritone, rich and vibrant. She has taught him that Turkish song about Istanbul, where virtue has long been forgotten. There is a round of applause and with the corner of her eye, she can see that her internuncio bows his head to her.

Monsieur Stachiev's voice is more and more garbled. He tells her that the Russian Empress herself never wastes a night with an untried man. One of her ladies-in-waiting has to pronounce the man able before she lets him into her bed. This is not a bad strategy and he intends to follow it – whose recommendation could possibly be better than Monsieur Boscamp's.

The internuncio is deep in conversation with the French ambassador. His head is bent, and he motions to the servants to bring him more wine. He must be talking about something funny for the Frenchman laughs and claps his hands. Then he looks at her, across the room, still laughing, shaking his head in disbelief.

'I need some air,' she says and rises from her cushion. Her hair is ruffled where Monsieur Stachiev has pulled at it. He is far too drunk now to remember what he does or hears anyway. She kicks his shin as she stands up, hard enough for him to wince, to have a bruise the next day and wonder where he got it from.

'A beautiful mare,' he says. He tries to rise too and follow her, but his legs wobble and he sits down. Before she gets out of the room she can see his head loll onto the shoulder of his companion on the left.

The internuncio comes after her, his hand is patting her

behind. 'You are a sensation, Dou-Dou,' he whispers. 'Just as I thought.'

'How would I know,' she says shrugging.

A tear rolls down her cheek. He sees it and wipes it off with his thumb.

Is this one of her 'moods', a recent appearance of a flaw in her otherwise remarkable disposition? A sign that she needs reigning in, more stringent discipline of the spirit. Is she expecting her menses perhaps? Has anyone been nasty to her? Cruel? Unreasonable? Has *he* done anything to make her angry? Isn't she well-fed, well-clothed?

Her new shoes have cost him a fortune, so why is she twisting her leg in this way. She will chafe the side and spoil the form.

'What is it now, Dou-Dou?'

'Nothing,' she says.

But he insists, and there is anger in his voice. Anger at these unreasonable expectations, he has certainly never encouraged. There is only one way to disarm him.

'In four months,' she whispers, defeated, 'you will be gone, and I'll never see you again.'

He laughs now, and kisses her. His tongue smells of oysters and white wine.

'Dear child,' he says pleased. 'You will forget me the minute I'm gone.'

'Never,' she says. 'I'll never forget you.'

He hands her a silk sack. 'Put this on,' he says. 'I've promised you would dance for them.'

'Now?'

'They are waiting.'

She can hear the sound of a citra, a peal of laughter, a loud belch.

'They think I've bought you from the Harem for a sack of gold. They want to see an odalisque dance.'

He points to a small room separated by a heavy curtain. Inside, on a dressing table, there is a mirror and a candle. Two cushions are stacked in the corner, but there are no chairs. The room smells of must; it has not been used for a long time.

He helps her out of her blue dress, taking care to fold it neatly and place it on one of the cushions. 'Don't be too long,' he says, pinching her cheek before leaving. 'Don't disappoint me. I want them to envy me.'

In the silk sack she finds a gauze shirt and pantaloons, a bodice embroidered with cekins, a long tulle shawl, and a small tambourine with bells. The skirt and the pantaloons are almost transparent.

In the small mirror, kohled, her eyes are even bigger, more luminous. Flaring.

Thomas

By the time he reached forty Thomas had seen so many deaths, that the death of his own father had melted into a multitude of agonies, last words, and death rattles. Valet to Marquis de Londe, a Parisian libertine of unsavoury reputation, his father was a man of no possessions. He thought Thomas, his only son, to be his justification for every blow he had ever taken, every humiliation of his position. Thomas could still remember his father coming to the little room in the attic they shared where rats chased one another behind the wainscoting. Before getting into bed he would blink his eyes and shake his head and shoulders like a dog shaking off the water after a plunge.

He shielded his son with his own arms, his own body. Only at the later trial Thomas realised that his father may have been shielding him from more than just blows, for the Revolutionary Tribunal accused the Marquis of sexual orgies during which little boys and girls had been tortured and sodomised. The Marquis, of course, denied all accusations and his father was no longer there to offer testimony.

The Marquis was sentenced to death on the 13th of Brumaire. His wife and daughter were guillotined the week after.

Gilles Lafleur, was only fifty when a carriage pole pierced him, pinning him to the stable door. A surgeon called to his bedside announced that it was a miracle he was still alive. When Thomas was a medical student he came across the description of his father's case. *A complete severing of the muscular and cartilaginous structures, including the cartilages of the ribs from the 4th to the 9th, wounding the pleura and lung.*

His father lived for five more weeks, to the great amazement of the Parisian doctors who came to see him and examine the pieces of lung protruding from his side. Proud of his sudden fame, Gilles Lafleur greeted them all with seriousness and ceremony. By then he was the number one Parisian oddity. Thomas's father welcomed such attention and would have proudly agreed for his mortal remains to end up on display for doctors to study and learn from, if anyone had asked.

Right before his death, in the bigger room on the first floor the Marquis allotted his favourite valet in the last weeks of his life, fingers smoothing the fine bed-linen meant to impress the doctors, Gilles Lafleur told his only son he wanted him to be a man who didn't have to bow to anyone.

That afternoon, back from a brisk walk around Berlin, he saw that two notes were waiting at the pension. In the first one, Ignacy, as Thomas expected, again called him a fool who would not bend his mighty notions of what was right. *Do come for dinner, though*, the note ended. *I need to forgive you.*

The second note carried a faint smell of camomile and soap.

> Doctor Lafleur, Countess Potocka insists she will not see another doctor and wants you to take care of her until the Lord chooses to call her to His presence. You will be well rewarded for your efforts. Come as soon as you can. The carriage is at your disposal.

The note (the handwriting *was* beautiful) was signed Rosalia Romanowicz, and Thomas could not hide a flicker of satisfaction when he read it.

PART TWO

. . . As Your Royal Highness knows so well, the slings of fortune have wounded me many a time, and I, remembering how the Pontian king Mitridat accustomed his body to poison, adapt myself to the challenges of the future believing that a small dose of pain every day will render me immune to what fate has in store. Nevertheless, to counter the calumnies of my enemies, to snap at the head of the vile gossip claiming that I enrich myself in Your service, I am enclosing this undisputed evidence of the meagre life I lead. I trust, Your Highness, that even one, most cursive glance at this pitiful account will suffice to prove my selflessness and devotion to My Merciful Sovereign.

Expensa:

D –, my landlord (for a very inferior apartment where mice feel more at home than I do)	ducats: 39
Table expenses (6 florins daily)	ducats: 120
Daily morning drink (1 florin daily)	ducats: 20
K –, my barber	ducats: 125

Washerwoman for one year	ducats: 24
Silk stockings a dozen, for one year	ducats: 24
Cotton stockings, ditto	ducats: 5
Firewood for one year	ducats: 24
Wax candles	ducats: 20
Tallow candles	ducats: 4
Tobacco (very inferior)	ducats: 24
Bed linen, (my old was too threadbare)	ducats: 50
Fur coat for the winter	ducats: 50
Gazeta, for one has to know what is going on this earth	ducats: 4
Journal, for Your Highness will not deny a man of the world the need to know the literary tastes of his times	ducats: 8
Books, paper, sealing-wax, quills, post	ducats: 12
Doctor and pharmacy	ducats: 24
Renting of a carriage, six times per month	ducats: 72
Wig maker	ducats: 6
Gold watch (after all a sign of my station in life)	ducats: 24
Shoemaker for very inferior shoes:	ducats: 2

Knowing Your Highness will not leave His faithful servant without consolation, I hasten to present another instalment of the story that has amused Your Highness so much.

Your humble servant.
Charles Boscamp

Mes amours intimes avec la belle Phanariote:

For a few weeks the internuncio delighted himself with his new mistress, but as once the demon of jealousy threatened to break the course of his antics, this time it was the demon of disagreement, shaking its snaky hair and kindling the fire with its bloodied hand, that was already thinking up ways of destroying their ties, at the same time, unwittingly, spinning the thread of fate that had brought our heroine to her present position.

Psaro, a Greek boy from the archipelago, and more precisely from Mykonos, poor, but with excellent calves and very dashing, Chevalier Psaro, well familiar with Hadja Maria's skills and services, slyly began visiting the house where Dou-Dou resided with her mother, staying, according to the reports of the internuncio's faithful informers, well into the night. These reports caused our internuncio some agitation and he decided to pay his young mistress an unexpected visit to see what he very much not desired to see. Psaro, having heard the noise at the front doors, escaped so quickly that only his shadow was spotted jumping out of an open window and disappearing into the side street.

The accuser of Dou-Dou's conduct who saw the man coming into the house with a silver sword and escaping without it pointed out, not without reason, that it should be sufficient to discover the place the sword was hidden to prove the girl's unfaithfulness. As all of this was happening, Dou-Dou stood with teary eyes, staring at her mother with an accusing glare, as if trying to say, 'Wasn't I right, Maman. Didn't I warn you?' Immediately, the internuncio and the valet began searching for the sword in the very room where, in separate beds, both the mother and daughter slept, and the sword was indeed found in the head of the mother's bed – or at least in the bed she said was hers – under the pillows. This discovery should have cleared Dou-Dou from the accusations and proven her innocence, but the internuncio's valet let it be known how Psaro boasted in front of him that he availed himself of the charms of both the mother and the daughter (one after another or both at the same time) and that the mother (having indeed enough time to do that) could have placed the sword under her pillows to draw accusations to herself.

Then another incident worsened Dou-Dou's situation, for a small boy who lived there and slept at the door of her room, said, without being asked, that his kokona[†] welcomed chevalier Psaro's attentions and that he saw and heard the indiscretions that went between them. All that – coupled with Dou-Dou's gloomy silence and her mother's swift disappearance (dear maman, without doubt, was terrified at the prospect of the storm over her head) – was the reason why a whip was produced and Dou-Dou was 'encouraged' to provide some more lively explanations. Bearing her punishment without a murmur of protest, Sophie repeated over and over again that she would willingly bear any whipping ordered by her beloved master, if she could get back his feelings for her, but this

---

[†] A name given to unmarried women one wants to honour, corresponding to the German '*Fraulein*'.

statement, however pleasing to the internuncio, did not shed much light on the matter. As a result the decision was made that Sophie would leave the Mission's house the following day, taking her mother with her; from now on Dou-Dou would live in Phanar, from where she had been brought according to her lover's whim and wish; she could keep with her all that was given to her, excepting a few intimate mementoes, like rings and a medallion with a monogram, which were immediately taken away, with the promise of their equivalent worth in money, and that she would receive a small salary until the time she found a husband. Then came a swift separation without even a word of good-bye that, our internuncio noted, left Dou-Dou despondent, while to him the entire scene felt lifted from Molière's comedy.

Having returned to his rooms, and feeling some heaviness in his heart, the internuncio called his Greek valet who – he had noticed it at the time – was crying during the scene I have described above. 'Why did you cry?' the internuncio asked. 'Is this girl a relative of yours? Or are you pitying me that I had to send her away?' 'No, Sir,' the boy said, 'neither this nor that. Pray forgive me, but I cried over the victim of all these lies and over Yanaka's‡ deviousness. For a long time this ingrate has tried to destroy the innocent girl and now he is congratulating himself on his efforts. Not longer than three days ago, he boasted that, soon, Mistress Sophie would be back to her old occupation of scrubbing pots and washing dishes in her mother's house.'

Confronted with such an answer of the servant-defender, his master ordered him to go to Dou-Dou's house

---

‡This is the name of the accuser, the same valet who would later on serve in Warsaw, in the costume of a Turkish sailor, as a valet to ex-marshal Rzewuski, and who must ponder in his heart the vicissitudes of fate, seeing his former victim in her present, uncontested glory.

and see what was happening there, without revealing, however, the nature of his visit. Nicholas, for such was the boy's name (and St Nicholas, it should be noted, is the patron of errant girls) returned saying that Dou-Dou was accusing her mother, who had in the meantime returned, that through her weakness for Psaro she had brought disaster on her own daughter's head. The mother was trying to console Dou-Dou with the hope that her lover would return and that, should that happen, the girl should beg to be heard and to explain everything.

'Swear on God Almighty,' she kept saying, 'and on our sacred faith that you are innocent. Tell him that as a daughter you couldn't betray your own mother, but now, should the internuncio demand it, you would gladly let your mother leave.'

'Oh, no,' Sophie cried. 'Indeed, I know him too well. Nothing will appease his anger, and I'll never see my beloved master again.'

'You do not know him well enough,' the mother said. 'He loves you. Surely, even now he must be already consumed by sadness, thinking of what has happened. Go to him right away, with this Greek valet of his. I guarantee you'll not fail. And when you return you'll not find me in this house, where, from my own indiscretion and weakness, you have suffered so terribly. It's right that I should be punished for my sins.'

To which Sophie replied, 'I would fly to him, I would throw myself at his feet and wet them with my tears. I would take any whipping, any punishment he would care to inflict on me, if I only knew that my beloved master would listen to his slave.'

As soon as the valet reported all this, the internuncio ordered him to fetch the girl, and this is indeed what happened. The prophecy of the experienced mother had been fulfilled, and the two lovers were fully reconciled in less than fifteen minutes.

BERLIN, 1822:

Laudanum

Thomas

Shivering with cold, Thomas woke the following morning, his last at Frau Schmidt's pension. He had already made arrangements for Pietka to take his meagre belongings to the von Haefen's palace. He tried not to think of the unpleasant conversation he had had with Frau Schmidt, who reminded him in an icy voice that he had made his reservations for the minimum of three weeks and that she expected him to pay for this time.

Frau Schmidt counted her money in front of him and, satisfied she was not cheated, walked heavily toward the kitchen muttering about the French always putting on airs and acting on their whims with no regard for others while she, a widow of a Prussian officer, had to make her living. Perhaps to punish him on his last night the fire had been allowed to die. He was shivering.

On the Great March from Moscow Thomas had seen men warm their freezing hands under the nostrils of horses. The death from cold, he thought, was not the worst. After all it came with a deadening of the senses so the victims slowly stopped caring. One could scream and hit them, and they would not move. Skin, flesh would peel away, all the way down to the bone, as if a human body were nothing more than a wax model of removable layers. Those who froze to death often had gentle smiles on their faces as if, in the last moments, the memories of their loved ones, of warmth and comfort became so real that they believed them.

At Berezina, where he got the touch of frostbite that permanently reddened the skin of his hands, Thomas saw a woman in a white muslin dress cut open a dying horse and dive inside, sabre in hand, in search for the liver. A wisp of a woman he would never have suspected of enough strength to kill a fly.

Austerlitz, Borodino, Moscow, Berezina. Thousands of wounded, many with necrosis and advanced gangrene, too late for amputation to help. No matter whether it was victory or defeat, it drowned in pus, vomit and congealing blood. He was surrounded by gangrene eating up healthy tissue in its relentless hunger, rats chewing on freshly cut limbs, maggots crawling in fresh wounds. The cries of the wounded were everywhere, their hands clutching his, begging for assistance. He had learned to be so fast, so incredibly fast.

Larrey had kept telling them that amputation was the only way to save lives. Nothing but a clean cut could stop crushed bones and dirt from doing their deadly work. 'Faster, faster,' he urged them on. 'We have to reach them within the first four hours. There is no time to deliberate.' Thomas's Parisian students listened in awe as he told them about Larrey's miracles: a Polish officer with general emphysema caused by a thrust from a Cossack lance cured with cups and wine embrocations; a Russian colonel whose severed nose Larrey re-attached to his face. In spite of perforated lungs, stomachs and intestines, bones smashed, lacerated and broken down into splinters, in spite of the gangrene, the swellings, the fevers, life clung to this world.

'Have you noticed,' Thomas had reminded Ignacy, during these long evening talks in Paris, 'how we stopped calling him His Majesty and the Emperor. How it is back to Napoleon or plain Bonaparte.'

Ignacy, Thomas thought, like most of the Poles he had met, was a man of little luck. When, at twenty-one, he thought he had found happiness at the side of Alicja, his father was killed in the last battle of the failed insurrection against the Russians, which had brought about the dissolution of Poland. Afraid of persecutions and anxious to secure her son's future after the final partition of Poland, Ignacy's mother left for Paris where she married again, an officer in Napoleon's Polish legion. When Thomas expressed his doubts that, in 1795, Paris was that much of an improvement on Warsaw, Ignacy was adamant. Even stained with the blood of the Terror, Parisian streets offered more hope he said. It was in Paris where Ignacy and Alicja's only child, Constance, was born.

In spite of Ignacy's protestations to the contrary, Thomas gathered that this was not an easy time. The two women did not get along. There were constant accusations of greed and thoughtlessness, tear-filled, silent days Ignacy couldn't stomach. He used to walk through the Parisian streets for hours, wearing out the soles of his shoes. It was only after Alicja's death from consumption, that Ignacy's mother declared her late daughter-in-law a saint. 'Or a mere angel, on her worse days,' Ignacy said with a wry half-smile. 'A saint *I* never cherished enough!'

A year ago, in January, Constance had asked to be taken to Rome, where she joined the Carmelite order. Once her vows were taken, she would not be allowed to lift her veil for any man, not even for her father. All Ignacy had left was her last portrait painted by a friend, the last image of her he was permitted to see.

Ignacy had hoped Constance would be Thomas's bride, that their bloodlines would unite in the next generation, but Constance wouldn't hear of it. 'It wasn't you,' Ignacy said apologetically. 'It was the idea of marriage that revolted her. She wanted nothing but to serve God. Do you understand?'

'Yes,' Thomas said. 'I understand.'

He understood the desire not to have anything to do with this world. This was perhaps the only thing about her he truly understood.

Gazing at the scar on his left wrist, a permanent reminder of the slash of a Cossack sabre, Thomas wished he could have seen Napoleon on Saint Helena, alone, without his epaulettes, his uniform, even without his kerseymere waistcoat. Naked. Just a man. Stripped like the men and women during the days of Terror, who were tied together and thrown into the river. The mob, roaring obscenities at them, had a name for this deathly embrace: *marriage revolutionaire*.

Rosalia was standing by the window, looking at the rain. She was waiting for him, she said, to show him to the room Frau Kohl had prepared.

'I insisted it needs to be close to the grand salon,' she said. 'I trust you agree.'

At that moment, in spite of the bright yellow dress, she seemed to him almost funereal. When she turned around toward him, he saw no trace of rouge or rice powder on her skin. Her translucent pallor was the result of long days spent in darkened rooms. Some ladies took small amounts of arsenic or were constantly bled to make their skin similarly look like alabaster. He never tired of denouncing such measures.

'In St Petersburg it must be snowing.'

'Yes,' he said. A flicker of unease was caused by the fact that she glanced at him, quickly, without seeing.

'Doctor Bolecki tells me that you are leaving for America. When?'

'As soon as I'm free,' he said, shifting to relieve the pressure on his knee. The pain turned dull. The rain was stopping.

'Aren't you free now?' her voice gently mocked.

'I mean when I'm no longer needed here.'

'That soon?'

'Yes.'

'Where?'

'To Philadelphia first.'

'And then?'

'I don't know yet. I'll see.'

The new room, he assured her, was more than satisfactory. Luxurious would be a better word. He had forgotten such wide beds existed. And all the space in the drawers.

'The drawers can be kept locked,' she said. 'The housekeeper has agreed to give me the key.'

He watched as she locked and unlocked the drawers one by one. 'It's better not to tempt the servants,' she said with a smile.

He was looking at her, aware of a growing layer of pleasure. Looking at her soft, auburn hair tightly pulled back from her face, her fine, narrow nose. The tiny lines around her eyes, the softening of the tired skin. She smelled of camomile and soap.

This is what he liked, just watching her. Watching as she moved across the room in her yellow dress, her hair dark against the nape of her white neck. He liked watching her hands when she smoothed the countess's bed, when she fed her lifting a silver spoon of broth to her mouth.

Her face did not register disgust with the blood and the pus, which was quite remarkable in a woman still young who – as Ignacy said – had been thrown into her role quite recently, by circumstances. She took it all as if there were no difference between a bouquet of flowers and the contents of the chamber pot. Yes, she was quite remarkable.

It wouldn't be long before the countess died, a few more weeks, perhaps not even that. Patients had astonished him before, so Thomas wouldn't insist on his predictions. Some clung to life longer, but even they had to let go. When this day came, he would be free to board ship for America. He imagined himself alone on the deck, open to the new world, the new life, unencumbered by what he was leaving behind.

> Their silks and satins we will take
> To make ourselves foot-rags!

It was the groom's voice, coming from the courtyard. The mournful tune and the sweet sounds of the bandura were haunting.

'What is he always singing about?' he asked.

Pietka was singing the same *dumy*, songs the blind *dziady*, old beggars, sang in Ukraine, Rosalia told him. They sang of Cossack flesh cut to the white bone; captives languishing for years in Turkish cellars; legs slashed by sabres, arms pierced by arrows; the lost freedom of the steppes; the destruction of the Sich. They promised death to Turks, Poles, and Jews, describing the pain that would be inflicted on them, the sweet taste of revenge.

'Payment in kind,' she lowered her voice, 'for what was done to them.'

It seemed to him that she shuddered.

'You wouldn't know,' she said.

'I've been to Moscow.' He tried to make his voice sound devoid of feeling. 'With Napoleon. I can imagine a lot.'

In the last post, she said, there had been a letter for the countess from the Tsar, thanking her for the poplar saplings she had sent him from her gardens in Uman. These were grown from the trees her late husband, Count Felix Potocki, had brought from Italy and planted in his Ukrainian estate.

'Now,' she said, 'you are serving the personal friend of the Russian Tsar.' Her voice reminded him of a flute – soft and warm, floating in the air, soothing.

'Bourbon is back on the French throne. Life is curious at times.'

She smiled and then, in an instant, her smile disappeared, a candle blown out.

'I have to go, now,' she said.

He stood up and walked her into the corridor. Her skirts rustled softly. She was still crumpling the handkerchief in her hand. If she dropped it, he thought, he could at least pick it up and give it back to her.

'Good day, Doctor,' she said from between two Grecian vases perched on twin marble columns, then disappeared round the corner.

'Good day,' he said to empty space.

Sophie

She will not be travelling alone. Carlo, the same Carlo who had once brought her – a girl from Phanar worthy of a king's bed – to his master, will accompany her. The internuncio wishes it. *A servant*, he has written, *in whom I have utmost trust*. Carlo and Monsieur Karwoski, an engineer from Danzig, with a pockmarked face that blushes easily and cold, sweaty hands. There is a nervous tinge to his voice as if anything she did could cause him some great misfortune. The Danzig engineer is the one who can write.

They are her master's spies, her chaperones, the guarantors of her good conduct. It has been nine months since the internuncio's departure and through all these long months she has been chastity itself. As her master demanded of her, she did not go back to live with her mother, but stayed as a lodger with Monsieur Boscamp's translator and his family, renting a small room where no visitors ever came, making sure her grief and longing for her master were noted. This journey too is a trial, a test. Every action of hers will be recorded, every word she utters will be included in the dispatches to Warsaw. Monsieur Boscamp – in mourning for his beloved wife and mother of his three children – may have sent for her, but he does not want trouble.

> Your slave will arrive soon on the wings of the wind, to help her Lord and Master in his mourning. Her tears will join yours over the grave of the lady whom she would have liked to replace in her final resting place, but whom she can only replace in her love.

'Don't go,' Mana says. Carlo no longer has her favours: too uppity, too jealous and taking to drink. Him she is not sorry to see go to that faraway Poland. 'Can't you see how men look at you? You can pick and choose from the best merchants in Pera. What else do you want? Why go where no one will be able to help you? What will you do when he tires of you or sends you to the streets?'

But nothing can be said that can stop her. She has seen so little. She is hungry for the world. The world is rampant with growth, fresh and so incredibly beautiful. The sun is brighter than she has ever remembered it, the wind warmer. Underneath the bark of the pine trees, sap gathers.

Every bud is a promise of a new shoot, a flower, a fruit. Birds swoop down from the sky. The old almond tree that grows outside Mana's house has burst into flower. Sophie breathes in its peppery scent and presses her palms against her cheeks, just to feel their warmth.

'Don't worry about me. I know what I am doing.'

She knows the secret of Lais and Phryne. The pleasure imagined is greater than the pleasure fulfilled. It is not merely her beauty that she relies on, but subtle promises. A glimpse of her ankle, a finger resting on her lips, a rustle of her skirt, a tremor of submission. How you have changed, the internuncio has said, just before leaving.

Mana grunts, but nods her head. 'Go then,' she says. 'But don't be a fool, girl. Watch out for yourself. Everywhere on this earth, you are either a married woman or a whore.'

Mana is afraid. That very day the carriage they were riding halted so abruptly that their bodies were thrown forward like sacks. The horse had stopped for the corpse of a young Turk, no older than eighteen, with a pale girlish face. His turban was lying in the dust. Death had come to him through his shaved neck, for this was where the bullet hole was. It seemed a sign, an omen; but for whom?

'He is a widower now,' Sophie says, smiling. 'Isn't he?'

> My beloved Lord and Master, the light of my days, the longing of my heart. There is nothing I wish for but to be at your side, and to kiss away your sorrow and your troubles. The only goal of my life is to bring happiness to your days, and to do everything in my power to soften the heart of your beloved King so that He would recognize the virtues of his loyal friend and reward Him as He deserves to be rewarded.

The journey is long and tedious. After two weeks – and there will be at least two weeks more before they reach Warsaw – she is no longer drawn to the sight of scraggy oxen (eighteen) dragging a broken-down Viennese carriage; or a whole line of mules tied one to the other and decorated with small bells; or a group of travelling Tartars, their women wrapped in yashmaks so that all that is left visible are their eyes and the heels of their shoes. She no longer hears the howling and barking of dogs or jackals. The carriage jolts and shakes her body until she is sore and nauseous by the end of the day. Every time the horses neigh their displeasure, she shudders at the grating noise.

Carlo and Monsieur Karwoski do not allow her to leave her bedroom when they stop for the night. They lock her door every evening after bringing her supper. The men play cards, drink wine, and talk to other travellers. She can hear Carlo's voice from downstairs, his loud laughter. In the flea-ridden rooms, no matter how much perfume she pours on herself, she can still smell the chamber pot. She hasn't been to the *hammam* since the day she left Istanbul, and her body itches at the memory of the soaping, the rubbing of the skin until the blood flows faster. Is there a *hammam* in Warsaw? The King has one, this she knows already, but would the King let anyone there?

> Your position in my households would be of the same nature as it was in Istanbul. You are not to expect anything more.

Why worry about the future, a voice whispers in her head. Ahead of her are still many days of travelling, of bone-shaking carriage rides, broken axles, mud getting inside no matter how tight she locks the carriage door.

More grimy inns, more lonely nights in a locked room, watched by the two men who should be her servants. Unless . . .

'The master,' she says with the faintest of smiles, 'intends to marry me.'

Carlo is listening, made uneasy by the conviction in her voice. This uneasiness tells her that his instructions must have been vague, and that he too wonders about their future in Warsaw. 'My fiancé,' she continues, 'listens to me. His love for me is such that he'll do everything I wish. I *might* wish your advancement, but why should I? Why should I think of your future when you treat me like a prisoner?'

She places the corner of her handkerchief to her eye, wiping away an imaginary tear. Carlo is not saying anything, but her words have had their effect. His sideways glances confirm it. What if this girl is right, he must be thinking. Surely her beauty and charm are hard to miss. Why would the internuncio not want to spend the rest of his days with her? What is so unusual about an aging man wishing for the warmth of youth to sweeten his last years?

That evening the door to her room is not locked and a jug of red wine makes its way onto her meal tray. After supper, she ventures out of her prison, a few steps along the corridor. The company downstairs is playing cards. The men are coarse-looking and loud. She opens the small window at the end of the corridor and watches the sky. The stars are glittering. The light of the full moon gives a leaden hue to the clouds. One seems to her like a crown.

You make me laugh, her internuncio used to say to her.

Funny how little she remembers of him: the feel of his hands; the smell of his body; the pressure of his loins on her belly; the powdery dryness of his skin. If she were never to set her eyes on him again, it would not hurt.

And yet she does miss him; misses the way she feels in his company; misses his voice that makes him owner of everything he speaks about.

When Prince Ypsilanti, the *hospodar*, the governor of Wallachia, sends servants to inquire of the identity of the travellers, she instructs Carlo to say that Lady Sophie Glavani from Istanbul is on her way to Warsaw to join the widowed Monsieur Charles Boscamp. The word fiancé is never pronounced, but there is enough doubt in the *hospodar*'s mind to err on the side of caution.

'Dear Monsieur internuncio is a friend,' Prince Ypsilanti says as he welcomes Lady Sophie of Istanbul at his Bucharest court. 'A benefactor whose favours are well-remembered in Wallachia.'

She turns her head a little to give him a view of her profile. His eyes do not leave her delicate nose, her full lips, her small round chin. He tells her that her beauty alone is reason enough for his dear friend to want her company in his widowed state.

'For eternity, if I could assure that,' she whispers, blushing. Her best satin dress with a lace collar got torn at the sleeve, and she has mended it too quickly. The tear shows, but only if one knows where to look.

Prince Ypsilanti won't hear of Lady Sophie staying at the inn. He calls the accommodation vile and the tavern-keeper a thief who adds copper to the water in which he boils cucumbers so they look green even if no longer fresh. She must accept his hospitality, the honours he reserves for his most illustrious guests.

'I hope, my dear lady, that you have not had anything to eat there.'

'No cucumbers,' she smiles at him with all the sweetness she can gather, thinking of a feather mattress and supper with oysters and roasted pheasants: a perfect gift from Lady Fate. A wave of bliss rushes over her. If she could, she would cry out at the top of her voice with joy.

When she leaves for Moldavia a few days later, yet another of the Ottoman vassal states, she is escorted by Prince Ypsilanti's guards, a lady travelling with two servants to join her fiancé. In Fokshany her arrival is greeted with a flurry of gossip and guessing. Monsieur Charles Boscamp is well known here. Visitors come to pay their respects, to catch a glimpse of her. She receives them all graciously, casting her eyes down. She lets their questions linger. 'Please, do not make me say things that should not cross my lips,' she begs. 'How unfortunate that what should remain secret is being dragged into the open before its time. The period of mourning must be observed. Madame Boscamp was an angel.' *How dare you*, her internuncio writes in a letter that reaches her, *spread such brazen lies about my intentions toward you. Daily I am exposed to questions why, I, a man of my pedigree and position, even consider joining my life with a woman of such base connections, a daughter of such a Mother and a niece of such an Aunt? What have I done to raise your expectations such? Have I not always been clear and straightforward about my intentions?*

Eh bien, she thinks as his anger chafes her. He won't make me cry. He has his own sins to consider. In Fokshany, being Monsieur Boscamp's fiancée elicits angry remarks of unpaid debts, of a business deal that went awry – a shipment of Persian carpets claimed lost but later seen in Warsaw by three independent witnesses ready to swear to what they have seen. Besides, in Fokshany there is someone else she would rather think about.

That someone is Prince Lysander bej Zadi. She was playing with puppies in the courtyard of an inn where she has found passable lodgings, kneeling on the flagstones, holding two of them in her arms, their pink tongues tickling her chin. He stopped his horse, and stared at her for a long time. Seeing him she put the puppies down and stood up.

'Are you a Goddess,' he asked, his eyes twinkling with amusement.

'A lady in distress,' she said, 'a traveller stranded in the quagmire of bureaucracy.'

'Stranded?'

'The *hospodar* of Fokshany is not helpful. He swears that Monsieur Boscamp's fiancée will not continue on her journey.'

'How is that possible?'

In Istanbul, she has been given a wrong passport, *yol-ferman*, useless for travelling outside the Ottoman Empire. She didn't know any better, then, having no one to advise her. She has been tricked. She knows who is responsible. Pangali, a translator for the Polish mission with too much influence at the Ottoman court, the fat fool who panted after her and whom she rebuked for his advances. A big, fat fool with foul breath. Punishing her in this under-handed way for she had laughed at him in public, sent him back to his boys he always preferred anyway.

Prince Lysander laughed. 'Do you always turn your admirers away?'

'Often enough.'

'What will you do now?'

Her servants, she has told Prince Lysander, have already dispatched word to Istanbul, and a proper passport is on its way. In the meantime, her predicament has attracted attention. Bread is three times more expensive for her than on the open market. The innkeeper demands one ducat per day for his flea-ridden hole, thrice his usual rate.

'Fokshany is a backwater,' Prince Lysander said. 'They do not know how to treat a woman of quality.'

* * *

She has only known him for a few days, and she is already filled with memories of him. Their eyes seek each other across the room. And even when they have to look elsewhere, each is constantly aware of the other's presence. He makes her think fondly of ordinary things – a pitcher of water; a quince on an earthenware plate; the bleating of a goat in the distance; being yanked from sleep before dawn by the prayers from the minaret; the smell of hemp and charcoal. She wakes up to the memory of his face, his eyes perhaps a bit too wide (but only perhaps), the long, narrow nose she thinks exquisite (the word has a taste to it, pungent and rich), the black tangle of his hair. She falls asleep recalling the sound of his voice. In her dreams she runs with him through the fields and he pulls her toward him and presses his lips on hers.

He brings her gifts and flowers. A jewel box of encrusted wood inlaid with mother of pearl. A branch broken off a flowering almond tree (spring comes later here, he tells her when she marvels). His eyes soften at the sight of her; his hands reach out to touch her. More than by her beauty, he tells her, he is stricken by the joy in her. He delights in her, walking briskly, impatient with time. Sometimes she is still like a child, sometimes she is a woman. A miracle he has stopped expecting.

'With women like you,' he tells her, 'the Greeks have nothing to mourn.'

She marvels at his olive skin. The smoothness of it. His way of waving his hand, impatiently, as if he were warding off a fly. Why shouldn't she believe love so sudden? When they are together, everything seems sparkling with possibilities, making it easier to ignore the sour faces of Carlo and the Danzig engineer. Their poisonous whispers, their warnings. Their attempt to close the door to her room and hide the key.

Her prince has another key, from the innkeeper. 'The power of *bakshish*,' he says laughing.

He asks her what she likes best in the whole world. Jonquils, the roasted skin of a lamb, still steaming from the fire. Singing at the top of her voice. Running fast through the garden, in the morning, when the dew is still on the leaves. The feeling that lives in her, the conviction that life is unstoppable, that miracles happen.

What he likes best are horses. Arabian, with their undulating necks. The dancers of the desert, able to last when other breeds fail.

He comes to see her every day. The very circumstances of their encounter conspire to join them together. Her forced stay in Fokshany is nothing less than a gift from fate, a gift he will not turn down.

'May the courier with your new passport take his good time,' he prays loudly, kneeling at her feet. 'May the deep waters open on his path and deep chasms slow him to a crawl.'

Even that would be too fast.

'Poor courier,' she says. 'How can my Prince be so cruel.'

'It's love that is cruel, not your Prince. Love that knows no pity but its own force.'

He has bewitched her. There is nothing he had to do to accomplish this, but just be with her, look into her eyes. Tell her that the black in them is softened with the languor of blue. She has not resisted. She doesn't want to. She gives herself up to love the way she gives herself to fate.

Watch out girl, Mana would have said. Don't be foolish.

But she is foolish. Foolish and very wise at the same time for she can tell that her infatuation spawns the passion he has for her. They are like twins, she thinks. What she wants he wants. What she wishes to be, he wishes too.

'How lovely you are,' he gasps.

He promises her the world. She will be his wife, cherished until death closes his eyes. If he could, he would pierce the heart of that man who calls himself her fiancé. That old goat who thinks he has bought this beautiful Greek girl with his gold, like a slave. Of whom it is said that he has lost his influence with the King and is now desperate for any position, begging for a few ducats on the account of past services. How could such a man make her happy in the way she deserves to be?

Words like these make her bold. Words like these erase the bitterness of memories she has kept locked away for months.

> On sight of hereof admit the Bearer to the sweet pleasures of Mon Plaisir, as well as the exploration of other Territories, including the Hills, Forests, and Forts, especially in the lower part of the Continent. As to Canals, let him have Ingress, Egress and Regress, in such manner as pleases Him, for the period of two Hours, and no longer, and place it to the Account of Your Kind and Constant Keeper.

How could I even think I might go back to that man, she thinks. What is it that he has given me?

Sophie Kisielev

Outside the carriage window two crows landed on the freshly ploughed and harrowed field. In the distance, the elm trees hidden in the morning mist seemed to stand still. After four days they were but halfway there.

Please, Sophie, my dearest daughter, hurry. I want to

bless you and my first grandson before I die. For months her mother's letters had been more and more alarming, but none had been that frightening. Why was it in Rosalia's hand? Shouldn't Olga have written to her own sister? Was she cross at her perhaps? Did she think Sophie should have guessed the truth? Refused to be comforted by her mother's lies? Know better? Feel the truth in her blood, in her heart?

Could her own sister have grown so bitter?

Monsieur Talski will tell you more when he brings you this letter to Odessa. But Monsieur Talski – her mother's steward – avoided her eyes, and said that Madame la Comtesse suffered a great deal. 'Everything in God's hands,' he said. *I wanted to send you your pearls, but M. Talski refused to write me a receipt for them saying that we are all mortal. I can't trust anyone with them without a receipt*. With the letter came a bank order for 50,000 roubles for the trip. There were assurances, too, for Pavel.

> Tell your husband, not to wait for His Majesty's permission, for it may come too late. He can always explain the circumstances that forced him to leave. Assure him that His Imperial Majesty, whose friendship and benevolence I have felt many a time, will understand his position and will not think it insubordination but a fine display of filial affection. The Emperor is not thinking of a war and, therefore, your husband has no reason to fear that he might not be allowed to leave for Berlin.

'Oh, just go,' Pavel said in the end, slamming the bedroom door behind him. She had not allowed him to touch her since Volodia's birth, pleading that she was still sore, but after he left, she found herself sobbing for hours in her bedroom. He would go to Berlin as soon as he got his permission, 'the very hour I get it' he promised, 'but I'll not disobey my orders hiding behind your mother's skirts'. This he said, as she was climbing the steps to the carriage, just before the footman folded them away.

The two carriages were speeding toward Berlin. Madame Kisielev's French maid, Colette, was in the other one, sharing the space with her clothes and supplies for the journey. Volodia and Katia, his wetnurse, were with her. Even with the superior Prussian roads, the constant shaking of the carriage was getting to her. Her stomach heaved, her legs hurt. The baby was crying, too, the poor soul. Choking on his tears, his dear face purple with exertion. If she were too late to see her mother alive, she would never forgive herself or Pavel and his insistence that there was no rush. 'You are no longer at her beck and call,' she remembered him saying, 'You are a wife and mother first.' To think that once she used to think of Pavel as droll and a bit awkward, in need of her love.

The carriage swayed and for a moment it seemed to her she could hear a knock on the door. 'Maman is dead,' she thought, her heart folding in fear. 'I'll never see her again.'

'It's the cord, Ma'am,' Katia said, cheerfully. 'The footmen never know how to tie it properly.'

It was the cord. She could see it, just above the window. Volodia's birth five months ago had made her fearful. She couldn't stand hearing people talk of babies dying or stillborn. She was still agonizing whether to inoculate her son against smallpox, an action her mother advised strongly. But Countess Sokolov's daughter had died shortly after being given the inoculation. Was it really because she was sickly and would have died anyway?

You are a mother now. I tried to hide the truth from

you for so long, for I wanted your heart to be light when the baby was growing in you.

Yes, she was a mother, and she was afraid. Her two brothers and an older sister were buried in Sophievka, among the flowers and the rocks. When she was little she stood by their graves and asked them to come and play with her. She even envied them for Maman said that they were angels, now. Hovering over the garden, hiding among the flowers, invisible, but all-seeing. She wondered if they liked watching her from the clouds. Now she wondered how her mother could have withstood such pain.

Volodia, her beautiful baby, had been born with his face down. The midwife didn't want to tell her that, but Sophie had found out anyway. Face down toward the earth, toward the grave.

'Please, Madame,' the wetnurse said, her smile revealing a missing tooth. Volodia was snuggled in her arms, and Sophie found the sight painful. When she insisted Katia put the baby in the wicker cradle, the baby cried. He also cried when she, his mother, held him.

'We shall stop soon,' Sophie Kisielev said. 'At the first post.'

This constant struggle over her own child was something Sophie had not foreseen even though many of her friends had warned her. 'You begin to fight for your baby with them,' they said about wetnurses. 'As if the milk in their breasts gave them all the rights.' Katia was unabashed in making her demands: beer in the morning; honey; big spoonfuls of jam on white bread, buttered. Everything Katia ate or drank nourished the baby and never in her life had she been so pampered. Sophie often caught the glimpse of the wetnurse touching the folds of fat over her hips with pleasure.

'I want to pee,' Katia said, still grinning.

There was a shadow of contempt in Katia's eyes, contempt covered with an elaborate show of affection and subservience. If Sophie could, she would have dismissed Katia long ago, but her milk was good for Volodia, and they both knew that with the first three wetnurses he had been vomiting curds.

'He has the General's eyes and his smile,' Katia crooned, swaying back and forth. 'My little hawk.'

The carriage was approaching the station and Volodia, sensing the change of pace, had woken up. Sophie insisted on taking him in her arms, and Katia relinquished the baby, pleased that he began to cry as soon as she handed him over.

'Bad boy,' she said. 'It's your own Mama. Your Mamochka. Don't cry.'

Sophie smiled at her son's tiny face, trying to calm him down. She rocked him in her arms. She kissed his tiny cheeks. But his eyes were closed and, wailing, he paid no attention to her.

'I'm hungry,' Katia said. There were two wet spots on her dress where the milk leaked from her breasts. 'You should eat, too, Madame General. You are too thin. Even His Highness Pavel Dimitrievich says so.'

An hour later, after the whole entourage had been settled at the inn, Sophie Kisielev came down to the dining room. She needed to stop thinking about death.

The proprietor welcomed her with a bow and pointed to the reserved, private dining room he kept, he informed her with another bow, only for his select guests. Two of his other guests were there already, an old, retired Prussian general with a wife who, Sophie decided, couldn't be older than sixteen. 'General Kolwitz,' he introduced himself. 'And Frau Kolwitz,' he said, his wrinkled face – powdered and rouged – beaming with pride. The young wife bowed and smiled softly, not able to hide her pleasure at the sight of her ringed finger which she placed on the edge of the table, the Belgian lace around her cuffs, and the string of pearls on her white neck. What do you know of me to judge, her eyes asked.

'Tell Comtesse Kisielev what we have seen in Berlin, my darling,' the General said, after they completed their introductions.

The General's wife was delighted to oblige. Her high-pitched voice brought back the memory of the carriage and the insolence of the wetnurse. Sophie tried not to wince as her ears filled with the exclamations meant to describe a military parade in Berlin. 'Such strength, such courage, such presence. Ah, the discipline of the soldiers who marched with one step! A giant machine of the army so well oiled.'

Frau Kolwitz leaned toward her and asked in a whisper, 'Is it a girl or a boy?'

For a split second Sophie did not know what she meant. Only when she heard, 'The baby,' she understood that their arrival must have been observed and commented upon.

'A boy,' she said, smiling. 'My first one.'

'How wonderful,' Frau Kolwitz said with such obvious rapture that Sophie's irritation disappeared. This was why, when they had eaten the simple meal of consommé and roast beef, she agreed to a game of faro. 'If I win,' she decided, 'all will be well. Maman will recover. Volodia will grow. Pavel will love me again, and I'll be happy.'

General Kolwitz was the *tailleur*, the banker. Five other travellers joined them around the oval table covered in green baize, one agreeing to be the croupier. She bet on the jack of spades. She doubled her stake. Tripled it. She won. Then she won again. She would remember this moment for years when as Kis (to her friends) she would be playing in the casinos of Monte Carlo, Paris, Vienna.

Separated from her husband, a beautiful woman in a lamé turban, collecting her winnings with gloved hands. Writing to her younger sister from her Parisian boudoir, knowing Countess Olga Naryshkin would think her a sentimental fool. *We both married Russian Generals and now we have to atone for the sins against our beloved country.*

Sophie

Every day she comes up with a new reason to stay in Fokshany: muddy roads; her own delicate health; rumours of brigands on the prowl.

The horse she is riding takes a sharp turn, to a clearing in the woods. Her two chaperones, ride past her, lost on their phantom chase. Lysander is waiting for her, his face beaming with joy that a simple trick could work so well. A beautiful carpet is laid on the grass, a basket is there with the delicacies she craves. ('Are you always that hungry?' he has asked.) Partridge pâté with cranberries, roasted lamb, fried aubergines. She claps her hands and jumps off her horse, right into this beautiful spring day, right into his arms.

He feeds her morsels of lamb, fresh figs, plump dates he fishes out from the basket. His hand brushes her cheek. It is a hot day and her skirt is slightly damp. He smiles and opens her blouse, so white against her skin.

Something has broken out of her. Something free, soaring, more precious than life. Everything that has passed, has led her to this perfect moment and, therefore, everything that has passed can now be forgotten. Love knows no past, cares nothing for what has been. Love wipes away everything that is not bliss.

Her arms touch the back of his neck. Her lips part to receive him. If ever there were gods in that other, ancient Greece, they couldn't have been more like them.

'I love you,' she whispers.

He is so hungry for her that his hands tremble with impatience. Fumble with the hooks and lace. Tear at the garters. She has to help him free herself from the clothes that try to hide her body. 'Wait,' she laughs. 'I'm not going anywhere.'

She is dazed by the sun, the wine, the food. Her Greek prince is the lover after her own soul.

In that meadow, impatience overcomes restraint. Pleasure washes over her like a spring torrent. In his arms she is without will. There is a force that links them together, a force more powerful than her own wishes. With him the world is before her. The world with no lies.

She has always been lucky, hasn't she?

She is still giddy with love when she wakes up the next morning in her Fokshany inn, her skin tingling, her lips swollen from his bites. Carlo is giving her a dirty look. She doesn't care.

'Why such a long face?' she asks cheerfully. 'Don't worry, Carlo, it's not your fault.'

'No,' he says with venom. 'It's not my fault that you've made yourself into a whore.'

Something in his voice strikes her, makes her sit up on her bed. The whole town of Fokshany is talking of nothing else but how Prince bej Zadi had his way with the internuncio's fiancée, thus avenging himself and his best friend the *hospodar* of Moldavia. Avenging himself for a transaction – a shipment of Arabian horses whose bloodlines turned out to be far from pure – in which the two had been the losers. Now, the dear internuncio is welcome to take what remains of the Territory the Prince has claimed with far more vigour.

This is not all.

The internuncio has not left many markings of his

exploits, the Prince says to anyone who will listen, being a mere potboiler in that department, for the *lady* in question is craving for the pleasures so long denied.

'You want to hear what else he says?' Carlo extracts a folded sheet from his breast pocket. His voice hisses with bitterness and fear. Carlo has been fooled and the Master will not forget such humiliation.

'No,' she says, but she cannot stop him.

> The rider must be very careful of her, as the eager volunteer in the field of Venus starts at full speed with dying looks, short breath and wishing eyes. Requires to be used gently, as she is very excitable, especially lately, having taken fresh instructions in the art of mastering new Manoeuvres in the amorous contest that can enhance the coming of pleasure.

'You are lying,' she screams and throws her shoe at Carlo who ducks and covers his ears. She can taste the bitterness of her tears, feel the flush of crimson on her cheeks. She should have known better, but didn't. Mana was right.

But was she?

What if it is but a cruel joke. Or the work of her enemies who envy her. There could be so many reasons. A prince has fallen in love with a commoner. A prince has been thinking of marriage.

'I don't believe a word of it,' she screams.

In her mind she can see him harried with grief. He has been admonished for his love, chastised for the choice of his heart. Told she is not good enough for him. Is he crying with pain now, thinking she may believe these vicious lies?

She sits down at a writing table:

> The cruel words that have reached me make me sick

with worry. Whoever is spreading these venomous rumours, whoever is trying to make me doubt in the sincerity of your heart should know that my love for you is stronger than that.

She places three kisses in the empty spot below and puts her name there. But Carlo will not deliver the message. From the window she spots a small boy who is helping the groom. The door to her room is locked again, so she throws the note wrapped in her own handkerchief and asks the boy to deliver it.

'Yes, *kokona*,' the boy says, but not until he picks up and examines the coin she throws down after her note.

She wants to climb down, lower herself on the sheets tied into a rope, run to her beloved, hear from his own lips what has happened. But she will wait. He will come soon, she tells herself. He will come to tell her how afraid he was she might believe these cruel words.

If you let them drink from the tit, Mana has often said, why would they buy the cow.

In the evening her throat is hoarse, swollen, her cheeks are hot with fever. She has to shield her eyes from candle-light and she is shivering. She feels something itchy on her neck, at the base of her hair. In the mirror she sees these are red blotches. When she looks closer she notes that the redness has spread to her neck and her face.

She screams.

'The girl has measles.' The doctor's voice is matter-of-fact, resigned. The calculation is simple. The contagion has entered her body and is spreading fast, weakening her defences. In her mouth there are small white spots with red circles around them. She needs all the strength now to fight death that wants to claim her.

For three long weeks she sees faces in her dreams.

Mana comes to soothe her but recoils as she sees her daughter's body covered with pus. Is that how you want your life to end, Mana asks her. She shakes her head and waits for a wave of heat to pass. In the dreams that come after that she walks through the desert without a drop of water. She lifts her flask and places it at her lips but nothing flows out. It is so hot that the air burns her feet and hands. Someone, Lysander, throws burning sand into her face and her eyes. She screams and screams and Carlo comes again and moistens her lips.

'The passport has arrived from Istanbul,' he says. 'We can leave as soon as you are well enough. Your mother sends you this.'

He slips something into her hand. A metal figure that quickly warms up in her hot hand: St Nicholas, the patron of travellers and errant girls.

'Has he come to ask about me?'

Carlo shakes his head. What more proof does she want?

'Don't think about this scoundrel,' Carlo says. In his voice there is compassion now. Perhaps this means she is really dying.

'I want to live,' she whispers, squeezing the holy figure in her hand. 'I so very much want to live.'

The Graf

There were four of them in the grand salon: Sophie, Olga, Rosalia and the Graf.

Graf von Haefen was sitting on the day bed, leaning backwards, his left arm extended on the arm rest, thinking that once the front rooms in the East wing were finished, he would ask Herr Schinkel to take a good look at this salon, too. Nothing too drastic, but the effect must be much simpler, more elegant. His wife had been right when she said that his father's tastes had been far too flowery, too ostentatious.

A Polish maid, the plumper one of the two, came in with a plate of lemon tarts. The cakes were a gift from the Graf's Potsdam housekeeper.

'These tarts,' Olga said as she stood up to serve him tea. 'Are the best I've ever had. Maman says so, too.' The samovar, the Graf noted, stood right where his father used to keep his favourite brandy.

The tarts were, indeed, delicious. The pastry was light and flaky, the cream fragrant with vanilla and lemon zest. Each tart was decorated with a candied slice of lemon.

'They come from the most precious of friends,' Sophie echoed, and Graf von Haefen thought once again how Olga's features lacked her mother's beauty. They were too sparse for her face, too reminiscent of the perfect mould not followed. It must be hard on her, but who could equal the divine Sophie who had once bewitched Berlin and Paris with her *beaux yeux* and her Greek costumes.

'My wife,' Graf von Haefen said, 'keeps telling me I should stop riding as if I were a young lad. She is sure one of these days I will break my neck.'

'How is her Ladyship?' Sophie asked.

'Quite well. Quite well. She asked again if she could come by to pay her respect.'

'I wish for no visitors,' Sophie said. 'Please indulge me.'

'Your wish is my command, my dear friend. This is what I said to Fredericke. It is no time to pay respect. Your illness . . .'

'I wish not to talk of my illness. You will have to indulge me again.'

Graf von Haefen was finding his new trousers too tight. Peg-top trousers, strapped under the instep that he knew would be getting in between his buttocks. They were a bow to fashion, or rather a sign of his stupidity, he thought, and proof of his Italian valet's powers of persuasion. As annoying as the high starched collar of his shirt, the upturned points chafing his cheek.

'Berlin has changed, *ma chere amie*, from the time, so precious in my memory when you dazzled us all here. More beautiful than Rafael's Venera, I swear. Driving us all to madness. I, for instance, still recall my own incredible foolishness, but don't worry. I shall be silent on this topic in the presence of your young daughter.'

The countess's smile was faint but visible.

'At that time,' the Graf continued having winked at Olga, 'I still thought that the German nation had a role to fulfil. A sacred role. Now we've been overtaken by the parvenu, by the vulgar. Jews and philistines have sneaked into our world, and now it is no longer ours. This little Levin woman I've been writing you about, managing to marry one of our diplomats! This is what terrifies me. They are baptised, their women marry into the best families. They change their names, but they cannot eradicate their nature.'

'My dear friend,' Sophie said. 'You are too sensitive.'

'Should we just despair and give in?'

'It might be time, my friend, to forget the affairs of the nation and think of yourself more.'

The Graf rose from his place as if to approach her, but sat down again, cursing his new trousers. He would make his valet wear them. He took another lemon tart from the plate. A few crumbs fell inside his waistcoat. Olga must have seen it, too, for she burst out laughing and tried to cover her outburst with a cough.

'Are you all right, dear child?' the Graf asked. He was just about to rush to her help, but Rosalia was faster. She too believed in a good slap to clear the throat. The tart, he noticed with some regret, fell to the floor, which was strangely bare without the carpet.

'Are you all right?' Sophie echoed. Olga was still coughing, her hand pressed to her chest.

'Raise your hands,' Rosalia said.

'The wrong way,' the Graf said. 'A piece of the tart went down the wrong way. It's nothing.'

The commotion suited Olga, he noticed, brought warmth to her cheeks and took away some of the harshness from her face. Definitely, more weight was called for. He was wondering if there was any truth in the rumours that Sophie arranged for her daughters to have a little romance with her friend Tsar Alexander in Tulchin, as a little investment in their future. The Tsar was a fool, of course. Always in uniform, his enormous feet decked with solid gold spurs, when everyone knew he never stirred out of his villa when Napoleon marched on Moscow.

'She needs a drink,' Sophie said. The concern in her voice annoyed him. He would have liked to be alone with her, have her attention to himself.

Rosalia poured Olga a cup of tea from the samovar, and she took a few sips. When she finally stopped coughing, he resumed his monologue.

'Oh, how easy it is to talk to you, my dear friend,' he said to Sophie, taking another bite of the tart, this time managing not to spill any crumbs. 'To know you understand all, share all. I feel lost in this new world. It has no place for me.'

'Perhaps nothing in this world is pure and unmixed. Perhaps our enlightenment always has to come at the expense of our pleasures.'

'You always say that.'

'I always mean it,' she laughed softly. 'Can I ask for one more favour?'

'But of course, dear friend. Anything.'

'Music,' she said. 'It's so quiet here, that I can hear my own thoughts. I long to hear some music.'

After he had said his good byes to Sophie – refusing to accept any more thanks for taking care of all their arrangements, including the daily administering of the accounts – and after he had closed the door behind him, Graf von Haefen turned to Olga who had accompanied him out of the room.

'I don't think laudanum is working, my dear Olga,' he said and his words extinguished the last traces of her childish glow. 'My eyes are still good. She is in much pain. Your dear Maman was clenching her teeth the whole time.'

Sophie

The letter in her hands is short. It is meant to dispel whatever hopes she might still have.

> Since I am about to enter into holy matrimony again, having gained the consent of my late wife's cousin, a woman of excellent connections and angelic nature, your arrival in Warsaw is no longer possible. I am pained, by the lies you have been so careless to spread about my plans toward you. They have already caused me a lot of embarrassment and, far more inexcusable, they have tarnished the memory of my beloved wife, especially in the eyes of my true fiancée.
> Charles Boscamp

The courier who delivers the letter into her hands smells of fried onions and the dryness of old age. He is on his way to Istanbul and says that Monsieur Boscamp's orders are direct and straightforward to take her back to her mother. A drop of saliva dangles from his upper lip, stretches to its limit and falls.

She is still weak from the measles, but the rash is gone. Her skin is more translucent too, and she is more willowy, more airy now than before. Even the old courier cannot help staring at her.

'Monsieur Boscamp,' he repeats, 'left me clear orders.'

She refuses to think of Lysander. Carlo is forbidden to mention his name. She is not interested. There is only that much a heart can take, that much that can be eviscerated, bloodied, destroyed.

She has slashed the white blouse she wore on that day. Slashed it into strips with a razor blade.

'I've been betrayed,' she says to the old courier. Her voice is calm and steady, but her beautiful eyes are drowning in tears. She lets the tears flow, until the old man, moved by her stillness, fishes for his own handkerchief and hands it to her.

'A man whose advances I've rejected, is doing everything to destroy me. My heart, I've told him, belongs to my beloved master. No promises, no force would ever sway it. In this very room where we stand now, I revealed to this evil man the secret of my heart and he left in anger. Before I fell so gravely ill, I'd been warned that he has sworn to avenge himself. To my own peril, I've dismissed his boastings. I trusted with my whole heart that nothing in this world could turn my beloved master against me.'

The old man is listening.

'Was I wrong?' she lowers her eyes. 'Is innocence always at the mercy of malice?'

The old man clears his throat. The skin on his neck is loose. It shakes when he swallows. She asks him if he has children.

He is the proud father of five, his youngest daughter is her age. She is married already and with child. A sweet and lovely daughter who has never caused him a heartache, unlike the eldest of his sons.

'Reckless?'

'Disrespectful,' he says. 'Thinking with the foolishness of youth that the world is his for the taking.'

'Disrespectful? To such a father?'

The old man suddenly frowns and stops talking. The matter is, she hears, that he has been warned. She is a temptress, Monsieur Boscamp has said, and a consummate actress who can wring a man's heart any way she pleases.

'Look at me,' she says. 'Does it surprise you that an arrogant youth who has always had everything he wanted in his life cannot take my rejection? That he wants my ruin?'

He shakes his head.

'Does it surprise you that he wants my master to turn me away from him?'

She sits down and clasps her hands close to her chest.

'Oh, if I could only stand in front of him and tell him what really happened. All I ask for is a chance to tell him the truth. Then, once he hears it, he can send me away. If this is his true wish, I shall not object.'

'Do what you need to do, child,' he says, giving her the money Monsieur Boscamp entrusted him with. The money meant to pay for her journey back to Istanbul.

'May God be with you,' he says and gives her a father's blessing, a sign of the cross on her forehead.

She kisses his hand as a daughter would. She has had enough of Fokshany and Moldavia to last her a lifetime. Tomorrow she will set off for Kamieniec Podolski. For Poland.

Every morning she makes herself get out of bed and dance across the room, swaying to the rhythm of her clapping hands. She forces herself to imagine the way her body gathers strength, her blood flows faster in her veins. When she catches herself repeating Lysander's name, or recalling the touch of his hand, her heart clenches, but then she wipes the thought out, makes it vanish.

The light of my eyes, he had called her. Are lies that hard to spot?

Kamieniec Podolski is a small border town. By now she has been everywhere. To the parish church, to the fortifications. She has even touched the white rock on which the fortress is built. Touched it and then smelled her own finger as if the rock were a flower that would shed its scent.

This is Poland, she tells herself.

A garrison town, the outpost of the Polish Commonwealth, a fortress erected to tower over the wild lands to the east, the realm of the Tartar hordes and Ukrainian *haidamaky*. A rabble, she hears when she asks about the latter, armed with pitchforks and cudgels. Riff raff who slash the throats of their betters, just as they did in Uman, a Potocki town three days' journey to the east. The orphans of the Uman slaughter are still waking at night screaming in fear, remembering the bodies ripped apart and the screams of the women. In his Krystynopol palace, not far from where she stands now, Old Count Potocki housed at least forty of these orphans, before families were found who would take them.

The Potockis, she hears, are Polish magnates, owners of many palaces, of vast Ukrainian estates that reach to the end of the Polish Commonwealth. Richer than the King, more powerful.

Kamieniec Podolski. She learns to pronounce the name without hesitation. *Urbs antemurale christianitatis.* The outpost of Christianity, the gate into Europe.

Beggars are called *dziady*. So many of them hobbling on one leg, waving stumps. Some singing long, melancholy songs, some pointing at their empty eyes or at the skin eaten with gangrene. Their hair is long and matted, their feet wrapped in bloodied rags. The Uman murderers, people whisper, bearing their punishment, their bodies branded with the signs of revenge until the day they die.

Perhaps, she thinks, she should return to Istanbul after all. Why fight what is coming at her with such force? So what if all the Istanbul Greeks must already have heard of her humiliation? Istanbul is not Bursa. Soon another scandal will come and people will have other things to talk about. But she doesn't want to go back. Journeys are like that. They make you unfit for return. Make you long for more.

Madame Czerkies, her landlady in Kamieniec, is delighted to have someone to talk to. Her days are long and empty ever since her husband departed from this world. From this vale of tears, she has said, from this domain of pain and sorrow.

General de Witt is the commander of Kamieniec. 'A noble, but a bit of a recluse. A miser too,' Madame Czerkies tells her. 'At the fortress,' she whispers with a smile, 'there are no servants. Prisoners serve the meals, chains rattling as they walk.' She bangs a fork on the pewter pot as she says it. They both laugh. Laugh so hard that it hurts.

'It feels so good,' Madame Czerkies says, 'to laugh like that. A blessing. They say that if God closes a door, He opens a window somewhere. Isn't it so very true?'

'How old is His Grace, the General,' Sophie asks.

'An old man with a sick, sick wife.'

'Lonely?'

'Yes, but not alone. There is a son. A major in the army, still not married.'

Joseph de Witt. Forty years old, with a mistress he keeps in an apartment in town. A married woman, the wife of one of his own officers. Not too pretty either, but cheerful and fond of singing.

'People say many things.'

'What things?'

'There was a baby, stillborn. His, people say, though the mistress swears it is not true. A duel that ended in a night of drinking and shooting at pigeons in the market square. Men amusing themselves. The usual.'

'Why is it that only men are entitled to their pleasures?'

'This,' Madame Czerkies sighs, 'is how the world was created. This is a woman's fate, a woman's destiny. It is on our shoulders that the burden of life has been placed.'

'A party, a soirée,' Sophie pleads. 'What is life without good company that would push away such gloomy thoughts?'

'Monsieur Boscamp,' Madame Czerkies says, pursing her lips, 'has been most insistent in his instructions. There should be no visitors. No officers, especially.' She shakes her head as she says it. 'I'm a respectable widow. I have a reputation to keep.'

'What harm would that do to have a few officers drink coffee in this beautiful front parlour?' Sophie pleads.

Monsieur Boscamp has written letters. Specified what Lady Sophie is entitled to, should she arrive in Kamieniec against his express wishes. Six *złotys* per day in expenses, including food. Not enough to replace the shawl torn in Moldavia. Not enough to buy a much needed new pair of shoes.

'I'm afraid, my dear,' Madame Czerkies says, 'that Monsieur Boscamp too is a miser.'

Madame Czerkies announces that Major de Witt has asked to come and pay his respects to Lady Sophie from Istanbul. Monsieur Boscamp will be very angry, but how can a poor widow say no to a commander's son, to a noble.

There is a chuckle in her voice as she says that. A note of defiance. They are two women after all. If they don't help each other, who will.

Sophie jumps up and throws her arms around Madame Czerkies's neck. The joy in her eyes spills and melts all uneasiness.

'Blessed is the man who will call you his wife. Whatever you touch, my dear,' Madame Czerkies whispers, 'turns to joy.'

Joseph de Witt, son of the fortress commander is a short, balding man. His face is pleasant enough though, and his eyes are dark and can be soft.

Lady Sophie casts her eyes down when she speaks. She smiles and blushes easily.

'My fiancé,' she says. 'The man chosen for me by my dear Maman. The man I hardly know but whose intentions are honourable, and I cannot afford to listen to my own heart.

'A pauper like me, brought up by a strict mother whose own life is a sad story of decline. How quickly an illustrious family can find itself in the street! How the wheel of fortune turns!'

She tells him a story:

'It all began with a beautiful woman.'

'As beautiful as you are, Mademoiselle Sophie?'

'More beautiful,' she whispers. 'I am but a shadow of her. Her name was Loxandra. She was my grand-grandmother and her father ordered her to marry a rich *Bey*.'

'So it is a sad story after all, Mademoiselle,' Joseph de Witt sighs. 'Love denied, exchanged for mere gold.'

'But this is not the end,' she says gently, touching his hand and then withdrawing her own swiftly as if catching herself at a transgression. 'It is merely a beginning. A proof that true love is worth waiting for.'

Just before the wedding Loxandra fell ill with smallpox and her beautiful face was disfigured. Her father, knowing that her fiancé could not lift her veil before the ceremony was over, forbade anyone to mention the misfortune. When the rich Bey saw the face of his bride, he recoiled. Nothing was left but for him to send her back to her father with enough gold to pay for his betrayal. These sacks of gold, this ransom, allowed Loxandra to marry a man who learned to love her for the beauty of her soul.

'Prince Lysander Maurocordato,' she says in a soft, lingering voice. 'But the story of happiness cannot last forever. There were too many children.'

She gives a stifled sigh at the memory of the family grandeur lost. Lady Maria, her own mother, suffered greatly from her family's impoverishment, wanting her only daughter to learn the manners that befitted her provenance. Find her a husband who would love and cherish her the way she deserved.

Monsieur Boscamp's visit was a gift from fate. A man of the world, in need of connections, he called upon Lady Maria asking for her help in meeting some of her illustrious cousins, the Maurocordatos. 'Alas, my dear Sir,' Lady Maria was obliged to say. 'My own family has closed its heart to me and my only child.' It was a tribute to Monsieur Boscamp's character that he had not turned his back on them, but, moved by the family's reduced circumstances he remained a frequent visitor at her mother's house.

'This is how I got to know *him*,' she says, flashing Major de Witt the most beautiful of her smiles. A shy girl, brought up by a strict mother, unable to know her own heart.

'Monsieur Boscamp was married then, so there was never a question of our future together. Only when he returned to Warsaw and when his own wife succumbed to her illness and left him a widower, the true nature of his interest revealed itself. He sent for me, to join him in Warsaw as his wife and to be mother to his orphaned sons.'

Major de Witt listens. He holds his breath and listens to her every word. The story is not long, but she makes it meander, slowly, dazzle him with its possibilities. An impoverished aristocrat, a shy virgin. Tempted on her way to Warsaw, tempted by pure love and the solemn sounds of the marriage vows. A chance he should not be prepared to pass by.

'And so,' Sophie says, blushing deep crimson, 'I'm on my way to become the wife of a man with whom I have never exchanged a word in private. A man who could be my father, whose children are as old as I am. But Holy Mary, Mother of God will not forsake me. She will give me strength to be a good wife to this kind and honourable gentleman whose name shall be mine in just a few weeks. Holy Mother shall give me strength to bear the burden my earthly mother wishes me to bear.'

There are tears in Joseph de Witt's eyes. Tears of compassion. Monsieur Boscamp, he tells her, alas, is not the man she takes him for. Many a door in Warsaw has closed in his face. It often happens that, once abroad, a man passes himself off for someone far grander than he really is. She wouldn't know that, of course, but . .

'I cannot listen to this,' she says. 'Please don't hurt me any more. Don't make it more difficult than it already is.'

'Is there anything that can stop you?'

'Nothing,' she says. 'All my life I've been taught obedience and respect. How could I let my own feelings interfere with my mother's wishes?'

'But surely your mother would not object to another proposal of marriage? From a man closer to your age and unburdened with children? A man whose heart is filled with love for you?'

'Love? Already?'

She laughs and withdraws from him before he can touch her hand. 'Can love be that swift?'

'Love is swift,' he says. He is not a poet but a soldier. His manners are simple and straightforward. He speaks what he thinks and what's in his heart.

'I love you. I want to marry you.'

'Monsieur Boscamp will not stand for such an affront,' she gasps. 'Won't he do everything to stop us? Your own father, who is his friend, will not allow this, either.'

'We won't tell my father,' he says. 'We won't let Monsieur Boscamp know of our plans. We'll get married in secret. No one will stop us.'

He describes to her the arrangements: a small wooden church in Zienkowice, a village near Kamieniec; an open carriage with six white horses; two of his own officers will act as witnesses.

On June 14, 1779, she is sitting in an open carriage lined with white velvet, drawn by six horses. But they're grey, not white. Sophie de Witt. Madame Sophie de Witt. Lady Sophie de Witt. The wife of a Polish noble.

The power of wishes, she thinks. The force of desire. The force of life.

Rosalia

The countess was awake, watching her. Looking at her blue cotton dress, her hair pulled tight. Too tight perhaps, not the way her mistress liked it, with a few ringlets let loose. You look like a wet bird huddling under a raft, the countess said on that first day in St Petersburg.

How lost she felt then, unsure. As the ship entered the

Neva she perceived a slight thickening of the horizon. Soon, it took on irregularities that seemed to her like a drawing made by a child's shaky hand. A drawing of onion domes, golden cupolas, of cloisters, whitened columns of schools and public buildings. This city, she heard a man say in Polish, right behind her, had emerged from wilderness at the command of one man, but she was not sure if the tone of his voice was one of contempt, respect, or fear.

'Your mother's dying wish,' the countess said that very first day, 'was to see you here with me.' A smile warmed her beautiful, oval face and large black eyes. The room was filled with flowers: yellow and scarlet roses, blown open, exposing their golden centres; lilies with creamy funnels crammed into crystal vases.

'Come closer, child,' the countess said. 'Closer.' Rosalia took a few more steps and felt a hand, warm and light as a feather, run over her face as if the countess were learning to recognize her in the dark. The hand travelled from her forehead, along her cheek, smoothing it as it moved toward her lips.

'A wet bird waiting for the sun to warm it up.'

'Blue does nothing for your skin, Rosalia. You should get rid of that dress.'

Doctor Lafleur, Rosalia informed the countess, would be paid 25 louis d'or per day. This, Doctor Bolecki suggested, would be only fair. There had been inquiries from Berlin patients. It was important to ensure that Doctor Lafleur would decline other offers.

Doctor Thomas Lafleur. It pleased her to say his name.

When she showed him to his new room, Rosalia noticed that the skin on his hands was red and chapped. The room would be very satisfactory he assured her, far more comfortable than his previous quarters. He thanked her for the trouble she had taken to make sure all was in order. And especially for keys to the drawers where he would lock the laudanum, the writing paper, the sander, the quills. For he always took notes of his patients' treatment: the dozes, their duration, and immediate reactions.

'In such matters, I trust your judgment,' the countess said.

Rosalia ran her finger over the wooden mantelpiece to check if it had been dusted. She lifted the eiderdown to see if the soiled sheets had been changed. Properly changed, for the maids were instructed that the fresh linen should always be old, softened by frequent washing. Unlike death, Rosalia had told Marusya, bedsores were avoidable.

'I want to be of use,' Rosalia said, noting that the night table should be cleaned again. There was a yellow stain on the doily and crumbs on the floor beside the ottoman.

The laudanum, she would tell Doctor Lafleur as soon as she saw him again, was working as well as could be hoped for. This morning the countess slept until eight thirty, and when she woke managed to swallow a few mouthfuls of strong consommé. Sacks with heated oats, another of Dr Lafleur's recommendations, were also far superior to the hot-water bottle.

Sometimes it seemed to her that the French doctor followed her with his eyes when she wasn't looking. 'Memory is so fickle, isn't it?' he asked when telling her he always took notes on his patients. 'It likes to play its tricks.'

'Doctor Lafleur says you need to drink more.'

'I'm not thirsty.'

The countess flinched. Bunched up only an hour before, the pillows had already begun to slip. One was lopsided, hanging over the bed side, threatening to fall to the floor. Far too big and too soft, pillows were quite useless as support. Perhaps, Rosalia thought as she rose to adjust them, if she rolled one up and then wrapped it in a sheet, it might stay in shape longer.

'Don't fuss, Rosalia. Please.'

'Is the pain gone?'

'If I don't think about it.'

'Would you like me to open the curtains? It is a beautiful day.'

'No.'

'Shall I read to you some more?'

'No. Tell me something instead.'

'What about?'

'Anything. Anything you want.'

In the morning, Rosalia saw a pair of crows sitting on the bare branches of the oak tree. Her father always said that crows had long memories. His own father used to poison them, putting arsenic in carcasses he left as bait, but one day the crows stopped eating the poisoned meat. For years afterwards they would never touch carrion until some other bird tried it first. Generation after generation of birds remembered.

'My father gave me a kite once,' she said. 'It was red and yellow and blue. Like a big parrot. I loved to make it fly, but someone broke it.'

'A boy?'

'Yes.'

'Did you like that boy?'

'No. He stuck his tongue out and said I didn't know anything about kites. But I did.'

The countess smiled and closed her eyes. There was a new hue to her skin, another shade of whiteness. Her voice came blurred, unsteady.

'I think I may be dead already. Sometimes time stops and it feels that I'll be here forever. Lying in bed, waiting for something that has already passed.'

'It's the laudanum. Doctor Lafleur says it is to be expected.'

'Doctor Lafleur doesn't know everything.'

There came another long moment of silence. In the distance Rosalia could hear Doctor Lafleur's voice, asking if the sacks of oats had been placed by the kitchen fire the way he had ordered. 'They have to be ready whenever I send for them,' he said. 'Ready at any time, day or night.'

The strange contraption that looked like a wringer made of brass, she had explained to Doctor Lafleur only the other day, was the machine from Tula she had the presence of mind to bring from St Petersburg. She showed him where the charcoal was placed and how perfume was poured so that fumes scented the rooms the machine was whisked through. Attar of roses was the countess's favourite.

Doctor Lafleur said the machine was most ingenious. His cheeks were flushed, for he had just taken a turn in the garden, as fast as he could. His gait had the awkwardness of a growing boy, the eagerness of hope tampered by restraint. Only in his case experience not innocence had caused it. 'But the air is quite warm outside,' he said. 'The bedroom could be aired. Fresh air will clear the blood.'

'You do agree with me, Mademoiselle,' he added. 'Doctor Bolecki tells me you are very fond of walking.'

He wasn't looking at her when he said that, and she noted this with disappointment that made her ashamed of herself.

It must have been the rustle of her petticoats that woke the countess this time.

'You are trying so hard to take care of me, Rosalia,' she said. 'What will you do when I am gone? What will you do when you have to look after yourself?'

Outside the closed door Rosalia could hear Frau Kohl scolding someone. A maid, for soon she heard a second voice, high-pitched, on the verge of tears. Something had not been done to her specification. A duty was neglected, a task was shoddily done. The maid hurried upstairs sobbing, and Frau Kohl gave a long sigh of exasperation.

Sophie

Her new father-in-law calls Joseph a fool. General de Witt, the commander of Kamieniec, has been bled three times, to relieve his heart from too much pressure. For two days he has refused to leave his room, screaming at anyone who approaches him. He doesn't eat, and drinks nothing but water.

On the third day she opens the door to his room. He is sitting with his back to the door, his eyes fixed on the fields, refusing to move.

'Is there anything I can do?' she asks quietly.

His eyes are a watery blue. They follow her as she comes closer and falls to her knees. 'Joseph should have asked for his father's consent,' she says. 'It's all my fault. I shouldn't have allowed him to take me to the altar without his father's blessing. I'm so sorry, Sir, to have caused you so much pain.'

'Dou-Dou. A daughter of a cattle trader and a whore.'

He points to the letter lying on his desk. A letter from Charles Boscamp warning him that a former *Greek paramour* of his might, against his express wishes, his attempts to send her back to Istanbul, appear in Kamieniec and make outlandish claims. *A harlot, a strumpet, and a liar*, he reads. *She tells her stories with such conviction that the wisest of men do not know where she has bypassed the truth*. This letter warns not to be taken in by her sweet words and the sighs of innocence.

'My daughter-in-law,' the General says, spitting on the ground. The blob of saliva is yellow and thick. Boscamp must be laughing now, telling the story to anyone in Warsaw who would listen. Anyone with half a brain. The swift ascent of his Greek whore. The story of these aristocratic connections Joseph repeats to anyone who would listen without laughing in his face.

She gasps and is just about to speak, but he stops her.

'Save your breath, you wretched thing. I'm too old to be fooled.'

She stands up and looks at him. General de Witt bears little resemblance to her husband. The husband who insisted on hanging out the bloodied sheets after their wedding night, who boasts to his officers about the size of her breasts and the smoothness of her buttocks.

Her father-in-law's eyes are piercing her skin as if he wants to penetrate the mystery of her body. The flow of her blood. Eyes of an eagle, she thinks. She lifts her head and looks right into them, without turning away. She has a business proposition, a fair deal that he, a man of the world, should appreciate.

What's done cannot be undone. What good would it do to reveal Monsieur Boscamp's warnings? Madame de Witt can be made the talk of the town, but will that really be what General de Witt desires? Wouldn't it be better if she, given the position she now has, made sure that de Witts rose in the world? Made sure that the son would succeed the father, or even rise higher than that?

General Joseph de Witt.

Alone, her husband cannot do it. With her beside him, all is possible.

She will leave her father-in-law with this thought. Let him think and make his decision. She will retire to her room and await her fate.

Her silk dress rustles as she walks away; the heels of

her new shoes click on the marble floors. Behind her she leaves a trail of attar of roses.

In the afternoon, Joseph rushes upstairs to her boudoir. He places a kiss on her lips and laughs. A horsy laughter at the triumph he attributes entirely to himself. His blindness will never cease to amaze her. There is the smell of vodka on his breath, and she rolls her eyes.

His father has summoned them both. To his official study. They are forgiven.

They walk in hand in hand. They fall to their knees. Two children asking for a father's blessing.

'I don't have any choice,' the General says. 'My son will have to drink the beer he has brewed for himself. Fools are not sown, they sprout by themselves. What has been broken cannot be made whole again.'

His daughter-in-law is now a Polish noblewoman.

'Don't bring shame to the de Witt name,' he says.

She bows in front of him, making sure he gets a good glimpse of her bosom.

'Your son's future is my future,' she says. 'His prospects are my prospects.'

For a while she believes it too.

Rosalia

Doctor Ignacy Bolecki appeared just as she began her walk in the palace garden. The air was cold but clear. She had thrown a dark blue overcoat over her pale yellow dress and put on her walking shoes.

'I was hoping you would take a morning walk. It's what I would have prescribed,' he said. 'Do you mind if I join you? There is a delicate matter I wish to talk to you about.'

There was an air of suave ease about him, she thought,

the self-assurance of a man well-liked, and the smell of tobacco, slight but persistent. His clothes were impeccably ironed, his cheeks clean shaven. A shadow of sadness was hidden deep in the very shape of his wrinkles. Aunt Antonia would have liked both his promise of solidity and the sadness. A widower, she would have stressed, a widower with a grown-up child, but not too old to have children of his own. What better could she hope for?

She extended her hand to him and he kissed it, a fraction longer than it could have been. A sign that there might be something more to this walk, in the expressions of concern over her health. The thought made her hurry her steps in the direction of the twin oaks. She slid her hands inside her fur muff. 'How it becomes you,' the countess said when she gave it to her for the St Petersburg winter.

'Madame la Comtesse,' Dr Bolecki said, lifting his top hat, 'thinks very highly of you.'

'The countess is very kind,' she said.

It pleased her to notice Dr Bolecki had to strain to follow her.

Dr Bolecki apologised for the French doctor's abruptness, for what amounted to the sentence of death. His friend was an excellent surgeon and a remarkable man, but he shouldn't have left the countess without hope.

'Sometimes he is so hard to fathom, Mademoiselle Rosalia. Maybe because he is French.'

'Madame la Comtesse wanted to know the truth.'

Doctor Bolecki hesitated, as if reflecting on her words. His steel-grey eyes kept grazing her as they walked. She tried to keep her own trained on the gravel path.

'Perhaps. Perhaps this is why Doctor Lafleur is going to America, and I'm staying. I'm not modern enough. However, my illustrious friend must be given some credit. He says you are the best nurse he has ever observed.'

'Doctor Lafleur is very kind, too,' she said, 'but I'm hardly a proper nurse. He must have noticed that too.'

'He is a kind man, I agree, but what he says about you has nothing to do with kindness. He merely observes facts. He is a man of reason. He says you are endowed with a natural ability to heal. A rare talent but easy to spot when one sees it.'

'I'm much obliged,' she said. A thought began flickering in her mind, wild, improbable, but strangely satisfying. A silly thought she should have dismissed right away but could not. What if Doctor Bolecki were sounding out her feelings on his friend's behalf?

'Your cheeks are gaining colour, Mademoiselle. A brisk walk I always say, is the best prevention against disease.'

He now walked in step with her, talking incessantly. The countess had called her 'the blooming flower of her sickroom,' but flowers needed sun and fresh air. Mlle Rosalia shouldn't forget to take care of her own health, to nourish her spirit so that she, in turn, could nourish the sick.

'I find it hard to leave her.'

'Such a sense of duty is your dear father's legacy, Mademoiselle. Obvious to see for anyone who has ever met him.'

She watched his teeth flash as he spoke, front teeth overlapping slightly. He was glad, he said, that he could offer her the gift of this memory, however short.

In Paris, his step-father had many illustrious visitors, and Captain Romanowicz had been one of them. He remembered him very well, for Captain Romanowicz had been particularly kind to his daughter, Konstancja. One incident he remembered well. Captain Romanowicz told his daughter that if she took a big metal sphere and removed the air from it, not even sixteen pairs of horses tied to both ends would be able to break it apart. Such was the power of vacuum, he said. He even brought her a sketch that showed the horses and the sphere. His own daughter, Rosalia, he said, was also fond of experiments.

'So you see, I've even heard of you before,' he said.

'My father died in Santo Domingo.'

Rosalia did not mention that her mother never forgave Napoleon for sending the Polish Legion, so eager to fight the enemies of Poland, to Santo Domingo to suppress the slave uprising. To kill the very freedom, she said, they wanted so much for themselves. She never forgave the secrecy of these orders, the fact that, until they reached the Manzilla Bay, they did not know what their God of War had in store for them. Her bitterness had never diminished. 'If your father knew where they were going,' she kept saying, 'he would have resigned. He would've stayed with us. He would still be alive.'

She never mentioned how close she felt to her mother in moments like that: joined by their loss no one else in the world could share in the same way, fused with pain.

'Your father,' Doctor Bolecki said, 'sacrificed himself for the following generations. Paid the highest price for the common good. Mademoiselle, dear Mademoiselle Rosalia. Such is our Polish fate.'

She listened.

That they have found themselves together in Berlin, he continued, was not perhaps a mere coincidence. Everything in this world happened for a reason. All lives were interconnected, linked to one another in most mysterious ways. Yes, life was a chain of events echoing one off another, their significance hidden until something innocuous, a chance encounter perhaps, a flash of realisation, revealed it.

She listened.

It would be his greatest pleasure if he were allowed to call upon her more often. There was so much they had in common. Didn't she agree?

'Yes, of course,' she said, blushing. 'Only I find it hard to leave the countess.'

'As I have said before, such a sense of duty is your dear father's legacy, Mademoiselle.'

'It is hard to compare his duties to mine,' she said.

One more turn and they would be heading back toward the palace.

'How do you like living in Berlin?' she asked, quickly.

He liked it well enough. Not as much as living in Paris, but well enough. He was closer to Poland and he had an opportunity to watch, firsthand, how Prussia governed itself. Such knowledge would one day be invaluable if Poland were to throw off the yoke of slavery. To know your enemy was half of victory he believed. He also believed that one should take one's lessons wherever one could. There were many others of the same mind, far less fortunate than he. She must have heard already of the recent reprisals that befell the Polish students in Berlin: the black list, the arrests, the expulsions from university. This poor fellow, Köhler, whose ill-fated notes from a clandestine meeting started the whole affair. Wasn't that the most frightening example of Prussian nationalism?

'I don't know enough, I'm afraid, to judge for myself.'

'Quite right. Quite right.'

Such a statement, he added, was one more sign of the superiority of her character. Remarkable and worthy of admiration, like everything else about her. There was a pleasant note of embarrassment in his voice, and she savoured it for a while. They were now approaching the palace gate.

'Is that the delicate matter you wished to speak to me about, Doctor,' she asked, aware of the playful note in her voice.

'No,' he stammered. 'No . . . Not at all.' What he wanted to tell her was far more mundane. Frau Kohl and

Graf von Haefen's butler noticed strange goings on in the kitchen. A very delicate situation. The Russian servants were taking liberties. The pantry was being raided, as if a troop of Cossacks went through it each night. Seven pots of jam disappeared two days ago, yesterday a whole quail pie vanished without a trace.

'And the cellar,' he added. 'The whisky is missing, too. At least three bottles.'

She wondered why Frau Kohl did not speak to her directly.

'Perhaps, Mademoiselle Rosalia, all you have to do is to make inquiries. Let the Russian cook know that nothing is overlooked. Frau Kohl said that Countess Olga was still too young and too inexperienced to manage the servants.'

He opened the palace door for her. A smell of chicken broth reached her from the kitchen. Then the servants' laughter. Marusya's was the loudest, straight from her belly.

'Yes,' Rosalia said. 'I'll see to it, of course.'

Later that evening, in her room, in her nightdress, she tried to see herself as she might seem to someone else.

The light caught in her auburn hair, highlighted the paleness of her tired skin, her hands chapped from washing. (Why don't you wear your gloves at night, Rosalia? Goose fat won't work unless you wear gloves.) The gauntness of her cheeks, the eyes tired from lack of sleep.

Admit it, she challenged her own reflection. You can never manage the lightness, the bewilderment of charm. The lightness that comes from thinking yourself invincible.

Never.

The cold of the room climbed into her, rising from the floor through her bare feet. She kept looking at her own reflection, the gentle slope of her shoulders, the disappointing flatness of her chest. Her skin was white and smooth, but that realisation failed to console her. And then her feet got too cold and she climbed back into bed, to warm herself up.

Sophie

'This is Warsaw,' Joseph says with an indulgent smile.

Two miles before Warsaw, there is the hill from which they can get their first good glimpse of the city. He points out the town walls, the Saint-Cross Towers and the Royal Castle. He points out Praga, the busy district on the right bank of the Vistula River, where they would be obliged to stay that night, waiting for the boat to take them across to Warsaw, the following morning.

She has waited for this moment for fifteen months. Fifteen months in a fortress where prisoners in chains did serve at the table, where her bones chilled to the marrow in winter, where she tried to keep boredom at bay with the help of dancing instructors, French tutors and riding masters. Fifteen months of pleading with Joseph, of pointing out to him the wisdom of being known at court, of securing the good graces of the right people. It is not that he has been reluctant to show her off. She could tell how pleased he had been when Prince Czartoryski, after his official visit to Kamieniec, made it known that the delightful and charming Madame de Witt is the only attraction worth seeing for miles around. But still he kept putting off the date of their departure. The time was not good, the roads too muddy, his own father too overwhelmed with duties to be left alone. 'Aren't you happy with me here?' he kept asking.

Happiness, she tried to make him see, was a tender plant. It needed room to grow, or it would wilt and wither. 'You do not wish to remain Major de Witt all your life?'

From his uneasy smile she knew this was the right path to take. Who, she asked him, would get the command of Kamieniec once his father dies? How could the King be sure that the son was worthy to step into his father's shoes? How could anyone advance in this world without powerful friends?

'You are not that jealous, are you?'

In the end, what made Joseph agree was a note from the King included in a letter to his father:

> Major de Witt, as your Sovereign I forbid you to keep your beautiful wife away from Warsaw any longer. The rumours of her charm and beauty have reached me from many most reliable sources, and I am eager to compare them with the original.

With the note came an offer. One of the King's apartments is waiting for the young couple who, both General de Witt and his son would have to agree, should take *their long overdue honeymoon journey.*

The King of Poland has invited her to Warsaw. This is happiness, she wants to tell Joseph, but stops herself. Joseph likes to tell her that the King is desperate for allies. The seventeen years of his reign, he reminds her, have been one disaster after another. One by one, the Polish provinces have rebelled, calling him a Russian puppet unable to steer his country in any direction. The friends he still has hear nothing but his long lists of warnings. The Russians are too strong to oppose directly, diplomacy has to be used, allies sought at all cost. All talk, no action. And where has it led us, he likes to ask. What other country in Europe has allowed itself to be cut up and devoured by its neighbours. He once showed her the map of Poland where, with red ink, his father had marked the territories lost in 1772, three slivers of land, one in the west, a bigger one in the east, and one in the south. 'Stolen by Russia. Stolen by Prussia. Stolen by Austria,' General de Witt wrote in thick, even letters. And isn't it true, Joseph likes to continue in his mark-my-words tone, that appetite, once aroused, grows.

She keeps it to herself, but she thinks the King may not be as wrong as Joseph thinks. What else is there to be done, if one is weak? What's the use of grand gestures and heroic deaths? She can see good reasons for powerful friends, for patient pressure, for quiet strengthening of the country. But such means have little respect among the men she talks to. Action, Joseph says. Any action is better than humiliation. Not that he himself is that eager to fight. Ordering his soldiers around, yes, she can see that. In a fury over some transgressions, yes. But smelling gunpowder, sleeping on the ground?

February is not the best month for travelling, Joseph grumbles. They are bitterly cold in spite of the pile of furs and a foot-warmer filled with hot coals. But travelling in winter has its advantages. The roads, frozen, are free from the sticky mud, and a sleigh offers a much smoother ride.

Stories proceed her. Whispers of delighted amusement at her exotic beauty, her mysterious past. Some swear she has been a Sultan's odalisque. Others that she is a Greek princess, impoverished by family misfortune. Prince Adam has praised her exquisite manners and her pleasing ways. She makes time pass like a dream, he has said. Boscamp's name is mentioned too. An elderly suitor tricked out of his prize by Major de Witt, left seething with powerless rage.

Good stories, she thinks.

She misses Mana and Aunt Helena. She wishes they could see her now. See how Joseph dotes on her, how unsure he is of himself. Of Lysander she also thinks, when such thoughts cannot be helped. Sometimes she sees a shadow of his smile on a stranger's lips, the sheen of his hair in another's. I don't hate him, she says to herself. He doesn't matter. In a way, she is right. He does not matter any more. But there are thoughts she cannot stop. Thoughts of betrayal, of ridicule, of rejection. Thoughts that make her look beyond words and smiles, turn them around, search underneath, sniff them to catch the slightest whiff of wavering. Of danger. Of weakening. She has always been a quick pupil. Twice in her life men have betrayed her, and there will be no third time. This is what she swears now.

'You will be so proud of me,' she whispers to Joseph a day later, after they are settled in their Warsaw apartment, still cold in spite of the bearskin thrown over the floor, in spite of the fact that the servants assure them that they had kept the fire going all last week in anticipation of their arrival. Still cold even after the shot of vodka Joseph insists on, vodka that brings colour to her cheeks.

'I promise,' she whispers and watches how he stretches his neck with pleasure.

He is proud. Proud of her dresses, of emerald silk and rose chiffon. Of the flowers that arrive in baskets every day to the delight of the servants who scurry to tell Madame the good news. Of the frenzied anticipation with which their appearance is awaited at parties and soirées, of long lost acquaintances who find him out and remind him of their connections and insist on inviting the lovely couple to yet another salon. Of the calling cards that arrive daily, carriages that stop to let out another guest.

Of invitations from all quarters, with the most important one, from the King, displayed on the mantle.

He is proud when Stanisław August, the King of Poland, receives them a mere week after their arrival in the capital, on 3rd March, Anno Domini 1781, while many others are kept waiting four times as long. When the King nods his head in appreciation of Sophie's beauty, when he leads her in the *polonaise*, holding her perfumed hand in his as if it were made of bone china.

And is she proud too?

She turns this question over in her head. And hesitates. Please him, Mana's voice says. It's so easy. Make your husband believe he too is responsible for all this triumph. Is this what her new friends refer to when they mention words like *savoir vivre* and gentle manners?

Pride, she says brushing his cheek with her lips, does not satisfy Madame Major de Witt that easily. Have you noticed, she asks, that in the invitations they have received so far, among all the calling cards she keeps in a carved box in her boudoir, one name is always missing?

He has not noticed. What name?

'The Potockis,' she says, her lips twisting in a nonchalant half-smile. 'Aren't they the most powerful of the Polish magnates?'

Count Felix and Countess Josephine, of the Pilawa crest.

'Most powerful?' Joseph is ready to question the reason for the hurt in her voice. The Czartoryskis, he points out, are as powerful as the Potockis, and there have already been two invitations from their Blue Palace.

But Sophie will not accept such consolations. The Potockis are the true kings of eastern Poland, the owners of palaces far grander than the Royal Castle. 'Too high a threshold for de Witt's feet.'

'Did they say it?'

'No,' she snaps with impatience. She does not know

what they have said or not. She is not interested in the Potockis or their bug-eyed children or their pride. She has other things to do. Other matters to attend to. Of more importance.

'This is what I said in the first place,' Joseph says with triumph. He has just caught her, he seems to be saying, in another display of her feminine inconsistency. Her lack of logic, so charming really. 'Just listen to your husband,' he says and pats her on her behind, now separated from his touch with layers of fabric and a cushioned bustle.

In March 1781, the Polish King, Stanisław August Poniatowski, does not look like the portrait of him she remembers from the internuncio's study. He is older, now, nearing fifty, his forehead more wrinkled, his robes less grand. But his large black eyes are warmer, softer and two dimples still form in the corners of his lips.

Besides, now she knows that it was only a copy. The real one is here, in Warsaw.

The three grand chambers on the ground floor of the Royal Castle have been turned into a studio. Painters, sculptors and furniture-makers work there together. Apprentices and students who come there, are allowed to copy the paintings by Lampi, Baciarelli, Grassi, Norblin, from the King's personal collection.

'Sometimes I feel as if the paths of our lives have crossed many a time,' His Royal Highness tells Madame Sophie de Witt. 'Perhaps we have lived before?'

The notion that souls may come back to earth for another life intrigues him. In the Hebrew Cabbala he has studied for some time now souls come back to atone for their sins, or to assist other souls in their journeys. *Gilgul,* he says, the rolling of souls from one body to another. The Hassidim believe in it too, although the

Talmud scholars assure him that there is no basis for these beliefs.

'If our lives crossed before, I could've been your slave.'

'Or I yours,' the King says.

She laughs and spreads her fan. There are real flakes of gold on her new gown. After the bored calm of Kamieniec, Warsaw delights her. The crowded streets, carriages, horses. Her apartment on Krakowskie Przedmieście, for which the King pays twelve talars each month. Joseph does not like Warsaw. 'Look at that whore,' he told her, pointing at a woman, her face obscured by a coarse shawl. She was carrying what looked like a small bundle of rags. Stopping beside the church, she put the bundle inside the trap door of a church, and rang the bell. 'Another bastard,' Joseph said, 'left at the mercy of the Church.' The woman rushed away, without looking back.

Better than leaving them by the Vistula, drowned in the mud. Better than strangling the baby with her own hands, or smothering it with a pillow. Life is always a better choice, even if it is nothing more than a chance at it.

'Ah, the joy on your face,' the King says. 'I could drink it.' He takes her hand in his, peels off her white glove and his warm lips touch her skin. She cannot quite name the pleasure she feels, but she wants to stretch this moment to the utmost. Her skin has preserved the touch of his lips and she can still feel it when he leads her to one of the students copying a landscape. Tubes of paint are piled up in a wooden box, colours bleeding, staining the wood. The painter's hands are speckled with colour, and there are spots of red and yellow smeared on his cheeks.

'This is how I would like a garden to be,' the King says, pointing at the luminous landscape the student is copying. 'The sky, the earth, the sea, the eternal forces of nature. But it is always the fire that dominates it.'

She asks who the painter is.

'Lorraine,' the King says. 'The worshipper of the sun.'

In a beautiful garden the sun should illuminate beauty, lead the visitors to perfection. In such a garden death would not frighten us any more. It would be nothing more than a moment of passage, leading us away from the passing pleasures of the body into the world of Reason.

'What does *he* talk to you about all the time?' Joseph keeps asking.

She is wearing a dress of pale pink muslin. The fullness of the skirt draws the eyes away from her thickening waist. In the morning she vomits. It's a boy, Joseph whispers with pride. You don't get sick like that for a girl. She sends him away to bring her pickled cucumbers and herring in oil. She demands oysters or a pint of beer. When her face gets bloated in the morning, she rubs her skin with a chunk of ice until the bloating goes away and the pink glow returns to her cheeks. She prefers to be seen in the soft light of the candles.

'God,' the King says, 'knows not only the laws of geometry according to which the world is built, but is also an artist creating according the rules of beauty. Beauty, together with Wisdom, and Strength is the basis of all knowledge.'

Yesterday, Joseph brought her a bowl of crayfish. Still warm, for he wrapped it in a blanket. From Jezierski's, he said, the best in Poland. He also brought her a pineapple, as sweet and juicy as she remembered from Istanbul.

The news of your blessed condition has brought tears to my eyes, Mana wrote. *May the Lord and All the Saints have you in their care.*

'God,' the King says, 'is the greatest of gardeners, for He has created the Garden of Eden from which, Adam, in spite of original sin, salvaged the last shards of light coming from the Tree of Knowledge. These shards of divine light, this primal truth, can only be retrieved when man returns to nature and begins to ponder its mysteries. If followed faithfully, Nature defies death with birth, decay with new growth. It makes no allowance for status or class, does not distinguish between kings or paupers. Naked we are all equal. We are all human. We all have the right to happiness.'

He picks up a book and reads to her:

> The Melancholy Garden is to offer a somewhat sombre atmosphere, cause sweet reflection and lead our minds toward the contemplation of the eternal. Thick, shady forests, an abandoned cemetery, ruins overgrown with moss, a chapel-tomb splendid in its isolation, a moonlit path by the lake where shadows bathe in the velvet darkness of the water, all are fitting ornaments there. In such scenery thoughts naturally wander toward death and parting, toward the sweetness of friendship and the pangs of love. The best for such a garden are trees sheathed in dark bark, with gnarled trunks and drooping boughs.

'Such a garden,' the King says, 'is nature cultivated by human toil, tamed by wisdom and tender friendship. Those who love gardens, love humanity itself. But not the formal gardens of the French. A straight line does not make for the shortest path. Human life is fraught with mysteries and secrets. Those who love gardens welcome that melancholy that seizes them in the labyrinth of paths and ruins, for they know that it is through this melancholy that they can free themselves from the shackles of the body.'

How much of the boy is still in him she thinks, in spite of all this talk of melancholy and death: a boy eager for another day, a curious boy whose mind cannot stay still.

His voice is soft and warm. She wonders what his face looks like without the powdered wig. Does he notice how his presence makes the students bend over their paintings, shoot furtive glances at them? She has heard that he likes to lecture them on the finer points of painting. He likes the colouring of Rubens, the contours of Veronese and the costumes of Rembrandt. He likes the blend of monumental and sensual.

'The way to the Truth leads through a labyrinth.'

'The way to Friendship leads through the language of the heart.'

'The way to the depths of one's soul leads through solitude.'

Wasn't it his fault, she has heard, that, in 1772 Russia, Prussia, and Austria helped themselves to slices of Poland? A price for the crown his lover put on his head?

Anything he touches, she has heard, turns to dust.

A builder of ruins.

He takes her arm and leads her out of the studio, to the visible relief of the students whose shoulders slump and whose eyes wander away from the painted canvases. She can smell her own warm body, the wafts of attar of roses she had smeared on her wrists in the morning. In his right hand, spotted with brown patches, a white handkerchief wavers.

'Is this a sign of your capitulation, Sire.'

'Absolute surrender,' he says. 'My life is in your beautiful hands.'

'You are pardoned then.' She touches his arm with her fan. Lightly, like in a game of tag.

Mystery shall not be revealed too eagerly. In the King's bedroom she stands still. The touch of his soft hand makes her tremble.

On the desk in his bedroom she has seen pages of the

digests his librarian prepares every day: digests of discoveries and theories, summaries of long books, files on things like serfdom or constitutional law in which she has little interest. A lightning conductor is another matter, drawing electric sparks from the clouds.

'That I'd like to see,' she murmurs.

'I'll show you one then. In Ujazdów. Tomorrow if you wish.'

The sounds of a harp reach them from the small antechamber beside the King's bedroom. The curtains are drawn. The servants have been told not to disturb them. Sometimes their footsteps can be heard, fading into the distance.

Above the desk a woman's face stares at her from a portrait. *If only a king can ask for your hand, then I will become king*. This is what he wrote to this *mistress of his fate* who gave him the Polish crown. 'Her true name is Sophie too,' he said with a lingering sadness. Empress Catherine, she has heard, has little patience with sentimental lovers.

'It is all forgotten now,' he lies. 'Even the most acute of pains, is dulled with time.'

She closes her eyes and lets his lips caress her neck, slide down her breasts, his fingers are writing something on her belly. 'Nothing,' he says when she asks what it is. He is a gentle lover who waits for her to follow. His kisses are soft and fleeting, like the wings of butterflies, like snowflakes melting on her body.

'Your skin is like fire,' he whispers.

He smells of pomade and good perfume. He doesn't touch wine or spirits. Not even to toast his infatuation, his delight and the moments of sweet oblivion.

How often she has dreamt of him. Once, in Istanbul, she vowed to become his slave. She would have held the towel for him in the Turkish bath, if he let her. Now, she laughs out loud at the thought. He has made love to her, and now puts his head on her breast and talks of his burdens. The kingdom is like a stone around his neck, weighing him down. Poland is a weak country between strong, ruthless neighbours. Should we side with Russia, Prussia or Austria? Play one against the other? Resist their meddling with our affairs? Play for time and strengthen the kingdom with reforms? Play for time and do nothing, not to upset the delicate balance?

She never lets her eyes off him. This is a man, she thinks, who likes women.

'Prince Potemkin,' he says, 'assures me that a strong union with Russia will not affect Polish sovereignty. Sometimes I can believe him. Sometimes I fear that the Russian power is too great to oppose. That it will crush us forever. That whatever we do we don't have a chance.

'Prince Potemkin,' he says, seeing bewilderment in her eyes, 'has been for some time the most-beloved favourite of the Russian Empress. He is a brilliant general. Catherine would like to see him rewarded with a kingdom. If he were elected to the Polish throne, once it becomes vacant, it would be in his interest to strengthen Poland, wouldn't it? And Catherine might listen to him.'

The sigh with which he says it means that the Russian Empress is no longer ready to listen to Stanisław August. It also means that these desperate measures *have* to be considered, if Poland is to survive – no more grand gestures, no more civil wars, no more discord – but how to do it in a country where magnates are richer and more powerful than the King?

In the night, surrounded by candles burning out, the King of Poland is confessing to her.

'Once, everything I was doing seemed almost divine in its purpose. Now I think of nothing but the predictability of human emotions, of greed and intrigue.'

She recalls what he told her of souls rolling from one body to another. She has thought about this for a long time. The world is split into layers, of which we know but an outer one. We are like blind men touching an elephant, asking if it is long and flexible Or stout and solid? It is a world of invisible connections, of lives touching.

'I'm tired of the human nature that always makes the same mistakes,' he says. 'That always moves in the same circles, in the same ruts. That destroys itself in the same way, by dwelling on the very thing that gives it pain. I'm tired of life.'

She touches his hand and says that it is the goodness of his nature, the warmth of his heart that makes him suffer like that, his sacrifices for the nation, for the betterment of his people. This is the fate of kings.

'Istanbul,' she says, 'where I come from, is the city of fires. A fire can start in one wooden house and by the end of the night the whole quarter can be lost. It is the wind that carries these fires from one house to the other, until they stop at the edge of the Bosphorus, or at the top of one of the hills, or if there are no more houses to burn. But then life returns. New houses are always built on the ashes of the old, new gardens bloom.'

He thinks about it for a while. A lesson from a simpler world, he calls it, a world where every moment has to be measured against life or death.

The German musicians

The German musicians gathered in the antechamber as the Graf had ordered. They unpacked their flute, violins and cello. The grand piano was already in the salon where they were to play.

Behind the curtain, a dying Polish countess wished to listen to music. They would hear her sometimes but they were not to pay any attention. Once she wished them to stop, a footman or a maid would come and tell them. If no one came, they were to continue playing. The countess was a grand lady, a great beauty whose name was mentioned alongside those of kings and queens. Their music was taking her mind off pain and death.

'Marais?' the first violinist asked, immediately deciding this would not be suitable.

'Komm maybe,' the second violinist suggested.

'Hoffnung might be better.'

'Beethoven?'

'Mozart,' the pianist said, to everyone's agreement.

The singer would come on certain days, the Graf's footman informed them. His Lordship's own choice, a beautiful soprano. Frau Hellmann. She would like to sing 'Wie Nahte Mir Der Schlummer', from *Der Freischutz*.

'She can sing whatever she wishes,' the pianist said. 'We are professionals.'

The doors to the countess's room opened, and the footman ushered them inside, holding a finger on his lips. They would have to learn to walk like cats, feeling their way around, for a thick, burgundy curtain was drawn across the room, cutting them off from daylight. They took their places, placed sheets of music on their stands. The footman lit thick wax candles that gave them enough light to see the scores. The grand piano was in excellent condition: polished, well-kept, no sluggish hammers. They were now to tune the instruments to it, as quietly as they could. This would be, they were told, a most satisfactory engagement.

They began to play. Mozart was a good choice. Then they would follow with Beethoven – the string quartet in F minor.

During their first intermission, they spoke of Berlin where, since the royal power would not have the people discuss politics or social matters, men fought over music. Now Spontini was pitted against von Weber. Spontini had been called a simplistic fool, and his Kappelmeister's salary of 4000 thalers had been declared excessive.

'The price of royal favour,' the violinist said.

'But the whole of Berlin from the Hallish Gate to the King's Castle sings *Jungfernkranz*,' the flautist said. 'What would you rather have?'

'The money,' the violinist laughed.

When the talk returned to their present engagement, they all came to the same conclusion that the worst part of it would be the uncertainty. There might be days when they would play for merely an hour; there might be days when six hours might pass and there would be no sign of the footman.

'How can we conserve energy,' the violinist asked, 'if we do not know even, in approximation, how long we are to play.'

But he had to confess that he liked the idea of playing to defy death.

Sophie

Warsaw is at her feet. Madame de Witt is the darling of the salons. Madame de Witt, a beautiful Greek, her past shrouded in delightful contradictions. Was she really a Sultan's slave, an odalisque, and did a mysterious European prince really buy her freedom? Is she really related to the Maurocordato princes? Why has she ever married this dreadful de Witt? Is it true that the King himself had to intervene, for the de Witts wanted to keep her immured in Kamieniec?

Monsieur Charles Boscamp requests the honour of seeing Madame de Witt.

He is a pimp, she has heard and a traitor who takes

money from the Russians. A coward who has feigned illness to avoid duels and who would invent any slander that might fetch him a few ducats. Even the King, whose judgement in people has to be doubted, has lost patience and turned away: 'Oh, don't even mention that despicable creature, my dear Sophie,' Princess Lubomirska exclaimed, holding her nose.

She makes him wait in the antechamber and peeks at him through the keyhole before letting him in. He is thinner than she remembers and stooped. Without a wig his head looks smaller. He is a man of earthen complexion pacing the room like a wolf in a cage. No, not a wolf, like an old, mangy dog hoping for a treat. His *Jewel*, his *Precious Stones*. How easy it had been to impress her then!

Don't spit on those below you, Mana would say. Think what they might do when you fall. From a crystal decanter she takes a sip of claret. Right from the bottle, without bothering with a glass. The claret warms her up.

'Monsieur Charles Boscamp,' the footman announces and the internuncio walks in.

She cherishes his uncertainty, the quick look at her dressing table, at the crystal vases of orchids and tulips, the silver brush and mirror, her string of pearls.

Not bad for little Dou-Dou, a daughter of a cattle trader and a whore.

'This,' she announces, 'will be a brief encounter. I don't have much time. Life is curious at times, isn't it?'

'My precious Dou-Dou,' he says, laughing. 'I *know* you.'

Underneath the layer of powder, his face is covered in blotches. Have his teeth been always so stained or is the morning light always harsh, unflattering? She winces at the thought of her old self. She wonders how she could have ever doubted herself, thought him powerful or attractive.

He sits down on a chair, without asking permission,

without waiting for her to sit down first.

'You are not as naïve as you seem to be, are you?' he says. 'You of all people should know that kings and princes care little for those beneath them.'

He spreads his legs. His riding boots are old, she notices. His cuffs frayed.

'*Some* princes,' she says. '*Some* kings.'

He shakes his head just the way she remembers, as if she were a child to be admonished. Outside the door the footman moves. One word, one scream and she can have Monsieur Boscamp thrown out into the street. The thought makes her laugh out loud.

'How little you know,' he sighs, looking up at the ceiling.

Balsam, when added to tar, ceases to be balsam but turns to tar; and tares, though sown in the finest field, will not become wheat. So, if a noblewoman marries a peasant, she will certainly give birth to an ignoble child. For what purity can come from such impurity, what perfume from such a stench? It is a wise proverb that goes: nightingales are not born from owls.

Piekarski from Przeworsk, a peasant's son and a bastard who now passes himself for a noble from Podolia.

Dobrzecki from Kaleniów, a merchant from Toruń who paid the Karwowski family to adopt him.

Nowacki, a Jew. His daughter married into the Wierzycki family.

His memory is as excellent as always, he can go on for

hours if she wants. There is a whole book of such revelations, a book she will find extremely popular among her new friends. No one who has ever sneaked into the Polish gentry has been spared. It's all there, proven beyond doubt. He likes to consult this thick book at his leisure. It offers him new lessons in the deviousness of the human nature. It might one day have a new entry:

> De Witt: His mother, Sophie Glavani, a Greek whore well versed in the knowledge of the school of Cytera and the mysteries of Paphos, has married into the de Witt family. His grandmother is a worshipper of Venus in Istanbul eager to service every passerby, circumcised or not, and is a famous procuress.

'This sounds just right. Will it be a girl or a boy, I wonder?' he says, looking at her belly. 'You never thought that by the time this child is born the past would be forgotten, did you?'

She knows he is right.

'Fortune, my dear Dou-Dou,' he says in that old voice of his, 'is fickle and can be easily smothered. Men like to believe the worst. The King might like to hear a story or two, a story of a kind one man of the world tells another. *Mes amours intimes avec la belle Phanariote*? The story of conniving, of false pretences, of virginity traded so many times.'

Outside, in the street, someone shrieks with a piercing scream that makes her hair stand on end. *Think*, she tells herself. What can you give him to buy his silence?

She can feel the baby move inside her.

'Do you want an enemy or a friend in me,' she asks. Her voice is light and cheerful. 'You still have a choice, *mon ami*.'

He clears his throat. To make a point of his strength he pours himself claret from the same decanter she had taken her sip only a few minutes before. This is her best claret, a gift from the King's cellars.

'You see, *mon ami*,' she says, smiling, 'there are enough valiant chevaliers in this city who would gladly challenge you to a duel and I've been told that you do not cherish the prospect much.'

This is no bluff. One word to Joseph would be enough. He is fast with pistols and his sabre. He has a good eye. Monsieur Boscamp's lifeless body would soon be lying on the Błonie fields. He knows that.

'You have two sons, don't you, Charles.' This is the first time she has called him by his name. A little moment once only imagined, now insignificant. 'And a daughter who should be married soon. Married well, I presume, which is not very easy given her father's reputation. Perhaps some people need to hear a word in her favour.'

He raises the glass to the light, admiring its crimson hue. Then he raises it to her. His eyes narrow, his lips twisted into a grimace. She can take it for a half-smile, if she so chooses.

'Your health,' he says, bowing to her. 'Madame de Witt. Divine Madame de Witt.'

> Your eyes are black and lovely,
> But wild and disdainful as those of a stag.

When he leaves she takes the decanter and smashes it against the wall. The crystal breaks into a cascade of glass and the wine splashes red across the wall and down to the floor. The maid who rushes in looks at her with questioning eyes.

'Clean it up, and help me get ready,' she says, trying on a new pair of white damask gloves. 'Tonight is Princess Lubomirska's *soirée*. I cannot disappoint a dear friend.'

Olga

Among the letters that arrived that day there was one from Jeroslav, her stepbrother, addressed to Olga personally. The letter had been dispatched three months before, from Odessa. It had been sent to St Petersburg and then, having missed them by a few days, forwarded to Berlin.

Olga took the letter to her room and closed the door. She broke the Potocki seal. *My dear sister*, Jeroslav began. Even in this opening she could hear his voice, the ironic twinge, the haughtiness of a Potocki. A better Potocki, a son of Josephine, *née* Mnishek. A distinction. subtle but significant, hinting at the delicate matter of provenance and lineage and the talk of cuckoo's chicks.

> I pray that these few words will find you, my dear sister, in good health. In such trying times one has to remember how delicate one's constitution is and how easy it is to abuse it.

She eyed quickly Jeroslav's long-winded exposé on the vicissitudes of life. She had no idea what her half-brother meant by the importance of upholding the highest of values and following in the footsteps of the golden tradition.

> As children of the same father, my dear sister, we need to help one another in times like this, and preserve whatever is still left of our patrimony. I have been given to understand that this clever little Jewess is gaining undue influence over your mother. I was told that your mother has made a far too generous endowment on her behalf, and that she is showering her with quite expensive and entirely inappropriate gifts. Could you arrange to have the girl's things searched before you leave for Paris? One

hears stories of ingratitude that make one's blood curdle. I have to warn you, my dear sister, that at the time of illness the mind is often weak.

Is it really insupportable to ask for the account of your mother's expenses, not of her own funds, of course, but those which, by law, belong to her children?

Olga read on quickly: about the pearls that should be hers but would, undoubtedly, go to her elder sister; about yet another endowment for Jan de Witt, son of that *disgusting* de Witt whom her mother had insisted on receiving in Tulchin after their father's death as if it weren't enough that he was paid off handsomely for giving up his rights to Madame de Witt. *I wouldn't like to suggest that it is all happening at our expense, yours as much as mine, but the unfortunate facts speak for themselves.*

She tore the letter to pieces and threw it into the fire. The paper smoked and smouldered for a while before disappearing in the flames. In the Tulchin palace where she had grown up, the palace now claimed by her brother Mieczysław in spite of Maman's protests, there had always been a grateful chorus of residents. Madame Czerkies, toothless, rambling on and on about the need for gratitude and the rewards kept in store for charitable hearts. Monsieur Trembecki going on and on about how only beans and water were good for you and how one should never touch animal flesh. They couldn't ever leave Maman alone, could they? As if she did not have her own children who could take care of her?

For it hurt to remember that when Olga offered to write to her sister and ask her to hurry, Maman said she had already asked Rosalia to do it.

She felt a chill strike her, thoughts a torrent of anger kept stale for too long. The sight of Rosalia in St Petersburg on the day she arrived, awkward in that black dress, her uneasy smile that grew so fast in confidence and that story of the books taken away from her at the customs. Olga's own elation at the thought that she would be free from those tedious tasks of helping Maman. The moments she must have missed, ignored, moments of immense importance, now so plain for everyone to see.

There is no need to trouble yourself. Madame la Comtesse is very comfortable.

Madame is resting now and should not be disturbed.

Madame had such a bad dream last night, but it is just a memory now.

Who does this Mlle Romanowicz think she is? What gives her the right to order me around like that? Does she think Maman cares for her more than she cares for her own daughters?

How quickly those who are lifted from the gutter forget their place. Claim what was never theirs.

But there are other thoughts too, one bringing a smile of satisfaction to Olga's lips. Rosalia, so freshly out of mourning, preening at the mirror; letting her curls fall loose on her forehead; asking Marusya for ice in the morning to rub her cheeks with; staring at the French doctor. Staring at him like . . . like a calf at a painted door.

Rosalia trying out her faded charms.

Yes, *Monsieur le docteur*. No, *Monsieur le docteur*.

Rosalia melting with hope.

At your expense, my dear sister, as well as mine.

Sophie

Their itinerary is: from Warsaw to Berlin, from Berlin to the town of Spa where all fashionable people drink their mineral waters, from Spa to Paris. From Paris to Vienna, from Vienna back home to Kamieniec.

As soon as they left Poland, in the first inn where they

stopped for the night she saw that Joseph signed them as Comte and Comtesse de Witt. This, he assured her, was the only accurate translation of their true station in life.

'Our real honeymoon journey,' he calls it. Delayed by a year and a half but so much sweeter for it. General de Witt's generous allowance has proved a good investment in his son's career, though Sophie likes to remind her husband that De Witt's money goes much further for all along the way their new friends are eager to offer their houses and carriages.

In the Berlin Lustgarden, firecrackers explode with loud bangs. Contrary to what Charles Boscamp told her once, grey stuffing does not stick out of the gilded chairs in the Berlin palace and the guests of the Prussian King do not leave the table hungry, even if many complain that the food is rather crude. Frederick Wilhelm of Prussia is a man of thrift, who believes in simplicity.

She is wearing a Greek chiton. It is made of one big rectangle of red silk woven with threads of silver and gold. The top edges of the fabric, on her shoulders, are fastened with golden clasps. Her hair is pinned up, adorned with pearls. Her laughter has a new tinge to it, impetuous and confident. On the day she arrived at court the King of Prussia asked her if she liked to dance.

'Always,' she said. 'Especially with kings.'

But the King of Prussia did not want to dance. He wanted to see her dance with one of his officers, Graf von Haefen. 'Will you indulge me?' the King had asked.

She would dance as long as he wanted, she said and let the Graf lead her through the waxed floor, to the hushed whispers of the guests. Bets were being taken, she heard, on who was more beautiful: Comtesse de Witt or a certain German Fraulein whose position in Berlin society had not been contested until now.

The verdict, her new friend Alfred von Haefen has informed her, was in her favour. He has not left her side for the last four days. He is beside her now, in the Lustgarden where the King and his guests have come to watch the entertainment.

A young juggler is wearing a costume on which blue, red and green triangles are linked with yellow braid. In his eyes, she can see the reflections of the flaming torches he throws in the air and catches with his deft hands.

In Bursa her cousins taught her to juggle with wooden balls and held contests around the bonfire. Diamandi always beat her then, his hands faster, his eyes more alert. He was a foolish boy, still herding sheep for his father. This is what Mana wrote with undisguised triumph, with a toothless wife and five snotty children. Mana does not believe in forgiveness, but Sophie likes to think that if it hadn't been for Diamandi, she might still be in Bursa.

The juggler is the first one in a long string of entertainers the King of Prussia has ordered for the evening. There will be fighters, wrestlers, boxers and fencers. A tightrope has been strung between two windows of the palace. A muzzled bear stands on his hind legs, awaiting its turn. She claps with delight. She has never seen a dancing bear.

Graf von Haefen already has a rival, young Prince Naryshkin from St Petersburg, another visitor to the Prussian capital, who has also placed himself firmly at her side. Both bore her slightly. All they can do is repeat what she has said or done or what has been said about her. The King of Prussia thinks her ravishing. 'If there are more such pretty faces there,' they repeat his words, 'perhaps I should visit Poland more often.'

The King of Prussia may prefer the love of men, but Comtesse de Witt has charmed him nevertheless. She sang him a drinking song about the myrtle of Venus and

Bacchus's vine. 'Once,' she whispered into the King's ear, 'I sang it dressed as a page.'

The juggler has finished his act and stepped aside. He is sitting on an oak barrel, watching the firecrackers, a half-smile on his lips. The torches, extinguished, are lying at his feet in a pile.

To escape her adoring companions, Sophie walks up to the juggler. The man is young and muscular, just the way the King likes them. As she approaches, he smiles awkwardly and stands up. She is a lady and the guest of the Prussian King. Her silk chiton sparkles with streaks of gold. He is very tall. Even if she stood on tiptoe she would reach no higher than his chest.

'May I,' she asks, pointing at the torches.

The juggler nods silently and picks up two of the torches. He watches as she tries to throw them into the air. She is clumsy at first, but soon remembers the secret of juggling. She has to throw them in the right way – not too high, not above eye-level, and always at the same interval. The juggler gives her one more torch. 'Three are easier than two,' he seems to be saying. She does not understand German, but she understands the vigorous nod of his head and big smile.

The body remembers. The hands, the eyes slip into a pattern once thought forgotten. A rhythm she can feel inside her. All that is left is to surrender to it and follow.

'*Gut*,' the juggler says. '*Sehr gut*.'

A small crowd is gathering around her, she can hear a hushed whisper, a gasp, a rustle of a dress. Behind her something is burning. The juggler is waiting for her to pause. As soon as she does, catching the torches in her hands, he lights them with a rag drenched in oil and motions to her to start again.

The flame is a distraction, for she already knows the secret of success. Absolute concentration. Refusal to look anywhere but at what is essential, what is in front of her, until the juggler steps right beside her and takes over. Only then, breasts heaving with excitement, her nostrils flaring, she closes her eyes and steps into a sea of applause.

Before the de Witts are ready to leave for Spa, a story makes its rounds in the Berlin salons. Graf Alfred von Haefen put on a blue coat and a yellow vest and stole Joseph de Witt's pistol. He made sure the de Witts were not at home and told the servants Major de Witt asked him to fetch something from his room. Pistol in hand, the Graf went to see his best friend and, in the friend's living room, declared that he was going to shoot himself because he loved Comtesse de Witt, and further life without her was impossible. Then, he made a great show of aiming at his heart, banging his head against the wall, and smashing a marble bust of Caesar. His friend, von Rutenberg, with the help of his valet, restrained the Graf and tried to calm him down. It was he who, the following day, brought Comtesse de Witt the very note her suitor had planned to leave for her, stained with his blood:

> Beloved Sophie, I do not shudder to take the draught of death. I do not tremble, for all hope is gone from my life. With a cold, unflinching hand I knock at the brazen portals of Death.

Comtesse de Witt pasted the note in her *sztambuch*.

The leather-bound *sztambuch* with gilded pages of best vellum paper is filling up with poems, sketches, and confessions. Calligraphed words adorned with dried flowers:

Beside you, my sweet countess, Venus herself stands outshone;

I have come, I have seen, I have been conquered;

To please her all eagerly sought . . .

Men, she has decided, do not always like to win. They too know that there is sweetness in surrender, a thick, sticky sweetness of surprising strength. Honey, as someone told her, can help move frescoes. A thick layer is strong enough to tear a layer of plaster off a wall.

Animal magnetism, this property of heavenly bodies, the earth, and all living creatures, renders us susceptible to our reciprocal actions. You, Madame, possess that force in concentration higher than anyone else.

Like light reflected and multiplied by mirrors.

Propagated and increased by sound.

A magnet?

A goddess?

Spa is no different than Berlin or Warsaw. Men follow her as if bewitched. Invitations pour in. Not a day passes without another tribute to her charm and beauty. Not a day passes without dancing, laughing and rushing from one salon to another.

In Spa her most ardent admirer is Emperor Joseph II of Austria. All he asks for is her presence at his side and undivided attention to his monologues on the quality of the sturgeons sent to him by Catherine of Russia, or on how ancient Roman and Greek monarchies differ from modern. The progress of civilisation, he likes to say, must be ascribed to stability. He likes to make her laugh at her suitors, their undisguised ardour, their jostling for her attention. 'Look, look at this tall chevalier who is staring at you,' he whispers in her ear. 'Is he a fool or a barbarian?'

Comtesse de Witt, the Emperor of Austria insists, cannot be allowed to proceed on her journey without proper introductions. In Paris, especially, she will be his protégée and this is why he entrusts *la belle comtesse* to the care of his beloved sister, the Queen of France. *A friend so special and dear*, he writes to Marie Antoinette in a letter he ordered copied for her, *who has warmed my heart. The word boredom is banished forever from the place where the beautiful Comtesse de Witt stamps her foot.*

Why does it delight her so much?

Joseph likes to read this letter to her, raising a glass across the table, in anticipation of further conquests. This and other follies men commit for her, lured by admiration, lust, or mere hope.

There is pride in Joseph's voice. Isn't a woman's worth measured with trophies of the heart, with games of conquest and surrender? Isn't a man's worth measured with the importance of his wife's conquests?

But then, one night, he touches her belly gently and places his hand on it, waiting. His hand is warm and soft and for a brief moment she thinks of Lysander's kiss, in that beautiful meadow. If he had truly loved her, would she still be there?

There is a scar on his right cheek and her fingers know its contours by heart.

'One of your future soldiers, Sir,' she whispers into his ear, 'is very badly behaved and kicks me in the stomach!'

From her dream that night she remembers sailing on a beautiful lake, its surface smooth and shiny. She dips her hand in the cool water and puts it to her lips. The boat she is in creaks and sways like a wooden cradle.

By the time they reach Paris she has seen enough to know that Joseph de Witt has his merits. He may be just a major in the Polish army with no clear prospects, curiously blind to the simplest of human desires, deaf to the finer points of elegant conversation, but – unlike other husbands she has seen – he is not jealous of his wife's advancements.

Sophie, Comtesse de Witt. Her travelling trunks are packed with Greek chitons and dresses of pale muslin and chintz, the colour of the spring sky. Her stockings are scarlet or the colour of ripe cherries. Sometimes she cannot stop herself from touching the smooth velvet of the carriage seat, the ribbed silk of her shoes, or smelling the sandalwood handle of her fan.

Every day her hair is transformed into a thick and frizzed mass of black curls, puffed and padded to surround her face and shoulders. She needs five chests for her hats alone.

In a letter to her mother she describes a Parisian lady sticking her head through the carriage window, for the height of her hair allowed no other way to travel. Paris, she writes is not unlike a district of Phanar, in Istanbul, where Maria Glavani lives now, thanks to her daughter's generosity. Lives in comfort though not yet in luxury, next door to a rich spice merchant whose wife impatiently awaits Sophie's sketches of Parisian fashions and her descriptions of the city. Sophie can almost hear this woman she has never seen, black lace revealing white skin, gold rings flashing, talking to her friends. 'Comtesse de Witt, my neighbour's daughter, says Paris is just like Phanar. The best families live there, the most select society. She's married to a Polish count now, a friend of kings and queens.

'One of the Phanariots, one of us.'

Comtesse de Witt has seen the crowd of pedlars and merchants in the corridors of Versailles, so *that the Queen cannot step out of her private rooms without breathing in the effluvia of their merchandise and tripping over the sellers who hope to entice her fancy.* (She is very fond of collecting elegant words. Someone in Berlin had assured her that she was 'dispersing seductive *effluvia*.')

Comtesse de Witt is also making sure to let everyone

know that her good fortune is not excessive and not without shadows. She complains that the fashions are exceedingly dear and, with her husband's limited resources, she can afford but an imitation of Chinese lacquer and very ordinary *chiné* for her dresses (lavender blue and shades of lilac are *de rigueur* – white too but patterned like marble or foliage). *If it weren't for the thoughtful gifts we receive from most illustrious benefactors, my dear Maman, I would have to blush with shame at the state of my wardrobe.*

Mana sent back words of caution. *Wishing for too much*, she writes, *can bring you down. Perhaps, now that the Lord has blessed you and you are with child, you should devote yourself to your family*. To her repeated invitation to come and live with her in Kamieniec, Mana always sends the same words of refusal. *Your happiness and well-being is more important than my comfort. With the money you've sent me, I lack for nothing here. May the Lord and Saint Nicholas bless you, my beloved daughter, as I bless you.*

So she does not tell Mana that Comte d'Artois has sent yet another bouquet of flowers, snow-white roses from his garden, and presented her with an ostrich feather for her hair. Or that Comtesse de Polignac, her new best friend, assures her that the Queen herself wishes to receive her in Trianon, where even the King of France is not always welcome and where, if he is too boring, clocks are set forward to make him depart earlier than he has planned. '*La Belle Phanariote*,' Marie Antoinette has said, 'my brother says that she knows the mysteries of the Seraglio.'

With Diane de Polignac, Sophie curls up like a cat before the fire. Their bursts of uncontrolled laughter annoy Joseph who makes a show of leaving them alone, just like any Parisian husband. They could have been sisters, the way they understand each other's moods, when to talk and when to keep silent.

Diane likes lists. Where you have to be seen: Opera, les Tuileries, the palace of Madame de la Reynière. Who should paint your portrait: Madame Vigée-Lebrun. What you absolutely must have: an ostrich feather for your hat.

They plan *tableaux vivantes*. Anchises, a shepherd tending his sheep on the wild scarps of Mount Ida, Aphrodite appearing to him clad in a gown brighter than gleaming fire, like an unwed maiden, filling him with sweet longing of the flesh. Or, Aphrodite redeemed, depicting the moment in which Hephaestos having placed an invisible net to capture his wayward wife with Hermes, and having called all gods to bear witness to his wife's shame, sees them overcome with desire for her, demanding her freedom.

In Paris days begin long past noon. Only tradesmen see the light of the morning. Real life prefers the dimmed hours of the twilight, moonlit promenades, the masquerades of the night. Sophie needs to learn so much, shed her provincial ways. Forget Kamieniec, Warsaw.

She is a good pupil. 'I don't have to tell you anything any more,' Diane de Polignac tells her friend with awe after Sophie manoeuvres her way past her creditors, her chin up, an act impossible only a few days before.

They talk of men. Of lovers. Of how love likes the drama of a perpetual crisis: a death threat, a fainting spell, a torrent of panegyrics and recriminations, a touch of jealousy. A lover should never be sure; never unthreatened, never bored.

A slave? No. You don't want to make them think that.

To this friend Sophie confesses her restlessness. Even in the most sumptuous of rooms, something compels her to stand up and walk from the curtained window to the door, from the bookcase to the ormolu clock. As if every room were a cage, every door an escape, a promise of something better. While Joseph complains about the tedious carriage rides, she welcomes any movement. She will not miss a ball or a hunt, not until the baby won't let her jump out of bed in the morning. She knows what's best for her. She knows that it is stillness that would harm her.

'Joseph,' Diane gasps. 'You can do better than de Witt. You should do better. I hope you do.'

Diane does not believe in husbands having much to say in the matter of their wives' daily occupations. A marriage is but a contract of two estates, of two independent people who lead their own lives. If a husband dares protest . . .

Joseph dares not protest. Sometimes in the rage he can evoke in her, she throws things at him, a slipper, a book, a jar with cream, a silver box from which the calling cards spill to the floor, and tells him to go away and never come back. Tells him she deserves better than the bowlegged major of a provincial fortress with a pockmarked face. He takes it as if it were a joke. He ducks her blows, and she does not insist. For now she delights in his surrender, in the fact that he has chosen to please and placate rather than demand. Perhaps he too knows that this is the only way to keep her.

For as long as he can.

Diane says she looks ravishing. She says that placing a soft kiss on her perfumed cheek. 'You look ravishing too,' Sophie gasps in return. They both laugh. There is no jealousy in Diane de Polignac, no resentment at Sophie's conquests. As if she lived for the moments when the two of them, loosening their corsets and kicking off their shoes, would lie down on an ottoman and recall the sweet moments of triumph. Have you seen the way Comte d'Artois looked at you? Have you seen his eyes?

'No,' Sophie lies. At the royal hunt the other day, when she outraced him on her grey mare and plunged her hand first into the bleeding neck of a slain stag, the King's brother had grabbed her hand and licked the hot blood off her fingers.

'Come,' she says to her friend. 'Forget them all. I have an idea.'

'What is it?' Diane asks, her eyes twinkling.

They throw off their gowns and jewels. They unpin their hair. The maids are aghast as they put on the simple dresses of servant girls. Diane's footman is ordered to come with them and not give away their disguise at the threat of instant dismissal. 'You,' Sophie says, lifting his chin with her finger, 'look like a man who would know where two beautiful country girls could dance until their legs can't carry them any more.'

The young footman looks quite dashing in de Polignac livery of blue and white, the livery he will have to exchange for something that would allow their disguise to work. If he is surprised, he does not let on. He isn't though. Mistresses and masters have their whims, better indulged without much thinking about. It is his role to keep his mouth shut and do what they want.

They would make handsome maids, he says, making both laugh with delight. But it is Sophie who spots the most glaring giveaways: powder on their cheeks, the perfume, the padding in their hair. Splashing themselves with water as if they were girls, they wash and put on thin, coarse dresses, laced at the front. Sophie insists they practise the way they will walk in the street, free from the wires that hold their gowns, lighter, faster. 'Like a cat,' she says, and takes a few steps.

'Like a cat,' Diane repeats and follows her, her hands flailing as if she needed to steady herself.

'Not like that,' Sophie insists. 'You'll spoil everything. Watch me.' She has taken off her shoes and wears a pair of maid's slippers. Her hips sway as she walks. A she-cat on a roof, red hot from the sun.

'Your turn,' Sophie orders. 'Just do what I do. Exactly what I do.'

'But you do it so well,' Diane says in awe, making her best imitation of Sophie's new gait. 'As if you were born in these.' She points at the dress she is wearing, at a tear on her arm, too hastily repaired, a thread hanging loose.

'Come on,' Sophie says, biting off the thread with her teeth. She is satisfied with the outcome of the rehearsal, with their new look. 'We are ready.'

The footman now wearing brown breeches and a white shirt open at the neck, says he knows of a dance nearby, in a tavern a few streets away. They could all walk there, if Madame wishes it. 'Madame is Flora from now on,' Sophie says. 'Madame de Reniere's undermaid, if anyone asks.'

'And your name is Lou-Lou,' Diane says.

'A milliner's apprentice from Rue-St Jacques.'

A walk filled with delights, a plunge into a throng of passersby: pedlars, vendors, servants, journeymen, soldiers. They are surrounded by women with babies at their breasts, older children holding onto their skirts, insisting on a treat or demanding attention; dogs sniffing them as they pass; beggars stretching out their hands, displaying festering wounds; a ribbon vendor who gives them a ribbon each for their hair and refuses the coins Sophie offers him. 'Take them for good luck,' he insists, pinching her cheek. 'For you and for me.' A young man in livery spots the two servant girls; he tries to catch them by their arms and steal a kiss. Sophie is faster then he, eluding his grasp. But she is too fast for all of them: a Swiss guard in his red jacket; a fishmonger trying to frighten them with a live lobster; a baker in a white apron who stretches his hands to block their way past his stall. It is Diane who is kissed by a drunk soldier with a foul breath; who gets her dress smeared with something white and sticky.

It is Diane who then has to be rescued by her footman who puts on an act of an offended suitor, ready to fight for *his* girl.

In the servants' dance hall, like all the palace ballrooms Sophie has been to, men sense her presence, note her every move. She draws them not just with her looks, not just with her unpinned raven black hair, the white skin of her neck, the radiance of her eyes, her full breasts showing under the thin dress. What makes men cast their eyes in their direction, for Diane makes sure she is at her friend's side, is more important. The raw vitality that radiates from Sophie, from the way she dances, her head thrown back, her body whirling: this is what makes the men vie for a place beside her.

For a while there is nothing else in the world but the music, the hot, gyrating bodies, the singing, the laughter that comes from deep inside, the rubbing of skins, of hips. They clap their hands, accept treats of fried pork and glasses of diluted wine. They listen to promises of walks and ribbons, and evade the questions that try to pin them down, make them reveal too much. No one really believes the story of a maid and a milliner's apprentice, but they are none the wiser. An insistent butcher who throws money around treating everyone to drinks, is told that Lou-Lou is a gypsy child, a runaway, and Flora, her friend, is the Polish mistress of a rich spice merchant. 'Polish?' the butcher says with a wink, pulling the skin under his right eye with his index finger. 'How come she speaks French so well.'

There is more dancing and more bantering with suitors. More pork rinds and bread, more sweet cakes and wine. But Sophie is already getting restless. She casts furtive looks at the door, grows impatient with the butcher's jokes.

'Let's go,' she whispers into her friend's ear.

Diane protests that they have not yet had enough; that the musicians are still playing; that it is still long before dawn, and that she has lost sight of the footman who should escort them back. But Sophie shakes her head.

'That's the best time to leave.'

As they walk back, alone, through the empty Parisian street, having given their eager suitors the slip after a surfeit of promises, Sophie kicks off her shoes. Her arm encircling Diane's waist, she is no longer impatient, no longer eager to put an end to the evening. With bursts of laughter, she recalls the highlights of their escapade. The butcher, half-drunk and sweaty, kneeling in front of her, begging her to marry him. She would never lack fresh meat, he said. She would have a house, an oak bed in her bedroom. She would have a servant girl. 'I was tempted,' Sophie laughs. 'But I liked your sweetheart more.'

Diane gasps in mock horror, recalling a tall, thin youth with buck teeth who tried to lift her up in the air, staggering under her weight. He was from Provence, he said, a winemaker's son. 'You have class,' he said. Diane had class and was wasting her time with her spice merchant. 'Come with me to my father's vineyard,' he said.

'Was that a proposal of marriage,' Diane wonders aloud, 'or just an invitation to a romp in the haystack?'

'A romp in the haystack,' Sophie declares with conviction. 'But then, after you made him taste your delights, he would marry you, my dear. On his knees, in a small wooden church, his eyes blind to all that is not you.'

'You must have been French in your previous life,' Comte d'Artois whispers into her ear. 'Where else could you have learnt the art of conversation that well.'

Princess de Lamballe leads them to the Queen. 'A bore,' Comte d'Artois whispers, his lips pursing in imitation of their guide. 'Your Majesty cannot possibly do this . . . cannot possibly do that . . . It is my duty, Your Majesty . . . my obligation . . .'

'Please, my dear Comte. We'll be overheard.'

'And then banished? Together forever: what a delightful prospect.'

Comte d'Artois doesn't care what Princess de Lamballe thinks of him.

'This is,' he says, 'what we have to put up with, at our own court.' The shackles of etiquette bind him. Tradition and duty are suffocating him. 'Dining in public,' he says, 'so that some chevalier from the provinces can boast to his Maman that he has seen Prince So and So or Comte So and So eat his consommé and, after hurrying to another chamber, still achieved the sight of Princess So and So tackling her dessert.'

The baby moves with such vigour that she has to catch her breath: a kick in her stomach, a stampede of tiny feet. 'He will be strong,' the midwife promised. 'A boy. I can tell from how they kick.'

Her *interesting condition* is carefully hidden under the drapes of her best dress. White with marble pattern that sets off her black hair and luminous complexion. That makes her eyes seem even bigger and deeper.

'Your first one?' Princess de Lamballe asks gently, wistfully perhaps. A childless widow, still young, who can see through the drapes of her dress with a soft look of approval that does not include the King's brother.

Sophie nods.

'I've heard it said, that you disapprove of card games,' the Princess says. 'Isn't that so, Comtesse de Witt.'

'Oh, yes,' Sophie says. 'Far too boring. And I have heard that ladies ruin their dresses for their laps get blackened with gold and they are forced to change twice in one evening.'

The Queen is playing with her daughter, *Madame Royale*, when they approach. The girl lacks her mother's grace and her small face has a seriousness to it that seems excessive. 'An old soul,' Comte d'Artois whispers into her ear. 'This is what they say, but I care little for old age, even in royal babies.'

Is she in love with him? Enough to make such moments tingle with pleasure. Enough to anticipate all stages of a romance: the seduction, consummation, and the inevitable parting.

She rewards the King's brother with a smile and a touch of her fan. There is a lightness to him she finds irresistible: the impatience with whatever is boring or simply annoying, such as a merchant asking for his money for the wine long ago drunk and forgotten. He is like a spoilt child aware of his charm. He wants her to admire him. This is not difficult.

Ma belle Phanariote, he calls her, *Ma plus belle Comtesse*. His hands touch her neck, lift her chin. At dinner tables his leg finds hers and travels up, ruining her scarlet stockings. But he is in no hurry, which Comtesse de Polignac tells her is a good sign. He is ready to wait for his pleasure.

His hands are soft and beautifully manicured. Every fingernail smooth and perfectly round. He walks with a slight hesitation, as if ready to bolt at the last minute, summoned by a more attractive alternative. She ran with him once, away from someone 'exceedingly boring', breathless, her baby crouching inside her, frozen with fear.

'My dear beloved sister,' Comte d'Artois says to the Queen of France. 'Turn your pretty head toward your guest.'

Sophie curtsies. The Queen smiles seeing her totter, almost losing her balance. And they both burst out laughing for they are both with child, their bodies fighting the same obstacles to grace.

'Comtesse de Witt, you have charmed one of my

brothers already,' the Queen says, beckoning her closer. A cloud of scent hovers around her. An *effluvia* of wild roses. 'Are you now claiming another one?'

Comte d'Artois frowns with pretend astonishment.

'But, my dearest sister,' he begins.

'Your Majesty,' Sophie interrupts him. 'I'm already claimed by the creature who has all my heart and whom I have not yet seen. But only another woman in the same delicate condition can understand how I feel.'

Princess de Lamballe smiles with approval.

Rosalia

She came to like the musicians: the tall, skinny violinist who bowed when he saw her in the morning; the pianist who liked to twirl his reddish moustache; the flautist, a Frenchman whose crooked teeth were too long for his face, yet the gentlest smile.

The day before Rosalia overheard the flautist talk of his Italian journey. He had travelled for the whole summer with just half a dozen piastrs in his pocket. He set off each day not caring where his feet would take him, looking for nothing more than the boom of the church bells or a flock of lapwings, the delights of freedom. He could always find shelter in wayside caves or shrines where the saint would look upon him with warm understanding. When he took out his flute, the music that came to him was mixed with poetry, with memories, and the sights before him.

Today was the day the singer came. The Graf had brought her in his own carriage. A lady with translucent skin, and a fluidity that suggested betrayals. She demanded a chaise longue to sit on while she was not singing, a pitcher with spring water for her throat, a glass that had no fingerprints on it and another small table for her scores. 'Hortensia,' Rosalia heard the Graf call her and saw how he squeezed her hand.

The musicians seemed unfazed by the singer's demands and treated her with obvious reverence. The flautist called her Frau Hellmann and offered to move to make space for her.

The door to the grand salon opened with a squeak that made the countess flinch. Pietka, Rosalia thought, would have to be told to oil the hinges.

'Good evening,' Doctor Lafleur said.

She could sense his presence or even the approach of it. She already knew the rhythm of his steps, always somewhat hurried as if he wanted to catch up with someone ahead of him. There was something deliberate about his movements, and something resigned. He was hesitant at times. The way he held the countess's wrist (like a porcelain bird), the gentle teasing of his questions (Only one glass of water? You do not listen to your doctor, Madame, but perhaps you are right).

Once he told her that the art of healing required observation and to be unobstructed, free from assumptions and judgement.

The countess tried to rise up, but the doctor stopped her. All he wanted was to stay here for a while. 'If you'll allow me, that is.'

'To watch me,' the countess asked.

'You can say that.'

'And what is it that you hope to see? How my illness is improving? I'm dying from sheer improvement, Monsieur le docteur. I can tell you that much myself.'

'I've never doubted you could. And even if I dared to, Mademoiselle Rosalia would have put me in my place in no time. Wouldn't you, Mademoiselle?'

'I would,' Rosalia said.

He sat in the leather armchair by the bed, crossed one leg over the other. From time to time he shook this leg, as if to wake it up. It moved her to notice how the fabric shone at the knees, stretched beyond its endurance. Austerity she thought. Refusal to indulge. Somewhere, already, she had begun hoarding moments, collecting, filing them in her memory for the future. She noted that he rarely smiled, but when he did, his whole face lit up and in it there was a glimpse of a boy he must have once been, a quick and curious boy with deft hands and bright eyes. She noted that fire attracted him, made him turn his face toward the flames. Catching the sight of his room, when it was being cleaned, his black jacket hanging on the chair she imagined him hanging it there and the very ordinariness of this gesture amazed her. She felt a quiver of pleasure at the thought, a pleasure that lasted for a long time.

Truthfulness, she thought, was in order. This steady basis of self-control she prided in herself now demanded an account of her feelings. His temporary absence always registered, always measured. Moments she would think insignificant otherwise filled up with meaning just because they touched on him. She collected them, like a magpie or a thief. The sight of his reddened hands, with their curling black hairs, so coarsely male against the waxen skin of the countess. The frown on his forehead when she asked him about America. The sight of his boots being polished, disfigured from wear, the shape of his feet melted into the brown leather. The curious moment, in the shadowy darkness of the hall, when she saw, or seemed to see, a flash of surprised delight in his face.

The countess was breathing hard but did not groan, so the pain must have subsided. The room was filled by the sounds of the flute.

With her chin pointing at the burgundy curtain, the countess said:

'Tell them to play something joyful, Rosalia. Tell them I'm not dead yet.'

Sophie

In her Parisian apartment sleep refuses to console her. At first she amuses herself by guessing what kind of a carriage passes in the street below. In the evening, cabriolets are always most numerous, swift and light, drawn by one horse. By midnight heavier equipages prevail, when the best of society return from the theatre and the opera. It is still before dawn when the heavy workhorses of the tradesmen begin their day.

Joseph insists she decline the latest invitations. 'They will miss you even more,' he says. She can hardly walk now. In her dreams sometimes the baby is born already and its pale lips search for her. When she bends over the cradle, she can smell sweetened milk and lavender and then something else, something she doesn't know how to describe yet, but something she will never forget.

The first pangs of pain seize her at dawn.

If only Mana could be here, with her. Mana who has sent a red string to be tied over the baby's wrist as soon as it opens its eyes. Mana who promised to pray for her daughter's safe delivery, to pray every day to the Holy Virgin, who knows well the woes of women, until the good news reaches her.

May this sweet child bring you as much happiness as you have brought me.

The midwife has gentle hands. She cannot count the babies she has brought forth to this world. 'Madame Sue is clean,' Princess de Lamballe assured her, squeezing her fingers as if to warm them. She also praised the wisdom of smallpox inoculation – an old custom of the Circassians, known for their beautiful daughters. The commercial people, she said, are always more alert to their interests. She too had it done, by a Parisian doctor, when just three years old.

Madame Sue demands a vat of boiling water to be placed in the room and orders everyone out. She places a sachet with dried hyacinth petals under Sophie's pillow for easy childbirth. 'No spectacle for the idle eyes,' she announces, limping across the room to close the door on Joseph and the maids who try to steal one more glance inside. 'We need peace.'

Madame Sue herself is not peaceful though. She moves about the room talking incessantly, her voice rising and falling. She does not require conversation. She does not expect to be answered or even listened to. But she does not stop.

Sophie listens. Time has slowed down, her pangs come and go at long intervals. What else is there to do.

'The Queen is due any day now. There must be a boy this time. France is in need of a dauphin, in need of the prosperity and tranquillity such a birth guarantees.

'When *Madame Royale* was born, so many of them came to watch that they sucked all air from the room and if it wasn't for the King, the Queen would have departed this world. His Majesty, May He be blessed, broke the window open and let in fresh air. So many people around her, and no one with the presence of mind to make sure there was a vat of hot water ready. Good for nothing, the whole lot, gossiping and scheming all day long. None ready for an honest day's work.

'When the Princess was born, all Paris rejoiced: the illuminations and *feux de joie*! Fountains spewing real wine, and bread and sausages were given out in the streets. And the theatres of Paris were free to everyone who walked in. One had to take the seat by noon, to assure oneself a place: the charcoal vendors were given the King's box, the market-women the Queen's.'

The Queen's fecundity pleases Madame Sue to no end. So many barren years had not been good for France or for the Queen. A childless woman can easily lose herself. It had been heartbreaking to see how she looked at the children of all her friends, how she longed to be a mother.

Madame Sue makes Sophie lie down. She wishes to check the progress of her labour. 'It won't be that long,' she declares. 'You are a lucky one.'

When Sophie resumes her walk, she is leaning on Madame Sue's arm. She is to keep walking. It is good for the baby. It is good to keep her mind away from the bad thoughts that hover over a woman in times like that. Let the earth pull at the child, Madame Sue says. Let the earth call. Outside, in the streets, the day is in full glory. A sunny October day, the 12th of October 1781. A Friday. This in itself is a blessing. She can take her time. She won't have to fear that her firstborn will see the world on a Tuesday.

She is twenty-one, not that young any more for her first baby, but she is strong and the baby is fast. By the afternoon Madame Sue tells her to sit in her bed, propped against the pillows. She has opened enough to push. 'This baby,' Madame Sue says, 'is no sluggard. This baby wants to be born.'

When she was coming into this world, Mana was in pain for two days and she almost died.

Push. Push. Harder.

Come, angel of the air. Have no fear of the evening cold. My arms are ready for you, my room is adorned with flowers. I'm waiting for you.

* * *

She pushes. She pushes hard. Blood floods her face, her eyes. There is nothing else in her but that force. She has no place for pain or fear.

Push.

Push.

Harder. Harder.

The baby slips out of her, so quickly that Madame Sue smacks her lips with delight. 'The first ones are hardly ever so good to their mamans.'

Come, nameless one, come into my arms. You speak no language, but I understand you. Come quickly, my treasure. Come to console me and fill my heart with joy.

Madame Sue stops talking. The baby has all her attention now. Sophie tries to lean forward, but the strong pain inside forces her to fall back. She can only hear the baby cry, with a scream she has been waiting for, a scream she will never forget.

'A boy. Little chevalier de Witt,' Madame Sue says, placing the baby in her arms. 'Ten fingers, ten toes, and lungs of iron. We can let the father come in now.'

Sophie is shivering. Her legs trembling as if she had walked through the Alps and reached a valley and her legs have carried her all this way. This is not from cold, but release.

The baby's eyes are closed. He is no longer crying. When she touches his tiny lips he begins sucking on her finger. This is a moment when time stops, when there is nothing but joy. This is the essence of love, pure, simple, unalterable. Love that will never wane, never betray.

'You are mine,' she whispers in his tiny ear, touches the tiny fingers. 'Nobody's but mine.'

* * *

Five days later, Marie Antoinette is delivered of a baby boy. The artificers and tradesmen of Paris go to Versailles with their insignia and music. Chimneysweeps carry an ornamented chimney, at the top of which a small boy perches. The chairmen carry a gilded sedan in which a handsome nurse and a little dauphin sit. The butchers bring slabs of good beef. The shoemakers make a little pair of boots and the tailors a little suit in the uniform of his future regiment.

> Long may this cherish'd dauphin wait,
> Ere he the throne ascend;
> And long with glory rule the state,
> Before his reign shall end.

In the great room of the opera house, at Versailles, the bodyguards – having obtained the King's permission – give the Queen a dress ball to which Madame Comtesse de Witt is cordially invited. Her Majesty opens the ball dancing a minuet with a private selected by the corps, to whom the King grants the baton of an exempt. Madame Comtesse de Witt gives her first dance to Comte d'Artois.

Thomas

A memory he had thought forgotten. The Parisian mob bursting into La Petite Force and breaking down every door until they found Princess de Lamballe. Dragging her screaming from her cell into the yard where she would be raped, tortured, and hacked to death.

Thomas could speak about it, in a way. He could say that the Princess's severed head and breasts were put on pikes and taken through Paris. 'Come and see,' the crowd yelled until the Queen came to the window and saw her friend's head. The mob, bloodthirsty, blinded by hatred and released from all restraints.

What he couldn't say was that he had been there, in the yard of La Petite Force. Pushed against the wall, seeing her white hand clutching at the bricks, desperately trying to stop time. His mouth opening and closing, his throat raw, his nostrils twitching at the smell of blood. 'What are you hiding from, Princess? From us? From your faithful servants?'

He was skinny and tall, but still just eleven years old. After his father had died, the Marquis de Londe had allowed Thomas to stay in his house. But Thomas did not have his father's patience to become a valet and soon his quick temper and irreverent tongue landed him in the stables. Then when the first stirrings of the Parisian streets came, the cries for freedom and brotherhood, he couldn't stay away. A stray amidst the revolutionary throngs, he lived from hand to mouth, stealing if no one wanted to give.

He couldn't speak of the feeling in the pit of his stomach, of the blood pounding in his temples, in his limbs. Or of his hands trembling when someone pressed a bloodied rag into his hands. A rag upon which, with the tips of his fingers, he could still feel the shapes of embroidered flowers.

It was not enough to reason that he had never been close to her; that he had been too young and too weak to have pushed his way to where she lay in her blood and vomit; that he must have imagined the sights that came to him on so many many nights. Sights so vivid that he woke up paralysed, feeling as if he'd just stepped on something soft, on something breaking under his foot.

Later, fortified by experience, he pointed out to his students that violent death was often kinder to its victims than it seemed to onlookers. He recalled the eyes of a little girl mauled by a dog. Parts of her throat were missing, blood was coming out of her in streams. And yet she felt no pain, of that he was sure. Her eyes gazed at him with bewilderment, not suffering. She was even smiling, telling him that her wounds were not important, that she was leaving and had no use for the body he held in his hands.

How he got back to the place where he slept, for he couldn't call it home, he never knew. He came down with a high fever as soon as he threw himself on the damp bed. He was smeared with blood that he hoped was his own. Now he felt that the high fever and heavy sweats were cleansing him. He remembered the martyrs in the paintings he had stared at in churches: stoned, clubbed, decapitated, shot with arrows. I feel like St Sebastian, he thought, but then the voice in his head whispered, 'Their bodies were mutilated because they resisted sin. You are not worthy to wipe their feet.'

He was sure he would die then, like a rat in his hole, alone, but he didn't. And he was not alone, either. When he attempted, on the fifth day, to stand up, he fell right down, only then noticing that someone must have been taking care of him after all for there was a jug of water by his bed, and a plate with small pieces of bread.

It took another day before he could dip the bread in water and put the morsels, one by one, into his mouth; before he could open his eyes and see the smiling girl with reddish hair, telling him how he had screamed and cried and how everyone had thought he would die.

'But you won't die now,' she said, brushing a drop of fragrant oil on his forehead with a small slender hand.

'Leave me alone,' he said. 'I *want* to die.'

She told him to please himself, but not before she went out of the room for she didn't fancy seeing yet another soul departing from a body. And then she left, hesitating a moment in the doorway, half turning around, as if knowing that the light would play with her hair and make it beautiful.

Dr Ignacy Bolecki's Berlin house didn't resemble his old Parisian abode on Rue St Jacques. The carpets and the furniture had been replaced by far cheaper and less ostentatious ones, despite Ignacy's obvious prosperity. ('There are more important things in life, Thomas. Causes greater than another ottoman.') No clavicord in the corner of the parlour. Only the collection of sabres on the wall of Ignacy's study was unchanged.

Ignacy embraced him heartily and led him to his salon. His arms flailed like giant wings. Gone was the reddish moustache of the Parisian days and the goatee. Ignacy's face was clean-shaven now, and he had put on quite a bit of weight. It suited him, gave him presence.

'Thomas, Thomas, my friend, come in,' Ignacy urged, ringing the bell. When a maid appeared, petite, in a dress that revealed neat ankles and black flat-soled slippers, he ordered coffee and sweets.

A small miniature of Ignacy's daughter, Constance, was standing on a side table. Her hair was carefully coiffured, the locks gathered over her ears turned her into a woman of fashion. In his zeal the painter had woven a string of pearls in between them, which she would surely have refused to wear. But her grey, almond shaped eyes, he thought, were true to how he remembered them, and this was not an easy feat.

'Mademoiselle Rosalia,' he could hear Ignacy say, punctuating his words with gasps and heaves. 'We went for a walk together and she told me that the countess has expressed a great liking for you. Did I tell you I knew Mademoiselle Rosalia's father? Captain Romanowicz of the Polish Legion. He died in Santo Domingo, like so many.'

'You did.'

'I must say I'm surprised at the way it all turned out, Thomas. Mademoiselle Rosalia said the countess was grateful to you for telling her the truth.'

He likes to say her name, Thomas thought, aware that the thought annoyed him.

That turn of events was of immense importance. Countess Potocka, Ignacy continued, commanded exceptional influence in St Petersburg's highest circles. Tsar Alexander was numbered among her close personal friends. Her gratitude could be priceless, her influence used to sound a few people out and keep an eye on others. Revolutionary ferment was in the air, and it was reaching as far as Russia. Some said that even among the officers of the Tsarist army.

'I hope you don't think too harshly of me, Thomas. I'm not thinking merely of myself . . .'

Thomas had known Ignacy long enough to know that. Never merely of himself.

Thomas stretched his legs, suddenly aware of the return of the dull pain in his right knee. An old fall from a horse, innocuous at the time, insisting on taking its toll. If he did not stop his friend now, he would be treated to speculations on the possible Polish uprising, the chances the Polish cause had for the support of the Enlightened Russians who, like the whole world, did not give a damn about anyone else but themselves. He would be asked what he thought about this or that speech at the Russian Duma, another proposal to end serfdom. The slightest increase of democracy in Russia, Ignacy would say, was a new chance for Poland. Speculations Thomas had heard so many times before. He had to stop him right away.

'Do fashionable Berlin women still promenade at five o'clock in the morning along that great canal, bordered with poplars and plane trees?'

This was something he observed fifteen years ago. It seemed so odd to him then. In Paris, society ladies would have still been fast asleep. But here they took their walks, breakfasted at eight and then slept through the hottest hours of the day. Thomas had offered this observation to his students as an example of the adaptability of human habits (a sensible one for a change) contributing a great deal to the remarkable state of freshness and good health among German women.

'Only in the summer months, Thomas,' Ignacy said. 'Only in the summer months.'

Sophie

Vienna is on their way back to Kamieniec from where General de Witt is dispatching impatient letters, complaining that other people have to tell him what his grandson looks like. This journey of theirs, he writes, is taking too long. She reads these letters, carefully noting how veiled the complaints are, how cloaked in the loneliness of an old man, the longing of a grandfather eager to see his only son's firstborn. *Sophie will agree with me*, he writes, *that a baby needs tranquillity and peace.*

My baby, she thinks, needs nothing but my presence. With her son's birth, something has changed in her, hardened. The mere thought of Kamieniec makes her shiver. How can this gloomy fortress be a good place for her son? The society of uncouth officers and their boring wives? The Potockis are the only family of any importance for miles around.

'My favourite sister writes that Paris misses you already,' the Emperor of Austria says. '*Misses Countess de Witt's beautiful eyes*, she writes. You will stay in Vienna for a while, won't you?'

Luckily Jan has taken to the new wetnurse, and she can leave him without worrying. 'Such a good baby,' the wetnurse flatters her shamelessly, knowing the shortest way to her heart.

Her menses are back. 'A visit from *dame Thérèse*,' she calls it now. In Paris one evening, Comte d'Artois had confessed his fondness for the 'seductive effluvia, vapours transmitted by the essence of life'. She replied smiling, that if he ordered her to bleed to death for him, she would.

'Vienna is already dear to my heart, Your Majesty.'

'I can see you've not been enticed to rouge your lovely cheeks,' Emperor Joseph of Austria says, putting his hand on her shoulder and leading her away from the curious ears of his courtiers. 'Some ladies, even here in Vienna, have made great progress in the art of painting. They lavish more colour on one cheek than Rubens would have required for all the figures in his cartoons. I suppose I look like a death's head upon a tombstone among them.

'Don't interrupt. I know what I am talking about. How lovely you look. It *is* true what they say that maternity brings out the loveliness of the female form. Would this husband of yours protest much if I kept you here? You hold him firmly in your little hand, do you?'

'Your Majesty flatters me.'

'When the King of Naples offends his queen, she keeps him on short commons and *soupe maigre* till he has expiated the offence by humbling himself. Only then does she permit him to return and share her bed.

'You are laughing. But this is such a sad story, my dear countess. This sister of mine is a proficient queen in the art of man training. My other sister, the Duchess of Parma, is equally scientific in breaking in horses. She is constantly in the stables with her grooms while the simpleton, her husband, is ringing the bells with the Friars of Colorno to call his good subjects to mass.'

The art of conversation comes to her like breath, without thinking. Mostly it means letting the men talk and remembering what might become useful. She never rouged her cheeks, for her face had never been touched by the scars of smallpox. No, luck had nothing to do with it, she tells the Austrian Emperor. 'It was my dear Aunt's foresight. When I was three years old, she took me all the way to Paris for my inoculation. Your Majesty can judge the results.'

'How cold you've become,' Joseph tells her. Is it the thought of Kamieniec, closer with each passing day, that makes him bolder? The hope that at home he could be her master?

The irritation in his voice annoys her. Each morning, when she is hardly awake, craving her first cup of coffee, he begins his accusations. She never listens to him; he is always the last to know of their plans. His valet knows more of her whereabouts than he.

'What precisely is it that you want to know?' she asks. Her voice is ice cold, edgy. As he stumbles for an answer, she can see the fear in his face, no matter how hard he tries to hide it.

It's not that he objects, she hears, but he is worried. He is her husband after all. She doesn't get enough sleep, just a month after giving birth, when her body is still weak, still vulnerable. Her headaches in the morning should not to be ignored.

'I've never felt better in my life,' she says, but her voice has lost its coldness. She recalls the moments when they sit together in the nursery and watch their son; watch the miracle of his first smile at the sight of their faces; breathe the same air. 'I'm the father of your child,' he tells her. For now, he knows, it is still enough.

'This is the fourth cherry you have picked from the plate, my dear Comtesse,' the Emperor of Austria says. 'Shall I take it you are fond of cherries? I grow them in my orchards. Sheep manure is best, around the roots in the spring.'

He amuses her with the gallery of his relatives, reflections in the funhouse mirrors. A brother who is too fat to walk. A sister who eschews men for she is too ugly for any to look at. Another brother who sells corn to his enemies in the time of war, and to his friends in the time of peace.

She laughs with him, protests what she calls his exaggerations. Invented to amuse the ladies of the court. Amuse her.

Delight her.

'And what do you make of Versailles, my dear Comtesse? Will you agree with me that the Queen's staircase and antechamber resembles the Turkish bazaars of Constantinople more than a royal palace. My sister does not dare to protest this barbaric custom. She tells me that a Frenchman is more easily killed than subdued.'

Perhaps she should have stayed in Paris. Diane had begged her to forget Joseph, not to go. How will you live there, she asked, not even trying to conceal her tears. Who will you talk to? Returns, she said, were always impossible, like relighting an old passion.

'I have little experience of the Turkish bazaars, Your Majesty,' she says, fanning her cheeks. 'However, I think your comparison is particularly apt.'

Rosalia

The countess did not need them for a while, Doctor Lafleur said.

After it was aired (Doctor Lafleur insisted on it), the grand salon smelled of the autumn garden, of wet leaves, smoke and freshly dug earth. The invalid would sleep at least until early morning. 'And so should the nurse,' he added.

He opened the door for her and she walked past him. She would remember that moment, the momentary closeness of their bodies, the black stubble on his chin.

As they walked toward her room, Rosalia told him the recipe of St Genowefa's balm that her mother had taught her: French olive oil, rose water, wax, red wine, and sandalwood. All boiled and mixed with Venetian turpentine and then, when it cooled, with powdered camphor. 'In the end,' she said, 'one gets a balm that can heal old wounds, rashes and pustules. Excellent at restoring circulation in frozen limbs. Or on the belly, to relieve stomach pain.'

He repeated the ingredients after her. She watched him as he did it, his head nodding, hands moving with the rhythm of his words.

'I have an excellent memory,' he said, smiling. 'I'll remember.'

Later, in her room, she wondered about memory. She remembered a long summer day in Zierniki in 1803, when she had felt purely happy. Apples and pears were ripening in the orchard. She was nine years old, no longer a child, her mother kept reminding her every time she complained about her lessons or the hours spent in the kitchen learning what Aunt Antonia called 'running a house'. The grass had been freshly mowed this morning and she loved the heady, sun-soaked smell of drying hay.

They were playing blind man's buff. Her cousins, Andrzej, Krysia and Anusia, hovered around her. Three shadowy figures whose shapes she couldn't distinguish through the mesh of the linen blindfold. The girls were wearing light summer dresses. Andrzej, back from his Warsaw school, almost a stranger but not quite, in breeches and a loose white shirt, open around his neck. It was his presence that occupied her thoughts so fully then: the sight of his muscular arms; the curious glances he surprised her with; the awkwardness that overtook her in her cousin's presence. The day before he had sought her out as she stole into the garden after supper. He talked to her of Warsaw, of his school. The teachers were tedious, he said, but his comrades were fine fellows. She liked the word 'comrades'. A bat flew above them. The lights of the salon reached where they stood, but she was watching the moon rise above the linden tree. They were second cousins, he said, stressing the word *second*, and he squeezed her hand.

When they returned to the house, Aunt Antonia gave her a dark, long stare. 'Andrzej has brilliant prospects,' she said. 'I won't let him throw them away.'

In the long months since her father's departure from the Livorno harbour, from where Napoleon's orders summoned him into the unknown, this had been the only time Rosalia had permitted herself not to think of him. That day it was Andrzej's laughter that rang in her ears, followed by Anusia's 'Not fair.' He was cheating again, letting Rosalia catch him.

Then the dogs started barking, fiercely, announcing a stranger. Removing the blindfold from her eyes, she caught a glimpse of a man on a chestnut mare, dismounting, walking toward the house, asking to speak to Madame Romanowicz. 'Concerning a very grave matter,' he said with eyes cast down.

Her mother closed the door to the parlour. From behind these doors, Rosalia heard the messenger's quiet voice, then her mother's anxious gasp, her scream, and the thump of a body falling to the floor. Before the man had the time to call for salts, she ran upstairs to Aunt Antonia's boudoir to fetch them. She held the blue bottle under her mother's nostrils until the stink of ammonia brought her back.

A dispatch was lying on the floor, the seal broken:

> Based on the testimony of two independent witnesses, it is concluded that Captain Jan Jakub Romanowicz of the Polish Legion died in Santo Domingo. A hero to his last breath he gave his life fighting for Poland's freedom. With deep sympathy, General Dąbrowski.

It was Aunt Antonia who picked it up and read it aloud. It was Aunt Antonia who threw her arms around Rosalia and let her hide her face in her bosom. The face of a daughter who could not yet cry for her father.

Later that day, still unable to cry, Rosalia pushed away Andrzej's hand as if he were the guilty one. As if it were his fault that she had stopped thinking of her father. That day she blamed herself for everything. She should have felt the moment of her father's death. She should have listened to her own heart. She should never have let her own thoughts betray him.

The messenger, fed and having drunk a shot of vodka with Uncle Klemens, left muttering condolences. He wasn't able to tell them much. Two witnesses had confirmed that Captain Jakub Romanowicz had been taken to Les Pères Hospital, and that he had died there of yellow fever.

It seemed to Rosalia that the shapeless sack he had left behind was somebody's skin, discarded in a hurry.

Her mother clasped the leather sack to her chest and begged to be left alone. Alone, she repeated, closing the door to her room with a thud. Every so often, Rosalia crept to the closed door. 'Maman,' she pleaded. 'Maman, please.' But all she heard were sobs, moans and what sounded like prayers.

The next day, when the breakfast tray was refused and returned to the kitchen untouched, Aunt Antonia called Doctor Farens. 'Do something,' she pleaded. 'This is not right. She might hurt herself.'

After his knocking was ignored, the doctor forced the door open. It gave in with the sound of breaking wood. Her mother was sitting on the footstool, feet bare. The mirror on the wall was covered with the pillowcase her mother had removed from her pillow. Her dress was torn at the collar, threads hanging where the fabric had been ripped open. Her face was scratched. Strands of her mother's black tresses were lying all over the floor, her shaved head revealing the geography of her scalp. Maman ran her hand over her head and then stared down at the palm of her hand as if it could tell her something she didn't yet know. Her face, without hair, looked small and bare. Frozen in apprehension, like a captured bird. A razor blade was lying beside her on the bed. She was muttering something Rosalia could not understand.

For years she had remembered it this way. The doctor taking Rosalia gently by her shoulders and leading her to her mother. His taking Maman's hands in his and checking her wrists were untouched by the blade. His picking the razor and giving it to Aunt Antonia who passed it on to the maid and told her to get rid of it. And his saying: 'Your child needs you, Madame Romanowicz.' Then the memory of Maman looking at the doctor's lips and then at her daughter, blood from the scratches drying on her cheeks in frozen trails. Then standing up slowly, as if each movement caused pain, stretching arms out to embrace her daughter.

And now?

Now she remembers more. She remembers the pitying looks of Aunt Antonia and the words she was not supposed to hear. *The child will have to pay for it, I suppose Her people, of course, will have nothing to do with them now. To them, they could starve to death.*

That poor girl, she remembers hearing, cheeks flaming red, her heart pounding.

But most of all she remembers shame at her own betrayal. The thought that if it were her mother who died, perhaps then no one would ever pity her like that.

Sophie

After their return, Kamieniec is not bad at first. Her father-in-law proclaims Jan the most beautiful and the smartest of all babies he has ever seen in his long life. He has taken to ignoring Joseph all together, and refers to her in all matters. He agrees the fortress is in need of changes, that it needs trained servants and new furniture. In the last few months, the de Witts have moved up in the world, changed their prospects and obligations. Her new friends have not forgotten Madame de Witt. The King is planning a visit, and so is Princess Czartoryska.

How she likes the clack of good china, the sheen of expensive fabric and the cold of the marble; the laughter around the table, the glances of desire. Sometimes she wakes up feeling that there are no limits to what can still happen.

If only Lysander could see her now, she thinks, and even this memory is a triumph. She hasn't thought of him for a long time now.

She is wearing her Parisian dress, the white gauze with mauve rosebuds, matching her velvet shoes. The dress Diane de Polignac told her looked ravishing on her. Her hair is pinned up. A white ostrich feather brings out the black of her curls. From Vienna a messenger comes with a gift. A basket filled with ripe, red cherries. Emperor

Joseph II wrote a note in his own hand. 'To *la Belle Phanariote* whose presence is sadly missed in Vienna.'

One is never a prophet in one's own land, Joseph reminds her. This is not an encouragement. He would like her to settle for memories, for sweet reminders of her triumphs. He is afraid that her success will bring out the worst in those less lucky, that resentment will breed around them. He talks of the power of envy, the wisdom of not seeming to want too much. Someone has already printed a pamphlet that calls her a king's whore and a woman with a heart of stone. 'An upstart,' Countess Josephine Potocka has been reported as saying, 'who should be shown her proper place.'

'I don't believe it for one moment,' Sophie says. She is ready to believe in the jealousy of a backwater town, the revenge of the petty gentry hard put to provide dowries for their daughters. Such people are best ignored, countered with indifference. But she will not believe that the Potockis think de Witts unworthy of their company.

In Warsaw, in Paris, in Vienna, she called on the best French families and was received with honours. Are the Potockis any better than de Polignacs or the Austrian Emperor? Their Krystynopol palace is but a short ride from Kamieniec. Why should Madame de Witt, having just returned from her journey to the courts of Europe, not pay her neighbours a visit?

Tuesday is the day when Countess Josephine Potocka is receiving and this very Tuesday she will walk into the grand salon of the Potocki palace. She will make sure that her eyes express her silent admiration. She knows how not to cheapen the objects she attempts to praise. It is important to notice expensive tapestries, but it is equally important to compare them to the ones in the Imperial Palace in Vienna, notice their perhaps somewhat finer detail; to admire a picture, and stress that it would complement the Queen's *private* apartments at Versailles.

When she is asked to take her place in the Krystynopol salon, she will tell Countess Potocka how Marie Antoinette looked at the Dauphin's christening. She will mention the sadness of her smile and the migraines the French Queen suffers from each morning. She will describe how beautiful the fireworks were, lighting up the sky over Paris, the sparkling explosions of light. She could also mention the curiously wide sleeves of the Viennese dresses, the music of Monsieur Mozart that thrills her more than anything she has ever heard in her life. And besides, she has greetings to pass on. From Prince de Ligne himself who remembers Countess Josephine Potocka fondly from a certain masked ball in Versailles.

She is with child again. Mana has sent her another red wristband. Little Jan wore his until it turned to tatters. Only then she allowed the nurse to remove it and burn the remains in the fire. *Wear this one yourself*, her mother wrote. *To avert the ill wishes of those who might envy you.*

Here, in Istanbul, her mother continues in her shaky hand, *I could be of use, share your joys. My grandson is stretching out his dear little hands, and I cannot hold him in my arms.*

In Krystynopol, four Cossacks in yellow jackets guard the front palace gate. Standing at attention, their eyes are trained on something in the distance, something far behind her.

She has heard stories about the Potockis. Bad stories, stories of cruel pride. She is resolved to pay no attention to them, resolved to be forgiving. The rich and the powerful always attract envy and evil tongues. Who among us is without sin and can cast the first stone?

As her carriage approaches the courtyard of the

Krystynopol palace, she sees the five carriages with the Potocki crest are hitched and ready to leave. Countess Josephine is leaning out of the carriage window and waves at her husband, who is still talking to the butler. The children are in the other carriages, watching eagerly as if they have been promised a rare treat.

This is strange, she thinks. The countess *is* receiving today. It *is* Tuesday.

Her humiliation is planned to the last detail. As soon as her carriage rolls into the courtyard, the Potockis leave. Madame de Witt is not to be spared the sight of the tail of their equipage. Someone must have warned them of her intentions. One of her own servants perhaps. Has she been foolish in her trust?

The approaching footman looks her in the eye with an insolence he doesn't care to hide.

'The Count and Countess have just left. They asked to tell Madame de Witt that they never expected the arrival of such an illustrious visitor!'

She does not avert her eyes. The skin on her cheeks does not betray her. Her hands stay steady and she manages a sweet smile. Pride, she chews on the mute word, turns it around in her mouth. The Potocki pride. She *has* been foolish, dazed with the ease of her conquests. She has assumed victory. How thin the shield is with which she has covered herself, with which she has covered her child. De Witt's name will never be enough. Is it a name or *le bruit*?

> Balsam, when added to tar, ceases to be balsam but turns to tar; and tares, though sown in the finest field, will not become wheat.

'On behalf of the servants, however, I shall be delighted to offer Madame de Witt her refreshments.'

'Thank you,' she says, managing a graceful smile. 'I wouldn't dream of causing such trouble. Pray, tell your mistress I'll come back at a better time.'

At home she rushes into her bedroom, she wants to lock the door, but Joseph is faster than she is. He forces his way in and watches as she throws herself on her bed, sobbing with rage. The bed sags as he sits beside her, and he unpins her hair, and loosens the laces of her corset. There is no I-told-you-so in his voice when he tells her he has never liked the Potockis. Never.

Remember what people say about them, he says. He reminds her how old Countess Potocka ordered a Cossack guard jailed for accidentally touching her gloved hand as he was helping her descend from her carriage. How she whipped her own ladies-in-waiting if they ever dared to exchange a word or a mere look with a man. Whipped them herself, he says right into her ear, having ordered them to strip naked first.

He does make her laugh.

The gossip she once dismissed. There is one story he reminds her of, the story of the first Countess Potocka. The story of beautiful Gertruda who should now be the mistress of Krystynopol palace, a story only a fool would ignore.

It was a bad time. *Szlachta* rose up against the new King brought to the Polish throne by Catherine's sabres. Brothers fought against brothers, peasants rose against their lords.

Plague had descended on the lands around Krystynopol, where Count Felix lived with his parents. People lit fires to cleanse the air, rubbed their bodies with garlic, carried mercury in their pockets, poured vinegar on hot iron and used the vapour to purify their homes. If one person showed symptoms of the plague, the whole town or village was forced to abandon homes and possessions and they were burnt to the ground. Crowds of the dispossessed wandered through the countryside. People from villages and towns still unaffected by the plague left food for them outside the gates, but many still died of hunger and illness and their bodies littered the fields.

Sin was spreading like wildfire for, faced with death, people forgot all restraint. All they wanted from this earth before dying was one last sweet moment of pleasure. There was fornication, there was rape and plunder. There was murder. Threats against *Pany*, the lords were uttered without fear. From Ukraine, old blind *dziady*, sang the triumphant songs of the Uman slaughter, and no one dared to stop them from singing.

Count Felix was young then, in the first spring of adulthood. An awkward child for an heir of the great fortune. He was shy and bashful, stammering if he had to speak, his voice breaking, his skin reddening with fright. In the Krystynopol palace his parents were busy with his sister's wedding to Prince Lubomirski. 'A great match,' his mother, Anna Elizabeth said, 'but not as great as the one I have in mind for my only son.'

The nights were hot, the air in the palace stuffy, polluted with the smoke coming from the fires. Felix was restless and lonely. He asked to be allowed to ride his horse through the neighbourhood, promising to avoid the town and the vagrants. All he wanted was fresh air, the feel of the wind in his hair.

After that he rode every day. His cheeks revived their colour, his steps became sprightly and quick. His proud mother was pleased. She didn't suspect the real reason for her son's transformation.

He had seen Gertruda a few months before, in the Krystynopol palace where she had been presented at his parents' court. The youngest daughter in the Komorowski family, she had just returned from Vienna. A distinguished family, her father stressed, perhaps no longer rich, but of impeccable lineage, a family of senators, primates, and poets. Beautiful as a doe, her thick brown hair and eyes the colour of hazelnuts, lips like ripe raspberries, sweet and full of warmth.

'Not worthy to kiss a Potocki's foot,' Anna Elizabeth said.

People say the young Count's first visit to the Komorowskis' manor was one of chance. He was thirsty, and wanted a drink of water. As son of their mighty neighbour he was welcomed with great warmth, perhaps even hope. Gertruda was a lovely girl, her disposition was sweet, her voice divine. If fate wanted her elevated in this world, who were the Komorowskis to oppose the workings of fate.

That night Count Felix had a dream. Gertruda was holding a metal bucket up to him brimming with water. She had just winched it out of a well. Her eyes were reaching right inside him, making him burn with heat and he couldn't stop staring at the snow-white skin on her neck. He woke up whispering her name and the sheets in his bed were wet. That day he paid the maid one ducat to wash the sheets before his mother could find out.

Three months later, Jakub Komorowski took Count Felix aside. The matter he wanted to discuss was serious. His daughter was expecting a child, an event he had to accept as the will of God. Human flesh was weak, but he had watched his young guest for a while. He was of the best opinion of his character and the sincerity of his feelings. Besides the happiness in his daughter's eyes could not deceive him.

'Am I mistaken, Your Highness, my dear neighbour?'

'No,' the young Count replied. 'You are not mistaken.'

'The baby will be a Potocki,' Gertruda's father said.

Seeing the Count's knuckles clenched white, he added, 'I know my daughter's honour is safe with you.'

The secret wedding took place right after Christmas. The bride was lovely in her white dress, its folds cleverly draped over her growing stomach. Her brown eyes shone without belladonna, her hair pinned on top of her head, cascaded in locks down her shoulders. The few witnesses were asked for discretion on account of the groom's parents who were hoping for a grand match for their only son. It was better to wait, they were told: to give the young time to plead their case; to give the young Count time to confess his love and his new commitment. After all he had done the honourable thing and he was happy.

Poor Gertruda. She did not foresee the power of pride. She was prepared to be shunned for a few months, to throw herself at the feet of the Potockis, and beg their forgiveness. She trusted the power of her youth – and the smile of her baby. A son, she hoped. Count Potocki, her son, whose tiny hands would reach out and melt the fury of his grandparents' hearts.

What did she think of when the Potockis' men, their faces smeared with soot, invaded her parents' home? People say they were dressed as Cossacks, and pretended to search for confederates. What did she think when they dragged her through the snow. In her nightdress, her feet bare, her baby whose first shy kicks she may have already felt keeping still inside her. What did she think about as she was suffocated under the furs in the sledge that carried her into the cold February night?

Yes, only a fool would forget Gertruda's fear. Only a fool would forget that Gertruda's body was thrown into the Rata river, and when the river returned it in the spring, the Potockis' *ekonom* buried it in the field. Or forget how quickly the love of the mighty ends: in the letters Count Felix sent from Paris, Rome, and Vienna, he begged his parents' forgiveness for his despicable moment of weakness and offered all his assistance in having this foolish marriage that had caused his beloved parents so much sorrow and tribulations annulled.

'God Himself did not wish for the Potockis' disgrace,' Countess Anna Elizabeth was to say when she heard of Gertruda's death.

But they had to pay for their sins. People say the old Potockis died within weeks of each other, terrified of every noise, every horseman clattering through the Krystynopol courtyard. That Anna Elizabeth's ghost came to beg a novice in the St Benedictine Order in Przemyśl to pray for the salvation of her soul and demand that her son completed the construction of the church. Her ghost left behind a wooden plank with the fiery imprint of her right hand, as proof of her words.

But, even when his parents' deaths freed him to admit the memory of his first wife, Count Felix refused to mention Gertruda's name, and he paid the Komorowskis lavishly to drop their suit so that nothing would stop him from leading Josephine Mnishek to the altar.

'De Witts, at least, have never murdered anyone,' Joseph says. 'Our name has not been tarnished.'

She lets Joseph peel off her dress. He lifts her petticoats, tickles her skin with his moustache. His lips are hot and dry. He breathes in her perfume, and beams with pride when his tickling makes her laugh aloud.

Thomas

In the grand salon he watches the countess move her head. Her arms, Thomas noticed, were wrapped in a Kashmir shawl. Hers, of course, his father would have whispered to him, was the real thing, not the English imitation to be bought for twenty pounds in London. Look, Thomas, pay attention, he would have said, his fingers pressing on his shoulders, as if he did not trust his son to care enough. Look how light it is, how smooth. Look at its sheen. It is woven from goat's hair not silk or wool, from the finest softest fleece of wild Asian goats.

'Am I awake?' the countess asked.

'Yes,' he said and gave her some sweet tea to drink. She swallowed a few mouthfuls.

'What time is it?'

'Late morning,' he said. 'The fresh air made you sleep.' The big clock in the hall had just struck eleven. She moved her nostrils, twitching at the smoke from the fireplace.

Her eyes, no matter how prepared he was for their luminosity astounded him every time. *So you think you know me, Doctor?* they seemed to tease him. It was the human fascination with the symmetry of perfection, he might have told his students. A willingness to overlook all manner of transgressions as if extreme beauty should be freed from restrictions of those less perfect and live the life of unreachable heights.

'My dear Doctor Lafleur,' she whispered. 'I've asked for a hot bath.'

'Baths are not the best for you, in your state, Madame.'

'This is what this dear child, Rosalia, told me, too. But I don't believe it is good to deny oneself pleasure. Someone told me once that sad people commit the worst crimes.'

The countess looked through him, as if he were not wholly there. The laudanum was still working, he thought, pleased. He held her wrist. The rotting discharge from her womb told him the tumour had become ulcerated. Each illness had a smell, each stage of it a different scent: German measles smelled like plucked feathers; scrofula like stale beer; typhoid like baking bread; yellow fever like a butcher's shop. This was the smell of rot. *Karkinoma*, he thought, the 'stinking death'.

'Does it bother you, Doctor,' she asked. 'To always see people at their worst.'

'No,' he said. Laudanum slurred her speech, slowed her down. She took longer breaks between words.

'Good. I want you to remember me from my best side. And I want to know you.'

Her pulse was weak and fast. Her heart might have been pumping with all its might, but there was little blood reaching her starving organs.

Animal magnetism – in his head even now he was still explaining everything to those eager young faces still hopeful that they would decipher the mystery of life – is a force of life condensed into a fireball that draws us all into it, a miracle of life, never still, never the same. He would have pointed out the element of constant surprise, that tug on the heart one could never tire of, for it never stayed the same. Is this how she made him feel better than he was? More important? Stronger than he thought himself to be? Hopeful, too, in some foolish way. Promising unexpected passages where he had hitherto seen only walls.

'I'm amusing you, Doctor. Good. I want you to smile. I have enough of these gloomy faces around me. I was right about you from the start.'

He could see that she was pleased with herself. She was very pleased, and made no attempt to hide this pleasure shining from those large black eyes of hers. 'What for?' she seemed to be saying. 'We both know, don't we?'

'Don't go.'

He hadn't been going to leave, but she must have seen him twist his body.

'I had a dream,' she whispered. 'A very long dream.'

She sank into the dream the same way she liked to sink

into the bath, slowly and gently. She floated over peaks of mist, which gave way under her, forming tunnels and caverns, coagulating into the faces of people she had met. They all spoke in strange tongues she couldn't understand. Then through one such misty tunnel, she was taken to a burial chamber where she saw men dressed in long, priestly robes. Their faces were set and grim. Her arms and legs were heavy as lead and she could not move them. She was but a corpse, awaiting burial.

The oldest of the men, with white hair and a glittering medal around his neck, poured scented oils on her body. She could feel the oil flowing, filling up the pores of her skin but still she could not move. The man cut her open and removed her insides. She was empty, just a shell of herself. And then another man, younger, his face covered with reddish blotches, began wrapping her up in bandages. When she was all wrapped up, like a cocoon, they placed her in a coffin and put her into a tomb. She had been there for a thousand years, waiting.

'You saved me, Doctor,' she said to Thomas. 'You took me out of my grave.'

It was the increased dose of laudanum that made her dream like this. Its telltale signs: the awareness of every passing second stretching into infinity and the vividness of images. He asked her how she had felt, entombed, and she answered that she felt absolutely still, like water in a calm lake, that everything around her had been suspended. She had had no impatience, no desire to do anything, to break the passage of time.

'Is that what death feels like?'

'That I don't know.'

'Do you think they are waiting for us?' Her voice was so quiet that he had to strain to hear her.

'Are the dead waiting for us, Doctor,' she repeated.

'No,' he said. 'I don't believe they are.'

'Do you always have to say what you think?' she asked, attempting a smile. 'You would ruin the best of parties with such atrocious manners.'

The curtain that divided the salon moved. Thomas could hear movement behind it, the throat clearing, the muffled knocks of objects upon the floor. The musicians were coming in.

'You should be warned. I like to meddle in other people's lives, Doctor.'

'In mine, too?' he laughed. She was tempting him, he thought, with illusions of his own importance.

'Especially in yours. For you are the man who likes to speak his mind.'

'Sometimes. In some matters.' He was trying to be cautious, thinking he should leave before the musicians were settled, to avoid the awkwardness of finding his way among the scattered instrument cases. The woman singer made him uneasy, especially the pallor of her skin.

'Tell me, then, my truth-loving friend, what do you think of my Rosalia?'

'Mademoiselle is an excellent nurse. You couldn't have found a better one.'

'You are not in love with someone else, are you?'

She had surprised him, after all. He was expecting a game, a tug of conjectures, a salon talk of half-smiles and half-truths. Her abruptness disturbed him and sent blood right into his cheeks. He resented that, too, and the sudden trembling of his face she could see. He began his withdrawal.

'I don't think I can answer that.'

'What a pity! Time is so short,' she said with a sigh. 'I wish you did. I would know what to do.'

He resisted the temptation of asking her what she would do. 'You must drink more,' he said. 'Much more.'

'You are not good to me, Doctor,' the countess sighed. 'You are not listening.'

'Oh, but you are mistaken, Madame. I pay the utmost attention to every word you say.'

'Then why are you hiding your desires?'

'Perhaps this is the best strategy.'

'Now you are talking like a soldier, *mon ami*, but I don't care much for war. I'm talking of simple happiness. You are not thinking of giving up love for the sake of your friend?'

'Madame la Comtesse,' he said, raising and folding his stethoscope, his face flushed. 'The matter of my feelings is mine alone, and this is how I wish it to remain.'

She did not try to stop him when he rose.

The musicians were tuning their instruments. Thomas parted the curtain and saw them standing at their posts. There was a smell of autumn around them, of burning leaves and cold wind. They did not take any notice as he passed by. In spite of all his efforts to move slowly, he had managed to knock over a violin case propped against the wall.

His speed increased as he went along the corridor, by now he was striding. From the walls generations of Prussian Grafs mocked him. The fat faces of epileptics who must have ended their days in a fit of passion that pushed the blood all the way to their heads looking down at him. Syphilitic fools who mounted their servant-maids and let their sins loose. Thomas walked faster and faster until his own vigour suddenly pleased him and he smiled.

PART THREE

Your Majesty, this is how we, harried travellers through time, arrive at the next étage *in the life of our delightful heroine – or as Your Royal Highness might prefer – to the following act played by her in the* theatrum mundi, *where all of us, for better or worse, play our earthly roles. But before I allow myself to dwell on the compelling evidence of Dou-Dou's growing powers of seduction, let us take a closer peek at the object of our scrutiny at this pivotal moment in her life:*

Her head resembles that of the famous Phryne, a Greek like her, and is worthy of Praxiteles's chisel. This head destined to conquer the hearts of so many – young and old, and even a few crowned ones – is adorned with the most beautiful eyes in the world, black and luminous, and red lips between which glitter her small, white teeth. Her chin is worthy of utmost admiration, the raven-black hair that she ties into a knot to reveal the nape of her neck, is like Daphne's, and her forehead and ears stun the admirer with their perfect proportions. This magnificent head rests on a neck and shoulders, unfortunately not equal in perfection. Dou-Dou's shoulders are shapely enough, but her hands are too big, like the ones of the antique sculptures in her country. The same can be said of her feet, far bigger than those we admire in women, resembling the ones depicted for us by the ancient sculptors.

After her neck and shoulders, come her breasts. I would have liked to compare them with the breasts of Phryne, of whom Quintillian says that when she stood in front of the court accused of blasphemy against Aphrodite (having impersonated her during the festivities), and when – in his defence speech – Hyperides bared her breasts asking if such divine beauty could ever offend the gods, she was immediately given a sentence to her liking. Unfortunately, if Dou-Dou were ever forced to do the same, she would surely lose her case. Her breasts are withered, shapeless and inflexible (perhaps because of the hot baths so favoured in this part of the world). They hang like pears on her belly, which, I must say is of rare beauty, as if trying to point to its perfection and say, 'descend and forget about us.'

The area of the mount of Venus is faultless. Its centre would have also been perfect, if it wasn't for a certain protrusion, visible in the fortress around the nest of pleasure, a protrusion that may deter more discerning men. That defect, however, Sophie is able to cover with the beauty of other parts. Her delightful little buttocks, smooth like silk, her milk-white thighs, her knees and calves could pass muster with the best sculptors of the world. This body, filled with natural charm in all its shapes and movements, with what modern Greeks*

---

* Doctors in Turkey maintain that girls, during bathing, (where everything is allowed, especially without the elderly chaperone who would have guarded such girls in the Padishah's harem) cause these protrusions themselves, by pulling at them, so that their clitoris is of a much greater size than in women of other races.

following the examples of the Turks call nouri, *the light of the body, is animated by a soul, far superior than many.*

Dou-Dou's soul is a well-functioning machine that allows her to move with astonishing agility. She is characterised by a rightness of opinion, quickness of mind, and finesse, far exceeding the average. She reasons with natural logic, even when she lies, so one could have taken her for a pupil of Aristotle. With her sophistry she has reached such perfection that she can get her opponent into a corner in the blink of an eye. Her penetrating intelligence is visible in her gestures, words, and thoughts. No man can escape her scrutiny, for she studies him so deeply that she can predict his dreams and desires. Her memory is angelic; her inventiveness, her perseverance in pursuing her wants, astound me.

She cares not for the future but lives for the moment, drawing happiness from every passing second. She shows no traces of whims, no sentimentality, no artifice, and is never boring. With the same self-assurance and courage she tells the truth and lies. She can tell stories, with all their little fibs, in such a way that the wisest of us would not know where she has by-passed the truth.

Never surprised at the turn of fortune, she does not show excessive joy or sorrow. Nothing, no ties of blood or friendship, will stop her from getting what she wants. Joyful and pliable, she knows how to stay on the best of terms with her friends and lovers so that no one leaves her company unhappy. A true coquette, she can draw advantage from every circumstance.

BERLIN 1822:

Opium

Rosalia

In the grand salon the countess was trying to raise herself up, fighting with the pillows as if she were drowning. Her mouth opened like a gash across her face. Fear, when it came with such force, Rosalia thought, maimed all.

'I don't want to die.'

At moments like that comfort did not come from words.

'Shhhh . . .' Rosalia whispered. She had wrapped her arms around her mistress and rocked her gently back and forth, shielding her with the soothing warmth of her own body, alive and strong against the dying one. The countess's head slid over her shoulder and onto her right breast, flattening it until it hurt.

'Shhh . . .'

'I have no legs. I have no hands.'

Her mistress's hands were indeed cold, her fingers moving with difficulty. Rubbing produced no effect. She needed help.

'Don't go,' the countess said, shivering. 'He is waiting for you to leave.'

Rosalia rang the bell for Marusya and told her to fetch

Doctor Lafleur. The maid crossed herself before rushing out of the room. Rosalia could hear her steps recede down the hall, her knock on the doctor's door.

'He won't make me cry,' the countess said. 'I won't let him.'

Moments like this were becoming more frequent. The lapses of time, the incomprehensible declarations. Only last night, the countess had begged someone not to go. 'Not now,' she muttered. 'Not now.' Then she wanted to know why the baby was crying so much. 'Does the wet-nurse have enough milk?' she asked. When Rosalia said there was no baby, the countess insisted her daughter had brought her grandson with her. 'I saw him just a minute ago,' she said. 'You were there too, Rosalia. I saw you take him in your arms and smile.'

Doctor Lafleur sent Marusya for the sacks of oats warming by the kitchen fire. Restoring the vital signs, strengthening the body weakened by bleedings was the first step in any crisis.

'Laudanum is no longer effective,' he declared. The time had come for pure opium. *Papaver somniferum.* He had it in his room. He would fetch it right away.

With Pietka's help, Marusya managed to bring five of the sacks. One by one, the hot sacks went under the quilt, and around her mistress's shivering body. The maid was now sobbing loudly, upsetting the countess even more. It was the dream the maid kept saying, that same old dream from St Petersburg. The dream of teeth falling out, a whole handful of them, the omen of death.

'What is she talking about?' Doctor Lafleur asked, frowning at the commotion. Marusya was trembling as if possessed, her hands covering her eyes, wiping the tears from her cheeks.

'She had a silly dream.'

Thankfully, the warmth was having its effect. The countess quieted down and closed her eyes. Her tousled hair encircled her head, making her face seem small. She was biting her lower lip. By the time Rosalia managed to send Marusya back to the kitchen, the shivering had stopped.

'Where am I,' the countess asked.

'In Berlin.'

'How did I get here?'

'We came here in a carriage.'

'Oh, yes . . . the carriage. I remember.'

'It should be reddish-brown,' Doctor Lafleur said, showing Rosalia the small cake wrapped in poppy leaves he had just brought from his room. He told her that in Turkey its bitterness was often disguised with nutmeg, cardamom, cinnamon or mace, but that he mixed it with honey and dissolved it in red wine.

The countess was fully conscious now, her eyes wandering through the room, resting on the votive lamp under St Nicholas, asking if the water could be changed. The flowers, she said, did not look fresh.

'I'll bring new ones,' Rosalia said.

'With this,' Doctor Lafleur said, handing the countess a glass he had just stirred. 'You will have a good, quiet rest.'

'If you say so, Doctor,' the countess said. She could taste the bitterness, in spite of the honey, for her lips curled in disgust.

'Close your eyes and think of something pleasant. A good moment, dear to your heart. You will feel that your body is getting heavier, that your pain is slowly leaving you. Rest, smile, sleep.'

The countess closed her eyes and moaned, but a few

moments later she was asleep already, her hands gripping the quilt. Hands so thin, Rosalia thought, that holding them felt like clasping a bunch of twigs.

'Pure opium,' Doctor Lafleur told Rosalia in a low whisper, as he prepared to leave, 'might buy us another week. Maybe two. The countess might be more sluggish though, even more absent.'

He was not looking at her when he said that, and Rosalia felt a tinge of disappointment.

Something was happening to her in this Berlin palace. Something unaccountable, frightening. Wild. She could not name it. She did not dare name it. There was an image she carried with her. On a hill top, a tower struck by lightning. High and mighty, once impervious to danger, now split in half by bolts of light.

It was to disarm this something that she threw herself into the day's chores. Idle hands she thought, were the temptation of devils. She shuttled from the sickroom to the kitchen, scolding, reminding, remembering the medicine, the clean sheets, the lotion for the bedsores. If there were moments of hesitation, she reminded herself what would happen if she let herself go. The maids would gossip in the kitchen letting the dust settle, the coffee grow cold before it was brought upstairs, the fires die or suffocate in ashes. The smoothness of days would disappear, eaten up by unforeseeable disasters. Life required drudgery, vigilance, eagerness to oversee and control the minutiae of every day. She was just that, an overseer, and she could not let herself go.

What else was there anyway? Acres of solitude?

Doctor Lafleur rose, bade her a good rest, and left. She could hear his steps grow fainter in the hall. Suddenly she noticed that the knuckle of her hand was bleeding. She sucked at it and waited. The blood did not come back.

'There is nothing for me here in Kamieniec,' she tells Joseph. 'For us,' she adds, seeing his lips twitch but actually thinking of her son. Still her only son, for that second one did not live beyond one short day.

Don't be a fool, Mana writes. *The evil eye is never idle.*

'If there is a door, open it.' Her old restlessness is back, her need to be on the move. She has tried to quench it with visits to Warsaw, to Lvov, to Vienna. Anywhere but here, in this backwater. This cesspool of gossip, of jealousy and spite.

How many times can one cross the same field, meet the same people, give alms to the same blind beggar, she says.

'Even my own mother does not want to live here,' she screams. A lie, really, for Mana refuses for quite another reason.

Please come, she has written, but her mother is forever offering excuses that shouldn't matter in the least. A wave of heat that makes a thought of a carriage a torture, some debt she needs to collect, Aunt Helena's recurring indisposition that requires her presence. *Two widows looking after each other*, she writes. *That's what we have become. Thinking of the time when you were with us. Always laughing, like a ray of sunshine, my dear Dou-Dou.*

Her mother is afraid she might spoil her daughter's luck.

Joseph nods. He has learned to close his ears to gossip. Her lovers are his dear friends. All he wants from them is transience. All he wants from her is swift impatience with each lover. All he wants from her is to keep her heart cold to everyone but their child. When she leaves

Kamieniec, he writes to her daily, asking her not to forget them. Reporting on Jan's every word, every antic, begging her to come back: without her, he is nothing.

'Jan too needs a future,' she tells him. 'You don't want your only son to command this.' She makes a sweeping gesture with her hand. Dismissive, impatient. Angry.

'Without you,' Joseph says, 'I cannot live.'

That much, she tells him, is true. Without her connections, he would never have become the commandant of Kamieniec. The position he curses now, for with the Russians and Turks at war, a commandant of a Polish border fortress cannot accompany his wife in her travels. If she only let him, he would have resigned his commission, but that she will never do.

Kamieniec is watching the progress of the Russian-Turkish war that promises to bring Istanbul to its knees and restore the ancient Byzantium under a Russian rule. By December of 1788, after a long siege, the Turkish fortress of Ochakov falls to the Russians and the ladies can take sleigh rides to see pyramids of frozen Turkish bodies blackened with blood.

With each victory, the Russian headquarters are on the move to Ochakov, Bender, Jassy, and Madame de Witt often accepts the invitations to balls and feasts there. After all, with the war dragging on, there is a great need for diversions. For balls and concerts, for witty conversations, and for genteel company to take the mind away from the hardships of war. For a beautiful Greek who understands what the Turkish prisoners say to one another, and who wishes for a Russian victory. 'A sad army can never undertake the toughest assignment,' Prince Potemkin likes to repeat.

General Potemkin, the Russian Prince of Taurida, chief commander of the Russian troops has a passion for what he calls 'Asiatic magic', scent boxes filled with Arabian perfumes, carpets interwoven with gold, a divan under a baldaquin, and beautiful women dressed in oriental costumes, lounging on the sofas around him. Princess Dolgoruka wears an odalisque costume for him. Countess Branicka announces her imminent arrival. Madame Lvov is coming soon with a young girl of fifteen, beautiful as Psyche.

It is in Ochakov where Madame de Witt displays her Greek chitons. The red silk one with golden threads, and the purple one, woven with silver. Her black hair is pinned up to reveal the curve of her neck. She declines the invitation from the Prince of Taurida to join his select company of sultanas. She prefers to be the bearer of secrets.

'You are a Venus and a Greek,' he tells her. 'Is there anything else I should know about you?'

She shakes her head. Caution is what she believes in now: small steps forward, followed by a swift retreat. In the next room, an orchestra is playing, of the best Russian drummers. When the Prince cavorts with Princess Dolgoruka, the drummers are asked to drum until just before the supreme moment. Then, his Grenadiers, with their hundred cannons and forty blank cartridges each, are ordered to fire.

'Tell me what is the best way to conquer a woman's heart?'

'Why?'

'To please me.'

'Mystery will please you better.'

He likes to talk to her, but even more than that he likes how she draws the looks of desire and expectations. He offers to make Joseph a governor of Kherson. His Empress, he tells her, would do whatever he wishes, so nothing is impossible.

'If I were your mistress,' she says, 'you'd already have forgotten me.'

She pretends to tell his future. She says that she can

see change. Someone now close to him has no more love in her heart.

He shrugs his shoulders and laughs. 'Anything else,' he asks.

'You will take Ismail within three weeks,' she says, taking another look at his cards.

'I have more infallible ways than fortune-telling,' he answers. When she asks him what these ways are: he says, 'General Suvorov.'

When in December 1790 Ismail falls, he shows her the letter General Suvorov has written: *Nations and walls fell before the throne of Her Imperial Majesty. The assault was murderous and long. Ismail is taken on which I congratulate Your Highness.*

'Wasn't I right?' he asks.

She is dressed in a Turkish tunic embroidered with roses and precious stones, made by Cortet et fils in Lyon, not by some cheap Russian imitator. She is sitting for the portrait the Prince of Taurida ordered.

It is better not to look too closely into her own heart.

Grigori Aleksandrovich Potemkin, the victor of the Turkish campaign, has asked her to come with him to St Petersburg. He has chosen the way she is to sit, hands folded across her breasts, a shawl wrapped around her hair and shoulders. 'My last sultana,' he declares, but she can see how he looks at his own niece. The painter, warned that one too daring look at his model would be enough cause for the Prince to cut his balls off and let his mastiffs chase him naked across the snow, is snatching short, nervous looks at her.

'The likeness will be striking, Madame la Comtesse, my Prince,' the painter says. His voice trembles, his hands are pale and smeared with paint. He is Italian from Turin, and new to Russia.

'Leave us alone,' she says to her prince and, to her surprise, he obeys.

The painter, obviously relieved at the Prince's departure, mixes colours on his palette and tells her about Russia. He has seen a Jewish wedding. The Jews of Russia, he has been assured, are always ready to marry someone. Three hours after Prince Razumov's order, the whole synagogue came to the manor with their choirs, jesters and the betrothed. He saw two orphans wed in front of the spectators, under a canopy. There were fiddlers and dancers and the jesters. The groom was carried around on a chair and the men danced most beautifully.

'I thought it most delightful,' he says.

She inspects his work and decides that one of her eyes looks crooked. It is also too big. She demands that he change it.

'It is because your eyes, Madame, paralyse me,' he says. His shirt is open at the collar, specks of paint stain his neck.

He says Russia is a country for artists and lovers. Women here have the charm of nymphs.

She reminds him that Prince Potemkin makes no vain threats and his mastiffs are known for their fierceness. No one would ever inquire what had happened to an Italian painter with a penchant for Russian brothels and vodka. That stops him mid-sentence and the portrait is declared finished. She still does not like the right eye.

A chill is coming over her too. Someone must have opened the door and let in cold icy air.

The portrait is called, 'Sophie, Comtesse de Witt.'

'Come,' she hears his voice, burly in the darkness of this giant room. Prince Potemkin. A lover who tells her to strip and covers her naked body with jewels as if they were grains of sand, whose hands leave purple bruises on her white arms. A lover who kisses her naked feet, who asks her to place them on a black velvet cushion like jewels and watches when the maids dust them with powder. A lover who would drop her the moment his eyes saw another, younger or prettier or just new.

His uniform, he has once told her, cost nine hundred thousand roubles. At his table she has tasted caviar from the Caspian, melons from Astrakhan and China, fresh figs from Provence. Today, she is his beloved, his favourite sultana.

She shivers at the sound of his voice.

One of his eyes is blind. A scar from the Orlov's sabre, he says, the scar of jealousy. But only the other day she heard him say that a tennis ball hit him in the eye and then a quack with his remedies finished it off. The remaining eye, though, is enough to pierce through her as if her body were no defence.

He is standing in front of her now, in this grand uniform, covered with decorations and diamonds, embroidery and lace. His head is dressed, curled and powdered, but she still remembers him in his morning gown, his neck bare, legs half-naked in large slippers, his hair flat and badly in need of combing. That one eye of his has the power to cut her off, encircle her in some invisible glass dome. This is what she thinks when she is with him. Of some fairy tale where she has been caught trespassing, of prison cells where she cannot hide, innumerable faces, gawking at her through the glass. Watch out, her heart warns her, with him you could lose all you've achieved.

This is the time to remember Lysander, the bitterness of her awakening, the piercing, suffocating pain of betrayal. The time to salvage what can still be saved. Instead she remembers the sunny meadow and the waves of joy. She remembers how he spilled thick, sweet wine over her neck, how it flowed across her breasts, through the hollow between them, down to her navel, leaving its trace on her skin.

I'll cry tomorrow, she thinks.

His impression of indolence and boredom is a disguise. Prince Potemkin will remember every word he needs to remember. Every name, every incident she ever mentions, every confession he has forced out of her lips.

'*Ma belle Phanariote*. Come to your prince.'

Once he took her for a ride in the country. Their horses, young and restless, strained to get away, pulled and neighed with impatience when the Prince forced his stallion to trot beside her. Not to talk of love or desire, but to tell her how the Empress when she entered the room always made three bows *à la Russe*, to the right, left and middle. Appearances matter, he said and grinned. Catherine, the Empress of All Russia is always right. 'How you love her,' she said, jealousy choking her throat. She tried to make the words sound calm and indifferent, but failed.

'Come here,' he says. '*Ma belle Phanariote*. Make me forget. Make me laugh.'

Gossip amuses him. Stories of Count Barecki who ordered a battle picture with himself as one of the generals even though he has never even owned a uniform. Of Prince d'Artaud in Versailles who offered her the key to his private apartments and when she declined said, 'Comtesse de Witt, you have no ambition. You do not love French princes.'

'People are fools, *ma belle Phanariote*. They will believe anything if they set their minds to it. Have you ever thought of that?'

He lies down, chewing a blade of grass slowly, staring at the sky. 'Talk to me,' he says. 'I like when you talk.'

She is trying not to think of the news from Istanbul. Her Mana has died peacefully, blessing her on her deathbed. *The only regret she had was not being able to see you and your son*, her Aunt wrote. But *you mustn't be sad, dear Dou-Dou. She wanted nothing more than your happiness.*

Princess Dolgoruka, she tells him, keeps a slave girl under her bed at night. If she cannot sleep, the girl is always there to tell her fairy tales. One story after another until her mistress tells her to stop.

'I have everything I ever wanted,' he says, his face red with too much blood.

They are sitting at the dinner table in his St Petersburg palace. The white tablecloth is embroidered with gold threads. Diamonds glitter among the fruit, making the bowls sparkle. 'I wanted high rank, I have it; I wanted medals, I have them; I loved gambling, I've won and lost vast sums. I have houses, palaces, diamonds. All my passions have been sated. I'm entirely happy!'

Funny, she thinks. How would it feel, having nothing to wish for anymore. She cannot imagine it.

Then, suddenly, the sound of porcelain smashing on the floor, scattering on the marble tiles makes her quiver.

Prince Potemkin has swept the priceless china plates off the table. He storms out of the dining room, crushing the broken pieces underfoot, kicking at whatever is in the way. She can hear a dog whimper. The guests in the Taurida palace sit motionless, unsure what to do next. She rises and follows him.

'You are the only woman who intrigues me,' he says when she finds him in his bedroom, fists jamming the pillow, a smudge of blood on his cheek. His hand is hot when he pulls her toward him, squeezing her breast. Her heart is pounding. His hair brushes her cheek, and now she can feel the heat of his breath. His lips bury themselves in her skin. She is trembling with joy. With desire. With fear.

With love?

All of it, she thinks, all of it at once.

Thomas

After the first dose of pure opium, Rosalia reported, the countess slept for five full hours, her body retaining warmth without the need for more sacks. Upon waking, she had a few spoonfuls of beef tea, a morsel of white bread dipped in red wine. The shivering stopped. So did the confusion. The countess was wide awake now, asking for him.

There was a new note in Rosalia's voice, he thought, scrupulously trying to avoid her eyes: a halting note of confusion, a trace of fear, perhaps too. Ignacy said she had lost her mother not long ago, and now she would have to bear another death. He fought the urge to reach out to her, to let her rest in his arms, to be of use.

'Please,' he said instead. 'Go and sleep. You need it more than anything else.'

A fly buzzed and bumped against the window pane.

'Yes,' she said, her voice flat, monotonous with weariness.

He opened the door for her and caught a waft of her scent: attar of roses from that perfume machine she had shown him, mixed with camphor and soap.

Having closed the door behind Rosalia, Thomas took out his stethoscope, opened it and proceeded to listen to his patient's lungs. Cancer liked to spread, he reminded himself. It could attack her lungs, her kidneys, her bladder. Like a cunning spy, it could surface in the most unexpected of places to take over a new territory.

'Is this what you came up with not to touch women's breasts, Doctor?' the countess asked.

'Not me,' he laughed. 'Laennec. He might have had other reasons, though.'

Stethoscope, he told her, was nothing but a long tube that carried sound. It let him listen to the sounds of disease: the creaking and rustling of the body. She smiled.

'What is it that you hear? The sounds of death?'

'Yes,' he said. 'Sometimes.'

'How does my death sound, Doctor?'

'It doesn't sound like much. It's not in your lungs. If it were, I could hear it.'

He folded the stethoscope and put it back into his coffer.

'Do you think God is punishing me?'

'No. I don't think God is concerned with us, Madame.'

'Is that what you believe?' she asked, the ring of irony in her voice. He had noticed the holy icon in the corner of her bedroom, with a prie dieu in front of it, though he doubted she could kneel in her present state. A votive lamp with its red light was always lit, though, and the flowers were always fresh.

'Yes,' he said. 'That's what I believe.'

The opium was working. She gave him a fleeting, coquettish look but didn't pursue the subject further. There was a softening of the body and a limpness in her hands.

'I want,' she said slowly, 'to see my first grandchild. My elder daughter is on her way here, from Odessa. Let's make a deal. You have to keep me alive until then.'

Her daughter, Thomas was informed, had married a Russian general. A brilliant man with a brilliant future. The Tsar had been most gracious to them. Her grandson had been pronounced a most charming baby. By the Tsar and Countess Razumov.

Each sentence was short, Thomas noted, clipped of unnecessary words. She was conserving her energy. He felt that it was his duty to meet her eyes as long as she looked at him, and he hated himself for his willingness to do so. What is it in this woman, he wondered, that makes me want to please her? He had never been impressed by opulence or by the incidence of noble birth that made a syphilitic cripple 'better' born than a healthy peasant. He was a child of the Revolution after all. So why was he lingering by her bed then, wanting her to notice his diligence?

'A deal, Madame,' he said. 'What will I get out of it?'

'That you will learn when I think you ready.'

'I don't know if I should trust you.'

'Perhaps you shouldn't, but you will.'

The countess was silent now, breathing hard. Talk, even that short, was too much of an effort.

'Try to eat more, Madame,' he said. Behind the burgundy curtain the musicians were taking their places. 'Mademoiselle Rosalia told me you had some beef tea today. That's commendable.'

'Is food all you can think about, Doctor?' the countess said, the reflected flame of the votive candle dancing in her beautiful eyes. She fixed them on him, narrowed like a cat as if she knew exactly what he had been thinking about, knew her own power over him. 'Is it because you are French?'

The countess and her entourage occupied but a fraction of the von Haefen's Berlin palace. The rest of the building was a maze of guest apartments, galleries, passages, and stairs. The palace, Rosalia had mentioned, was to be renovated, and the signs of the coming changes were all around. In one room the hunting trophies had been taken down and propped against the wall. In another, the walls had been stripped of old wallpaper and freshly plastered.

As long as the opium was working, Thomas reflected, he would be able to develop the routine he had longed for. Early morning: check on the progress of the night.

Then breakfast, followed by the monitoring of the haemorrhages and the level of pain. Same in the evening, combined with a review of possible remedies: applying calming lotions to the stomach area still irritated by Dr Horn's blisters and camomile compresses on the eyelids. Watching for the first signs of bedsores. But here, he was ready to concede, Rosalia was most capable on her own. As long as the opium worked, he would have time to go to the Graf's library and do some reading. Find some accounts of America, perhaps.

Passing the vestibule on the way to the library he saw that it was raining heavily, streams lashing on the windowpane. Dampness in the air would flare up in rheumatic joints and old wounds. His own knee had reminded him of it already.

The maiden fair
Through the forest went
Evil she muttered
Roots she extracted
The moon she stole
The sun she ate. . .

Pietka's voice reached him from downstairs. It had been Rosalia who offered this translation a few days ago, but it was fixed in his memory. The groom was playing his bandura again to the amusement of the fat cook whom Thomas had caught adding pearls and gold coins to the broth she was making for the countess. 'It's an old cure,' she said and gave him a defiant look daring him to forbid it.

Thomas liked the library. He liked this big, rectangular room lined from floor to ceiling with mahogany shelves, decorated with portraits of ruddy men who must have preferred the pleasures of the flesh to the dusty volumes they were now forced to look at. Many of the shelves were empty; the Graf must have moved his favourite books to the Potsdam palace. Thomas took the thick, leather-bound volumes off the shelves, touched their spines, ran his fingers over the gilt-edged pages, letters stamped with pale gold. Rousseau, Diderot, Voltaire. Right next to them, Locke's *Essay Concerning Human Understanding*. Cervantes, Racine, Molière; he had read them all in his student days, in the cold garret smelling of rats and faeces. Then the old maps of the world with their compass roses, the holy cross marking the east.

On the top shelf he found Marquis de Sade's *Justine*, *Juliette*, and *The 120 Days of Sodom*. Beside them, *Venus in the Cloister, or the Nun in her Nightdress*, *The Bordello or John the Fucker Debauched*. Published, he noted with a wry smile, 'At Incunt, c/o Widow Big Mound's.'

Thomas was not surprised. Why would generations of Prussian Grafs be any different to French aristocrats? Dr Brown did have a point. Indulgence, after all, was the direct result of over stimulation, bringing the weakening of the desired effect and the need for more stimuli. He had seen men vomit black from overdosing on *pastilles à la Richelieu*, candies laced with Spanish fly that promised to make them potent.

The rain had stopped. Through the library window he saw gardeners raking wet leaves and pruning shrubs. Thomas resumed his search through the shelves. Goethe's *Die Leiden des junger Werthers*, he had read some time ago in English, the story of an artist who kills himself because he is in love with a woman engaged to someone else. In its time, he recalled, the book had caused a sensation. A small army of men in blue coats and yellow breeches plunged into self-induced states of melancholy and blamed it all on the book. He used to wonder why.

Feeling a draught coming from underneath one of the

shelves, Thomas wondered if the shelf might be a hidden door, like the one his father showed him in Marquis de Londe's palace. Removing a few books, he found a lever, and after a shrill squeak, the shelf gave in, revealing a small, octagonal chamber with marble floors, slightly on an angle, sloping toward a gutter that ran around it.

In the semi-darkness he saw that most of the windows had been nailed shut, but he managed to open one, letting in enough light to see the paintings on the walls. The Rape of the Sabines, Susanna and the Elders, Leda and the Swan. Beside the paintings there were large, gilded mirrors, from the ceiling right to the marble floor, in the rich rococo frames of the last century. The room was cold and smelled of mice. The door leading to it, the backside of the library shelf, was well padded and covered with black leather. Two scarlet ottomans stood in the middle of the room, beside them a rack with whips. Cane whips and cat-o'-nine-tails that Thomas remembered seeing in the Marquis de Londe's collection. His had been made of hemp, the ones here of iron and brass.

A Parisian tribunal would have made a great deal of his discovery. At the Marquis de Londe's trial a metal chair was offered as evidence. 'A rape chair,' the prosecutor said. One of the men who had brought it in, tall and very thin, was asked to demonstrate how it worked. Sitting down on it, his body triggered a mechanism that clasped him in a grip, putting him in a horizontal position and spreading his legs.

Thomas took one last look at the secret chamber of the von Haefen palace, the whips, the red ottomans, the paintings covered with a thick layer of dust. He left the room, closing the padded door behind him, making sure he had secured the lever and covered it with books.

Sophie

She has new bruises on her wrists where he has grasped her. In Russia she often hears of men who could wrestle bears: Prince Potemkin is one of them. His seeing eye takes on a strange brightness as if he has been drinking, but there is no wine or spirit on his breath. 'He is mad,' someone whispers behind her. 'If you cross him, the Prince of Taurida will strangle you with his bare hands.'

Once he told her he would kill her, if she deceived him. That her cuckolded husband would not touch her, he was sure. 'I've brought that miserable de Witt here,' he told her, 'I opened a chest filled with jewels, and I said, "Choose, *batushka*! You can have whatever you ask me for, or you can have Sophie."'

He is my wife's friend, Joseph insists to everyone – most generous, a benefactor. Her eyes he avoids, trying to make himself invisible. If he does not move, perhaps nothing will change.

She has lost her balance. Even with her eyes closed she can see her prince. With her whole body, she can sense the moment just before he enters the room or the moment before he decides to leave.

Once he took a knife and made a cut on her thigh, and then another, like notches on a musket for slain enemies. He smeared her blood on her thighs and then, with his bloodied fingers, he smeared his own lips.

'Swear,' he said. She swore on the Virgin Mary that she would never betray him. She knelt in front of the holy icon and prayed aloud, begging the Holy Virgin to bear witness to her love. Then the touch of his hands on her cheeks was gentle and soothing.

'Look at them,' he said and placed his hands in front of her eyes. She looked at his big red palms, veins criss-crossing under his skin.

'What do you see?'

'The hands of my lord and master,' she replied.

Her meekness pleased him for a moment, but then he shook his head. This was not what he wanted to hear.

'Kiss them,' he ordered, and she pressed his hands to her lips, thinking he should be bled for his cheeks were too red.

'You have just kissed the hands of the man who shall one day wear the crown of Poland,' he said. 'There are no limits to what my will can achieve. No one can stop me. The Empress has already given Poland to one of her lovers. Now she will give it to me. All I have to do is ask.'

He squeezed her hands until the joints cracked, piercing her with his eyes, but she did not flinch.

'I'll be your king,' he said. 'And you might be queen.'

It is his arrogance that weakens her, his absolute absorption in his own needs. His confidence that nothing will ever be withheld from him, that he could change the destiny of men and nations. He never cares if he pleases her or not, and she doesn't know how to defend herself from him. One moment he is hurting her, another he is falling at her feet, begging her to forgive him for his harshness.

What is happening to her? Once she preferred sure bets in matters of survival. Once she vowed no man would deceive her again.

If only Mana were alive. Her mother, a shadow in her memory, a touch of her hands wiping the sweat off her brow, a gentle kiss on her forehead. But it's too late now. She is dead and buried in Istanbul cemetery, next to her father. *I pray for your happiness everyday, thanking the Lord that He has kept you in His care.*

'*Ma belle Phanariote*, were you really a Sultan's odalisque?'

'Perhaps.'

'Is it true that the Sultan is the only man in the Porte who can see every woman unveiled?'

'Yes.'

'You are the most intriguing of women. A minx.'

'You always say this.'

'I sometimes say this.'

'What is intriguing about me?'

'A feeling that these beautiful eyes can see right into my heart.'

'I'm a quick pupil, my Prince, and I have always had excellent teachers.'

She bends over him and caresses his hair, the nape of his neck. Laughing, he catches her in his arms and pulls her down onto the floor. He frees her breasts from the corset. The shiver of desire rushing through her body gives her strength to reach out and stroke him.

'What is it that you see?'

A spoilt child who will never be happy with what he gets, she wishes to say. 'A man who always gets what he wants,' she says.

'Liar.'

His arms tense as he rises over her. Anger is erupting again, a fit of passion carelessly triggered. Like an avalanche called into life by a scream.

She softens her body like a kitten before a fall. He has struck her before. He loosened a tooth in her jaw, drew blood.

'Does it hurt?' he asks with a fiendish smile, his hands diving inside her, tearing at her womb. She screams.

'You like it, don't you?'

She shakes her head.

'Liar,' he says. 'This is what your secret is. You have never said a word of truth in your life.'

She nods her head. Nods it again and again.

'And now?' he asks. A dark threat in his voice makes her skin tingle. It sends her somewhere soft and dark, like a waterfall pulling her with it into its depths.

She screams again. But he is kissing her now, her Russian bear. Biting at her lips, her neck, squeezing her breasts.

This moment frozen in time rouses her out of complaisance. It brings her right to the edge of a precipice and forces her to look down into the darkness, the void. It makes her stare death in the face and not fear it.

In the Taurida palace, her prince falls asleep on the carpet. He is so big that Sergey has to come with three other footmen to carry him to bed. When the footmen leave, she takes a handful of jewels from the jar he keeps next to his bed and slips them into the pocket in the folds of her dress. Her petticoats are ruined, she thinks, and so are her silk stockings. Her lover is breathing hard, snoring and moaning in his sleep. The name he mutters is not hers. A bear skin has slipped off him, and she lifts it from the floor and covers him before she leaves.

In the end it is death that puts an end to her folly. Death that lays its claim on her lover's body. In Jassy, where she has followed him, in the same headquarters where he celebrated the fall of the Turkish fortress of Ismail.

'I'm going to die soon,' the Prince of Taurida tells her. 'I'm so tired.'

He is fifty-two years old. He has defeated the Turks and on good days he still makes grand plans for the future. They have just come back from St Petersburg where Catherine, his Empress, gave balls and festivities in his honour. Where, to please him, she presented Madame de Witt with a pair of diamond earrings and a bale of fabric for her new wardrobe.

'You won't die,' she says. Only yesterday he refused to send for her. When she came anyway, Countess Branicka's carriage was already there in the courtyard, so she did not go in. She won't mention it, though. Today is another day. Better. Brighter.

'I'm so heavy,' he complains. 'The earth is calling me.'

He kisses her on the lips. 'You'll have to look for your king elsewhere, *ma belle Phanariote*.'

She looks at his bloated face, the livid shadows under his eyes. She kisses his hand, drenched in perfume. On her way in she has overheard the servants going over orders for the Prince's meal: ham, salted goose and three chickens, *kvas*, wine, and vodka to drink and more perfume to drown the sweat.

1791 is the year of change. The kind of change she cannot ignore.

Catherine, the Prince tells her, is watching the Poles with growing annoyance. The partition of 1772 turned out to be a lesson lost. Revolt is brewing again. Revolt against Russian influence. There will be no more royal elections. In the new Polish constitution the throne has been made hereditary to eliminate the vying for power; *liberum veto* has also been abolished, no longer could one noble veto a bill. The King is stronger now, the Cities Act has enfranchised many townsmen. Peasants may have remained serfs, but are now under the state's protection and complete freedom has been granted to all immigrants who return to Poland, which means that any peasant from the partitioned areas could, by escaping to Poland, become a free man. Catherine of Russia has written to him: 'How dare they alter the form of government that I guaranteed?'

'Listen, *ma belle Phanariote*,' the Prince of Taurida whispers. 'This is the beginning of the end. Soon your beautiful eyes will see the end of Poland.'

She doesn't understand.

He tells her that the Polish *Sejm* has changed the basis of the voting system to limit the powers of the nobles, to strengthen the cities. All to shake off the alliance with Russia. To encourage the French disease, the Jacobin revolutionary fever that will not stop until all monarchs are beheaded. Poland is sick, he tells her, and has to be quarantined. For the sake of the European future, the disease has to be stamped out. Eradicated. This is what he keeps telling his Empress to do, but she is tarrying.

Sophie has heard that triumphal arches have been raised in front of the Royal Castle in Warsaw; that public balls are given to celebrate the new constitution, a hope for a better future – for a stronger Poland able to defend its borders, a Poland free from Russian meddling; that the crowds in Warsaw cheer, 'The Nation with the King, The King with the Nation.'

She has heard that the whole world is in awe of the Polish reforms. *Homme-roi* the poets call the King. Polish morning dress has become fashionable in New York. *Happy prince*, Edmund Burke has written, *Happy people, if they know how to proceed as they have begun.*

The whole world, Prince Potemkin says, is filled with deluded fools who will forget the word Poland as soon as it is wiped from the map of Europe. He shows her the dispatch from his Tsarina. Catherine of Russia orders her general to prepare for an invasion.

His face is flushed with blood.

He won't die, she thinks. He cannot die. Not him. Nothing matters any more: Poland, Russia, revolts, wars. For him she would do anything. Her knuckles are white with pressure. She is biting her fingers until she draws blood. She prays and cries and makes wild offerings of penance and sacrifice. She will lay in front of the holy icon for the whole night, she will sell her jewels and give all the money to the poor.

'You have to make your choice, *ma belle*,' he says, squeezing her hand painfully tight. 'Countries are like men. You leave one to go with another. Will you side with us or them? Russians or Poles?'

She is scared of her own thoughts. She is not ready for her own conclusions.

It is Joseph who tells her the tragic news. Prince Potemkin, their dear generous friend did not want to trouble her with his pain. This is why he did not send for her on the last morning of his life. He was noble to the end.

The Prince woke up tired – Countess Branicka has told the story of this last morning – too dizzy to stand up unsupported. She was with him, when he asked to be driven to the country and when he ordered the carriage to stop. His Cossacks carried him from his carriage. He said that his bowels felt as if they were filled with liquid lead.

He didn't want to be with me, Sophie thinks. He chose her, instead.

She wants to tell Joseph to stop, to go away and leave her alone, but she cannot *not* know.

Once out in the field, the Prince of Taurida asked for his bedding to be placed on the ground. Countess Branicka was holding his hand. She knew it was the end. No one had to tell her. Tears were streaming down her cheeks, tears the Prince tried not to notice. He tried to say something, but death was quicker.

'Enough,' Sophie screams.

'I'm sorry, darling,' Joseph says. This is why she has begun to hate him. For his frightened look, shifting gaze, the flutter of his eyelids. For the declarations that make him the butt of jokes. *The Prince is not my wife's lover but just a friend because, if he was her lover, I would break any connection with him.* She hates him at this very moment for the obvious hope he still has that she will come back to him for consolation. For the hope that his ruses have worked. That he has withstood her passion – he will never call it love – her folly. That he has weathered the storm and could now breathe out with relief.

How mistaken he is. How wrong. She has had enough of this marriage, this miserable comedy. She has had enough. Enough.

Countess Branicka is wearing black. She repeats the story of Prince Potemkin's death over and over again. She has written up her account for the Empress, with a few embellishments, of course. It was Catherine's name, the Prince tried to say before death stopped him.

There is no place for Comtesse de Witt in this narrative.

In Jassy, the doctors who open Prince Potemkin's body find the innards awash with bilious fluid. The stench is such that even embalming cannot get rid of it.

Sophie cries so much that she has no more tears left.

Death, she thinks, can be a release.

When a door closes, a window is opened somewhere.

Rosalia

'Mademoiselle Rosalia. I hope I'm not intruding.'

Dr Bolecki assured her that he had not abandoned his patient, in spite of his unconditional trust in Doctor Lafleur's skills. As much as his practice allowed it, he was going to continue his visits to Graf von Haefen's palace. After all he might have a thing or two to learn from his esteemed colleague. As he sat down beside her, she smelled cigar smoke and coffee. His shapely hands rested on his lap.

'I'm glad to see you resting,' he said.

'It's just for a short while. The countess is still asleep.'

Doctor Bolecki had brought her a book from his own library. A book of Polish folk songs simple as the people who composed them, but beautiful nevertheless. It used to be his daughter's favourite. The daughter he had hoped would marry and give him grandchildren, but then she chose God instead. Perhaps it might lift Rosalia's heart too, bring her some respite.

'Thank you,' she said.

'Not at all, the pleasure is mine,' he said, bowing slightly.

He wanted to tell her something that might amuse her. Only the day before he had a most curious visit. A young man, a poet, had come to see him. The young man had arrived in Berlin from Göttingen over a year before, where he had suffered the pangs of unrequited love. 'What a surprise to be referred to a Polish doctor,' he had said. 'By Graf von Haefen himself.'

The young man was remarkable. Germans, he said, were far too willing to look at Poles through their own spectacles and find them wanting, but he respected the Polish nation for its struggle.

'Was it why the young man came to see you?' she asked. It pleased her that Doctor Bolecki smiled.

'He came to ask me to cure his headaches. They were so strong that they were splitting his head.'

The pain was like liquid lead streaming inside his head. His eyes were also prone to infections, which was particularly unfortunate for a poet and a student of law. But anyway, he was digressing, this was not why he was telling her the story. For the young man had spent his whole visit praising the charm of Polish women. He called them *the altarpieces of beauty, the angels of the earth whose gazelle eyes made heaven out of earth.*

'I thought he had suffered from the pangs of love in Göttingen,' Rosalia said tartly.

'What better way to cure a love-sick heart?'

She laughed.

He laughed too.

'If you allow me to express interest in your fate, Mademoiselle,' Doctor Bolecki continued after a short pause. 'I'd like to ask what you will do after . . .' He made an uneasy gesture as if he wanted to encompass the countess, her illness and her position in this household.

'I don't like to think about it,' she said slowly. 'It's not the first time my life will have turned upside down.'

'Forgive me,' he said, rising and kissing her hand. 'I shouldn't have asked. It's too soon. All I want is to know you will not disappear from my life.'

'I'm not an apparition, Doctor. I don't turn into thin air.'

'Is that a promise?'

'It's the truth.'

'In that case I should be satisfied.' His voice was solemn, too solemn perhaps, she thought. It made her uneasy, but also it flattered and pleased her. As if his seriousness proved something, made something whole again.

She cast her eyes down to the floor, watching the patterns of the wooden mosaic, the chessboard of light and dark squares. Then the tassels on the curtain caught her attention, tempting her to play with them the way she did when she was a child.

He told her that he worked too hard because he found the emptiness of his house too hard to bear. He told her of his visits to Mietskaserne, the former barracks of North Berlin were now converted into housing: 2500 people lived in 400 rooms, sharing just a few privies outside. Two families to each tiny room which the women put a cord across and hung their washing on. They all, even the children, worked in factories or the iron foundry. Their pockmarked faces were pale. Consumption and scurvy were rife.

'Old dreams, Mademoiselle, of freedom for all men,' he sighed. 'Where are they now?'

He is a good man, she thought. A man who will not disappoint me.

Sophie

It is 1791, in the Moldavian capital of Jassy where the Russian army is savouring its victory over Turkey and are about to sign a treaty with the Porte, trouble is brewing.

The Polish magnates have arrived to ask for Russian help. As her prince predicted, while the new constitution may be hailed in Warsaw as a victory for the new Polish spirit, a manifestation of Polish political independence, not everyone is happy with the reforms. Those who oppose them point out that, with Prussia and Austria at the ready, separating the Polish cause from the Russian is folly. Wouldn't it be better to seek help from our Slavic brothers, they ask. They call the King misguided and fooled by the radicals; claim that he has abolished *aurea libertas*, the golden freedom of the Polish nobles, the quintessence of the Polish Commonwealth, giving power to burghers and Jews. How could that, they ask, strengthen Poland?

Count Felix Potocki, Count Seweryn Branicki and Count Franciszek Rzewuski have come all the way to Jassy to seek out Prince Potemkin's help in ending the Polish folly. In Warsaw, they are called traitors to the Polish cause. Here in Jassy, they are the realists, the saviours.

'A political faction,' de Witt calls them. Since the Prince's death she has come to call him de Witt in her thoughts: Joseph suddenly seems too intimate. De Witt thinks that the Polish magnates are right. He too spews indignation about the new constitution, the reforms and the dreams of independence. The King has always been an impractical fool, a builder of ruins.

He has learnt a new phrase 'legalising injustice' and he repeats it *ad nauseam*. The new constitution is legalising injustice. Taking rights away from the nobles is legalising injustice – allowing the contagion of Plunder and Equality to spread.

She tells him that he hates the King because he is jealous. She tells him that she cannot stand him near her; that only her son's presence stops her from packing her things and leaving.

'Potocki has come to see Prince Potemkin,' de Witt smiles, 'but now he'll attend his funeral. If he came a bit earlier, he would have begged you to help him. Then our footman could've told him we were not at home.'

Does he really think she wants to hear it?

The constant dreams in which she seeks consolation disappoint her. When she wakes up, only fragments remain. Someone's hand over her mouth, stopping her screaming, the sound of a bucket falling down a well with a loud splash.

'Let's go home,' de Witt says. 'There is nothing for us here.'

He may think that the magnates are right, but he doesn't like to take sides. It is always better to wait through times like that, hedge your bets. She would have agreed with him at other times, but now his mere presence in the same room chafes her. The thought of returning to Kamieniec is enough to make her slam the door in his face.

In the salons of Jassy, everyone has something to say about the Polish question. In Warsaw, the talk is all of strengthening the army, rebuilding the economy, enriching the cities, regaining the long lost powers but here, in Jassy, she hears that according to the new constitution, any burgher can now claim equity with a noble. Isn't that a harbinger of the same movement that now holds France in its deadly grip? The French King was stopped on his way to Varenne and returned to Paris, a prisoner of the common man. What will come next? The public hangings of aristocrats? Peasants slashing the throats of their betters as they did in Uman?

You'll have to choose, her Prince had told her. Are you with the Russians or with the Poles?

'If only it were that simple,' Count Potocki says when she asks him the same question. The balls have all been cancelled in mourning for the Prince, but the salons of Jassy are full. Count Bezrobodko has taken over Potemkin's place, and holds court every day. And in his residence, Madame de Witt is a cherished guest.

Count Felix Potocki's estate extends over half of Polish Ukraine, a million and a half hectares of land and 130,000 serfs, his yearly profits around three million Polish *złotys*. She hasn't had to do anything to attract his attention. His eyes haven't left her face.

Her question would be simple, Count Potocki tells her, if the reforms had the slightest chance of accomplishing what they promised. But they are bound to fail and will plunge Poland into more chaos. Isn't it better to stop it all now, before it is too late, to salvage what can still be salvaged?

'Let me put your question in a different way,' the Count says. 'Would you rather side with the Russians or the Prussians? Which is the surer bet for the future of Poland?'

'You have no doubt that the reforms will fail?'

'None whatsoever. I know my countrymen. I know my king.'

Do I want him, she thinks. She is thirty-one and, she hears, more beautiful then ever. If she doubts that, no one knows. Beauty is not merely in the smoothness of skin. Smitten, drunk with hope, Count Potocki no longer thinks of pride.

She recalls his face that day he stepped into the carriage in the courtyard of the Krystynopol palace. The palace is now sold, for Count Potocki has a new residence in Tulchin. Here is the Count too grand to receive Madame de Witt. This could be her triumph, if she cared. If it mattered in the least.

'My wife,' he says, his cheeks flushed, 'is busy with her own life. We have *never* agreed on most important matters.'

She could tell him that it didn't matter. That she has forgotten all about the day when the Potockis were showing Madame de Witt her proper place in the world. She doesn't.

Count Felix Potocki can't stop following her around. In every fibre of her body she can feel his desire. For him there is no one but her in this room. He hears nothing, sees nothing, understands nothing. The powdered wig lightens his face, giving him an innocent air, but there is a smell of unease around him. He is patient, waiting for the right moment to approach her again. She walks away, quickly.

On 12th October her little Jan will be ten. She had planned a lavish celebration, but after Prince Potemkin's death, she will have to settle for a little private party; twenty guests, no more; red velvet chairs and napkins. She will raise a toast to him, tell him he has been her hope and her happiness. Her only happiness.

What do you want to have most of all, she asked him. He said: a brother.

She held him to her heart and buried her face in his hair, breathing in the wood smoke and saddle soap for he has been to the stables again. She too would like another child. Children are the greatest treasures, Mana would have said. May you be blessed with many.

The room is too hot. A waiter passes by with a tray, and she motions him to stop. She picks a glass of champagne. It is cold, a mist of frost hanging to the outside of the glass.

Letters that come from Paris are full of foreboding. *A la lanterne*, the mob cries at the sight of a carriage. It has become unwise to go out, to dress up, to remind the world of one's existence. Diane de Polignac has been hinting at her desire to come to Poland, hoping for a hospitable home where she could wait through the worst of times. Perhaps, my dear friend, you could help? Princess de Lamballe, however, refuses any suggestion of leaving the Queen's side.

She sees Count Potocki make a few steps in her direction. She looks straight at him, and then turns on her heel and leaves the room, running away as if it were his presence that scared her.

Joseph is still up when the carriage brings her home. There is the sharp smell of vodka on his breath. She slams the door of her bedroom and sprays perfume everywhere. The curtains, her pillows, her hands, her hair. Attar of roses.

The last gift from her prince.

'Oh, Madame,' her French maid, Paulette, says in the morning. 'The flowers are so beautiful. But alas there is no card.' But then she whispers, 'Sergey says he has seen the men who delivered them. They were wearing the Potocki livery.'

The flowers have filled up the living room and her boudoir. Roses, daffodils, lilies, orchids: crimson roses; white lilies, tulips of a beauty she has not seen before. He must have sent to his own greenhouses in Tulchin.

She picks one rose from the bouquet and pins it in her hair. A red rose from the most beautiful bouquet. Paulette hands her the Venetian drops. One drop enlarges the irises, adds fire and tenderness to her eyes.

She may be wearing his rose in her hair, but she still avoids the count that evening. As soon as she sees him take a step toward her, she turns away to someone else.

If he is close enough to hear what she is talking about, she changes the conversation from politics to her memories of the Prince. 'He was like a father to me,' she says, fanning her face. 'I'll never forget him. Nothing else matters, in the face of death. No dreams. No desires.'

After supper, she lets herself be persuaded to sing, and for her little recital she selects a Greek love song. The song, she explains, is about a beautiful Greek girl waiting for her long-lost lover, waiting in vain, her heart bleeding. As she sings, she holds her hand to her heart.

The song fills her eyes with tears. When her audience applauds and asks for more she excuses herself and asks to be taken home.

'My heart,' she says, looking right into Count Felix's eyes, 'cannot forget its loss that easily.'

Thomas

When he decided to prolong his stay in Berlin, Thomas had hoped he and Ignacy would go back to the carefree intimacy they once enjoyed, but now his own heart insisted on recalling his friend's limitations. Both real and imaginary, Thomas was honest enough to admit. For why should he suddenly find his friend's cheerfulness annoying. Or his whistling. Or the sudden care Ignacy put into tying of his cravat, the amount of starch in his collars, his insistence on walking rather than taking the carriage for it made the blood flow faster.

They had met at the entrance of Nicolaikirche and, after a quick stroll through the narrow streets, settled into a small corner tavern, right behind the Castle Bridge. The thick wooden table was covered with carved initials. *H.P. for W.H.* framed in a heart was pierced with an arrow.

'Soldiers who are brought back away from the battlefield, Thomas, tend to lose their sanity. We have seen that often, haven't we? But the ones who are kept near the sound of cannon fire, no matter how severe their wounds, stay sane. I think that this is no coincidence. As long as we still have a hope of fighting back, we will survive. I'm going back to Poland. To fight back.'

'We shall drink to that, then,' Thomas said and motioned to the waitress at the empty table in front of them.

'Europe, Thomas, is not a monster. We are not all madmen.'

Ignacy was right, chastising him like that. Despite all his caution and his talk of reason, Thomas realised that he was falling into the old trap of the dismissal of what is left behind, the fallacy of all nomads. If what was to come must be better, then what we leave behind must be made hurtful or worthless.

A fat waitress with a ruddy face placing tankards of beer in front of them winked at him and bared her blackened teeth. There was a certain lightness about Ignacy that evening, a playfulness even, in his refusal to pick up a fight, and it was melting Thomas's resentment. Ignacy patted him on the back.

'Remember that song we used to sing?'

> Release me from the dry concern
> Of listening to their moaning
> And from your votary ever turn
> Old dames with colic groaning.

In Paris, in their student days, they used to walk together at night, arm in arm, singing this song. They called themselves Napoleon's sons. After all, if it hadn't been for Napoleon, they reasoned, neither of them would have become a medical student. When was the last time they had sung together like this?

'Come on, Thomas. You haven't forgotten, have you?'

No, he had not forgotten. His voice was rasping and off tune at first but soon they were singing in unison:

> For patients, oh, to me impart
> The gay the young, the witty;
> Such as may interest the heart.
> This prayer, oh, grant in pity!

The small tavern was full of men, gesticulating wildly, Greek volunteers, Ignacy said. It was like fever, spreading through the delirious body. 'Today it is the baker's apprentice, Thomas. Tomorrow, the cobbler's son.'

Lieutenants passed themselves up for colonels. Colonels for generals. Committees had sprung in every German city, it seemed, collecting funds for the descendants of the brave and honourable Greeks, the fathers of European civilisation.

'Just listen,' Ignacy said.

One of the men, a short, pimply fellow, had climbed onto the bench. 'Nature has set limits to the aspirations of other men, but not those of the Greeks.' The man spoke in a booming voice, surprising in someone of such small stature. 'The Greeks were not in the past and are not now subject to the laws of nature.'

Another of the group, his mop of curly brown hair like a Cossack hat, was raising a pitcher of beer shaped like a riding boot and intoning a song. One by one his companions joined in, and then he took a deep draught and passed the boot on to his neighbour. The pitcher was so shaped that once half-empty the beer would flow with an unpredictable force, spilling onto beards and faces, causing much amusement and jostling.

'Small armies of men trek to Marseilles,' Ignacy said, 'from whence these committees hire ships to transport them to Greece.'

'Oh, but this is sheer madness, Ignacy. I bet they are

an absolute nuisance when they actually arrive. The Greeks must think them mad.'

'Human beings have to dream, Thomas. Without such foolishness we would all remain slaves.'

The group of men burst into laughter. The boot was working.

'I choose to dream too, Thomas. I too have hopes for my country, for myself. Hopes other men would call foolish.'

Something in Ignacy's voice warned him not to interrupt.

'Sometimes not stopping to fight – no matter how hopeless the struggle – is all that matters, Thomas,' Ignacy concluded. 'We are doctors. We've seen it often enough.'

They sat in silence watching the merriment of their neighbours, sipping their beers until the tankards were empty. Then they rose to leave. The afternoon was cold, but the sky was clear. If there were enough moonlight tonight, the street lamps would not be lit.

'What do you think, Thomas,' Ignacy said as they reached the end of the street. 'Am I too old to marry again? To have another child. Or two.'

'Not too old for a battalion.'

'A whole army.'

'If you only wish.'

'Mademoiselle Rosalia, Thomas. I have reasons to believe I'll not be refused.'

Since Thomas could not say that the declaration came as a surprise, he decided that it was the abruptness of Ignacy's words that he found annoying.

'So soon?'

'I'm not that young anymore,' Ignacy laughed. 'I don't think I can wait. There is so much we share. A common struggle. A common dream. Her father gave his life for Poland and she hasn't forgotten it. Do you think I'm foolish?'

'No,' Thomas said. 'I don't think you are foolish at all.'

But Ignacy continued as if he hadn't heard him. There was his loneliness, the empty evenings he longed to fill with simple pleasures. With a good woman at his side, he would still be of use for many years. There could still be children. Past mistakes could be repaired. But most of all they would share the Polish struggle.

Silent, intensely wishing this talk to stop, Thomas counted his own steps, from one to ten, and then back again. He was still doing it when they walked off the Castle Bridge passing an empty carriage, a driver asleep on the dickey. Then, he stopped.

'This Herr Sertürner, Ignacy, the pharmacist you told me about. Hasn't he been doing something here with morphine?'

On that matter Ignacy was sceptical. There were rumours of course. Sertürner was not much respected in Germany. He had rubbed too many people the wrong way, he liked to pose as a misunderstood genius. The story was that Sertürner had taken morphine himself. 1.5 grains within forty-five minutes. The results had been disastrous. Reddening of the face and enhancement of the vital forces was soon followed by nausea, dullness in the head, then sharp stomach pains, followed by extreme palpitations. He had had to swallow strong vinegar to induce vomiting. 'Morphine is more like poison, if you ask me.'

'But it's the same thing as Derosne's salt. Remember that lecture he gave at the Societé de Pharmacie? Or almost the same.'

'You are not thinking of giving it to the countess, Thomas?'

'Magendie had some good results with it, using much smaller doses than Sertürner's though. One of his patients even called it "divine balsam". I've brought some with me from Paris.'

The sound of hymn-singing reached them from behind the shut doors of the Nicolaikirche.

'Anyway, my cautious friend,' Thomas continued, 'I don't think I have much choice. I still have opium, but it will not work for longer than a few days.'

Ignacy gave him a quick look, as if he were still checking the soundness of his decision. The hymn-singing had stopped.

Having bid good-afternoon to Ignacy, Thomas continued to the von Haefen's palace, to check on his patient before the end of the day. He might see Rosalia too, a thought that came before he could stop it. As he was passing its wrought-iron fence, Thomas ran his cane over the spikes until they rang.

'You are a fool, Thomas Lafleur,' he said to himself, crossing the courtyard. 'And you will die a fool.'

He could see her at Ignacy's side as a bride. Her hands healing the sick, bringing comfort to the young men in hospital beds. The daughter of a hero who would comfort them with the story of her own return from despair, of her doubts assuaged, of her devotion rewarded. For Ignacy would undoubtedly make a good husband. There was tenderness in his friend, that he had often seen. He had gratitude for moments of warmth, for companionship in a common cause. There was a strength in him, that would help her past all doubts.

It was then that he spotted Pietka combing the chestnut mare. The horse stood motionless, waiting for the next stroke of the brush.

'It's a warm afternoon,' Thomas said, stopping. The Cossack must have heard him speaking to himself for he was stifling a laugh.

'Yes, *varm.*' Pietka was chewing tobacco, his jaws moving.

'She like me touch her,' the groom laughed, pointing at the mare whose ears twitched in anticipation. 'Like woman. *Nyet?*'

'How would I know?' Thomas said, smiling, in spite of himself.

'You know not? You doctor?' Pietka was laughing again, showing blackened teeth. 'She like it. I like it. No true?'

'Yes,' Thomas had to concede. 'Of course,' he added, as Pietka's hand patted the mare's rump.

Sophie

The note that waits for her in the morning says: *I know the rose that has touched your hair, for once I held it to my lips.*

'Read your lessons to me,' she tells Jan and he reads her the story of King Sobieski who – in 1683 – defeated the Turks at the siege of Vienna. A Polish king who saved Europe from annihilation.

'What's annihilation?'

'It's when someone wants you dead, you and all your children – everyone you know.'

He ponders on the thought for a long time. 'Your father too?'

'Yes,' she says. 'Your father too.'

'Is this true?'

'Yes,' she says. 'This is true. I never lie to you.'

It's Prince Potemkin's money that has been paying for the tutor, the French governess, the pony, and the horse. De Witt shrugs whenever she mentions money. 'What else do you want. I've never had half of what this boy has had in his life.'

'And look at yourself now,' she answered, regretting it

at once. If he heard them, Jan would frown his forehead and give her a pained look.

'You don't really like Papa,' he asks. He does it often, she thinks. Saying something that makes her think he knows more than he ever lets on.

'No,' she says. She does tell him the truth.

'But why?'

'I cannot tell you.'

'Why?'

'Why don't you like cauliflower?'

'Because I don't like its smell.'

'Why don't you like its smell?'

'I don't know. I just don't like it.'

'See. You cannot tell me.'

'But Papa doesn't smell like cauliflower,' he says, and she laughs and blows him a kiss.

As Jan bends over his lesson, copying King Batory's story into his notebook, making each letter as even as the previous one, another note arrives.

That rose in your hair knew more happiness than I dare to dream of. You must forgive me for a past wrong, for I cannot forgive myself.

She writes back.

That rose touched the sorrow of my heart, but it did bring me consolation through its beauty. For that I am grateful.

'Come, Madame, please take a look,' Paulette says.

When she leans out of the window she sees a motionless carriage with the Potockis' crest, planted in the street like some strange animal, crouching in anticipation.

'Go and ask his Lordship what it is that he desires.'

Paulette comes back smiling, another bouquet of roses in her hands. And a beautiful English saddle for Jan, a birthday gift.

Just a small token I dare place at your feet without fearing you might reject it.

Olga

The rain had stopped. Outside, the late morning sun illuminated the edges of the grey clouds. For an instant the countess's younger daughter was tempted to throw the windows open, to feel the cold air penetrate deep into her lungs, chilling them to the point of shivering.

When little she had often prayed to be sick. Illness meant having Maman sit beside her bed and tell her stories of a poor slave girl who found an old oil lamp and rubbed it clean, thus releasing a genie who would fulfil all her wishes. To feel Maman's cool hand smoothing her forehead. To hear her turn away visitors, tell them she could not receive anyone at a time like that, could not go anywhere. Wake up in the middle of the night to see her mother asleep in the armchair by her bed, as if there were no one but the two of them, no other children, no servants capable of replacing her in her vigil.

'You cannot die,' Olga whispered, 'I won't let you.'

Her mother opened her eyes. Closed and opened them again.

'The frills,' she said. 'Around your collar, Olga. They look quite vulgar. I so much prefer smooth lace.'

'Yes, Maman.'

'And this dress, darling. You have a stain on your cuff.'

Her sister may have been older, but it was Olga who always knew which of her mother's friends was her lover. Knew it with her whole body, sensed it in her mother's smell, in the new edge to her voice, the catlike movements swifter than usual, rounded with grace. It was like spotting a false note in a piece she knew by heart; it required no effort. She just knew. She always knew, even when too little to understand what a man and a woman did when alone together.

She hated knowing it. She wanted to bang her fists against her mother, but all she could do was to hide the turmoil inside and wait. Wait for her mother's inevitable signs of indifference, her eyes fixed onto the ceiling, her hasty excuses.

Agaphya Ivanovna, the cook, had asked to see Olga, wringing her hands as she spoke. There were things the young mistress needed to be told about. A lot could be done to ease the countess's sufferings if *some* people around here listened. If *some* people did not think themselves better than they were. She would give her mistress cow's urine to drink, and mix a spoonful of cow's dung into it for good measure.

Dried and powdered bat could also be added to her drink, to give her blood more substance. She had known of a woman cured by such a drink, taken daily in the morning and at midnight – a mother of five who went on to have three more.

Goat's tallow was also good, almost as good as putting the skin of a cat on the hurting part, but the cat had to be skinned alive so it would take the pain away.

'Come closer, Olga. I want to see your face.'

'I'm right here, Maman.'

'There is a letter on the tray, from your sister. She is on her way.'

The letter had been sent a week ago, by a courier.

'When did it come?'

'Last night, I think.'

'You didn't tell me, why?'

'Rosalia says she might be here tomorrow. Or the day after. It's because of the baby. One cannot travel that fast with a baby.'

* * *

Her mother's eyes were closed again, her breathing shallow but even. In the corridor Olga could hear Rosalia's steps, determined, strong. In a moment the door will open, Olga thought, and she will come in. This Jewess, this stray, who had sneaked her way into her mother's heart.

Olga stood up and walked toward the bed, her body tensing in anticipation. The steps slowed down, and then turned away. Her mother groaned.

'I don't want to remember her like this,' she thought.

Through tears, Olga looked at her mother's face, the skin melted on the bones. 'This is how she will look in her coffin,' she thought and felt her throat contract and stiffen, as if she were choking.

Sophie

Count Felix Potocki is a shy man.

He comes up to her the next day, his hands trembling, eyes clouded. There is so much uncertainty in these eyes, she thinks. Curious in a man who commands so much. Not a handsome man. Lips too thin, eyes bulging. There is no surprise in him. She can foretell all his pronouncements, finish his thoughts for him. She does not like herself much these days. She feels detached, remote, as if what is closest to her did not exist. She is still sore, still hurting.

You'll have to look for your king elsewhere, ma belle Phanariote.

She thanks Count Potocki for his most thoughtful gift. Her son is delighted, she assures him. 'You know,' she says, 'how to find your way into a child's heart.'

'I try,' he says. 'I try very hard.'

Silence follows, awkward and sticky. He doesn't know what she thinks of him. Sometimes he is filled with hope, sometimes despair. He is still struggling for words; he doesn't know what to ask her about or what to tell her. If he were a fruit, she would feel him for ripeness. The image of it makes her smile.

'Am I that funny?' he asks.

She shakes her head.

'Why then?'

What made her laugh, she explains, is the memory of her son when he was still little. How he demanded a wooden ark so that he could put all the animals inside and save them from the flood. Once she caught him trying to pair an elephant with a lion. She protested that they wouldn't fit together. Oh, but *they* think it is a good idea, he had said.

'A smart boy. Your only one?'

'Yes,' she says with a sigh. 'My only one.'

He stops as if surprised at the turn of the conversation. A blush flashes on his cheeks and disappears.

'Our paths have crossed before,' he says. 'This is a sign.'

He reminds her that he was staying in Warsaw when she came there for the first time, that they exchanged a few words of introduction.

'Risking your wife's displeasure even then, I presume,' she says, unable to refuse herself this little victory.

'I blush at the memory of her bitterness, Madame. Your beauty is too much for a small heart.'

'How is her Ladyship?'

'I don't want to talk of her. Please.'

Seeing the pain in his eyes, she smiles.

'I'm sorry,' she says. 'My heart is not immune to bitterness either.'

Count Felix Potocki does not believe in coincidence. All life is interconnected, he tells her, all moments in which two souls come together have deep meaning. It may be hidden at the time, unrealised, but it is there. It offers a chance to touch the essence of existence.

His voice falters slightly when he talks of destiny and fate. God is the Great Engineer of human fate, sending us onto the checkerboard of life with instruments to help us in our journey. When fates cross, when circumstances bring two souls together, one has to bow one's head to the influence of the Grand Design of Life.

'How beautifully you speak,' she says. 'I've never thought of life in these terms.'

'Life or death,' he says. 'We have to choose which side we are on.'

'Life,' she says. 'I chose life.'

'But death is not to be dismissed, either. It frees a spirit and releases it from earthly obligations. There is peace in this release and the chance to forge new passages, make detours in the paths of life, surrender to new love.'

'How would I know if it is God and not the Devil who sends such temptations?'

'The Prince of Darkness cannot tempt with love. His domain is envy, shrewdness, cold calculations, and not the tenderness of the heart.'

'I believe you,' she says, and places her warm hand on his. '*Mon epilda.*'

'*Epilda?*'

'It's Greek,' she smiles. 'It means hope.'

He kisses her hand softly and places it on his heart. His lips tremble as he whispers her name. The pale, thin lips of a Potocki. If she plays her cards well, Countess Sophie Potocka sounds so much better than Madame de Witt. After all with money and influence marriages can be annulled. Josephine and Joseph might well find themselves in the same boat. Josephine and Joseph: another example of divine coincidence?

The thought makes her laugh aloud. Upstairs in her

bedroom her coffers are half filled with her dresses and shawls. The maid has been told to pack only the best.

'You make me so happy,' she answers the questioning look in Felix's eyes. 'The happiest I've been in a long time.'

'What if he doesn't marry you?' Joseph says, a tinge of sadness in his voice. Resigned sadness, but wistful still. 'What if his wife won't allow it?'

He knows that he has lost her. She has heard that he has taken to drinking and gambling but whenever she sees him he is always sober. She shrugs her shoulders.

'You are not my mother,' she says.

Joseph de Witt knows that marriages can be annulled. A good lawyer and well-paid witnesses can prove that Sophie Glavani was forced into an unwanted marriage. Forced at gunpoint, when she, a young virgin on her way from Istanbul to Warsaw, naïve in the ways of the world, accepted de Witt's hospitality at the Kamieniec fortress.

He will do whatever she wants, he assures her. He will swear whatever she wants him to swear. It is Josephine she should worry about. If she does not agree, what will happen to her then?

'Let me worry about that,' she says. For a brief moment she wants to take his hand in hers. Once he has agreed to let her go, her resentment evaporates. Her impatience with him, her anger. They have a son. A child they both love. A child Joseph promises to let her see whenever she wants. A child she can provide for better than he can.

She is not that sure of victory, but she will not let anyone see it. She tells him how generous Felix has been to Jan and to him. A hundred thousand roubles and a small estate in Ukraine is just the beginning.

'I can be a better friend than wife,' she says.

He nods and smiles, relieved in a way. In the past

whenever she threatened to leave him, he broke down and tearfully begged her to stay. Now he too has discovered that the anticipation of pain may be worse than the pain itself.

No, she will not tell him of her doubts. Of her feeling of want, like a wild, untamed cat, pacing the cage in which it is locked. Making hungry rounds in search of something that would make escape possible. She will not tell him that what she wants is never what she already has, that a dream made true ceases to soothe, that only the impossible has the power to entice.

Thomas

'Tell me something amusing, Doctor,' the countess asked.

'I'm not good at fashionable talk.'

'What makes you think it's fashionable talk that I want to hear?'

Another defeat, he thought amused.

He told her that at the battlefields, when there were not enough instruments and dressings for the wounds, the patients survived more often than in hospital. The human body, left to itself, would often heal. There was a force in all living beings, a powerful force. For a long time he had suspected that many cures prescribed by him and his learned colleagues were nothing but obstruction. The only way to save the best of humanity was to give it space and time to develop according to nature.

'But this force won't help me,' she said.

'Not any more. It has carried you until now, though. It has made your life possible.'

'You are telling me to be grateful for the life I have had.'

'In a way,' he conceded. 'I'm not boring you, Madame?'

'On the contrary. You make a lot of things easier. Tell me more.'

He told her of his one-time mentor, Corvisart, dazzling his students with his diagnoses. At the bedside of a wounded soldier, Corvisart lifted the dressing of the wound, touched its edges and smelled its pus. 'Look and observe,' he said. Then he placed his hand on the patient's chest to feel the heart beat and asked all his interns to follow his example. 'What do you feel?' he asked them, and one by one they described the slight purring, like that of a cat. 'The mitral valve will not open completely, gentlemen. It's his heart that'll kill him,' Corvisart said. 'Not the wound.'

'Have you felt it, too?' the countess asked.

'Yes, but I didn't know then what it meant.'

'And was he right?'

'He was right. Corvisart was always right,' he said. He had loved proving it to them in the operating theatre, that old magic trick the opening of the heart to reveal its faulty valve.

'What does it?' she asked. 'What damages the heart?'

'Emotions,' Thomas said. 'Passions, fits of anger, fear, distress at the horrible times we've all had our share of.' His voice rose, and he almost forgot he was not lecturing his students.

'Like a criminal killed by the unexpected news of a pardon, or a lover struck by the paroxysm of passion.'

She lay motionless, considering his words.

'How do you cure a sick heart, then?'

'I would let time heal it. Unlike some of my mentors I don't think we, doctors, are actually doing that much good. I try not to harm. I amputate a shattered limb to prevent gangrene, if I still can. I remove a tumour to stop it from spreading. I leave the rest to *vis medicatrix natura*, the healing power of nature. Corvisart, of course, would not agree.'

'So what would Napoleon's great doctor have told me?'

'That nature doesn't heal. That life brings about its own end and the psyche can damage the soma. He would have told you to think of the cases in which nostalgia brings about the diminishing of life force. He would have told you to use all the means at your disposal to force the sadness out of your heart.'

She laughed.

'And you don't think he could be right?'

Sophie

She has gambled and lost. When thoughts like this come, she doesn't know how to defend herself from them.

She has been Felix's mistress for two years. Three months ago, in April of 1793, she gave birth to a boy, Konstantin, whom she calls Kotula. Unlike Jan who cried often when he was a baby, this son of hers watches everything in silence, his eyes full of calm inquiry. Now she is pregnant again.

He has failed her, Felix says. She left her husband for a man who has been declared a disgrace to his country; whose wife laughs at his requests for the annulment of their marriage, telling him that Madame de Witt can be his whore if she wishes, and bear him even more bastards, but that there will be only one Countess Potocka at his side.

In Poland, or what is left of it, Felix Potocki is called a traitor and a fool. Right after that fateful trip to Jassy when he fell in love with her, the Russian Empress summoned him to St Petersburg. Fanning his anger at the King she convinced him that he should lead a confederacy against the reforms and the new constitution. A confederacy of Targowica, named after one of Potocki's towns, would then ask Catherine of Russia for help to restore the old Poland, perhaps even make him its next King.

Catherine of Russia outwitted him.

As Felix predicted, the Polish troops were no match for a hundred thousand Russian soldiers, but the Empress did not intend to share her victory with anyone. All promises were forgotten, all assurances abandoned. Instead of the restoration of the old Poland, there was another partition, and there would be no more Polish kings. When he arrived in St Petersburg to protest, the Empress stomped her foot and reminded Count Potocki that his own estates were now part of Russia and that his loyalty was to her. He still doesn't want to talk about it.

A traitor and his whore, the pamphlets call Count Potocki and his mistress. *The infernal pair*.

They move from one rented palace to another. She has already lived in Cherson, Lvov, Grodno, and Minsk. They do not dare go to Warsaw even for the shortest of trips after an old man forced his way into their carriage there. 'Get out of Poland, you and your whore,' he yelled. The footman stopped him, but not before the man spat full in Felix's face.

'Do you still love me?' Felix asks.

'You are all I've got,' she says.

It is at night that Felix wakes up screaming. He won't tell her his dreams but he still believes in the power of confession. 'I never thought it would end like this,' he whispers. He means the Russian invasion, the partition. 'All I wanted was to stop the King, to defend our freedom.'

He asks if she believes him.

'Yes,' she says. 'I believe you.'

'Will I be punished?' he asks.

She holds him in her arms. In the nursery, Kotula is fast asleep. He is a quiet, sweet child, a little angel. For a moment, before she makes the thought vanish, she thinks of a rabbit in a dog's mouth, its limp body carried so gently the teeth do not break the skin. She wishes for a daughter now that she could teach to walk like a cat. Jan has written that his tutors are very pleased with him. How his handwriting has changed, hardened. For his little brother, he has sent a jar of the best Kamieniec honey. Dark and smelling of the grassy meadows *so that his whole life is sweet.*

Felix kisses her on her cheek, like a little boy, with gratitude and relief. Moments like this soften her heart. This is not the end of a Potocki, he says. He is making more and more outlandish plans. They could go to America. Buy the biggest estate there is and live far away from human envy and scorn. For this he has enough money in the London banks alone. They could be happy there, just the two of them and their children. What do they really need but each other?

'I miss you even when you are asleep,' Felix whispers. 'Without you I wouldn't have the strength to go on living.'

From France, the news is not good. In January the Jacobins executed the French King. Marie Antoinette is in prison, awaiting her fate. Diane de Polignac writes that the King showed courage beyond anyone's expectations, taking off his coat by himself, stepping firmly on the scaffold. *The world has lost its meaning*, she writes, *nothing will ever be as it was before.* She is safe for now, in Switzerland, relying on the hospitality of old friends. *Thank you, my dearest Sophie, for Count Potocki's generous help in making sure we stay in comfort*, she writes, *but do please assure me that I'm not making your situation awkward and causing you trouble.*

Perhaps America is not such a bad idea, she thinks. Bad times cannot last forever. Lately her old restlessness has returned, her hunger for change. She longs to smell the ocean, to feel the sway of waves under her feet. She longs to forget about Poland, Russia, France – to start again, to make no mistakes this time.

'I'll go wherever you want,' she says.

But Felix rapidly forgets all about America. Hamburg, he decides, will be far enough from the turmoil of the Warsaw streets. He tells her that in a voice that he believes is calm and assured. 'Until sanity prevails,' he says. 'Until people here listen to reason.'

The news of the hangings come when she is in Hamburg, with Felix. Her belly is still sore from labour, her breasts heavy, and ache merely from walking. The scent of flowers, nauseates her. In the morning her head spins and her maid needs to support her when she washes herself. It is July of 1794 and Nicolai, their second son, is two months old.

'He is beautiful,' Felix says whenever she urges him to look at the baby, but she has noticed that he never smiles when Nicolai burps or twitches. Babies are not that interesting, he tells her. He prefers when they have grown up a bit, when he can talk to them.

He lives for news. Poland has risen to fight the partitioning powers. The insurrection, led by Tadeusz Kościuszko, has just had its first victory over the Russians at Racławice, but it is in Warsaw where tempers are running high, where those accused of selling the Polish freedom pay with their lives.

Felix insists he is not a traitor. He is guilty, yes. Guilty of miscalculation, of too much trust. He has made a political error and he is paying for it. Paying for it with his own name, his own shame. What he cannot stand is that she is paying for it too. This is not the life he wanted for her, not the life he wanted for his children.

His children. Does he mean Kotula and Nicolai too?

The life he wanted for her is one of quiet, peace and contentment. The life in which she could be proud of his love for her.

The Hamburg Poles pretend not to see them in the street. Their calling cards are refused at the door. But Hamburg is not a desert, she points out to him. French exiles are flocking here too. There is French theatre and opera. There are English chop-houses. There are balls in Bosoltroff where they are always welcome. She would like to go there as soon as she feels better.

'Didn't I tell you that in Jassy?' Felix says, slapping the paper with his hand. 'They are a Jacobin rabble! It was not enough for them to provoke Russia. Now they want to murder us all.'

He reminds her more than once of the fate of his Tulchin neighbour, Princess Lubomirska, who left her husband in their Chernobyl palace and ran away to Paris with her lover. She was guillotined in spite of all the diplomatic pressure on the French. He likes to repeat the word *guillotined.* On the day of her execution, her own mother saw her in a vision, swathed in muslin, disappearing behind a long row of closing doors in the Chernobyl orangery.

Kotula is next door. 'Ring-a-ring o' roses, A pocket full of posies,' the English governess sings to him. He has learned to clap his plump hands and to blow bubbles of spit. He is too young to have a governess, but they could not find an English wetnurse and Felix wants him and Nicolai to speak English. There is no more mention of America, but there are hints of buying an estate in England for them.

From Ukraine letters come every week. Josephine has chosen to ignore Madame de Witt and her bastards. Instead she reports that the price of wheat has risen, that the Uman steward needs to be let go, for the summer palace is in a bad shape. What, a year ago, would have been the simple matter of repairing the roof, now means replacing the rafters and rebuilding the upper storey. There is news of the Potocki children, the dogs and the state of the Tulchin garden. There is gossip too: in Chernobyl Princess Lubomirska's ghost appears to her own peasants returning from their fields, her eyes wide with terror. 'Run away,' she begs. 'A terrible disaster is coming. This land will become poisonous and barren. You, your children, and your children's children will perish here. Run away as far from this cursed place as you can. Run away for in this land there is no hope.'

Felix reads the paper to her: a proof that he has been right all along.

> *. . . At noon, on the 28th of June 1794, right in front of the old town hall in Warsaw, the gallows were waiting. The crowds teemed with hatred. 'Death to traitors,' the women shouted, putting the children on their shoulders to let them see better. 'Hang Moscow's lackeys.'*
>
> Among those who died were Prince Antoni Czetwiertyński, Bishop Ignacy Massalski, Hetman Piotr Ożarowski, Józef Ankwicz, and Charles Boscamp.
>
> For years they had been selling off their country, bit by bit, fattening up on Russian and Prussian money and the end they met with was just. Trembling with fear the traitors were led to the gallows. Prince Czetwiertyński cried and kissed the hands of the executioners but that cowardly act did not stop the execution and he was hanged in front of his own windows. Ożarowski's son, looking at his father's convulsions, said: 'This man stopped being my father when he betrayed my country.' Having read a sign over the gallows that such is the punishment for the traitors, Ankwicz tried to defend himself. 'Everyone took money,' he said. 'Everyone

signed the act of partition. When everyone sins,' he asked, 'will you hang everyone?' Boscamp gave the executioner a few ducats and asked for a quick and easy death. 'Are these the same ducats you have taken for Poland's partition?' the executioner asked and, taking hold of his private parts, he twisted them so hard that the miserable traitor turned black in the face. The crowds cheered and danced with joy. At three o'clock a gust of wind came and brought in black, heavy clouds. It felt as if the world was about to end. Rain poured down, heavy and vicious, turning the streets into muddy streams. It was the rain that drew the crowds away . . .

His voice is tense. 'The justice of the mob,' he says. 'Will they not stop until we have rivers of blood flowing in the streets, like in France?'

She thinks: Charles Boscamp is dead.

'How long before Polish peasants start slashing our throats?' Felix continues. 'Raping our women? The way the *haidamaks* did in Uman?'

The cup is shaking in his hand and some coffee spills on his dressing gown. She takes the cup from him and puts it down on the breakfast tray. He tries to mop the stain with a napkin.

'The *true* nature of the common people is now revealed,' he tells her. 'The common man is a murderer, a violent beast, a monster.'

Charles Boscamp is dead, she thinks.

Life is so short, Dou-Dou, so fleeting. Shouldn't we suck the pleasure out of each moment?

Did Boscamp die thinking of her, wishing he could see her one more time?

She remembers that party in Istanbul. The sounds of the citra in the next room, the laughter of the men, the musty room where he wants her to change into the gauze shirt and pantaloons. 'I've promised you'd dance for them. Do not disappoint me.' She remembers the taste of her tears, the spasm of fear at his anger. She remembers thinking: *His whore. I'm nothing but his whore.* She remembers her eyes in the mirror, lined with kohl, flaring.

Life is curious at times. Someone said that, but she cannot remember who it was.

A traitor and a Russian spy? He betrayed her too. Despite his promises, he tried to sell his revelations, the true story of *la belle Phanariote*, many times over. Fragments of his manuscripts still surface where she least expects. They won't stop either, with his death. There will be always someone ready to pass them on.

Worn stockings, she could have told him. In the sea of lies about her, one more story does not make a difference. There is nothing she has in common with that trembling girl who stood before her master in Istanbul, fearing he might send her back to her mother. Nothing but a name.

Felix reaches for *Nouvelles Extraordinaires de Divers Endroit* to confirm the account he has just read. He is silent, but she knows that, in Warsaw, his portrait was hanged on the gallows.

Pamphlets make their way into their house, their carriage, appear in most unexpected places. The piece of paper Kotula was playing with turned out to be one of them, another one she found pinned to her cloak. There are crude drawings of Felix on the gallows: *The Targowica leader, the murderer of Poland.* There is Felix hiding behind a woman whose full breasts are spilling out of her low-cut dress: *I've killed my first wife, my country, and my honour. Now I'm hiding behind my whore.* The servants cry and swear they do not understand how it is possible. Felix has dismissed five grooms and two maids already.

If she can, she burns the pamphlets herself, before Felix can see them. But she cannot burn his wife's letters. Countess Josephine begs him to repent, to return to Tulchin, to abandon Madame de Witt and her bastards. *I've assurances from someone very trustworthy that the younger one is not yours, Felix.*

Boscamp is dead. What did Cleopatra say when Hailes despaired: *If you find him sad, tell him I'm dancing.*

Rosalia

'I'll sit with the countess,' Doctor Lafleur said. 'Get some rest.' She was holding a candle, watching its flickering flame. Melted wax gathered, dripping down the side.

Was he sending her away?

This was one of these moments she didn't know what to do with. Unspoken words seemed to stretch between them, like swampy fields. She had a feeling she misunderstood him all the time, that his words lured her into illusion. There was also the humiliating thought that, unlike hers, his life had endless possibilities – the very nature of which allowed him to wait and hope. What could she bring to weigh against such freedom? Nothing. Nothing at all.

This memory could still colour her cheeks with shame.

In the end all she had to do was to push the little pillar and the drawer snapped open, revealing the loose sheets of vellum paper and some letters. A pack of cards was wrapped up in a piece of black silk.

A woman whose name was but a squiggle thanked her mother for her help and asked God to bless her and her child. *When everyone turned against me and con-*

demned what I had done, you found it in your heart not to judge me. May the Virgin Mary hold you in her special care. The letter meant little to her and she quickly put it away.

There wasn't anything Rosalia was looking for. Her prying was more a petty act of defiance for her mother's silence, for feeling pushed away.

Before he left, Jakub kneeled and hid his face in the folds of my dress, as if he were drinking from my belly. I was thinking that if only I hadn't told him I was expecting a child, he would have taken us with him. He tried so hard to avert my attention from that drowned ship and from Fiszer's refusal to go on this unknown mission. 'There is no other way,' he said. 'You know I wouldn't ask you to stay if I didn't think it best.'

'I've left my people for you,' I said, 'but you won't leave yours.'

I was so angry with him then that I pulled my hand away and wouldn't let him touch me. I told him he was taking away the only reason I had for believing that I did the right thing. That without him there was no place for me, no family, no people I could call my own. I knew he wouldn't change his mind, but I wanted him to know how much I was hurting. For this I'll never forgive myself, either.

When he left I went with Rosalia to the harbour. I heard her count the ships and I told her to stop. Counting anything was bad luck my mother and Aunt Hannah always said. The evil eye would know where to look. Later when Rosalia was flying a kite Jakub had given her, I tried to kill the bitterness in my heart but couldn't. Poland, I thought, was like a bloodthirsty beast that demanded its sacrifice from each generation. It would never have enough, and it would always take the lives of its best sons. I sat on the bench at the harbour long after the sails disappeared over the horizon, feeling as if my life had ended, as if everything I'd ever done had brought me to this moment of utter loneliness. Time, I thought, was a thief, stealing life a drop at a time.

'I'll be back soon,' Jakub said. 'Life is not over, Miriam.'

He called me Miriam. 'Sweet little Miriam,' he whispered into my ear right before stepping on board.

A fear gripped me, a thought: What if he never returned. 'A bad hour,' my aunt used to call a time like that. A time when the worst thoughts come true. I tried so hard to undo that thought, to wipe it out from my heart. In church I kneeled in front of the Virgin Mary to whom, Jakub once told me, King John-Casimir consecrated Poland making Her our Queen. A Jewish Queen of Poland, I kept thinking, she will understand me. I have given enough already, I prayed. I have given up my people, my God. I didn't cry when I had to raise my child in exile, not knowing where we would live from month to month. I followed my husband faithfully all the way to Livorno harbour, I went wherever his duty and love for Poland called him. I tried to be a good wife and a good mother, not to burden anyone with my own pain. I taught my daughter to pray for Poland and to call her father a hero. Shouldn't I be spared?

Now I know it was already too late. Now I know so much more. 'A Jewess will always be a Jewess,' I've heard Antonia say to Klemens.

There were two letters in that brown sack. The first one was written a month before the yellow fever took him, so faint I could hardly make out the words. 'Why are we here, so far away from Poland,' he asked. 'We were told we would be maintaining order among our equals, but we are maintaining the French order over slaves.' He wrote that the negroes attacked them mostly at night. They heard the singing first, then voices of women and children, a short burst of a song and silence. Then another burst came from another direction, then another long silence and another song. They were armed, watching around them, waiting. The negroes emerged out of the forest, threw themselves at them, and then disappeared into the darkness as if nothing but phantoms.

The French assured him that they had no intention of bringing slavery back. Napoleon was only stopping the rebellion from destroying the country. The light of freedom cannot be stopped at will, they said, denied to some and bestowed on others. He wrote as if he tried to believe them.

The second letter was shorter. Jakub was writing it from hospital. He could already feel sharp pains in his eyes and he knew what was coming next. He had seen enough of his soldiers die of the fever. He wrote that he had heard rumours of Polish soldiers crossing over to join the negroes in their fight for freedom, four hundred of them. 'I pray,' he wrote, 'that these rumours may be true.' Then the last lines were so faint it took some time before I could read all the words: 'Oh, Miriam, my sweet Miriam, I wish we died that day in Uman: holding hands, innocent, together.'

Oh, Jakub. My dearest, my beloved. Once you told me that we could change our destiny and still find happiness. When I lay awake at night I think that I brought this death upon you, that you had to die for my sins, die so far away from Poland, from everything you loved. I wish I had enough strength to have stayed in Uman and accepted my fate, to be the mother of Jewish children who would not be ashamed of me, who would cherish my parents' names and carry their dreams into the future.

Underneath, below a thick line, in different ink:

My daughter should never have been born. I know I will lose her as I have lost the others, like I lost the one Jakub hoped would be born in Zierniki. And even if she lives, she too is going to suffer for my sins.

Rosalia let the vellum pages drop to the floor. The injustice of these words was so enormous. Was it proof of what she had suspected all along, that her mother did not love her? The reason why Maman always reminded her of her duties and never of her pleasures?

My daughter should never have been born.

She closed her eyes and thought of the sea, of that ship that had sunk, that ship her father didn't want them to know about. She thought of the kite she had never managed to fly that afternoon for it kept falling down and there was never the tug of the string she knew should have come. Of the boy who had broken it and ran away from her to his proper family – to his father who had not gone away like hers.

'You opened the drawer, Rosalia? You read my private papers?'

Her mother's face was red with anger, ugly, in some unspeakable way, and distorted with pain.

'Don't you see this is a wicked thing to do? Dreadful, terrible thing!'

She could hear the voices in the garden of her cousins quarrelling. The maid was telling them to stop right this minute or she would call Madame and they would be sorry.

'Why did you write that I should never have been born?' she asked. Her mother acted as if she hadn't heard her, as if her question did not exist, had never been asked.

'Don't you know it is wrong to pry through other people's things?'

'I know, Maman.'

'Then I want you to promise that you will never ever do it again.'

'I promise.'

And even if she lives, she too is going to suffer for my sins.

Rosalia would have promised anything, anything to erase the sting of those lines she would try to blot out of her mind forever, to stop her mother from looking at her with such anger and disappointment.

'I want you to go to your room now,' she heard. 'To think of what you have done.'

'When I die, Rosalia,' she heard just before Maman closed the door behind her. 'You may read it all – when I die.'

Sophie

Felix is talking to her. He has realised something.

'Think of what has happened to the ancient Greeks. They have not died without offspring, so their descendants still walk the earth. Some may have become Turks, some Italians. Some may still be Greek, their blood flowing in your veins.'

They have now been in Hamburg for two years. Kotula is in the room next door, playing with the English governess. He has already begun to speak. 'Catch,' he cries. 'Catch me.' He is not allowed to call Felix *Papa*. 'My Lord,' Kotula says, kissing his father's portrait goodnight the way she has taught him. 'Kiss kiss love love.' Nicolai is still a baby. Boisterous, demanding attention. Ready to scream with anger when anything crosses him.

She thinks of the sea in Istanbul. One clear night, she remembers, when Mana was asleep, she climbed onto the roof of their house. The sky was strewn with stars, luminous and tempting. She tried to look beyond them, into the black void from which they had sprung but the nothingness did not hold her attention for long. Instead, she gazed at the spread of the sea, recalling how she stood on its shores, watching the rolling crest of the waves, thinking that the white foam was like Belgian lace on a rich lady's cuffs. From the roof she could hear the dark waves, their edges splashing on the pebbles of the shore. Mana later found her there, staring into the distance. 'Hope is not a course of action, Dou-Dou,' she said. 'You need something much stronger than hope.'

'Think about it,' Felix says.

She doesn't know what to think. At moments like these, it seems to her that he is losing his mind, that the barrage of accusations, the gossip, the pamphlets and the jokes have finally cracked him open. He is unsure of her. He eyes with suspicion any man who comes up to her: young or old, handsome or ugly. He wants to know what she thinks of them, relieved if she pronounces them boring or pompous or foolish. If only he could marry her, he says. Right now. Right this minute. He trusts the power of the Potocki name more than he trusts himself.

'Think about it,' he repeats.

For who is he, he asks her. If fate had not thwarted him, he could have been the King of Poland. Wasn't his blood purer than that of Poniatowski? But does he have to remain Polish forever? Does he have to remain Polish when his countrymen would have drowned him in a spoonful of water?

He has had enough. Tulchin is now in Russia. So is Uman. His estates, his Ukrainian estates are part of the Russian empire and this makes him a Russian subject.

'I'm Russian now,' he declares. It is the Polish cruelty, he tells her, that makes him say these words, words that once would have seemed to him vicious and evil.

'Russia is where my home is. Russia is where we shall live.'

Countries are like men, ma belle Phanariote. You leave them when a better one comes along.

She has hardened. She is not like Felix, she thinks; she will not be judged. People can say what they want, but she will not care. She is her own judge, her own conscience.

Lovers come to her in her dreams. In the darkness she never sees their faces, but her body feels the grip of their fingers, the bite of their teeth. They are wild, ruthless in their desire, unstoppable. Strong from a life of struggle. Forged like iron, tried and true, without a scrap of excess in their bodies. To these lovers she surrenders with moans that wake Felix up.

'Who is Lysander?'

'A cousin of mine I grew up playing with. He drowned when he was twelve. His father carried him through the field, his body limp, his hands dangling. His eyes closed. All I could think of was: I will never see his eyes again.'

The ease with which lies flow no longer amazes her.

In Lvov her divorce trial is proceeding smoothly, thanks to Felix's money. Joseph has raised no objections to the witnesses' accounts. Madame Czerkies of Kamieniec has sworn that Lady Sophie Glavani, a virgin from Istanbul, was taken away from her house by Major de Witt, taken by force and by force brought to the Zienkowice church where she was wed to her captor. In a few weeks she will have to go to Lvov and give her own sworn testimony confirming the same story. Then she will have to wait for Josephine's change of heart.

For now she has consolations. She has a new passion: fans. When a fan is trimmed with down it catches to the lips, like gossamer. And then there is swanskin. When she touched this thin parchment for the first time she thought that's what it really was. Swan's skin. But then she was told that this fine parchment was made from the skin of an unborn lamb, then limed, scraped very thin, and smoothed down with pumice and chalk.

Luxury too has to be learned. Tasted first, before it yields all its pleasures. Like wild honey, Siberian apples, and smoked sturgeon. Like Utrecht velvet and Moroccan leather.

'We are going back to Russia. I've already informed my wife that I wish to live in Tulchin with you. You will have whatever you wish,' he says, holding on to her, smothering her with impatience, making her into someone she doesn't know. 'My Sophie. *Zosiu, Zosieńko.*'

She is not sorry to have left Hamburg. She is travelling alone, for Felix has been summoned to St Petersburg by Catherine of Russia, and she needs to go to Lvov. But *alone* means with Kotula and Nicolai, Kotula's two English governesses and one French, Nicolai's German nurse, her Polish housekeeper and her French maids. *It is the true Tower of Babel*, she has written to Felix. *Endless quarrels and bickering and I have to solve and judge. Mrs David told me that she would prefer to command a whole troop of grenadiers than one wetnurse! Only the English governesses cause me no trouble, and I worried about them the most.*

In Poland, the last desperate insurrection against the Russians has ended in defeat, just as Felix had predicted. In 1795, the last, third partition erased Poland from the map of Europe. Kościuszko and hundreds of his officers and soldiers are prisoners in St Petersburg; and those who managed to evade capture have left the country, a wave of exiles searching for means to fight for Poland, assessing alliances, choosing with whom to side. She has seen a group of them in Berlin, on her way from Hamburg. Five men draped in the Polish flag on a street corner, giving out leaflets, on the lookout for Prussian guards. Men with tired, bloodshot eyes, appealing to the conscience of Europe.

Hope is not a course of action she wants to tell them.

Stanisław August, the last King of Poland, has been forced to abdicate and become a *guest* of the Russian court. Catherine does not want him to gather sympathy for Poland at the palaces of Europe.

Sophie refuses to think of him like that. For her Stanisław August will always remain as he was on the day she saw him for the last time. In the Łazienki palace, kissing her hand, three times. A man with a thick, seductive voice and a half-smile on his fine, narrow lips. She has asked Felix to make inquiries at the Russian court. Perhaps something could be done to ease his fate, something however small. She has always believed in the power of small steps, little imperceptible victories, twists where steps are impossible.

On her way from Hamburg to Lvov she has made some pleasant discoveries.

In Nieborów, the Radziwiłł estate a few hours' ride outside Warsaw, Madame de Witt is received with an open heart. Count Potocki is not a traitor to everyone. He is still a Potocki, after all. He still has his millions in spite of all that has happened. Felix's influence in St Petersburg is also not to be discounted, now that so much of Poland is part of Russia. More than ever, one needs good friends at the Russian court.

A transformation, she thinks. Away from her, Felix has become better, more attractive.

Here, in Nieborów, it matters that he loves her. It matters that he wants to marry her as soon as Josephine gives her consent. It matters far more than she has hoped it would. All these burdens, these passing troubles, the uncertainty, the humiliations, her hostess says, will soon be just a memory.

'The truth can only be found in oneself, in peace and solitude, my dear friend,' Princess Helena Radziwiłł continues. 'One should not dwell in the past or nurture bitterness for what cannot be changed.'

The Princess wraps a cashmere shawl over her loose muslin dress, tied with an embroidered sash. 'I'll be your guide,' she says, slipping one hand under Sophie's arm. Her cheeks are flushed with pride. Arkadia, the Princess's garden, is her beloved treasure.

The most beautiful part of Arkadia, the Princess tells her, is the temple of Diana, built at the top of the lake. It catches the rising and the setting sun. In the evening the last rays of sunlight are reflected by a crystal mirror, guarded by two stone lions. The mirror wrapped in the wafts of smoke coming from censers placed at the temple's entrance.

'Earth, Air, Water and Fire meet here,' the Princess says.

Dove pace trovai d'ogni mia guerra, she reads the inscription over the portal. 'It is from Petrarch. Here I find my peace after each war.'

A beautiful garden is a place of solitude and true friendship. It will admit only those whose spirit is pure. 'Oh, my dear friend,' the Princess says. 'Without it, I would not have survived the turmoils of life.'

Arkadia is not big, but her guide is clever. While winding paths may deposit her where she has already been, every vista is different, every stone, every ruin has a story. From afar, she can hear the children laugh. The two 'kittens' delight Princess Helena's children who refuse to leave the guests alone.

And to think, she wants to say, that in Hamburg no one wanted to shake our hands. But she will not dwell on the miseries of the past. Every day is a new day. Every day is new chance. In a few months she will be free to marry again. As soon as Josephine consents, her children will be Potockis, not just 'kittens' without a name.

That afternoon she sits down at her desk and writes to Felix:

> Mon ami.
>
> We have arrived here late yesterday. I took a bath which I needed badly. Princess Radziwiłł among her family is a sight to behold. Before dinner the children played some music. They are all very talented. I am enclosing the score for a polonaise composed by Krystyna. Please dance it at the first ball you give in Tulchin. I know you will be giving balls, you have told me that a thousand times. You said that as soon as you arrive in Ukraine you want to chase the sadness away from this country, extinguish the memory of the murders and the defeat.
>
> Kotula is right beside me as I write this. The Princess and her daughters have fallen for him. He is so adorable and funny. They all speak English here so he is now on friendly terms with all the Princess's daughters.
>
> After dinner we all went to visit the Arkadia gardens. It is impossible to imagine anything as

beautiful and as romantic. You know Arkadia, but you saw it ten years ago. Can you imagine how far young trees can grow in ten years and how the investments made this enchanting place even more beautiful. Princess Radziwiłł is a charming woman, and I am learning so much here. As I walked with her I thought of you and your love for the countryside and quiet domestic life. I am sure that a woman like her would make you very happy.

But returning to Arkadia. I am in love with it. There cannot be a flower or plant in the world that is not here. As I was walking there, in the middle of the summer, I was re-living spring. The plantations are beautifully cared for and every tree seems to say: I like it here! Do you know that, with your means, one could have an Arkadia, or a place even more beautiful than Arkadia in just two years? Mon ami, shall we? Could we have a garden like that in Ukraine? And once we have our garden could you get organs there, the same as Princess Radziwiłł has in Arkadia?

A moment ago the maid came and brought me your letter. I fall to my knees, mon ange, for all the wonderful things you write about me. Even if I am not the way you see me, I shall try with all my might to become such. I will resemble the beautiful portrait you have painted, and I shall be happiest if, through these efforts to please you, I make you happy. And if one day my tenderness will let you forget all the sufferings you have been dealt, will let you taste the happiness of domestic existence, then you will look at no one else in the world but your Sophie. I am part of your world, for I believe you do love me.

Our boys are so charming, mon bon ami. I have read Kotula all you have written for him in English. He listened with great attentiveness and then ran to my bedroom, took your miniature did his 'kiss I love' to it ten times and asked, 'Where is my dear Lord? I wish very much to see him. Pray, Maman, go with me to my Lord. I am a good child.'

Our separation has made it clear to me how much I love you. It brought back all the sentiments you have evoked in me before. In Hamburg, sometimes, I thought I loved you less than I loved you in Jassy, Cherson or Grodno. But since I have parted from you I realise it is the reverse, for I love you more than ever. Before I loved you to distraction, but I still could make some plans; now I cannot do that. My only dream is to please you and to love you until the day I die. You know well, mon ami, that before my head plotted and schemed all the time; now I am calm and my soul is quiet. If not for the troubles with the divorce trial, if not for the deep longing to be free and to devote this freedom to you, I think I might not think of anything at all. I would entrust all my happiness to you, bon ami; if you don't build it, there is no one in the world who could, so accept that you are the lord of my destiny and I shall devote my time to caressing our little angels.

Nicolai is as beautiful as the love I give you. I don't like looking at him for I don't want anyone in the world to be more beautiful than Kotula, but I cannot stop myself from hugging and kissing him. I never thought that his big lips would become so shapely, or his eyes so black and luminous. He is made to be painted. This little one will outshine Kotula. In Tulchin, we shall not show him to anyone. We will make sure Kotula strengthens his reputation before Nicolai enters the world.

Adieu, mon bon ami.

Sophie

Thomas

'How does one die of yellow fever?' Rosalia asked him.

Her eyes were reddened, her cheeks streaked with tears, but she offered no explanation. He didn't ask for one either. Her face, he noticed was paler than usual. All this waiting for death was taking its toll. She never complained, of course, but he had never expected her to.

He didn't ask her why. It was a painful death he told her. Sometimes it began with a general feeling of sickness, exhaustion and depression. Most often, however, it came suddenly. Very sharp pain appeared in the eye sockets, feet, loins and stomach. Then came quick shivering fits, followed by a dry fever. The patients' face became flushed, tears flowed from their glazed eyes. The upper chest burnt with fever, but the rest of the body was cold.

He stopped, wondering if he should go on. Something in her face worried him, something fluid, threatening to spill. She was not one of his students, he reminded himself. Should he really tell her of the fear of suffocation; a face turned livid, thick whitish-fluid covering the parched tongue which changed into black incrustation; of faeces black with blood; spotty patches on the neck, chest and shoulders. Or of the final moment when utterly exhausted the patient would not be able to raise his eyelids. Only the tremor of ocular muscles would announce imminent death.

'I beg you,' he said. 'Don't ask more.'

Her lips were trembling. He could see that other words were on the tip of her tongue.

'My father,' she whispered. 'died of yellow fever in Santo Domingo.'

He stood up and poured her some brandy from the decanter on the marble sideboard. This was not the first time that he had blessed Frau Kohl's housekeeping skills. She took the glass in her hand and raised it to her lips.

One sip. Then another. He wanted to tell her to slow down, but seeing the colour return to her cheeks he stopped himself. What could he tell this woman, still young, and so consumed with mourning. This woman with eyes only for the dead.

'I'm so sorry,' he said. What else could he tell her? That Napoleon had cared nothing for the Polish freedom, or anyone else's, and that it was this ruthlessness that made him who he was. That if her father lived he could well have died in the fields of Russia, beaten to death by peasants who paid two silver roubles for the privilege? Should he insist as Ignacy would have done that deeper meaning should be forged out of pain? Meaning that never lessened with time, passed on to the next generation, in a relay of duties, of obligations. Thomas couldn't argue with such noble sentiments but wished that it wasn't so, wished that she could be spared.

The brandy had made her cheeks pink. This was one of these moments when she looked more than pretty, her face lit by the shy November sun, her hazel eyes warm and moist.

Vis medicatrix natura, he thought. This is what will force the sadness out of her heart.

Sophie

She thinks: Between God and the Devil, there is uncharted territory. Is it foolish to hope she won't be lost there?

Felix is so proud of himself when he brings her here for the first time, into this Ukrainian gorge littered with reddish boulders, just a short ride from his Uman summer palace. 'It will be so much better than Arkadia,' he says. 'You will see.' They dismount and the servants hold their horses. He takes her hand and pulls her to follow him to the spot where the river falls down the slope.

'Your garden,' he says. 'Look.'

With Felix everything is possible. From Africa and Italy will come the trees, fallen giants dug out of the earth, their roots wrapped in moist burlap, crossing the sea and dragged with chains from the ships in Odessa: plantains, Wejmut pines, poplars. The nettle tree, so solid and heavy that it would sink in water. The Turkish filbert from Caucasus, able to thrive in complete shade. She will watch them propped in enormous holes, watered day and night until they take root in alien soil. Until it seems they have always grown there, until they are no longer foreign. The Uman serfs will toil around the clock, lighting the way with torches, moving the streams, digging up the lake. Then the birds will start coming, crimson, black with orange patches, blue and green. She will ask the gardener where they are from, thinking that they too must have been brought over from Italy or France, but the man only smiles. 'They are from here,' he will say, 'from our Ukrainian groves.' He calls them cardinals, orioles, and evas.

'Your wishes,' Felix kisses her hand, 'are my orders.'

She says she wants peacocks, and so peacocks strut along the paths of her garden. She wants music and the orchestra is summoned and hidden beyond the bushes so that no sight of men will spoil her mood. She wants the little huts built, teeming with life, and he will order his serfs to live there, dressed as hermits and shepherds.

Felix has far grander plans. He can already see a big lake fed by the cascading water. A hidden lake into which a visitor would be taken by an underground tunnel. He likes the very idea of a subterranean journey, a moment of reflection between night and day, between death and life. A moment in which confronted with the memory of past sins, the soul will free itself from them through the hope of the future.

'I would like that,' she mutters.

On that lake there will be an island of Circe, but unlike

in the *Odyssey* where on such an island Greek sailors were turned into pigs, here animals will achieve human form for, in this blessed garden the sins of the flesh will be overcome, darkness conquered, and souls born again.

Countess Josephine Potocka refuses to talk of the divorce, so Count Felix is promising her another Arkadia.

'More beautiful,' he vows. With grottoes where the guest can hide from summer heat; with secluded spots where they can ponder the vagaries of fate; with vistas that take away one's breath; with a 'Greek forest' named in her honour; with boulders scattered as if by a giant's hand; narrow paths suspended over precipice; vast, gloomy meadows turned into the Elysian Fields.

Le jardins de Sophie.

Sophievka.

There is an engineer he already has in mind. An expert in hydraulics. Metzel his one time aide-de-camp, meticulous to a fault. He has seen the first plans already.

'Kiss me, my *Epilda*,' she says. She lets herself be careless, forget caution. In her womb she can feel another child stirring. Her own love, she assures him, is so overwhelming that she will agree to any fate. 'I'll be your slave,' she says. 'Your mistress forever if I cannot be your wife. Nothing you do will change it. Without you there is no life for me.'

'Look,' she tells Felix, knowing that he sees nothing but her delight. In his gaze she sees no danger of passion receding. He believes her like a child might.

Epilda. The giver of hope.

Olga

Olga thought herself a bird in a cage. Her sister should have been with her now, as should her brothers. She should not be alone with death.

I'm not like Maman, Olga thought. Her body was delicate, bone-thin, frail. Her mouth too large for her face, her eyes but a pale copy of her mother's. They were black, but too small, shining, but without the force her mother could effortlessly summon. The force that made men adjust their cravats, and follow her with their eyes wherever she went.

Rising from her bed Olga twirled her skirt out in a spiral of silk taffeta. Her brothers often teased her that they could encircle her waist in one hand. She could hear the French doctor come out of the library. He was talking to someone now in a booming voice.

Quickly Olga rubbed her cheeks to make them red and loosened her hair. She sat on her bed and spread the skirts around her, making sure her feet showed. She had taken off her slippers and was wearing white silk stockings. She began to sob.

The door to her room opened and Olena came in, but Olga waved her away.

'My head,' she moaned, 'my heart. Call the doctor. Quick.'

The French doctor did not look alarmed. He felt her pulse. His thin hands were warm, reddened. She wondered why he couldn't make the redness go away. He was a doctor after all. Quite handsome too, in a manly way, even if a bit short. She watched the hairs on his thumb raise slightly.

'It's the pain in my heart,' she said, pointing to her breasts. 'Right here.'

From his leather case Thomas took a stethoscope and placed it to her chest. For a moment she listened to his breathing. There was the smell of snuff around him. He said that he heard nothing unusual, just agitation: no doubt it was caused by the situation she found herself in.

'I'll give you a few drops of laudanum, Mademoiselle,' he said, and she hated the compassion in his voice. 'It's a difficult time for you. You mustn't be too alarmed by moments like this. We are only human.'

At her sister's wedding she drank far too much champagne, loving the lightness it gave her. She danced without stopping, giddy with happiness. Before her new brother-in-law, Pavel, took her by the elbow and asked her to take a turn with him in the garden, she had danced a waltz with the young Count Naryshkin. 'You are more beautiful than your sister,' he said. Sophie, the bride, her cheeks flushed, was looking at her from across the room with a look of warning. 'It's your *joie de vivre*,' the Count said.

'Try to calm down,' Thomas said. 'Take a deep breath.'

She stared at him when he poured some water from the decanter, added a lump of sugar, measured the laudanum, and began to stir it all together. His eyes took in her dishevelled dress, the frills of her petticoat, the shape of her small feet. She wondered if he too thought he could encircle her waist in one hand. Perhaps she should have let him see her spin out her skirt. See her in a twirling of taffeta. Hear the rustle of the fabric.

She drank the laudanum slowly, making a face. In spite of the sugar, the bitterness was there, right under the surface. When he reached to take the glass away, she grasped his hand and pressed it to her heart.

'Can you feel it now?' she asked. 'It's even stronger than before.'

He removed his hand from hers, peeling off her fingers one by one.

'You shouldn't get agitated. Please. I'll ask Mademoiselle Rosalia to sit with you.'

That Jewess, she thought, watching the doctor leave the room in a hurry. Jeroslav was right. She should have her coffers searched. It was all so unfair. Wasn't it enough that she had to watch Rosalia's hands? Make sure her mother was not robbed on her deathbed? That vulture, already counting the ducats she would get, scheming to get her mother's dresses, her jewels. As if it weren't enough that Maman were dying. That this horrible, half-empty palace gave her shivers. That she was suffocating here.

The door opened quietly. She didn't have to look to know it was Rosalia. She could recognise her steps anywhere.

'Go away,' Olga snapped. Hiding her face in her pillow, she could still feel Rosalia's hands adjusting the throw on her feet. The flash of hatred that hit her was like a bolt of lightning.

'Leave me alone, you sneaky Jewess.'

The satisfaction, a long forgotten pleasure of getting even. Like screaming at her brothers in the nursery. It didn't matter for what. The sight of crimson on Rosalia's cheeks made her go on. This and the suggestion that Doctor Lafleur should be sent for again, right away, to bleed her perhaps.

'Oh, run after him,' Olga screamed. 'You think I don't know what you really want? But he doesn't want you. And my mother won't help you.'

Only when the laudanum began to work, the sharp edge of this anger dissipated. Her eyelids heavy, Olga surrendered to the sweet calm enveloping her.

Sophie

On the way to the Uman palace, her coachman takes the wrong turn at the crossroads. It is a Sunday and the carriage rolls through a village with its thatched roofs, cranes, pots left to dry on the wattle fences. She parts the curtains to take a look at the maze of paths leading from one whitewashed hut with red window frames to another, at the gardens overgrown with lilac bushes and sunflowers.

There is something about this village that makes her think of Istanbul. The smell perhaps, of dust and heat. The feel of the hot earth under her foot. The hunger in her for that other, forgotten world. I am me, she remembers thinking, and nobody is like me. The seedlings are pushing through the soil around an old oak tree. 'See how many of them have high hopes,' the internuncio once asked. 'How many, do you think will be allowed to grow.'

Charles Boscamp. But she will not think of him. Or the gallows in Warsaw where his tortured body swung for hours, lashed by the rain. Every day is a new day.

There is a fair in the village and soon her carriage is slowing down, its path obstructed by the thickening crowds. 'Like locusts,' Felix would have said at the sight of so many carts, platforms, heaps of fruit, baskets, bast shoes, painted plates and bowls. Deafened by the squealing of pigs, the neighing of horses and cackling of hens. A woman is selling dumplings, a small stove right in front of her, pan at the ready. She keeps the dough under her skirt. She licks her fingers so that it doesn't stick to them, pinches a piece of dough from a bowl, and throws it into the pan.

She doesn't know these people, Felix would say, urging the driver to get them out of there. He has tried to frighten her with his stories of runaway serfs, army deserters, *haidamaks*, pointed out to her the Uman well once filled with Polish corpses, the synagogue where the Jews were burned alive. The orphaned children from Uman stayed for months in his father's palace, before arrangements were made; so many orphans, their eyes wide and empty.

'You have never known such fear,' he said.

You only strive after that which is bred in your bones, Felix. You only see that which appears to you.

Nobody can see all the trees, Felix. Only God can see the entire forest.

* * *

By the village inn she can hear the tapping of heels and the first tunes of a Cossack dance. A young man outside of the tavern is holding a bottle of vodka in one hand and a small bowl in another. '*Pij*,' he coos to passers by. 'Drink, brother, it's Matwij Szpon who is paying!' She sees men stop and drink with him, wiping the bowl with the rim of their white shirts. If anyone refuses, he pours the vodka on the ground and spits after the fool.

As the carriage rolls past the inn, she spots a convent. A small, unassuming wooden structure, hardly worthy of its name. This is where she will go, she tells the driver. This is where they can ask for help. Inside the convent gates, a small group of Ukrainian women in their colourful kerchiefs are drinking *kvas* and mead, which a bald monk is selling.

She gets out of the carriage, relief in every tired muscle. She sends her maid to the nuns to announce Countess Potocka's unexpected arrival and notes, with satisfaction, how they rush to bring refreshments and get a room ready for her. In the morning, she is reassured, one of the novices will lead the coach back to the main tract and she can proceed on her way.

'The Virgin Mary Herself has guided you here, Your Highness!' the prioress says, raising her hands to the heavens. 'For our needs are indeed great.'

She motions to her maid to drop a handful of ducats into the alms bin. They rattle against the bottom.

Beauty is cheap, my Dou-Dou. Being of use is not.

In the cell where the nuns have prepared her bed there is a painting on the wall, an amateurish effort by some local monk. She holds the candle to it and sees that it depicts the Last Judgement. The angels with their trumpets are waking the dead. The flames of Hell cover at least half of the canvas. Among these flames – rather crudely rendered, like giant tongues – stands Lucifer, his hoofed legs big and contorted. In his big, hairy hands the prince of darkness is holding the chains to Hell, where a multitude of sinners are being tortured, each in a different manner. The painter, anxious that the moral of his painting be not missed, has added white clouds which emerge from the sinners' lips, each adorned with an inscription.

Feeling better after a meal of cheese, black bread, and a mug of mead, she amuses herself by staring at the sinners. A cruel lord is being flogged, the same way he used to flog his serfs. A miser is being forcefed gold coins. A Jew in his black gabardine has vodka poured down his throat. Beside him a pale-skinned woman is being tortured by a small wiry devil who applies tongs and liquid tar to her private parts with a passion that makes her laugh. Another devil is defecating on the woman, while yet another pours liquid gold on her naked breasts. The inscription from the woman's mouth says, *This is what will happen to you for your sins.*

Kotula, Nicolai, and baby Helena are taken away from her one after another, in one week. Taken by scarlet fever, the same rash on their chests and necks, the skin of their fingers rough and peeling, their tongues red, the colour of strawberries. Their breaths drag from sore throats, their hands wrench away from hers, fighting off some terrifying shadows. 'I'm right here,' she whispers into their hot ears, but they never hear her. Death takes all their attention, all their strength.

Helena will not grow up, will not marry, will not give her grandchildren. Kotula and Nicolai will never call her Maman, again. Despair tastes of ashes. It numbs her. It denies all hope.

'I want them buried there,' she says to Felix. 'In Sophievka. In my garden.'

She is still only his mistress. *Does Madame de Witt or*

whatever she calls herself now perhaps think herself a female Napoleon, grabbing what is not hers, Josephine writes to Felix. *If this is so, please remind her what I have already stated many times before. There is only one Countess Potocka at your side.*

'A church in Uman,' he says, 'would be a better place.'

She thinks: Not the parish church where generations of Potockis have been buried, but the small St Anthony's church where his bastards would not draw attention to themselves.

She thinks: Better than the grave in the field where Gertruda's body was buried, the unborn child still inside it.

Every fibre in her body tells her to please him. To tell him his wishes are her orders, but her defiance will not be quenched.

'They are children,' she screams. 'They don't want to be among stones.'

Felix looks at her, pain in his bulging eyes. 'Sophie,' he whispers. 'My dear.' He never meant to hurt her, he says. Never. She can have whatever she wants.

A priest will consecrate the spot in Sophievka. There, at least, she can imagine her children's souls rising from the graves to play tag in the Elysian Fields, sneaking into the Grotto of Thunder where the water lashes like rain in a storm. Or taking a ride through the underground tunnel to the upper lake and playing hide and seek in the pavilion on the Island of Love.

She crawls into bed and lies motionless for days, refusing to see anyone. She cannot even pray. After a while tears don't come either, just dry heaving sobs mixed with fury. If God is punishing her, she is thinking, He knows what He is doing.

Every day she can hear Felix outside her bedroom, his steps coming closer, stopping, and turning back. Is he disappointed by the force of her pain?

When she finally gets out of bed, her face pale, she finds him in the music room, playing the piano. A waltz. The sleeves of his jacket are rolled up and she almost chokes at the sight of the black hairs on his flabby skin.

'Too much grief,' he says, seeing her in the doorway, leaning on the door frame for support, 'is a refusal to trust in the Lord's mercy.'

She does not go away. She does not close her ears to music.

This is not the end, she thinks.

Rosalia

Anger blinded her, making her pace her room, wrench the curtains to close them, and then open them again, a torn-off golden tassel left in her hands, making her throw herself on her bed, and hide her face in the pillow.

Sneaky Jewess. Her mother's daughter. *Their women. Their blood.* Was this what her father gave his life for?

You will have to suffer for my sins, Rosalia. For no fault of your own.

She stood up, straightened her dress and looked into the mirror. Her hair had come undone. A crease from the pillow was imprinted on her right cheek. One deep breath. Another one. 'Count to ten,' her mother would have said. 'Before you do something foolish, count to ten.'

In the mirror her eyes seemed dull and lifeless, her skin yellowed and sagging. This was a face she hardly recognised. *He doesn't want you, either.*

No one saw her when she sneaked through the servants' door. After the morning rain the air was cool, the pavement still wet. Sunshine peered through the spaces between the buildings, the wind touched her cheeks and cooled them down. Only for a few minutes, she thought. No one will notice I'm gone.

She walked along Unter den Linden. By the university, she crossed the street to avoid the crowd of students, shouting and screaming. One climbed on a wooden butterbox and gesticulated wildly to bouts of laughter and applause. His clothes reminded her of a jester: blue, red, green, yellow mixed together. His orange hat had a feather in it and he was waving it now, as if conducting an orchestra.

> I wish I had enough strength to have stayed in Uman, a mother of Jewish children who would not be ashamed of me.

She walked quickly, her heels clicking on the stone trottoir. In front of her a tall, stocky man in a top hat and peg trousers bowed to a woman who acknowledged his greeting with a tiny movement of her head. An elegant woman, in a heavy cape, trimmed with ermine. Then he crossed to the other side of the street and disappeared from view.

Dr Bolecki spotted her before she saw him. He was standing by the print shop, his hands behind him, holding his cane.

'Mademoiselle Rosalia,' he exclaimed. 'Where are you bound? Can I be of assistance? Are you all right?'

'You mustn't inconvenience yourself on my behalf,' she said, admitting she was only intending to walk. She had felt a momentary weakness but that had passed.

'But I need a walk as much as you do,' he protested. There was a lightness about him, a certain agitation she had not seen before.

It occurred to her that he too might be going to America. The picture in the print shop he had been contemplating was of a ship. A clipper with white sails, billowing in the wind. Two men on board were looking back at the shore.

But this suggestion brought a deep peal of laughter.

'I'm going back to Poland,' he said. 'Unlike my good friend, I don't believe one can start a new life. I don't believe in escapes.'

He extended his arm to her and she took it, noting that in this Berlin street, Dr Bolecki was a popular figure. She soon stopped counting how many men bowed to him and stopped to inquire about his health, and how many times he raised his hat in greeting. Her presence at his side, she noted, caused curiosity, but he made sure they were not disturbed for longer than a passing exchange of pleasantries.

He was tired, he said, of Berlin. Here he was turning into a doctor of fashion and that did not suit his character. A few grateful patients was a nice reward for his efforts, but he was still young enough to expect more from life.

A man in a black frockcoat leaned from the carriage window and bowed to them. Dr Bolecki bowed back.

'That's Herr Trommer,' he whispered with a smile. 'I cured his gout and he never paid his bills. Last time he saw me, he ducked so fast I thought he would smash his head on the floor. Only the other day, however, the fellow sent me oysters. A small barrelful. Do you care much for oysters, Mademoiselle?'

'No,' she laughed. 'Not that much.'

'Oysters, of course, don't keep,' Dr Bolecki said.

They walked for a while, until they came to the small square lined with trees. With a white handkerchief that he retrieved from his coat pocket, he wiped a wooden bench for her and invited her to sit down.

'You mustn't get exhausted,' he said. 'No one is without limits.'

She smiled.

'I can see big changes coming,' he said, sitting down

beside her. Immense changes that could release untold human energy. At such moments, opportunities seized with wisdom made everything possible. The trick was to know how to act, to contribute to the force that could transform the world and use it to one's advantage. Thoughts like that were the chief reason why he felt so elated. He was a man of action. He needed real challenges.

You are growing old. She would be nine and twenty soon. The borderline of embarrassment, not the time to dream. She saw the stubble that was beginning to darken Dr Bolecki's cheeks.

From the same pocket that had held his handkerchief, he retrieved a folded piece of paper. It was a poem, he said, that an old friend sent him from Vilnus. He read the first lines:

> Bez serc bez ducha to szkieletów ludy
> Młodości podaj mi skrzydła . . .

'This,' he said looking straight at her, measuring the effect of his words, 'may be the awaited promise of rebirth.' The poem was written by a young poet, Adam Mickiewicz, singing the praises of simple feelings and longings, uncluttered by the shackles of cold reason. The news from Poland had given him new strength. The young, he was sure, would atone for the sins of the past generation. The young would change the course of history, wipe off the shame of the partitions, of the squandered fatherland. They were generous. They were noble. They remembered the sacrifices of the past, the heroic deaths of men like her father. Here, Dr Bolecki bowed to her, raising his top hat.

'The Poles are not the only ones. The Greeks will rise, too and restore their ancient glory,' he said. 'The whole world will be renewed.'

He was a doctor, he would be needed, for the young would not stop at words alone. There would be another insurrection, he was sure of that. Not right away perhaps, for the groundwork would have to be laid, but soon. The sacrifice, as always with great common struggles, would be great, but the stakes were even greater. *Measure your strength with the force of your desires*, the young poet said. How right the young were. Heroes like her father had not died in vain. Sacrifice was a torch passed from hand to hand, into the future.

Rosalia listened as he leaned toward her, his grey eyes fixed upon her.

'The past is only important when it makes the future possible,' he said. It was the duty of the living to make sure their heroes did not die in vain. At his side, she could be of help to countless young men whose lives she might save. He knew he was right. She knew it too, he said.

'Mademoiselle Rosalia. This may seem sudden, but I've given it a lot of thought. I'm asking you to become my wife.'

A long indrawn breath. Another one. There was concern on his face, hope and the shadow of uncertainty. His hand was trembling, she could see with the corner of her eye. With him, she thought, I would not waste my life.

'You don't have to answer me now. I just want you to know of my intentions. I'm asking for nothing but hope,' he said.

She could see herself placing her hand on his, quieting the tremor. She could see him at her side, shielding her from pain. These were good thoughts, precious.

'I can give you hope,' she said.

She did not pull her hand away after he had kissed it and told her that she had made him the happiest of men.

With Josephine residing in St Petersburg, she is true mistress of the Tulchin palace where the inscription above the portal says: *May it always be the home of the happy and the free*. Her bed is draped in pearly sheen. Everything in her bedroom is new, untouched by the past. The furniture is white, the walls pale grey. The colour is called *cuisse de nymph effrayée*, like a thigh of a terrified nymph. Her step-children are forbidden to cross the threshold of this room. Nothing here will remind her of Felix's wife who is plotting against her, hoping her husband will *regain his senses*, turn his mistress away.

Hope is not a course of action.

In this world, Dou-Dou, you are either someone's wife or a whore.

Felix loves me, she mutters.

He does love her. His eyes burn when he catches her look across a crowded room. 'Nothing is as good as this,' he whispers in her ear, burying his face in her hair. 'Nothing.' The Uman summer palace is a hundred *versts* from Tulchin, two long days of a carriage ride; there she has also ordered new furniture and new drapes. She wants it to feel hers, for this is where they stay when they visit her Uman garden. Sophievka is growing more beautiful each day, a testament to Potocki's love.

She is thirty-eight years old.

She is with child.

In St Petersburg, the eldest of Felix's children, Yuri, is searching for an ally. His father's anger at the constant news of gambling debts and bad company needs to be softened, disarmed. This is his fourth letter to her:

> My father accuses me of ingratitude. You must feel, my dear Madame la Comtesse, how much my heart is

saddened by such bitter words. You, Madame, whom my father loves and whose judgement he trusts without reservations, please find it in your heart to defend me. Please try to make my father forgive my transgressions and assure me another chance to redeem myself in his eyes. For my part, I promise to continue my attempts to convince my dear mother that the course of action she has taken will only hurt us all. I hope that soon, I might be a harbinger of good news.

In the morning room Felix smiles at the sight of her. His eyelids are reddened at the edges. Letters and dispatches are scattered on the table. The Lubomirskis, their neighbours, have sent them a basket of tulip bulbs for Sophievka. '*Semper Augustus,*' he says, holding the flesh-coloured bulb up to the light. 'How very thoughtful.'

She sits down beside him. Mornings are not kind to her. Her mind is sluggish, dazed with sleep. Every morning she rubs her cheeks with chunks of ice, to bring up the colour and firm her skin. Felix wakes up at dawn. He has already taken a ride through the fields. His hair smells of wind, black earth and burning leaves.

This is the way he likes their days to be. The two of them, together, exchanging news. The price of wheat is up. The price of mutton is down. The steward of the Uman estate is asking what to do with the flock of sheep – sell them one by one, or as a herd? They will have to go to Uman soon, check the progress on the garden, mediate the disputes. The chief engineer Metzel, a strange man who never smiles at her, is making enemies. Mathematics is the key to all knowledge, he told her once. The kindest rumour that reaches them is his declaration that all people fall into two categories: they are either 'mathematicians' or 'cattle'.

'What are you reading now?'

The papers and dispatches bring disturbing news. A week ago, on February 12, 1798, the former King of Poland, Stanisław August Poniatowski, died in St Petersburg, and speculations abound as to the cause of his death. He had a cup of bouillon in the morning, and by the evening he was dead. The Tsar was his last visitor. In France a young general, Napoleon Bonaparte is shipping his army from Tulon to some undisclosed location, which is news most troubling to the English, Felix says. From Italy rumours arrive of legions formed from Polish exiles and prisoners of war, getting ready to fight at Napoleon's side for the resurrection of the lost motherland.

Felix's voice is agitated. He doesn't like the new Tsar, Catherine's son. Calls him a deluded madman, unworthy of his mother, left to steer Mother Russia at this time of turmoil. Predictions increasingly fascinate him: trajectories of comets, patterns of floods and droughts, the swarms of locusts, the shape of bones found in the steppes. All these signs point to a time of confusion and spilled blood. There will be a war, he says, there will be slaughter. He refuses to go to St Petersburg. He refuses to go anywhere. He wants to live in peace, with her and the children.

The King is dead.

She closes her eyes and sees him bending over her, his kisses reaching deep into her womb in a teasing dance that will never be. It is the force of regret that surprises her. For years she has hardly thought of him at all, but now she can think of no one else, of nothing but the longing of her body, the dull pain of desire.

Quickly she mutters a prayer for him, a prayer for the dead. She will order a mass in the Tulchin chapel for his soul.

'Any news from Yuri?'

Felix takes his eyes off the letter he is reading. He frowns, reluctant to think of what annoys him.

'Yuri is in trouble again.'

'Perhaps you are too severe with him.'

'Two million złotys in debt. They say he doesn't sleep, he doesn't eat. All he does is gamble.'

'He should live here with us. In his father's house. You said yourself that St Petersburg is not good for a young man. Here, we can make sure he does not fall into bad company.'

Felix gives her a puzzled look, but now the thought is planted in his head. She will make sure that it is not abandoned. Perhaps he has not been the best of fathers: too indulgent, too willing to let his wife spoil Yuri, give in to his childish whims.

'Josephine is still spoiling him,' he says. Still making excuses for all his transgressions; still protecting him from the consequences of his foolishness; making him waste away his life, his future.

When Felix is angry, his voice quivers and his mouth twists. Without a wig his head seems so much smaller.

'A young man needs a good example,' she says. He needs discipline. He needs to ride at his father's side each morning. Learn to take care of what one day will be his.

'Think of this unborn child,' she says, placing his hand on her belly. 'Our baby will need a brother.'

It is Yuri who informs his father that Countess Josephine has finally agreed to a divorce. On the 28th April, 1798 (17th April the Russian style) the marriage between Count Felix Potocki and Madame de Witt, *née* Glavani Celice de Maurocordato is performed twice, first by a Roman Catholic priest, second by a Greek Orthodox one.

There will be no more bastards.

Some gambles pay off, she thinks.

Hope, sometimes, is enough.

When they arrived in Berlin in the late afternoon, the courtyard of von Haefen's palace was covered with straw to muffle the sounds of the wheels. Her mother's groom, Pietka, who held the door open for her and unfolded the step was silent, too. In Uman, he would have whistled with joy to have seen her.

News of their arrival had caused a commotion. Lights appeared in the windows, doors opened and closed. There was a lot of ruckus with bundles and baskets and hampers carried into the hall.

This must be Rosalia, she thought when a young woman rushed down the marble staircase. She had a tired, drawn face lit up by a lovely smile, pretty, in spite of dark circles under her eyes. 'Rosalia Romanowicz,' she said in a quiet, resigned voice. 'Madame la Comtesse will be so happy. She has talked of little else for days.'

'How is Maman?'

'The pain is coming back. Doctor Lafleur . . .' But Volodia's crying made her stop in mid sentence. 'May I see him?' she asked.

Sophie Kisielev was just about to say that the baby was tired, that they were all tired, that she wanted to see her mother right away, but then changed her mind. Maman had written that Rosalia had been of great help in the last months. Katia was scowling, but did not dare to protest. Rosalia leant over the baby who watched her with interest, big blue eyes fixed on her face.

'May I hold him please,' she asked.

Noting Katia's growing annoyance, Madame Kisielev nodded permission. The baby, cradled in Rosalia's arms, did not protest.

The wetnurse would not concede defeat. She was listing the christening gifts Volodia had received: the silver set that consisted of a beaker, a dish, a spoon, a knife and a fork. They were decorated with vine leaves and the knife and the fork were inscribed, *To Volodia Pavlowich Kisielev from his Grandmother Sophie Potocka*. The beaker was covered in babies jumping around naked, big fat babies with plump hands and knees.

Then there were the apostle spoons.

'That is enough,' Sophie Kisielev interrupted, annoyed at herself for letting Katia go on for that long. Then Volodia yawned, and his body stiffened in Rosalia's arms.

'Oh! He's just having his little pee, Miss,' Katia laughed, seeing alarm on Rosalia's face. 'You'd better give him to me.'

Two German grooms were already taking the luggage upstairs. The rooms, Rosalia assured her, were ready. Bright and far enough from the grand salon not to disturb the invalid. She had made sure the fire was kept lit for the last two days. There would be no draughts.

Olga arrived breathless, having run down the marble stairs, and threw herself into Sophie's arms, crying. She seemed taller and thinner. In her eyes she could see fear. Maman, Olga said, already knew of her arrival and was waiting.

'She's been asking for you every day,' Olga said.

'How is she?'

Olga lowered her eyes and shook her head. 'Is that your son?' she asked instead, her voice on the edge, extending her hands to Volodia. Katia gave a sigh of satisfaction when Volodia began crying as soon as he left her plump arms.

'What's wrong with him?' Olga asked.

'Nothing is wrong,' Sophie snapped. 'He's tired. We all are.'

PART FOUR

I've heard that, in Kamieniec, one of the Armenian merchants painted a mural right over his store, depicting an old, naked man, his shrivelled balls crookedly falling to one side. On both sides of the figure, there was an inscription, cleverly broken into two: CURVA VITOVA. *In utter innocence, anyone unfamiliar with Latin was told that the inscription meant 'crooked balls' and referred to the old man's shrivelled instruments, but the whole of Kamieniec reeled with laughter, repeating 'curva vitowa': Madame de Witt is a whore.*

A delightful story, my reader may say, but I'm not one of the galliardours, Your Royal Highness, these troubadours or singers known for blackening the reputations of beautiful women and thus bringing on themselves cruel punishment, like Vidal from Toulouse who, as Nostradamus tells us, was deprived of his tongue (it was cut in two) for having offended a beautiful young woman in his songs. I also remember what old Athenian theologians so wisely maintained: that if God Almighty were angered by all human transgressions, then no creature would be more unhappy than the Creator, for He would have to be torn, ceaselessly, by the emotions caused by human sins. Shouldn't we thus assume that our Lord has acquired a somewhat thicker skin and shouldn't we, perhaps, follow His divine example?

Thus, it is best to say, My Merciful Sovereign and Benefactor, that we have arrived at the point of our story where it might be necessary to drag a sponge over Dou-Dou's scandalous life and respect her in her new position in this vale of tears. To her most appropriate would be the saying, Quantum mutatas ab illa! Oh, how different you are from the creature you once were! Or even: Omnia homini, dum vivit, speranda sunt. As long as one is alive all is possible . . .

BERLIN, 1822:

Morphine

Sophie

A finger cut by a piece of glass, the blood hesitating for a moment before pouring through the edges of separated skin. A lash of a whip across her back and her buttocks. A candle flame on her finger, pinching her skin with heat. Bruises from jealous fists and heels, scratches on her face and arms, hair pulled out by the fistfuls. A slap on her cheek, so hard that she could feel a loosened tooth and taste the salty blood. The pain of a body falling off a galloping horse, the dull thud when she reaches the ground, the radiating pain of the fall. The pain of childbirth, of her womb opening to release the baby's head, pain that makes her shiver, her teeth chatter.

A warm stream of saliva is flowing down her cheek. By the time it reaches her neck, it will cool down.

Felix is standing at the foot of her bed, dressed in black. Alive but like a statue of some dark hero, his hands crossed over his chest. His eyes, she thinks, are like two empty holes. If she lets him look at her for too long, she will melt. How is it, she asks him, that what was once most fervently desired becomes so bitter? Where in this pain-ridden body hides the source of defiance? Why one soul gives up in despair while for another the highest mountain is but another challenge?

'You are dead, Felix,' she mutters. 'You should know everything now. Tell me.'

Refuge of sinners. Comforter of the afflicted. Those who pray to the Virgin, pray with faith and constancy, will always know the power of her healing. Is it really true that on a Saturday the sun has to shine because it is the Virgin's day?

Scarlet stockings are the most alluring. A flash of red from beneath the black velvet. Her hands are made of wax. She has never liked her hands. They were too big, too clumsy. She has never liked her feet either. And lying down means she cannot toss her hair.

'Tell me.'

How can a despairing soul be freed from itself? How can a way be lit for thoughts that stay somewhere too deep to be touched?

'This pain is God's punishment for your sins.'

She feels drops of water on her lips, cool water smelling of rose petals. She is dreaming it all and yet the dream seems as real as if she lived in two worlds, one underneath the other, transparent like a mountain stream. How like Felix to think God would always be on his side.

'You betrayed me with my own son.'

Pain is breaking through her, tearing raw pieces from her womb. She wants to scream, but the scream dies in her throat. Felix is stopping her. No longer still, he is now kneeling on her chest, clutching at her throat.

'Do you really think you can fool God?' Felix says. 'Make up for what you have done with a few good deeds? You who care only for yourself.'

She wants to protest. He doesn't know her. He will never know her. How can he be her judge?

The faint sound of horses' hooves penetrates the closed window, the grating of carriage wheels. She runs her tongue over parched lips. The pain is leaving no space to breathe, no movement, no thought that she can call her own.

Who said that?

'It's called morphine.'

The bitterness slid down her throat and spilled into her stomach. The doctor was watching her. She remembered a flock of birds in Istanbul, no bigger than robins. No one had ever seen them settle. They were always in flight. Mana said they were the souls of the women whom the Sultan had ordered drowned.

'Is it very bitter?' Rosalia in that grey dress, pulling a grey shawl over her shoulders, her lips twisted as if the bitterness of the drug touched her too. She was a soul most gentle, a child frightened by her own desires. What was she doing here, in that unbecoming dress, buttoned up to her chin?

An orphan's heart is always hungry.

Bitter.

Very bitter.

'Slowly,' the doctor said. 'Take a small sip.'

Bitterness that spread from deep within her. Depth without end, without limits, filled with words and storms that were welling up, breaking through her.

Mea culpa. Mea culpa. Pray for me for I have sinned.

'Your daughter is here.'

Rosalia was steadying herself, holding on to the edge of the bed. On her face was a frown of resolve, a shadow of resignation.

Do you know what it is to always eat with another's mouth?

Move according to another's will?
Speak with another's tongue?
Feel with another's heart?
Which is the graver sin: betrayal or resignation?

Outside the grand salon the clock struck twelve. Midnight, she thought, had become more like space than time, a territory filled with shadows. A vast land of perfect stillness where past and present live side by side.

The floor beside her bed was empty.

Sophie Kisielev

In spite of the French doctor's fears, Maman was fully conscious, seated on the empire bed, the folds of her dress, the colour of olive leaves arranged as if she were a doll, an ornament in this glittering salon. The bed was covered with a golden throw.

Sophie ran to her mother as if she were still a little girl and her Maman had just returned from one of her trips to St Petersburg or Kiev, her arms loaded with gifts, her voice filled with surprises. She ran so fast, holding her breath, that the muscles in her neck locked in a spasm only her mother could soothe. She didn't have to talk to the French doctor or to Olga. She didn't need Rosalia's furtive looks. She could see death in her mother's face, in the whiteness of her skin, in that strange elation of her eyes – wide open, fixed upon her.

'Maman,' she sobbed and threw herself at her mother's feet. The smells of the journey still lingered on her dress: the horses, the inns, the smoke, the peculiar smell of the carriage, of leather and damp upholstery.

'I've waited,' her mother said. In her voice there was no reproach. 'I knew you would come.'

'It was Pavel, Maman,' she said. 'He kept me from leaving.'

That sounded childish, she thought, an accusation, an excuse. If she had insisted earlier, he wouldn't have stopped her. He didn't stop her in the end, did he? Still sobbing, Sophie took her mother's hand in hers. Skin and bones, she thought. So little life left. She was angry at Pavel, at herself.

'Why didn't you tell me earlier, Maman?' Her voice was sounding just the way it used to sound in childhood when she was cross, her eyes were filled with tears. 'I should've known.'

'You were in no condition to help me,' her mother said. 'I wish I did not cry so easily. I cry so easily these days.'

Unlike Olga, Sophie had no time to get used to the sight of her mother, the skin melting on her face, the disappearing muscles, the sores in her mouth. Even with the windows covered at all times, the light was too harsh, too revealing. Even in the darkened room, a dying body couldn't be hidden.

'My children,' her mother said. 'I have my children. I have always loved my children.'

Why this insistence in her mother's voice? Why repeat twice that Jan was writing to her every week? That his wife always added at least one line of her own, even to the shortest of notes. That they had planted the tulip bulbs from Sophievka by the pond, commissioned a painter to paint them when they bloomed.

'He doesn't know, does he?' Her half-brother, the eldest. Always spared from the bad news, from problems. Given far too much. Too often. Pavel did not like him at all and soon called him a spy.

'You'll take care of the youngest ones. Bobiche and Olga need you. They are still children. Promise me that. See that your sister marries well. Alexander will help you. In my will I've asked him to help you.'

Alexander, her elder brother. If she ever called him her

eldest, Maman always objected. Don't ever forget Jan, she insisted. He is your eldest brother.

'I promise.'

Sophie Kisielev wiped the tears off her cheeks, slowly regaining her breath. Her mother kept talking. The pearls were for her (they had to be restrung soon) and so was the furniture from the Uman palace. She had asked Rosalia to make a list of what would go to whom. The will was ready. Had been ready for some time. It was deposited with Monsieur Rashkin in St Petersburg. There were provisions for everyone except Mieczysław. This son of hers who cared for no one but himself had already taken more than his share.

'I can die now,' her mother said. 'In peace. I know you will do everything I ask you to. Twelve thousand roubles will go to the servants.'

'You won't die.'

But Maman did not listen. Her fingers drummed a staccato rhythm on the side of the bed. As if time passed too slowly, as if it needed to be urged on.

'I want to see my grandson now.'

Sophie Kisielev wanted so much to tell her mother about her fears, cry out all her pain, her premonitions, her uneasiness. 'You know how to make men love you,' she wanted to say. 'Teach me.' But all she could do was sob like a lost, frightened child until the doors opened and Katia came in with Volodia.

'Volodia resembles His Highness Pavel Dimitrievich. Like two drops of water,' Katia managed to say before she was ordered to leave. She did it reluctantly, staring at them as she walked toward the door. From behind the curtain came the soft sounds of a flute.

'My first grandson,' Maman said, taking Volodia in her arms, which were so thin that her bones showed through them. '*Mon epilda.*'

Sophie Kisielev was grateful that the baby did not cry. She was grateful for the tears of joy in her mother's eyes, for the tenderness in them. If such were her last memories of her, she would take them gladly.

Was the French doctor really good, Maman, she asked. Could he be trusted? He did say that Volodia was a healthy baby. Tired, of course, he was tired, the poor dove. That's why he cried all night. And also because Katia liked to carry him when he cried, and he had got used to it now. Katia was also healthy, even though her own child died of smallpox. In Odessa the air was mild, even in winter. The palace needed renovations, but it would be just right for them. Tulchin, in the end, was always too big, wasn't it.

Her mother smiled.

'Maman, Pavel said he doesn't like when I call Volodia "my dove".'

She knew not how to make her husband love her. She wanted her mother to tell her what to do. If only she could stretch out the time they still had, make it last longer. By a day, an hour even. She clasped her hands to stop them from trembling. She was trying not to cry.

'Do you ever think of Papa?'

Her mother gave her a soft, indulgent look.

'Yes,' she said.

'I don't remember much of him, Maman. Just that he always wore this long black jacket and it used to frighten me. Once he took me to a strange room where there were apples and pears on shelves. He peeled an apple for me and asked if I liked it. I said I did, even though I didn't.'

'You weren't even four when he died. You can't remember him much. He loved you,' her mother whispered.

'Are you all right, Maman? Am I tiring you?'

'No, *ma cherie*.'

There was a twitch on her mother's face, a spasm of pain.

'Go, *ma cherie*,' her mother said gently. 'Tell the doctor to come here right away. Tell him I need more of his medicine.'

Sophie

Her ankle is well turned. She has always liked satin bows on her shoes. Gold on black. Shiny. A picture: Felix lifting her shoe, holding it up to his nose. Breathing in and out. Her smell, her effluvia. 'You are all I've got,' he says.

If only he had stayed that way, she could have found it in her heart to love him until the end. But something happened to him. Something dark, sticky and feverish, spilling out of the dreams from which he wakes up screaming. Frightening her, frightening the children.

Each morning before breakfast, he drinks a glass of water in which his valet has tried to dissolve a teaspoon of tar. The tar turns the water brown and oily. It never fully dissolves, only softens, and black patches stick to his teeth long afterward. 'I know what I am doing,' he says when she objects. This is his doctor's remedy and he trusts his doctor more than he trusts her.

He is still giving balls and dinner parties, theatricals and fêtes. He has to, being a Potocki. He is lord of the Tulchin palace, lord of the Uman lands. He still owns Ukrainian towns, villages, and vast expanses of the steppes. But when guests arrive he lets her be the hostess and withdraws into his rooms. He may appear reluctantly toward the end of the party, a tall man in black wandering through the rooms, silent witness to their merriment. She could have sworn that often the guests do not recognise him.

In his dreams, is she the Devil's child? The temptress

for whom he has sinned? The cause of all his fears, of all his transgressions?

She has tried reasoning with him, urging trips to St Petersburg. They have a house there that needs supervision. The new Tsar, Alexander, does not resemble his late father, and is awaiting their presence at his court. What's wrong, darling, she keeps asking. There is no war, there is no slaughter. Why all this gloom?

And why now: when we have our children, our friends; when the old turmoils have died; when the past is forgotten?

'Forgotten,' he repeats back at her. There is derision in his voice as if she tried to tell him that the sun is black and trees grow with their roots up in the air.

Sometimes she succeeds though. Sometimes she can still make him laugh. Sometimes he lets her take his hands and pull him toward her. Softly she kisses his lips, his eyelids, and feels him stirring, feels his hands touch her breasts. How gentle she has become, how careful not to extinguish his passion with a movement too free, too daring. He likes when she whispers into his ear: My Lord, My Master, My King. He likes when she lets him lift her skirts, when she lies under him motionless and soft like a rag doll. But now even such moments are rare, and when they pass she sees him in the Tulchin chapel, prostrate on the floor, praying long into the night.

Mea culpa, he mutters. *Mea culpa. Mea maxima culpa.*

There is a resident in the Tulchin palace, a man she cannot stand. His name is Monsieur Grabianka and he does not leave Felix's side. He calls himself the King of New Israel, claiming that *superieur inconnu* has given him the secret of prolonging human life, that he possesses three tears shed by St John the Baptist, capable of healing all sickness. He talks of helping Man return to his state before the Fall, to restore the power he has lost through sin. If his mission fails, Monsieur Grabianka predicts great changes in the world. She may have little patience with his speeches, but she remembers that in this new world, servants will take away the possessions of their masters and an Anti-Christ from France will conquer the world.

'A crook,' she says, 'a charlatan.' If she could, she would have sent him packing long ago.

'A holy man,' Felix says, 'who has come to show me the way to salvation.'

The holy man likes to stand in front of a mirror and stare at his white teeth. He is fond of expensive brandy and roasted game. He speaks in demented puzzles Felix ponders over for days. 'The Word stepped down to earth from above, to teach the children of Jacob. The children closed their father's lips and the Word lost its power.' That she refuses to listen to the voice of this holy man is another sign of her weakness. She gathers she should be grateful for the word 'weakness', undoubtedly suggested by the *holy* man himself. He does not dare call her evil. Not yet. He knows he might still need her. So, for now, she is merely weak, a woman, a vessel that needs to be filled.

'Listen to me please,' she begs Felix on the rare days he is still hers. In the morning his face is bloated, red. Sometimes the tips of his fingers become purple and he is short of breath. 'Your health is failing,' she tells him. 'This is what brings on all these thoughts.' But when she suggests a trip to Spa, or a consultation with one of the St Petersburg doctors he dismisses her words. His problems, he says, are not of the body.

'Can't you see?' she asks Felix, angry at his blindness, at the quiet stubbornness she knows she cannot change. 'All he wants is your money.'

'That is what people said about you,' he answers. 'Was it true?'

He has answers to everything she says now. He dresses in black, because he needs to remind himself of the sins he has committed. He despises vanity. He does not dance, because dancing brings forth the Devil in the human soul. He does not touch wine or spirits for only the strongest souls can handle such a potent stimulation.

The strongest soul, she assumes, is that of Monsieur Grabianka.

'Such a comment is beneath you, Sophie,' Felix answers and walks away from her. She knows that he has made a new will. He will leave most of his money to his children by Josephine – Yuri, his firstborn, will get the biggest share. Her children are provided for, though she has been told that their share will be modest, and she can administer their funds until they come of age. Potocki's widow will be left penniless.

Is this your penance, Felix? she wants to ask. You want to punish me for your own sins? Is this what my stepchildren convinced you is just? Is this what will bring you peace in the afterlife?

The law is on his side. She has not brought any dowry to the marriage so she is not entitled to anything. 'I call it injustice,' Yuri tells her, pressing her hand with his, sliding it up her arm. 'I'll never allow it, as long as I live. You will have my share of the fortune, I swear it. All of it.'

Her stepson's love for her is like a disease. It claims him in feverish bouts, in spells of maddened desire. He cannot sleep, he cannot eat. He swoons and falls to his knees. His lips when he kisses her are hot and dry.

General Kisielev

Pavel Dimitrievich Kisielev was a thirty-four-year-old general in the Tsarist army. His career had been spectacular. He had taken part in the 1812 campaign against

Napoleon, he had been aide-de-camp to the Tsar himself, and a commander of the Second Army stationed in Tulchin where he had courted and won Countess Potocka's elder daughter.

General Kisielev's carriage was now approaching Berlin. The much awaited permission from His Majesty, Tsar Alexander, for a short leave, had arrived on the fourth day after his wife's hasty and, he must call it by the name it deserved, hysterical, departure. With the permission came his passport. Had his wife agreed to wait, as he asked her to, they could have made the journey together at a much lower cost. The carriage was thick with dust, the horses were tired. In the carriage – rebuked, his valet had kept silent – General Kisielev had a long time to think.

General Kisielev considered his wife's reactions excessive and unpredictable. Sophie was a new mother, however, and he had been warned that women's characters changed when the first baby arrived. He had felt that change already. His Sophie had been teary and impatient all the time, accusing *him* of being callous. In that last week she had talked of nothing but Maman. General Kisielev had used to think that as mothers-in-law go, his wasn't the worst. At first he thought her most charming and even – if he had to be honest – seductive, but then he changed his mind, even before the scraps of these vicious rumours began reaching him.

Now he could see quite clearly what his wife, the favourite daughter, wouldn't. Her constant manipulation of everyone around her, the planting of doubt here, jealousy there. Jan de Witt, the son from the first marriage, so clearly favoured in financial matters, was now in the Tsar's secret service. A despicable man, always ready to offer one a drink, or boast about his amorous conquests. To think of it, always trying to make friends with young officers, getting them to talk too freely. Alexander, the first of the Potockis' children, would never question his mother's word, so was always in charge of her affairs. Only Mieczysław, the younger one, miserable boor that he was, had dared to oppose her. Grabbed what he thought was his and turned his Maman out of the Tulchin door. But that, of course, was never mentioned.

A daughter of a Greek cattle trader and a whore. His wife refused to listen. She would not foul her own lips, she had said, with vicious rumours.

'Her blood,' she said, 'is flowing in your son's veins.'

General Kisielev opened the curtain of the carriage window. The houses of the German peasants were so much more solid, more prosperous than the huts of the Russian serfs. That was wrong, he thought, poverty bred discontent.

The possibility of ordering the world, of making life run an efficient and predictable course, fascinated General Kisielev, especially after his visit to Gruzino, General Arakcheev's estate. His Imperial Majesty had been impressed too. The Gruzino serfs lived in houses made of bricks. They worked ten hours a day, except Sunday. Woods and thickets around the estate had been razed so that lazy serfs would have nowhere to hide. Pig keeping, private plots, vodka were all banned. All peasants carried with them their punishment books at all times where their offences were listed and punishment recorded. Women offenders were made to wear iron collars and to pray to be forgiven for their sins in front of the whole church. In the libraries and schools peasant children, scrubbed clean and attentive, learned to read and write. Everywhere they went, there was order and cleanliness. General Kisielev was not surprised when the Tsar ordered the construction of military settlements based on the Gruzino model. If only he had thought of it himself first.

As the carriage rolled on General Kisielev's thoughts went back to his wife and the letter she had sent from the first station. *My heart is heavy with fear, and I'm afraid, Pavel, that I will never forgive you if I'm too late to see her*. It was evident to him that every frown he had made, she must have carried in her heart. *Your detachment, your refusal to listen to me, pains me greatly. You are my husband and I love you, but I'm not one of your soldiers.*

Under other circumstances, General Kisielev's thoughts would not dwell on women for that long. Women complicated things too much, wavered and changed their minds. The miseries of the boudoir, as he used to say, were best treated with laudanum and a visit from a milliner. All women were good for was the few moments of pleasure one could snatch away from their greedy claws.

The birth of his son had filled General Kisielev with pride. He would have a successor, a confidant, a soldier. The baby needed his mother now, but soon he would have to watch more closely over his upbringing. Women would only fill his heart with their stories, their sentimental nonsense and make him too soft.

'Faster,' he knocked on the roof of the carriage. The carriage swayed as if hesitating for a moment and then it rushed forward with a heavy lurch.

> Tell your husband that he should leave without waiting for the permission to arrive. His Imperial Majesty has always been a warm and considerate friend of mine and I guarantee he would not object to an act of filial obligation.

Well, the old girl had infinite confidence in her fading charms.

Fools! The Potockis, like all Poles, were fools. Rash,

impatient fools, who, on one day, would prostrate themselves in front of the Russians only to stab them in the back on another. He should have found a Russian woman to marry: a woman who would not turn up her nose at black bread and pickles, a woman whose family would not shame him.

To calm himself down General Kisielev looked through the carriage window again. It was cold and damp in November. The air was filled with smoke; Prussian peasants were burning leaves and dead branches in the fields. Peasant women bent down in the field, presenting their ample behinds. He recalled the latest wetnurse his wife had taken for Volodia, a plump, cheerful Russian girl whom he liked to surprise as she suckled his son. Her breasts were white and full of milk, her body big and rose coloured, her hair pale white like fields of wheat. Around her he felt the pull of the earth, the world of simple pleasures. Of hunting trips when he would trek through the snow-covered land, of falling asleep with his clothes on, of smashing ice to melt it over the fire to brew tea, small bits of grass still trapped in it. Of staggering into the icy night to relieve his bladder right there on the snow bank, watching the steam rise from the stream of his urine. His desire for his own wife had nothing to do with such images. Before Volodia's birth, Sophie submitted to his embraces without a protest but without passion, her body too soft, too pliant. Not that he resented it too much, especially when he considered Maman's reputation. In the end, a wife and a mother had other functions in life and a man could find his pleasures elsewhere.

Olga, however, was altogether different. The thought of his 'little sister' pleased him. During the wedding feast, she had dragged him into the garden and kissed him hard on the lips. 'It's the champagne,' she whispered. 'Please forget it.' She fled, before he had time to recover.

Sophie

In Tulchin, Felix is dying. It is January 1805. A winter so cold that birds fall frozen from the sky.

The snow has covered the Tulchin garden. Cold, melting under her hand. Melting on the tip of her tongue, freezing flesh. The *hammam* is empty. The unborn baby has stopped her from taking steam baths. Her skin is clogged and rough. Itchy at the elbows and knees. The doctor is adamant. Unless you want to lose it, he has said. She is forty-five years old. In the nursery, every morning after breakfast, she likes to watch her children at play. The maids praise them, good little angels. Little Sophie's gentle ways. The boys are already like little men, red with anger if anything refuses to go their way, the squabbling, the big tears, the pushing and shoving. But it is still so easy to make them forget, turn their attention elsewhere, toward the lark in the sky or a tickle on the tummy. Would you like a little brother or a sister, she asks them. 'A brother,' Mieczysław says, hands on his hips. 'But smaller than me.' So smart for his age. Always knowing what he wants.

There will be no baths. She doesn't want to lose her baby.

Her bastard, Felix said. He spat the word at her, flanked by his two daughters – Josephine's daughters of pure blood – Victoria and Ludwika, restored to their rightful position at his side. The real Potockis. A Greek whore, they call her behind her back. Her rule is over, their eyes tell her. She has lost. She is not invincible.

Dreams visit him, dreams Felix describes with flushed cheeks and clouded eyes. Dreams of fiery wheels, of smashed cups spilling their content into the ground, of a shaft of light that shines right into his eyes, blinding him. There are nights when he sobs and prays, stretched on the chapel floor, begging for God's mercy. Once he came to her saying that he saw an angel pass by the open door of his room, clad in a luminous gown, smelling of incense.

'That,' he said, 'is a sign that forgiveness is still possible.'

She has an image of a thicket growing between them: thorns and brambles, spikes that tear the flesh. A thicket denied, lied about. In his presence she is always generous and cheerful and at ease. It is Felix who trails her with his darkened gaze, who makes everyone conscious of his ugly squint, slipping off her, dissipating, withering.

Is there still time? Can she still turn it round?

She is not allowed to cross the threshold of his bedroom until he sends for her. She is not allowed to touch his food. Why would I want to poison my own husband, she has asked. Is there anyone else who would lose more with his death? In this country a widow is left with nothing – unless her husband chooses to provide for her.

He has been a coward, Felix tells her. She has been his punishment on this earth. His Gehenna. His Sodom and Gomorrah for which there is no other place after death but Hell. Every time he touches her, he purifies himself with holy water and salt.

He points at the faces of their children, asking, which ones of them are truly mine?

Remember Gertruda, Felix? Remember the child who was not even allowed to be born? Where were you then? Its father?

'Repent, when there is still time. Fall to your knees and beg the Lord to forgive you for your sins.'

When he breathes, his nostrils widen and twitch. Every so often his breath is hoarse, and he clears his throat as if about to choke. His right eye is bulging more than the left, and both are always rimmed with red. There is a smell that precedes him, of tar, camphor and unwashed flesh. A festering smell that reminds her of rotting roots in the muddy Tulchin pond.

'You have betrayed me with my own son. My children were right. I was a fool not wanting to believe them.'

God's will, God's punishment. God's grace, and God's forgiveness. Those last two are reserved for him of course. For her there is nothing but damnation and the fires of Hell.

'You have no shame,' Jeroslav says. This stepson of hers who once said he should have plunged a dagger in her back, right after the wedding. Before *they* were born. Her children. The Potocki blood has been thinned. Balsam has been diluted with tar.

She bites her lip and feels the warm flush rise to her cheeks.

'Wouldn't you rather slash my throat,' she asks, daring him to withstand her look. He cannot. With all his hatred for her, he cannot look into her eyes.

Does he – like his elder brother – dream of touching her skin? Is she his temptress too? Should she remind him of the rumour that he was fathered by his mother's footman?

Anger is gathering in her. She wants to break his smugness, his calm. Jeroslav is sitting in his favourite armchair, his legs stretched out. Her maid is saying that she has seen him sneak into the stables. Has he taken a fancy to one of the milk-maids – or grooms?

The child moves inside her. Its kicks are weak and furtive as if it were not sure about life. Her skin has erupted with blotches and at night she wakes up drenched with sweat. Last night she dreamt of Kotula, Nicolai, and

Helena. Three souls frolicking among the clouds, playing ball with the stars. She woke up with her face wet with tears. What if she dies with this baby? What if her little ones were left to the Potockis' mercy?

Her old friend, Diane de Polignac, writes to her often. Long letters filled with longing for the past, dismay at the zest with which the upstarts assume new privileges. In Santo Domingo, Napoleon's sister, Pauline Leclerc, orders her black slaves to carry her around the house and warms her feet on their bellies. *The years of exile have taught me to expect the unthinkable*, Diane writes.

I won't die, she thinks. I'll not give him that pleasure.

She takes a deep breath, feeling the air inside her. She moves her hands, her arms, her feet.

'Shame,' she points out to her stepson, 'is a luxury I cannot afford. Unlike you I wasn't born with a silver platter next to my bed, a silver spoon in my mouth and hundreds of servants to wipe my arse.'

He winces when he hears the word *arse*. Good, she thinks. The baby is due any day now. Jeroslav stands up and pushes the armchair away.

'I hate you,' he says, before leaving. 'I hope this one kills you.'

'The morphine is beginning to work,' the French doctor said.

She raised her hands in the air, marvelling at their translucent pallor.

'Is the pain gone?' Rosalia asked.

'Is it gone?'

'Is it?'

She could almost believe that she might stand up and dance, fly through the room on the wave of happiness. The pain was still there, but strangely as if it were in someone else's body. As if she and the woman in this empire bed whose womb was rotting inside her were not one and the same.

'What is it that you feel?' the doctor asked.

He was like all the men she has met, hungry for all he could not understand. Wondering what her body was telling her, wishing he could record the rhythm of her heart, register each flow of the life force that washed over her, weigh and measure the progress of death. When she was gone he would write it all down, document the case of the Polish countess, dying of cancer, given a dose of morphine.

'Now you are earning your keep, *Monsieur le Docteur*,' she told him. 'Now, you are worth your weight in gold.'

Thomas

Asking a foreign power to intervene in the internal matters of one's own country does not necessarily have to be a betrayal. The monarchists in France asking for a foreign intervention against the Revolution were not traitors, but political opponents.

Thomas had heard such arguments before, Ignacy made sure. But, in 1792, in Poland, there was no civil war. The May 3rd constitution united everyone. King Stanisław August supported it. The nation supported it. The leaders of the Targowica faction: Felix Potocki, Franciszek Rzewuski and Seweryn Branicki, *were* traitors.

'The best one can say about them,' Ignacy liked to repeat, 'is that they didn't know what they were doing. Catherine II, the greatest whore of Europe, Thomas, was dying. Death was already waiting for her, in her water closet. But it wasn't fast enough for Poland.'

There was a consensus in Ignacy's circle that had it not been for the Targowica, the Russians would have swallowed the reforms of the new constitution. The war with

Russia and the third, final partition of Poland could have been prevented. For before Targowica there had been political cards to play. One could have set Russian interests against those of Prussia, whisper into the Emperor's ear that a stronger monarchy in Warsaw would weaken the Jacobin dreams.

Every Sunday afternoon Ignacy received guests. His cook prepared Polish dishes: bigos, pierogi with kasha and thick sour cream, borsch. Sometimes, in response to special request, other dishes were made, some of them almost embarrassingly simple, like a bowl of boiled potatoes with pork lourdes.

'Do please come,' Ignacy said. 'It's not on bread alone . . .'

Topics of conversation in Ignacy's singular salon did not surprise Thomas. Every participant of the gathering had once been Napoleon's soldier. Captains Przybylski and Grójecki had gone all the way to Moscow, Colonel Sorek was with Marshal Poniatowski when the Marshal threw himself into the currents of Elstera. 'Did he really say, "God placed the honour of Poland in my hands and only to Him I shall surrender it,"' Thomas had asked. Ignacy shrugged and said that it didn't really matter, that was what the Poles wanted to remember.

The air of the salon was thick with snuff, cigar smoke and brandy. After spending time at the bedside of the dying, gatherings like this one, often felt slightly indecent. But it was precisely this indecent vitality that drew Thomas into the arguments that erupted in this room. One by one Ignacy's guests came up to him, keen to explain yet another aspect of the political situation. He was French, after all. He could have missed the point entirely.

'Fulhams, Doctor Lafleur, loaded dice,' Captain Przybylski said. 'I caught a fellow once. His dice were drilled and weighted with quicksilver to favour fives and sixes. All the scoundrel needed were three small veins of mercury, a drill and some burrs for hollowing. He could get a pair that favoured the ace and the deuce. Or fives and sixes. "High men" he called them.'

Captain Przybylski was a strapping man with reddish streaks in his hair. It took Thomas a moment to realise that the story of his encounter with a hustler had not been brought up in vain.

'After the Congress of Vienna the Tsar of Russia calls himself the King of Poland! General Zajączek has conveniently forgotten his allegiance to Napoleon and became the Tsar's right hand in Warsaw. Konstantin, the Tsar's half-sane brother rules over the Polish army. The Arch-Duke swears he will drag the last traces of the French disease out of their bodies. Napoleon's *gragnons* are now being treated to good old Russian discipline. The number of suicides has quadrupled. The lashes are back. The traitors have won and we are left to pay for what they have done.

'They call it luck,' Captain Przybylski sighed. 'A fulham, I say, and high men. Then the world quickly forgets the victims.'

The Poles, with all their faults, Thomas thought, had his sympathy. A nation betrayed, quartered and denied existence. He could see why they would feel cheated. Ignacy, however, did not believe in doctored dice. He would rather look for some mythical, exclusively Polish sins to explain his country's fate, sins that would have to be redeemed with more sacrifice, with more blood. As if other countries were better and more worthy. Thomas liked the fulhams theory better. Fulhams and high men, he must remember that.

Captain Grójecki's estate had been part of Prussia since the first partition of Poland. Now Captain Grójecki's youngest son had joined the Prussian army. 'This,' the Captain declared, 'is good.' He liked to think that his son was learning from the masters, that one day he might use what he had learned against his own teachers. 'When the right time comes,' he said with a knowing smile. Captain Przybylski, who had been waiting for a pause in the conversation, nodded and wrung his hands. Soon the two men were lost in a discussion on the merits of Prussian discipline and tactics.

Thomas sipped his coffee. The Poles made excellent coffee, and Ignacy's household was no exception. Freshly roasted beans made all the difference.

'Mycielski!' Captain Grójecki's voice again captured Thomas's attention. 'Small world, I tell you. I knew his father in Kraków.' For a while the conversation hovered around Captain Mycielski's amorous exploits in Berlin. Duelling might be considered foolishness by some, but obviously not by a dashing Polish captain in the Prussian Guards who had already been challenged a dozen times by jealous husbands. With pistols, too, not sabres like a mere hot-headed Jena student. A well-known society lady had taken ill on his account. 'Not the only one,' Thomas heard. There was an undercurrent of admiration in these voices, he thought, the Polish love of panache. In the end the consensus was that with Captain's Mycielski's slender waist, his broad chest, his hair, the calves of a Greek hero, who could be faithful to one woman?

'One would make all the rest unhappy,' Captain Przybylski laughed, smoothing his reddish hair, with, Thomas decided, quite a dose of wistfulness.

A maid approached Ignacy and curtsied. Her flaxen braid was tied around her head like a crown. Ignacy bent to listen, but then shook his head and sent her back to the kitchen. When the girl closed the door behind her, he rang the small silver bell. With some reluctance, the room fell silent.

'Gentlemen,' Ignacy said. 'We have gathered here not

just for excellent company and for the memories of past glory, but to keep our souls alive with hope. I have something for you today. General Dąbrowski's last will from which I want to read but a few sentences. *Keep in purity the national spirit, unite in morality and be like one man, then all evil will abandon you.*'

General Dąbrowski, the creator and commander in chief of the Polish Legion in Napoleon's army – the Legion so cruelly decimated in Santo Domingo – had died three years earlier in Winna Góra. He asked to be buried in the jacket and cap of the Legion. Three bullets were to be put in his coffin, the bullets that had been extracted from his body, souvenirs of close calls. Beside the bullets the General wanted three sabres, one from the 1794 Insurrection, one from the Polish Legion, and one from the battle of Berezina.

> Your future is great and illustrious, but trust yourselves only and build this future on your own strength. For only your strength will get back what the foreign powers have taken away from us!

'These are his very words,' Ignacy said. 'He wanted us all to carry them in our hearts.'

What followed was a mêlée of voices. Thomas didn't have to understand Polish to know what made these aging men jump at each other's throats. Chances had been missed, mistakes made. Now at least two positions were being violently argued. One was that Russia should never have been trusted. Those who entered into alliances with Alexander were traitors. Traitors like those who signed at Targowica. The other view held that political realities could not be ignored. Alliances had to be made according to need. If Poland had to walk with Russia for a while, so be it. Was it really that different than walking with Napoleon? Losing so many good men in Italy, Spain or

Santo Domingo? If Polish soldiers were to get their military training in the Prussian army, that's where they had to go. These were times of stealth and subterfuge.

'I have enough,' Ignacy said to Thomas, defeated by the cacophony of voices he hoped to bring together. 'You see, my friend. We are a condemned nation. Only a miracle can save us.'

Thomas held out his hand to squeeze Ignacy's arm, but his friend was already up waving his hands.

'Friends,' Ignacy cried, his cheeks flushed. 'Countrymen!' His voice drowned in the agitated noises of the flaring arguments, until the maid appeared again.

The bell that sounded this time was a huge brass one. When the ringing stopped Ignacy announced that the food was growing cold and the cook, God forbid, might be upset. All the kasha, pierogis, borsch! The thought of such waste was enough to quench all divisions.

'What more proof do you want. Food unites you. Poles are very reasonable people,' Thomas said.

'Never for long, my friend,' Ignacy laughed, putting his hand on Thomas's shoulder. 'Never for long.'

Later, after everyone had left, Thomas and Ignacy sat together in the salon watching the fire burn itself out. Sex was the need of the body, he used to tell his students. He tried to evoke Minou, her red hair, her lisping voice, her black lace and scarlet stockings. The image when it came failed to please, or even distract. Something had happened to him in this grim German palace. Something it would take a long time to extract himself from. Something he had long since stopped expecting.

'Come with me to Philadelphia,' Thomas said. It was an impulse, a foolish proposition, but he felt better after having said the words.

Ignacy shook his head.

'It wouldn't help me, and it won't help you, Thomas.'

What Ignacy wanted was a moral cauldron in which to cast a new Polish heart. Drown all these dissenting voices, drown all doubt. 'An uprising,' he said in a low voice, a whisper almost. 'Against the Russians.' He had already heard rumours of clandestine organisations forming among the young. Destiny now ceded to a new generation. The young were whispering already that one should measure strength by the power of dreams. The young, he told Thomas, had forgotten the cynicism of their fathers. Napoleon, for them was a symbol of human dignity and freedom. The Dąbrowski mazurka, the song that started with *Poland is not yet dead as long as we are alive*, had a line in it, *Bonaparte showed us how to win*. This was what the young wanted to remember, Ignacy said.

Will you make her happy, Thomas wanted to ask.

'Did he really show you how to win?' he asked instead as Ignacy saw him off to the door. From Santo Domingo only a handful had returned, but to what? The Russian campaign? Over dinner Captain Przybylski had told them of a gruesome discovery. In the dark Russian forests between Borissov and Studzianka, Russian serfs had unearthed a mass of leatherwear, strips of felt, scraps of cloth and shako covers of the Grande Armée. Beside all this there were bones: Human and animal, skulls, tin fittings, bandoliers, bridles, scraps of the Guard's bearskin.

'Corpses covered in mud and sand, whole vehicles buried there,' the Captain had said, 'have formed an island. That's where the grass grows now.' Then, leaning toward Thomas, he added, 'And forget-me-nots.'

Sophie

The footman announces that Count Yuri has arrived.

'Ask him to wait,' she says.

In the mirror she inspects her simple house dress, white as snow, a bright red ribbon under her breasts drawing attention to itself, and away from her pregnancy. The footman stands motionless by the door holding a cashmere shawl, should she need it to cover her arms. She motions to him to fetch her workbag.

Her fingers pushing the needle through and retrieving it on the other side, she thinks of the baby. She would like another daughter and name her Maria, after Mana.

Yuri when he walks in is shivering. His blond wavy hair is matted and stuck together. His clothes are put together in a haphazard, slovenly way, testifying to many hours spent with a bottle in questionable company. His beige breeches are smudged with wine, his shirt open at the chest, yellowed at the collar.

In his pocket she sees the outline of a pack of cards. She has heard that this morning he lost ten ducats to his own footman on a wager consisting of nothing more than guessing the length of a straw, half-hidden under a dinner napkin.

He approaches her with nervous steps and tries to kiss her on the lips but she makes a sudden turn and his lips brush her cheek.

'How much have you lost today,' she asks.

Yuri tries to laugh.

'I won,' he says. 'Two hundred ducats.'

'From whom.'

'Karwowski.'

'He has no money.'

'But I won it anyway,' he says and tries to kiss her belly. The thought that there is a baby inside her, a child that is his own flesh and blood moves him. Death is no longer frightening, he has told her. He can think of the future, now. A future with her and his child.

'If you don't gamble it all before that,' she says sharply.

The walls of her boudoir are her favourite colour, *cuisse de nymph effrayée*. It was the right choice, she thinks every time she looks at them.

'Will you eat something, Yuri?'

'No.'

'You should. I insist.'

'All right then,' he agrees. A small thing to please her. He is so thin that she could count his ribs.

She points at the mother of pearl inlaid table where the servants have placed Chinese tea cups, without handles, and *zakuska*: Small round canapés with smoked salmon and sturgeon and round slices of egg sprinkled with red caviar.

She eats hungrily. He pecks at the egg, making a face as if forced to swallow wormwood.

The pregnancy has made her legs swell, and he kneels beside her and slowly massages her calves and feet. His hands can be gentle and strong. She closes her eyes and feels the baby move inside her. A boy, she decides, kicking and elbowing his way. I'll have to think of another name.

'Remember the first time I saw you,' Yuri says.

A constable brought him from St Petersburg in a black carriage. Felix's first born, the prodigal son who has stolen his mother's silver and pawned it to pay his gambling debts. He had been caught drunk at the Winter Palace, so drunk that he leaned out of the windows and yelled, *Come here everybody so I can puke all over you.* Appearances matter, she told him then. The late Empress knew that well. You could not have caught her yelling her contempt from the palace window.

'You were wearing a blue dress,' he says, 'with a small bow right here,' he touches her swollen breasts. 'You were wagging your finger at me. It was such a bright day, the air so pure, I could smell the mowed grass. And I thought I had never seen a woman that beautiful in my life.'

He leans back as if to see her better. There is sweat on his forehead. He should drink two glasses of milk every morning; avoid draughts and dampness; and be in bed before ten, the doctor said.

'That's when I fell in love with you,' he says. 'And you? When did you know you loved me?'

Before she can come up with an answer, his body is racked by a cough that stains his handkerchief red. It is his suffering that moves her. He is a child, in spite of his twenty-nine years. A weak, spoilt child who has never known what it is to want anything. A man-child who pushes himself inside her like a slippery snake, eyes begging for a sign – a gasp, a moan of pleasure – the lover's alms.

'They will not stab you in the back,' he says, when he recovers his voice, her protector. 'I won't allow it.'

He'll swear to it if she wants him to, swear on St Yuri, his patron saint, that he will not let his brothers and sisters destroy her. He has made sure that, if he dies, she and her children get his share of the Potockis' fortune. 'What is mine is now yours,' he repeats over and over again, kissing her protruding belly.

She wants to ask him what he would do if this baby takes her life, but she doesn't. Hope is not a course of action. She doesn't want empty promises he can forget at the first glimpse of a deck of cards.

These are not promises, he assures her. He will marry her and give her everything he owns. He has made his will. If he dies before her, everything he owns will be hers.

'You are an angel,' he says. 'Without you I would've sent a bullet through my head hundreds of times.'

He is right though far too dramatic as usual. Without her he would have drunk himself to death in some brothel. In St Petersburg a whore once told him he was of no use to a woman. He had no blood left in him, she said and sent him back home with a bottle of vodka. He gave her ten ducats anyway. He still might manage to drink himself to death, if the weak lungs do not claim him first.

'Run away with me,' he begs. 'Let's leave this cursed place. They hate you here. I can feel it. They are praying for this baby to kill you. No one has ever been happy here. Let's go to Italy, or Spain. Where it's warm and where our baby can grow strong.'

'You should go, darling,' she says softly. 'Go to Spa. Go to Barèges. The waters there are excellent. I'll follow you when things settle down here. When people stop talking. They always stop. They always find something else to amuse themselves with.'

'You know I can't be alone.'

She smoothes the hair on his head gently. It is thin hair, just like Felix's but not yet grey. Her voice is soothing, calm. His love for her has already done enough damage, risen enough brows. Appearances matter, Yuri, she wants to tell him. This is not the time for foolish gestures.

'I have four other children, Yuri,' she says, 'besides this unborn one. Do you wish me to forget about them?'

How big the tears are that flow down his hollow cheeks, how white his lips, the strained look, the sorrow. His very soul is in these eyes. Sad and wistful and yearning for something that always eludes him. She promises she will join him as soon as she can. As soon as the baby can travel with her, as soon as the most pressing matters are resolved. Her reasons cannot be dismissed. What she needs to do is to build their future together, build its foundations. His brothers have already threatened to take her to court. She needs to go to St Petersburg, make sure the Emperor understands her delicate situation and to form alliances, entreat the protection of friends.

'If you let them touch you, I'll kill you.'

Her face turns into a grimace of disgust. Jealousy she cannot take. Not anymore.

'I'll kill them too. All of them.'

He staggers. Petulance is not endearing. Neither is sulking. She longs for a manly man; for arms she can wrestle with; for the smattering of danger, of blood.

'You are so impractical, my love,' she says. 'You would want us to live on air, but I can't. If you are like that, it falls to me to be reasonable, to do the right thing.'

Her arguments convince him for the moment or perhaps it is something else. A thought of some wager he might propose the minute he leaves her room. Yes, he agrees, she needs to stay in Tulchin for a while and then go to St Petersburg, but in this case he will go with her. She needs his protection more than ever. His word against the lies of his brothers. They have never liked her. Always sided against her with their mother, always scheming against her.

'You are sick,' she reminds him. 'The doctor said you will not live through another Russian winter. St Petersburg is bad for you even in the summer. Do you think that seeing you lose your health every day is going to help me?'

There is another tear in his eye. It swells and begins rolling down his cheek. There is so much wavering in him and so little strength. Is that what her baby will inherit?

'I want you to get better,' she says. 'I want you to love me. To come to me like you used to, every night.'

He smiles as she slides her hand inside his breeches and squeezes him, softly at first, then harder. He laughs and kisses her on the lips.

That night the footman wakes her up, the flame of the candle in his hands flickering. In the dark his pallid face looks ghostlike.

He doesn't have to say it. She knows it already. She can feel death in the air. She is a widow.

The blood rushes to her head and the waters break. The baby has decided that the time has come to enter this world.

Rosalia

Now that Madame Kisielev was here, she found herself unemployed. After the morning duties, her presence at the countess's side was no longer required. The daughters were at their mother's side and she was urged to take some much needed rest.

Blood – Rosalia thought – was always thicker than water.

'Death without pain,' Doctor Lafleur said. He had waited for her outside the grand salon. He would walk her to her room, he said. She should lie down. Put her feet up on a pillow. Rest.

'Yes,' she said. 'I will.' She was trying to remember how she had longed for such moments only a few days ago when the duties of nursing had made mockery of sleep.

'The miracle of morphine.'

The end, she thought. This is how it will all end. The countess will die and he will leave for America. She will never be allowed to forget. Forget what her life could have been.

The success of morphine had made Doctor Lafleur exceedingly optimistic. Perhaps, at last, this was the much awaited means of controlling pain. Not just for a chosen few, but for everyone. Perhaps even eliminating pain all together, even though there were bound to be adverse effects. With prolonged use, it might stop working, of course, but still, given the gravity of the patient's condi-

tion, this might not be much of a concern. Yes, what they were both witnessing was nothing short of a miracle.
So soon, she wanted to ask. Why so soon?

Before he left for Santo Domingo her father gave her a present.
'Go on, Rosalia. Listen to it,' he said, putting a big piece of amber to her ear. He had just rubbed it against a piece of fur and she could hear a tiny snap. Then a spark touched her.
'Is it for me?' she asked and then saw that inside the amber there was a tiny fly sitting on a piece of a leaf.
'Yes,' he said. 'For you.' With the corner of her eye Rosalia could see that he was holding her mother's hand.
'Go to sleep now,' her mother said, and kissed her. Her father kissed her too, and tickled her ribs the way he always did, sending her into fits of laughter.
Lying with her eyes open, listening to the noises of the house, she heard her parents' voices in the room beside hers. 'I cannot take you to the unknown. Not in your condition,' she heard. Her mother's crying could only mean that her father would be leaving soon. Leaving without them.
She remembered wondering about the little fly caught in the amber. Amber, her father had said, was resin that used to be soft and sticky but that had hardened with age. She wondered if the fly struggled or whether it had died instantly. She wondered what the world was like at the time when the fly was alive.
The day before her father left, in the street, they saw a wagon filled up with quartered carcasses of cows. A swarm of big green flies circled over it. Every so often a big drop of blood fell on the paving-stones.
What can be worse, her mother said, than the memory of happiness at the time of sorrow?

* * *

'The miracle of morphine, Mademoiselle Rosalia,' Doctor Lafleur said, recalling the bliss on the countess's face. 'Happy memories, marvelled at and left to float again.'

He stopped in mid step as he was telling her this, and it seemed to her that he was lingering on purpose, that he too wished this moment to last longer. He watched as she brushed the hair from her face.

He would take morphine with him to America, Doctor Lafleur continued. He would present Magendie's results and his own observations, lecture on the benefits of moments when pain was pushed aside. The true gift from the Old World to the New.

She watched him gasp then as if something important had escaped his memory and now, at that very instant, had to be dragged back into the light. Something that had to be said.

A delusion, of course, one more phantom of her fancy. Behind the closed door of the grand salon she could hear Madame Kisielev's sobs. Then came the soothing voice of the countess.

'Is that not a worthy gift?' Dr Lafleur asked.

That afternoon, alone in her room, Rosalia drifted into a shallow dream in which she was flying. Flying over the city, the red tiled roofs, the gardens. It was enough to think of a direction and her airborne body took her there without effort. She flew over fields of poppies, hovered over trees, peeked into bird's nests where chicks opened their beaks so wide that she could see their little flicking tongues deep inside their throats. Then she aimed for the white fluffy clouds, and wrapped them around her face like a gauze shawl.

This sense of elation, the gift of the dream, was still with her when she awoke. She jumped out of bed. The floor was so cold that the soles of her feet tingled. An old tune came to her and she hummed her mother's favourite song:

> Were I a gleaming star
> In Podolia skies
> I would swing to my love's window
> Gently, gently as the wind blows
> To shine in her eyes,
> To shine in her eyes.

'What will you do when you no longer have me to fuss about, Rosalia?' the countess had asked her. 'What will you do when you have only yourself to think about?'

What is the use of a life, she wrote in her diary, *in which the dreams are more important than anything that passes during the day?*

Sophie

Her son is born on the day her husband dies.

Yuri is holding the baby for the first time, amazed how tiny he is, how fragile. He kisses the tiny nose and cheeks before putting his son back into the bassinet next to her bed. In his mourning ensemble, Yuri is even paler than before. He did not see Felix before he died. The prodigal son has not asked for forgiveness and has not been forgiven.

'Our little boy,' Yuri says, 'will be named Bolesław.' It is the ancient name of Polish kings. It means, *he of a greater fame*.

'Bo-les-lav,' she tries to repeat after him, but on her lips it comes mangled and split. The name is too heavy for a baby anyway. She will call him Bobiche.

'Have you suffered much?' Yuri asks, putting his hand on her now strangely flat stomach. She can still smell blood, behind the incense the midwife has burnt. And the urine that escapes her, just like that day in Bursa, when her father's whip slashed her buttocks. That's what these babies do to you, the midwife has said. Some ladies cannot leave their homes without leather petticoats to stop them from wetting their dresses. Once she no longer hurts, she should pull the muscles inside her and hold them for some time. Do it every day. It will help.

The bed creaks when Yuri sits beside her, smoothing the lace frill on her pillow. The smell of fried bacon around him is a good thing. He has had his breakfast. There is black dirt under his fingernails. Are your fingers in mourning, she used to ask the children.

'No,' she says. 'And I don't remember pain anyway.'

She is grateful for her heart still pumping blood. She is even grateful for the torn skin. For the muscles contracting, for her body so small now under the quilt, so empty.

There is a certainty about Yuri she has not seen before. Her maid said that Count Yuri had never left the room next door when Madame was in labour, not even when the news came of his father's death. She had told him to get some sleep, or eat something, but he refused. As if he could help, her maid said. As if any man could help at such times. This morning, she also said, he was in the stables before breakfast, asking for the grey mare. He would ride every day, he had told the grooms, from now on.

He is not trying to lay his head on her breasts.

'I'll take you with me,' Yuri says. 'I'll not go alone. We'll get married in Rome. The Pope can marry us, if you wish. And there will be more children, more sons.'

In his voice there is triumph. His eyes are shining from

it – or could it be the fever. The cough has stopped, he tells her, as if he were reading her thoughts. He has not felt better in months.

'Staszewski says I resemble my grandfather,' he says. Staszewski is the old footman who has always eyed her with a frown.

'Has he not noticed that before?' she asks and turns her head away. How cool the pillow is, how soothing to her hot cheek.

'He says I've always resembled him, but he has never noticed it so clearly.'

The king is dead, long live the king. Yuri is the patriarch now, the firstborn son of the Potocki clan and he likes his new role, imagines himself changing. At least for the time being, until the novelty wears out.

'Yes, my darling,' she whispers. Her lips are parched again, but Yuri does not see it. He also does not notice that he is pressing her hair hard against the pillow. She cannot move her head without pulling it. 'We'll do as you wish. As soon as we are all well enough. But now let me sleep. I need my strength back. The doctor says I've lost a lot of blood.'

He bends over to place a kiss on her forehead. It is a soft, fatherly kiss, a stamp of approval.

The maid has aired all her black dresses and bonnets for the mourning, all black crepe, black lace. The veil she has worn after her children died. In its folds her old tears must still hide. Salty stains, invisible but to a mother's heart. Felix's body is in the Tulchin chapel, awaiting the funeral. How unhappy they have made each other. How sore.

•

You are water, and I am fire, she told him once. It was in St Petersburg, at a ball in the Winter Palace. She remembers an enormous room, lit by hundreds of candles, music filling it in excited waves. The rustle of silk, the tinkle of epaulettes, sables and spurs. Perfumed moustaches that brushed her fingers as she gave her hand to be kissed. She wore a dress of silk taffeta with tassels and her best diamond necklace, the one Felix had bought for her as her wedding present.

'My dear friend,' the Tsar greeted her. 'We've been waiting for you with much impatience.'

To Felix it was yet another tedious duty to get over with, but she felt so happy, so elated. She wanted to dance, to laugh, to feel the eyes turn upon her as she passed. She was Countess Potocka, she was beautiful, she was the Tsar's most keenly awaited guest.

'Sire, what a wonderful idea,' she said to him later that evening, interrupting a long conversation about inventions that would – the men were sure – change the course of human history. It was artificial insemination that was enthusing them.

'How wonderful, Sire!' she said, her eyes twinkling. 'Now, instead of going through all the farce of royal weddings, an ambassador could be sent over with a good sized syringe!'

She could see His Majesty's eyes narrowing with merriment. He extended his arm to her, and they danced to the accompaniment of hushed whispers and more laughter as the story of her wit made its predictable rounds.

Felix, she could see, was not laughing. She could spot him wandering round the room, talking to people who sought his company. He was not looking in her direction. She could feel the ill-humour gathering, his irritation with the noise, the smells of sweat, perfume and melting wax. If he could, he told her many times, he would never leave Tulchin. Why bother with these throngs of sycophants and schemers.

'So that they don't forget you,' she said. He was not convinced. Besides, he said, he wanted to be with her.

Alone. Without these constant distractions. Without having to elbow his way past the throngs of her admirers.

Why did she never have enough?

The music tore her away from these thoughts. The music, the laughter, the eyes following her. The poems to her eyes printed on dinner napkins, rings with her miniatures on them, notes delivered in bouquets of flowers. The chase is all I want, she tried to tell him. The very thrill of it, the rush of hot blood in her veins. How could she tell Felix that this was life itself. That, without it all, she was suffocating.

Tired from dancing, she stopped to pick a glass of champagne from the tray a footman offered her. Drops of moisture gathered on the cold glass. She could see Felix coming up to her, a solemn, relentless march past the crowd of dancers. Soon, so soon, she would feel his hand on her shoulder, hear his whisper. 'We are leaving, Sophie,' he would say. 'I'm too tired.'

Being his widow, she thinks, will be so much simpler than being his wife.

She is grateful for this baby sleeping so peacefully next to her. For his even breath, the big blue eyes that open for a few moments before they plunge back into sleep. For the tiny yawns, a small fist clutching to her finger. For the sweet baby smell she breathes like perfume. She is grateful for life.

Thomas

In the evening the countess had summoned them all to the grand salon. She had dressed for this occasion; the sleeves of her dressing gown were trimmed with white fur. He saw how she touched it with her fingers as if to remind herself how it felt. How she raised her own hand to the light and looked at it for a while. For the first time in many days, the windows had been left uncovered.

One of the better days, Thomas thought, when morphine was working its magic. A day when good memories came, when not a moment seemed wasted on pain. With the corner of his eye he could see Rosalia remove the string of tallow from the candle and roll it into a ball. The music from behind the curtain seemed listless to him, in need of a stimulant.

The countess talked incessantly. There was a gown remembered, embroidered with flowers and pearls. 'Pints of pearls,' the countess said, her eyes fixed on her elder daughter. 'And now I don't even know where it is.' There was a certain St Petersburg ball where every lady was presented with a gift. Hers had been a bunch of asparagus which opened to reveal a roll of love poems tied with a red garter.

Life was filled with puzzles, the countess said, curious puzzles that defied reason. Near Archangel, in Russia, there was a district where at sunset almost everyone became blind. Old and young. Men and women. As the evening approached everyone hurried home, for otherwise they would not be able to find their way there.

'How would you explain that, Doctor Lafleur?' she asked but did not wait for his answer.

She had seen it with her own eyes. She was travelling in the region with her husband and some boatmen were rowing her party to land. When the sun set, the men said it was impossible for them to go any further. Their eyes did not change in appearance, but they swore they could not see the water or the land. 'It is all the same to us,' they said. In their voices though, there was no alarm. They had always been like that.

'Imagine that,' the countess said.

Thomas tried to imagine a world where, in the twilight, all objects became indistinguishable as if greyness drowned them. A world that changed its face every night, blurred what would be again clear in the morning. A world in which, every evening, sight gave way to touch and hearing.

A world forever divided, forever altered by its own shadow.

'She sleeps so much more now,' Rosalia whispered to him. 'Much more peacefully than before. Does morphine affect her dreams?'

She turned around when she asked this, as if caught in a gust of wind. A wisp of her hair was curling over her forehead, softening her face. A flash of auburn, a promise, but not to him. Ignacy was already talking of folding his Berlin practice. Would Thomas know a good doctor who might want to replace him?

'Yes,' he said, aware that this simple answer would not satisfy her. He wasn't sure what else to say. The countess, when he had asked her about her dreams, laughed and said they were her own. You will just have to imagine them, she said, when you report on me to your learned colleagues. Or, if your imagination fails you, my dear Doctor, invent your own.

They were to play a game called 'secretary'. The five of them, the countess, Madame Kisielev, Olga, Rosalia, and Thomas. Each was to write a question on a slip of paper, and then draw these slips at random. Once the question was drawn, they were to reply to it most truthfully, writing one's answer underneath the question, and put the slip of paper back into the pile. At the end, they would read all the questions and answers aloud.

Parlour games, as far as Thomas was concerned, were nothing more but an amusement for empty minds. The means of passing the time if one had too much of it and nothing useful to do. But this time was an exception. The playfulness of this very moment was significant in itself. In his medical notes he would call it *a manifestation of euphoria*. After the second dose, he would note, the patient experienced an illusion of strength, of timelessness; a long period of giddiness; a temporary release from death.

'Hurry up, Doctor Lafleur,' the countess said. 'We are all waiting for you. Surely you can think of a question you would like one of us to answer, can you?'

But it took Thomas at least another minute before he came up with a question that did not sound utterly silly or pretentious to him. At first he wanted to ask about hope. *What is the virtue and fault of hope*? perhaps, he thought. But then it seemed too transparent. He decided against it. He would ask about lies, instead. He folded his slip of paper and put it into a bowl.

He could see that Rosalia hesitated too before writing hers. A frown, a pouting of lips. A long moment of deliberation as if this was an important choice.

It was Rosalia who read it all to them:

What is that illuminates your future?
That what was bright in my past.

What makes love and hatred similar?
A single look can bring them to life.

What makes life worth living?
That what makes death bearable.

Why lies attract?
Because truth closes too many doors.

What is the virtue and fault of hope?
That it can deceive.

'In Tulchin,' the countess said, leaning back on her pillow, 'we used to play it all the time. Remember, Olga? We had living pictures too.'

The talk was a sign of strength, but it was the manner of his patient's speech that pleased Thomas. The sentences were longer, punctuated with the waving of her hands, with giggles and laughter. The memories that came were also joyful. A drunken guest in her garden was found praying to the bust of Voltaire whom he had taken for a holy figure. A neighbour who had had the windows in her ballroom painted black so the guests would not know when the sun rose and kept dancing as long as she wanted. Three Polish princesses bribing Prince Poniatowski's butler and sneaking into his bedroom at night dressed as Greek nymphs only to be sent back, for he arrived, *enfer et damnation*, with his actress lover.

'Sitańska. She used to ride with him in the carriage all over Warsaw. Naked,' the countess said.

'Marshal Poniatowski?' Thomas asked. Was this the same man who threw himself into the waters of Elstera talking of Poland's honour. He must ask Ignacy about this.

'He *was* quite dashing,' the countess said. 'He had excellent calves.' In candlelight, with her head thrown back she seemed carefree and radiant. 'Just like his uncle, the King.'

There was more. The countess told them how in Warsaw, at Madame Ogińska's, she staged *Five odalisques in a seraglio*. 'Four nymphs bending over me,' she said. 'I was lying on a red ottoman, dressed in white tulle, so transparent that you could see through it. I was supposed to be asleep. They fanned my face, my breasts. The most beautiful women of Warsaw. The King was very pleased.'

Thomas could hear their laughter echoing off the walls, coming back, and disappearing again. A reminder of other times, he thought, but then corrected himself. No, not a reminder. Just a pocket of joy in the time of sorrow. A moment to cherish. To draw strength from.

Behind the curtain, the pale soprano was clearing her throat.

'My nipples showed through the tulle,' the countess said, still laughing. 'The King said they looked as if the bird of love had been pecking at them. Is it true what I hear that the young guards in Berlin are particularly fine looking?'

Olga giggled again.

From behind the curtain the pale soprano sang something in Italian. Her voice was trembling with angry fervour. The only words Thomas could make out from the lyrics were: *larve* and *ruine*.

Sophie

She is still weak after her *accouchement*, but she wants to see Felix's body. She wants to do it alone, without her stepchildren watching her every move. As she was pushing her little son into the world, she could feel their hatred focussed on her, the tentacles of poison sticking to her skin.

Hatred haunts this big sprawling palace in Tulchin, its long corridors where generations of the Potockis look at her with disapproval from their darkening portraits. Men dressed in long crimson gowns, their waists encircled with embroidered belts. 'The dress of a Polish noble,' Felix told her when he brought her here for the first time, 'the salt of the earth. The descendants of Japheth.' There were three of them, Noah's sons. When their father lay drunk, it was Ham who derided him while Japheth and Shem covered Noah's nakedness. 'A servant of servants shall he be unto his brethren,' Noah said of Ham. This was why

Japheth was the patriarch of all nobles, Shem of all Jews, and Ham, cursed for his sin, of all the peasants.

Laughing, she had pulled him toward her. Let all these descendants of Japheth see their son kiss her lips, her neck. Let them watch him on his knees lifting her petticoats, impatient to touch her skin.

You bring so much joy into my life, Felix said then. You make me want to live.

'Papa died cursing you,' Ludwika said when she came to see her new stepbrother. 'And him,' she added in the direction of the cradle. Her face was empty and stern.

Words like that are best ignored. Fear can only claim the ones who let themselves be frightened.

Ludwika was so plain, so devoid of charm, an awkward child with narrow, pale lips. Once she took a steak from her plate, carried it like a flower into the salon and then put it inside the grand piano. At another time she emptied a bottle of ink on her writing table, wiped it out with her cashmere shawl and then cut the stain out with her scissors.

'Go back where you came from,' she said. 'Go back to Istanbul.'

One small blessing was that Monsieur Grabianka was nowhere to be found. Her maid, asked to make enquiries, was told he had left for St Petersburg in disappointment. In the end the rumours of disinheriting Yuri and paying the King of Israel's debts proved to be just rumours. Perhaps Felix did not want to punish her that much after all.

With the maid's help, Sophie puts on the heavy mourning dress of black crepe and black stockings. It is still strange to touch her flat belly, to know that the baby is not there any more. Her head spins and she holds on to her maid's arm for a while, to steady herself. She will have to wear her mink cape too. The big hall is chilly, and the chapel will be freezing.

'Shouldn't you wait, Madame,' the maid asks. 'One more day?'

The day before he died, Felix called the children to his side, their children, Alexander, Mieczysław, Sophie and Olga. She, his wife, was not even asked to come with them. The doors were closed all the time. When they were let out, she asked Alexander to tell her what his father had said. 'Papa said he was not feeling well,' he told her with his usual seriousness. 'That I should be a good boy and look after my brother and my sisters.'

Felix did not allow the children to kiss him, but he asked them to repeat a prayer after him, a long prayer they didn't understand.

'Is Papa angry at us?' Alexander asked. It was his voice that had frightened the children, low and stern. And his long blessing from which Alexander recalled only one phrase, *absolve from sin.*

Felix refused supper that evening. Prayed and asked to kiss the holy icon of Saint Yuri. It would give him strength to fight the evil around him, he said. The forces of sin, poisoning his blood. Then he fell asleep, peacefully, and did not wake up. Ludwika noticed it first, in the morning. He was so motionless, she said. So peaceful. Now, in the Tulchin chapel, his body is lying in state, dressed in the grand uniform of the Russian General, his last public office. The Potocki Cossacks guard him. Every day more people come to pay respects: neighbours, servants, serfs.

What has been done cannot be undone.

The maid insists on holding her arm to stop her from slipping on cold marble tiles. Two flights of stairs, a long walk through the East wing, then another flight of stairs. By now, one of her stockings is threatening to slip down.

'I should have asked the footman to carry you, Madame,' the maid says. 'What if you start bleeding again? Doctor MacFarland insisted that you should not stand up for another week.'

'Don't fuss,' Sophie says, but she has to stop a few times and rest. The baby has sucked her strength away. The doctor said it should be her last.

As soon as they approach the chapel, she knows that something is wrong. The Cossack guards are sprawled on the floor, asleep, their shaved heads shining with grease. Empty bottles lie about, some of their contents still trickling on the floor.

'Oh My Lord,' the maid gasps, clasping her hands. 'Holy Mary Mother of God.'

'Wake up you wretched fools,' she screams, 'Countess Potocka is here.' The Cossacks do not even open their eyes. One of them is snoring, another grins, his eyes half-opened, rolling eyeballs revealing the whites of his eyes.

The chapel door is closed.

'What if someone is still there,' the maid asks, her lips trembling. Her foolish head is filled with nonsense. The dead rising from their graves, drinking the blood of the living.

She pushes the maid aside and opens the door to the chapel. In the dusk her eyes take a few moments to adjust before she can see clearly. The coffin is empty.

A few moments pass before she spots her husband's body crumpled on the floor. A shrivelled, pale white body with sutures from the surgeon's cuts, his penis but a limp fold of skin nestled in grey curls of hair. The uniform is gone and so are the rings from his fingers. The maid grabs the yellow *żupan* off the drunk Cossack's back to cover the Count's nakedness.

'Don't look, Madame,' she begs her. 'Do not look.'

But Sophie cannot stop looking.

Her husband's lifeless body is lying like a shapeless sack. Without his finery, he looks lost, abandoned. Smaller than in life. Cold.

Thomas

In his room, suddenly angered by his own exuberance of a few minutes before, he looked at his red hands, at the sabre scar above his wrist. The palms of his hands, when he stared at them, were two vast territories, creases crossing and leading off the edge, some ending like tributaries of undiscovered rivers. He had always considered palm reading to be one more manifestation of the irrational desire to make the future pliable, to mould it according to human dreams. So why was he staring at his hands?

The feel of the carpet under his bare feet pleased him. The muffled patter of his heels. He hummed as he washed, rubbing his skin hard with a cloth, feeling his blood flow faster and skin tingle.

America. Dreams of wilderness, waiting for those who want nothing from the old world. The ingenuity of free minds, unshackled by old dreams. *Kein Koenig dort*, as the Germans repeated with awe. They, from a nation of thousands of princes, knew what it meant to say the New World had no king. The common man given a fighting chance. Science allowed to penetrate the recesses of nature for the betterment of mankind. Perhaps, like the Boston sailor he read about in von Haefen's library, he would travel further north, take a position of a doctor on some ship. He would learn from the natives, observe their cures. He would collect samples of their remedies. If opium turned out to be the source of morphine, what other undiscovered plants might he encounter. At forty he was not too old to make his own discoveries.

Alone.

There would be disappointments, of course, there were bound to be. Ignacy was right to remind him that America would not be free from sin. That there would be greed there, pettiness, jealousies and hatred. Yet such thoughts did not diminish the pleasure he felt at the contemplation of the New World. He was a doctor. He knew that the well nourished, human body could perform miracles. Given proper nourishment of the spirit, human beings could rise to new levels of experience. Even if they failed, these would be very different failures.

Outside his room, in the hall, he could hear the quick, short steps of a woman. His heart quickened when the steps seemed to stop in front of his door and the woman, whoever she was, hesitated. Then she moved on, with what could be reluctance. But this could have very well been an illusion.

Sophie

I may have renters, she writes to Diane de Polignac, *but I'll have no owners.*

Yuri is in Paris, on his way to the Pyrenees where his doctor insists the waters are his only cure, telling everyone he meets that his Sophie is on her way there to marry him. Diane is horrified at the sight of him. A skeleton with fiery eyes, his hands hot as the desert sand. *Is this the kind of love you want*, she has asked.

Diane is writing her memoirs. She wants to preserve the memories of the murdered, record what they said and how. She has visions of muslin-clad figures, their dresses stained with blood. In these visions she can sometimes recognise Princess de Lamballe, Marie Antoinette, Princess Lubomirska, red velvet ribbons around their necks. Scarlet red, drops of blood detaching themselves from the fabric, flowing down their breasts. *We were spared*, she writes, *to record what has been lost.*

Joseph also likes to recall the past. In his estate just four hours' ride away from Tulchin, one of Felix's gifts to sweeten his loss, he bores guests with stories of his friendships with kings and queens, stories that grow fatter with each retelling. He sends her gifts of wild honey and kasha from his fields, claiming that the soil there gives it a taste she would not find anywhere in the world. Jan visits him often, now that the second Madame de Witt is buried in the village cemetery, and tells her that her portrait is hanging over the mantle. She too sends him gifts: pineapples and lemons from Sophievka, bottles with the strengthening tonic he swears by, lists of guests at St Petersburg balls and, though not too often, greetings from those who still remember him.

To herself she mutters her bewilderment. Why look back? Why grow old before your time? Before death steals what is possible?

She counts her own years with reluctance. She may have turned forty-eight, but time has been kind to her. Time and her own skill of concealment. Not everything should be revealed. She would not go as far as Princess L who kept her slave hairdresser caged in her St Petersburg palace, but she does have her secrets.

The three years that passed after Felix's funeral were not good. Yuri lingered in Tulchin for a while, lord of his Ukrainian estates. Not a role that suited him. If it weren't for her, he wouldn't know the difference between a poplar and a cherry tree. Wouldn't have the patience to check the accounts, review the leases, answer the petitions and requests. Would never ask himself why his own valet managed to give his two daughters a million *złoty* in dowry each. 'Two million,' she has pointed out, 'is what you get from your estates in a year.'

She so easily could reduce him to tears. He would kneel at her feet, beg for forgiveness, swear he would never place a bet again. He swore by the holy icons, by his love for her, by his own son, while gamblers continued to flock to the Tulchin palace like crows to a carcass rotting in the steppes.

In the end, he too was relieved when his doctor ordered him to go south. Now, he may talk about their imminent marriage to her friends, but in his letters to her he is less courageous. He begs her to drop everything and to come to him, but he no longer believes she will. Mostly he thanks her for repairing what he had spoiled, for since he left his income has doubled. With this money she is paying off his old debts and sends him an allowance each month, which is always enough to cover even the most outrageous expenses his valet submits. She does not question how anyone can possibly need ten dozen new shirts, three months in a row.

From March to the end of August, she lives in the Tulchin palace, but she does not like it much. It is too big, too unruly. As often as she can, she takes the children and her guests to the summer palace in Uman, from where they make daily trips to Sophievka. For the winter they all move to St Petersburg, where she also keeps a house.

Her stepchildren have not given up. They are digging up lies and rumours, hoping to deprive her and her children of their meagre share of the Potockis' fortune. Throw mud and some of it will stick, they believe. Throw enough and she will drown.

'They want war,' she says. 'They'll get war.'

A widow, she also says, knows the price of freedom.

Lord Alexander Hamilton Douglas likes to tell her that his forefathers were the Celtic rulers of the British Isles and that makes him the only legal heir to the Scottish throne. He likes to stand behind her and twist her pearl necklace gently around her throat until she feels the beads begin to choke her. 'You will kill me,' he mutters into her ear.

'In St Petersburg, *mon ami*,' she tells him, 'only fools trust fate.'

He no longer announces his presence, but takes his favourite seat in her salon, right by the samovar. He likes the way the water inside hums for it reminds him of the sound of wind on a Scottish moor. The servants no longer ask what he would like but bring him a shot of vodka on a silver tray. He likes it with a slice of black Russian bread and a pickle. 'Just like the Russians do,' he says, wiping his mouth. 'Learn from the masters.' The maids giggle every time he tries to catch his breath afterwards.

Once she had asked him to put on a mask and walk with her in the street at night. He grabbed her hand, when a woman stopped them. A woman wrapped in rags, with red cheeks, rouged by the cold, her breath smelling of vodka. 'Great Lord,' she muttered and grabbed onto the tails of his fur-lined coat. He gave her a rouble.

Monsieur Senator Novosilcov does not like Lord Douglas. 'Cold like all Englishmen,' he says. 'I have to agree with His Majesty's opinion that he is far too conceited.'

Of her St Petersburg friends Nicolai Nicolaievich Novosilcov is the most influential. He linked his fate with Tsar Alexander when His Majesty was still just the Grand Duke, living in fear of his demented father. Now he is reaping his rewards – he is a senator, a member of the Tsar's inner council. Nothing is difficult for him, nothing impossible. He has already made her eldest son, Jan, his protégé and placed him in the Tsar's service. Your boy will go far, he assures her.

Cher Senator does not like Yuri, either, and is very

pleased that young Count Potocki has left for warmer countries. Men take advantage of her, he explains. They avail themselves of her warmth and kindness, her generous spirit, and squander it all in the end. 'This fool will gamble you away, if you let him,' he warns her. 'His Majesty has little patience with him.'

His jealousy touches her. It is so solid, it could be carved like stone.

Tonight I shall tell everyone that I'm indisposed, she writes to him. *I shall refuse all invitations. Please come as soon as the children are asleep. The servants will show you to my boudoir.*

'This is the way I want it,' she tells him, placing his trembling hand on her breasts. She laughs when he blushes. She laughs when he kneels at her feet and presses his lips on her hand.

St Nicholas, she tells him, has always been her favourite saint.

Nicolai Nicolaievich likes to enlighten Countess Potocka in the ways of the world, dispel her delightful naiveté, and reveal to her the true nature of power. Some corridors of power have to be trodden with caution. Appearances matter, but alliances matter more, the right alliances, well maintained. In the courts of St Petersburg, he tells her, the Tsar's word is all that counts.

'You are right about Yuri, *mon cher ami*. His soul is so weak. I tremble at the sight of a letter from him. And about Lord Douglas.'

'I hear he is being recalled by his King,' Nicolai Nicolaievich says with a smirk. 'His mission here has not been too successful, I'm afraid. I wonder if His Majesty should not be told that he should thank *you* for it.'

The art of interpretation, he tells her, is the art of making sense of what may, otherwise, be overlooked. Any messenger knows that. Countess Potocka has to make sure His Imperial Majesty knows of the vile nature of her stepchildren's conduct. Their efforts to take away her good name, to declare her marriage *null*, to make her children bastards. To deny her grief over her husband's death, grief His Majesty should be reminded of.

Making sure cher Senator sees tears in her beautiful eyes, she thanks him for his advice. He is right in everything he says. In this cynical world, sometimes a helpless soul finds its guardian angel.

'The children adore you, Nicolai Nicolaievich. Yesterday Alexander said he wanted to grow up to be just like you. I asked him why. Because, he said, Nicolai Nicolaievich has a good heart.'

Would infatuation, she thinks, be enough? To know what a man wants is the secret to everything. Really wants, she thinks. Senator Nicolai Nicolaievich Novosilcov is not a rich man. To maintain his position he has to keep a house at a proper level.

She writes to him:

> I beg you to accept 6000 ducats, to cover the cost of your coming journey with His Majesty and your expenses here in St Petersburg. I'll not hear of any objections. I assure you this small sum is not of great importance to me, however your refusal to accept it would cause me great distress. I warn you not to bring up this topic when you come to see me, dear beloved friend, for you would only make me very, very angry. You have noticed already that I can be quite a despot and you have confessed to me how much you like when I tell you, 'This is what I want.' Well, I assure you now that I want you to accept my small gift.

The musicians

The afternoon did not promise to be anything out of the ordinary. The voices from behind the curtain ceased, and the musicians started with a potpourri for violin with themes from Rossini. The countess, Mademoiselle Romanowicz told them, had liked what they had played the day before, especially the sarabande. She was quieter, too. Other than an occasional groan no sound reached them.

They could always count on Mozart. Or Komm and Hoffnung.

They could smell her illness. The sour odour of infirmity, the attar of roses, the thick, dust-filled smell of the bedding that had not been aired. Two mattresses had already been burnt for the blood.

'Perhaps we should try Marais after all,' the violinist said, even though he had opposed this choice before.

'We can try,' the pianist said.

They played one of the *pièces de violes*. Then another one. They had played together for the last six weeks, and the practice had worked its magic. The music that had once started timidly was now strong, their sound more and more generous and vibrant.

The singer was late. Her absence was a relief, and the musicians exchanged gleeful looks every time their eyes wandered to the empty chaise longue where Frau Hellmann liked to recline, awaiting her turn. 'Making sure we get a good look at her feet,' the violinist laughed, with a touch of malice.

They were still absorbed in the music when the door opened. At first they expected the singer, but she would have walked in briskly, without hesitation, and whoever it was just stood there.

The violinist turned back first and saw that someone was pushing a young man forward. The man stood in the open doorway, flushed, uncertain what to do next. A black silk scarf was tied around his eyes. A strikingly handsome man, the violinist would always remember, in the uniform of the Berlin guard. He had a classical jaw, a narrow nose, a wave of thick, blond hair over his forehead and the body of a Greek hero.

They stopped playing. The young man removed his blindfold and tucked it inside his guard's jacket, opening it at the top. The candlelight made him blink, but he was already smiling in anticipation. Obviously the divine guard was no stranger to such sweet mysteries.

'Come here,' a voice commanded from behind the curtain.

The man gave the musicians a quick look of victory and took a few steps forward. The curtain opened, held by an invisible hand. The musicians could see the empire bed covered by a golden throw. The countess was lying down, propped on several pillows. Her face, in its deathly pallor, seemed of another world.

The young man turned his head toward them, as if wanting to check what they thought of it all. His blue eyes narrowed, and he smiled with consternation. Obviously he was expecting someone else to greet him.

'Come here,' the countess said, motioning him closer. The violinist would swear afterwards that the dying countess was devouring the man with her eyes.

The young man took a few steps toward her and, before the curtain closed behind him, the violinist saw that the man was transfixed by the sight, more like a statue than a man of flesh and blood.

'*Merci* . . .' the violinist heard the countess whisper, before they began another piece.

Later, when he told this story in Berlin taverns, the violinist would add what the whole of Berlin was whispering about. The young man he had seen was Polish. Captain

Mycielski, the most handsome of the Berlin guards. All the French doctor ever told him was that someone, a beautiful lady, wanted to see him. A lady who did not wish to be known. This is why he was taken for a long, mysterious journey through Berlin, in a closed carriage. He was blindfolded all that time, left to wonder what manner of sweet surprises awaited him. He wondered which one of his mistresses had come up with this delightful plot, toying with his desire. Hiding from a jealous husband, perhaps, as she summoned him to a place of love.

The carriage stopped and he was led upstairs. He was still blindfolded and didn't know where he was until a hand pushed him through the half-open door. He saw he was in a magnificent salon, divided by a burgundy velvet curtain with golden tassels. It was then that he was asked to enter.

A beautiful Polish countess – Berlin gossips repeated with gasps of disbelief, sending the story off on its rounds as far away as St Petersburg – a few steps away from eternity, wanted to lay her eyes on a handsome man one more time in her life.

Sophie

She can hear the music, coming from the garden. The musicians are cleverly hidden in the bushes, behind the table set for tea. Sweet, soothing music, rises and falls like waves in the sea.

The afternoon in Sophievka, speckled with sunlight. They have all come here from the summer palace in Uman, to see her garden. The meadow has been freshly mowed, if she bends she can see the cropped blades. Smell too the sweet aroma of drying grass and clover. From the distance she can hear the sound of scythes being sharpened on whetstones.

They are all there, waiting for her: the children with their governesses, l'abbé Chalenton and the guests. Count Kapodistrias who keeps asking her to help him get a position at the Russian court. 'Russia will always be at war with the Turks,' he assures her passionately, kissing her hand every time she promises to do all she can, whisper a word into His Majesty's ear. Isn't He showing her His benevolence in her troubles? Isn't He helping her defend her inheritance when her stepsons challenged Count Yuri's last will? Surely the influence she has over His Imperial Majesty cannot be discounted. 'We, the Greeks, have to remember where our hopes are. Our fatherland needs us.'

'You overestimate my abilities, my dear friend,' she tells him. 'I merely amuse and intrigue, and His Imperial Majesty likes to be flattered. A few words against me could turn him away from me.'

'I do not believe it.'

'You do not wish to believe it. You wish to be deceived.'

What a tedious lover he has become. Where is that gaiety that captivated her once, the days when he amused her with the gossip, her surprise at seeing him climb up the wall to her bedroom window? The Greek songs he sang for her and the children.

> Rain, rain, dear Virgin,
> Send snow and waters,
> To moisten our vineyards
> And our gardens . . .

Now he sulks for days whenever she laughs off his desire to marry her. But why would she want a husband again? Why would she want to give up her freedom, the sweet possibilities of widowhood? To suffer a husband's bouts of jealousy from which, unlike now, there would be no escape? To lose control over her children's fate? Four years ago she lost her husband. A few weeks ago a letter had come from Yuri's valet that his master died peacefully, leaving everything he owned to her and her children and – in the last letter he ever wrote – asking his brothers to respect his last will. They won't of course. Yuri is buried in a small cemetery in Barèges, and her stepchildren are taking her to court. *My brother's last will was written under duress, in a state of mental anguish*, Jeroslav has written to the Tsar.

If it weren't for Nicolai Nicolaievich, she might worry.

'I thrive on betrayals,' she likes to whisper into her lovers' ears. 'Watch out. This is a fair warning.'

The crystal glasses sparkle in the sun. Count Kapodistrias who will never become her husband is trying to get her attention by clinking a knife on his wine glass. She should tell him not to wear black. It makes his skin look sickly.

She stops to take it all in. It is a scene of immense beauty. Her daughters, Olga and Sophie, in their white muslin dresses, the boys, Alexander, Mieczysław and Bobiche, in their green velvet ensembles. Count de Lagarde, his eyes upon her every move, raises his glass to her. A sweet, silly man, still young looking, still hoping she might let him into her bed. But his footman has more life in his eyes than him – and far better calves. For now poor de Lagarde is busying himself translating the poem about Sophievka, trying to impress her with poetic nonsense. All nature is a garden, he maintains and her Ukrainian shepherds are philosophers of nature, watching after the flocks of deer that graze on the Elysian fields. They are the solemn students of the natural we should all be learning from.

'If I ever let nature rule, my dear friend,' she has told him, 'my shepherds would cut my throat. What makes you think they are any different from the Parisian mob? And what of the deer? The deer would eat my saplings and ruin my lawn.'

She has offered to show him the ha-ha fence her architect put in to keep the deer away. A sunken fence, invisible from afar, but one the deer could not cross.

'My tribute to your beauty, Madame la Comtesse,' de Lagarde is standing up, clearing his throat:

O! des filles d'Adam, Vous, la plus acomplie,
D'un mortel trop sensible, inestimable amie,
Tant que vous daignerez habiter parmi nous
D'un sex vous pourrez, extiter le courroux,
Mais de l'autre plus juste, enlevant les suffrages,
Vous obtiendrez l'amour, l'estime et les hommages.

She claps her hands and says she is flattered.

'Your ear for poetry, Madame,' he whispers, his leg seeking hers under the table. She laughs and pats his shoulder with her fan. She might go to the Crimea with him, after all, just to amuse herself. He makes her laugh with his stories of the Ukraine. 'But, my dear countess, the women here. I saw a whole group of them, all naked, swimming in the river, splashing around like ancient nymphs.'

This is all he sees. He glories in the expanse of wheat, fields of watermelons, vastness of the steppes. He talks of colour and texture. Once he bent and took a clump of soil between his fingers. It was black, almost purple in the sun. 'I should have been a painter, Madame la Comtesse. But then I would have painted nothing but you.'

Little Sophie waves to her and rises from the table, hands outstretched. In a moment she feels a slender arm embracing her waist, a smooth cheek begging for a kiss.

Her most loved daughter is still a child, a beautiful child.

'Maman,' little Sophie says. 'Monsieur Allen has given me this.' In her hand is a sketch of her in profile. A fairly good one, she has to say, the lines bold and sparse, yet able to suggest the likeness and the softness that warms her child's face. 'He said I was going to be as beautiful as you are.'

'Of course you will,' she whispers. She finds it all so amusing. This summer day with the sun slowly withdrawing, the buzzing of flies, the coming and going of the servants silently following a familiar ritual. The blood flowing through her body, warm, plentiful. Her heart is beating steadily, her skin smooth as velvet. There is no past and no future, just this moment in time, and she is right there at the head of the long table, listening to her children. Alexander made his horse jump through all the barriers today. Mieczysław, with a frown across his forehead, declares that he could teach the frogs to obey him. Bobiche just smiles from Olena's arms, even though, at four, he is far too big to be carried around like that, and waves his plump hand at her. Olga wants to know what games they are going to play after dinner.

Monsieur Allen has been painting Sophievka. She has taken a liking to him, a Scot with a reddish moustache and hands which betray the evidence of his experiments with a burnt patch of skin and a nail broken in half. For Monsieur Allen is also an amateur chemist and a passionate lover of machines. As a child, he confided, he saw a silver figure of a lady who danced, holding a bird in her hand. The bird opened its beak and flapped its wings. Ever since, he has striven to create intricate systems of wheels and levers.

'What do they do?' she asked him once, but he only smiled.

'Nothing,' he said. 'But I like them that way.'

At Sophievka he asked to be shown the hydraulic system that pumped the water from the river to the fountains. He marvelled at the sketches, but insisted that the design could be improved. She likes him.

The French maid is hoping he would notice her. She preens herself like a hen, and feigns interest in his structures. She is a silly woman, for the eyes of Monsieur Allen follow the stable lads and young footmen. He is discreet, but Sophie is too well attuned to human desires not to notice. Today he must have found gratification for there is a change in him. Most of the afternoons he has been silent, lost in his thoughts, but today he laughs loudly. 'Not a minute longer. Not one more minute,' he says. 'The children can't wait for their games.'

'Charades,' her little Sophie exclaims. 'Maman, let's play charades.'

L'abbé Chalenton is explaining to Mieczysław that frogs do not possess enough intelligence to be trained. Their bodies are nothing but simple mechanisms of stimulus and reaction. Her son's eyes darken and his jaw sets.

Sophie laughs. She knows that this happiness will not last, but such thoughts have never troubled her. There is a lightness in her, a giddiness she cherishes as the music caresses her ears. She can feel de Lagarde's hand covering hers, hear him whispering his silly love.

In a moment Mieczysław will point in the direction of Uman and ask, 'what's that?' and they will all see the red glow of fire. The music will cease, the servants will huddle together and point toward the glow and they will all begin to smell the first wafts of smoke. She will later learn how one careless spark was enough to ignite a wagon full of hay and how the wind scattered the flaming tufts all over the town. And then, for days, after the fire has been extinguished, she will smear balm onto the burnt skin of children, and distribute money and clothes to those who lost their homes. 'Our little mother,' the serfs will call her and kiss her hand and promise to pray for her until the day they die.

In her mind, softened by morphine, she floats away from them all, watching the diminishing figures of her children and guests, mere puppets now. But what she is floating toward is still hidden.

Somewhere a soprano is still singing:

> Even when clouds hide it,
> The sun still shines in the tent of heaven . . .

Pavel Dimitrievich Kisielev

The carriage was slowing down, rolling along Unter den Linden, into the courtyard of von Haefen's palace. General Kisielev took note of the straw carpet laid on the stones, muffling the horses' hoofs, and the tallow candles in the lanterns. The dusk was obscuring the faces of the servants and now, at times, they seemed to him little more than shadows.

After making sure his valet was alert enough to take care of his luggage, he let himself be shown upstairs. He was hoping his wife would be there, waiting, but a man greeted him, introducing himself as Graf von Haefen, his host.

'Welcome, General,' he said with a frown. 'Welcome to Berlin.' He must have had cognac not long ago, for General Kisielev could smell it in his breath. He too would have liked a drink, but he was not going to ask for it.

The Graf was pacing the room, limping slightly as he walked. If General Kisielev had any doubt as to the seriousness of his mother-in-law's condition, it would have to leave him now.

Small, hurried steps approached. The door squeaked open.

'Pavel, my darling,' his wife threw herself into his arms. 'You've come after all.' Her face was reddened from crying. Olga came in, too, walking just behind her sister, watching him through narrowed eyes, her face gaunt and pale. He kissed his wife's tear-stricken cheeks, and enquired about his son.

'He must be feeling Maman's pain, my little dove,' she sobbed. 'He couldn't sleep all night. The nurse carried him in her arms.'

He had forbidden such mollycoddling, but he was not without feelings. This was not the time to exert his will.

'Thank God, you are here, Pavel Dimitrievich,' Olga said.

General Kisielev noted that her pale face looked good in the blue silk, and that she clasped his arm strongly with her bony fingers. Her waist was so small he could have encircled it with his hands.

'You must be very tired, Pavel Dimitrievich,' Olga said. 'Our host will forgive us. Won't you, dear Graf?'

'But of course,' the Graf stammered. A schoolboy caught at something shameful, General Kisielev thought. His cheeks were far too red. Don't they have a doctor here who could bleed him.

'Let me show you to your room, Pavel Dimitrievich,' Olga said. 'And then you should go and see Maman right away. The French doctor says the confusion has cleared. Only he doesn't know for how long.'

Sophie

Something is happening to her. Something she cannot control.

She can feel a man's lips on her nipples, sucking the blood out of her. His hair under her hand feels limp and thin. She tries to push him away, but her arms are cottony and soft. She tries to scream but no sound comes through her lips. Out of all the things in the world, it is weakness that she fears the most. The kind of weakness dogs and horses can smell on the human skin.

Someone comes into the room. A man, young, with firm olive skin, black hair falling over his forehead. Lysander? How could that be? But it is him and joy at his presence overcomes her. How has he escaped time? For her, life has become an act of camouflage: false hair, rouge, rice powder, the remedies from her gardens. First strawberries mashed into a pulp absorbed by the skin, cucumber slices on her eyes, honey, bee pollen, oats soaked in buttermilk. He doesn't need any of this. His skin is radiant and smooth, the way she remembers it.

Her chest is heaving, her nostrils widen. What will she say when anyone comes in? She will say that Prince bey Zadi is an old family friend, from long ago. From Istanbul.

'But I'm dead,' Prince bey Zadi says. 'A boating accident on the Bosphorus,' he adds with a roguish smile.

He is not lying.

'You will always astound me,' she whispers into his ear. She marvels at the warmth of his hands. Her breath is hot and moist. Lysander, when he turns toward her, fixes his eyes on hers. They are black, bottomless.

She can feel the silky smoothness of his tongue on her thighs.

'Madame de Witt's bastards have no right to my father's money,' Jeroslav says. She cannot see him, but she can hear his voice. Why has Rosalia let him in?

I want to wake up, she thinks. I do not have time for hatred.

*   *   *

'Why cannot you trust me?' Felix asks. 'Why are you fighting me all the time? Who are you without me?'

He is bending over her, his face livid. He is pointing at his heart. When he died the doctor who opened him up said his kidneys were rotten from an overdose of Spanish fly. Is that what he worried about in the end: making love to her?

Was she mistaken about him after all?

She thinks. He cursed me. He cursed this child I carried in me.

'Why cannot you trust me, Sophie? Why have you never trusted love? Why have you let the Devil into your life?'

How distant the pain has become, how blurred. A presence she can marvel at but not be drawn into. The French doctor is the man who can kill pain.

So why would she talk to a ghost?

'Drink,' a voice says.

A man's voice, tempting, soothing.

'One more sip.'

She feels the familiar bitterness on her tongue, its slow progress down her throat. There is another kind of knowledge, Doctor, she should tell him. The knowledge of blood and guts and unchecked growth. The knowledge of the body: of teeth, eyes, limbs. The knowledge hunters have when they stroke the blood-stained fur and feel the shape of the skull.

She has always been lucky with men. This one will also do what she wants. All she has to do is ask.

'I'm yours, flesh and blood,' her own son tells her. 'Like you I have no shame and no regrets.'

She would like to close her eyes and make him disappear. A pile of crates is waiting for her in the Tulchin hall. Her steward has a detailed list of the status quo.

Nothing has been omitted from it, not a ribbon or pin, Mieczysław tells her. How calm he is, how sure of himself.

'I haven't taken anything that belongs to Maman. No dresses, no jewellery, no furniture.'

A draught of cold air envelops her shoulders. In one of these crates there must be a shawl she could wrap herself in.

Tulchin belongs to him, Mieczysław tells her. His stepbrothers, thanks to her clever scheming and her lovers' influence in St Petersburg, have no part of it. Jan has already got far more than he deserves. After all he is de Witt, not Potocki. As to his brothers, Alexander is too weak to fight him, besides he doesn't care for Tulchin. He would much rather live in St Petersburg or Warsaw. And Bobiche?

We had better not talk about Bobiche, Maman.

She remembers this son of hers from a day long ago, his fingernails bloodied from the lice he had squashed. 'Go and wash your hands,' she said. 'No,' he said. 'And you can't make me.' She did make him though. Two maids held him while the third one washed his hands with soap. Brushed his fingernails hard, making sure no blood was left. When the maids let him go he spat in their faces and ran away. 'Let him cry,' she said then. 'This is all he can do.'

He is looking at her with curiosity, as if she were an animal in a cage. A giraffe perhaps, with its impossible neck. He is waiting.

'This is my home,' she tells him in the calmest voice she can muster. That her own child can turn against her she cannot accept. Not yet.

'How many homes does Maman need?'

This man, she tells herself, is my son.

'Maman can live in Uman, if Maman wants. Maman would be close to her garden.'

His face when he says it, is almost joyful. He is the most handsome of her sons and the strongest. She has seen Marusya leave his room with her cheeks flushed, and with trembling hands.

What scares her is his voice. Perfectly level, almost bored. There is nothing to explain. He is who he is and he sees no reason why he should feel ashamed of it. Her presence in Tulchin bothers him. He wants to be alone. He resents even her coming and going. He has his own pursuits and his own life.

'What life? What pursuits? Screwing the maids? You think I don't see it?'

'So you do see it. I was beginning to doubt.'

'God will punish you,' she says. She is that helpless against him.

'I do not hate you,' Mieczysław tells her. 'I just do not wish to see Maman again.'

There is nothing she could say that could change his mind.

'Let us not seek for perfection,' he recites a line from something he must have read, 'which nature never produces.'

Pavel Dimitrievich Kisielev

In the grand salon, he could see the shadow of death in the wasted flesh. And yet in her eyes, wide, and as intense as ever, there was no fear.

Courage had always held General Kisielev's respect. Even in this woman whose meddling was causing the rift between him and his wife. She had outwitted him once already, he thought. For four years she had kept him waiting before she set the wedding date. Four long years of longing he had mistaken for love. But now he had the upper hand.

'So you've come to see me, at last, Pavel Dimitrievich. To see if I'm really dying?'

Bowing, he took the countess's hand in his and brushed his lips over it. Briefly. She did not, as he had expected, withdraw her hand after it, and he had to put it down himself, on the silk eiderdown. A hand so transparent he could have crushed it in his fingers.

Better to have it done and over with. He would also have to talk to that German, von Haefen, and take over the arrangements. The body would have to be taken to Uman. Mieczysław had already made it clear that they would not be welcome in Tulchin.

'You know I'm always glad to see you, Countess,' he said, standing over her, breathing in herbs and perfume. Underneath he could tell there were the other smells of blood and rotting flesh.

'I want to talk about my daughter,' the countess said. He hadn't quite expected it, but he should have. It was like his wife to come crying to her mother, and enlarging their little disagreements.

'You don't love her. I made a mistake. I should have sent you away.'

She was whispering now and he had to bend over to hear what she was saying. He had disappointed her. He could not make her Sophie happy.

Anger made his voice shrill.

'Perhaps you should have trained her better,' he said.

He saw no reason to keep silent. Now, once and for all he would extinguish this false glow, her affected sighs and hints at the cherished friendship with her beloved Emperor.

Her eyes measured him in silence for a long time. Cold eyes, he thought. What would she do? Scream at me, call the lackeys? Protest perhaps, and tell me more lies?

'You are not bad, Pavel Dimitrievich,' the countess said,

'but you have never learnt what's important, which is a pity for such a brilliant man.'

'A daughter of a cattle trader and a whore.'

Later in his life General Kisielev would often recall this scene, still puzzled at the memory. He had expected shame and contrition. Or at least angry denials and a show of fading power he could ridicule. For in the end, he thought, it was all about power. Always about power.

'So you think you know what I am and whence I come. You think this knowledge is enough. You want me punished for my transgressions. You would like to be my judge. Why would I let you do it, *mon general*? Why would your judgement be of any importance to me?'

She was looking at him as if he were a mere boy who needed to be taught a lesson. She was laughing at him.

'Your revelations do not interest me, Pavel Dimitrievich. You'll forgive me but my time is short, and I only have enough of it for really important matters.'

Her voice was cold as ice. She knew she could not make him love his wife, but, she had made sure her daughter was free from him if she ever wished it. These were ironclad arrangements, she assured him. Sophie's share of the money was secured, out of his reach. Even if his wife died, that money would never be his. It would go to Volodia and other children, should there be any – legitimate or not.

'My daughter is free and she will remain so. You can use what she wants to share with you as long as she wishes to. If she chooses to find her pleasure elsewhere, then, *mon general*, you'll have to give it all up.'

She rang the bell beside her bed with strength he had not suspected.

'I don't know anyone in St Petersburg without some sinful secrets, *mon general*. Do you?'

On his way out he saw the Jewess on the way to her room. She gave him an annoying look as if she knew what had passed in the grand salon. Was she listening behind the door, he thought?

Sophie

The waves of music carry her away. The soles of her bare feet sense its throbbing rhythm. She will not listen to anyone. She will be the judge of her own sins.

This is not a memory. This is what she wishes for.

Her body smells of jasmine oil. She sniffs at her own wrist and remembers from a time long gone breathing in the smell of her own skin, and her childish wonder at her own body. Her long hair loose, brushing her shoulders, she dances through the sweet disorder of the room. She dances toward this stranger with a body of a Greek hero, his eyes wide open, staring at her in bewilderment. His Prussian uniform is lying crumpled on the floor and she steps on it in her dance.

Before he has the time to chide her about it, she covers his eyes with her hands and laughs as he wriggles out of her grasp. He takes her hand, his warm lips closing on the tips of her fingers. With her free hand, she ruffles the hair on the back of his head. His body is half-hidden in shadow, but she can feel its every inch.

The flames of the candles dance on the walls, chasing one another like children at play. A shadow flutters over the spider web. Her breasts are full, her body limp as if she has forgotten how to stand. She could count each hair on her body; her hand when it touches the edge of the nightstand is caressing the wood.

The scent of candle smoke drifts into her nostrils. She pinches the candle and feels the softness of wax between her forefinger and her thumb. Gently she rolls it into a ball and lets it drop on the floor. There is no reason to rush, is there? She still has time.

Rosalia

In her bedroom, Rosalia closed the door and turned the key in the lock. Slowly she took off her dress and petticoats. The dress fell off her, like a discarded skin. She unlaced her corset and let it slip to the floor. A thought crossed her mind that she shouldn't let her clothes lie on the floor like that but it seemed to her that if she were to bend and pick them up, she would snap in two.

When she had nothing on but a cambric chemise, she sat on the edge of the bed and unpinned the tresses wound over her ears. Her hair took a while before it relinquished the shape of the braids. With a hard brush she brushed her hair, massaging the tired skin of her scalp. Fifty times one way, then another fifty in the opposite direction. When she had finished the hair was thick and supple and little ringlets had begun to form around her face. It was auburn with the shine of copper, abundant and thick. From her room she could hear little Volodia screaming in pain or anger. The baby wailed and choked on his tears.

> In you, like in me, flows the blood of your forefathers, fugitives from Egypt and Palestine, whose hearts harbour the oldest memories of the human race. I tried to erase this knowledge from my heart, to forget that to be with your father I have betrayed my own people and my God. I have been warned that everything born of such betrayal is tainted. I have been warned that my children, for no fault of their own, will have to pay for my sin.
> I shall pray for you, my beloved daughter, to have the courage to follow the path of duty.

Rosalia stood up and walked to the mirror above the chest of drawers. Surrounded by auburn ringlets her face seemed smaller. She stared at herself as if she were some outlandish animal. As if one careless gesture would send her scurrying into the thicket. Slowly she ran her fingers over her cheeks, her mouth, her neck. She opened her chemise and let it slide down her shoulders to the floor. Like her mother's, her skin was milky white.

With her hands she cupped her breasts. Her nipples hardened. She thought of little Volodia's hungry, toothless mouth closing over the milk-laden breasts of the wet-nurse.

Her body's whiteness seemed ghostly. A few more years and her lips would lose their fullness. Even now she knew that part of the loveliness she watched was a gift from the soft glow of the coals and the flame of the candle. In the morning the sun would reveal a harsher picture.

Only the day before the countess gave her a box of *agate arborisée* set in gold. Rosalia protested that such a gift was far too valuable for her to accept, but her mistress insisted. It was her *gage d'amitié*, she said. Once she had intended to have it buried with her, but now she changed her mind. 'Beauty should not be buried,' she said. 'Don't you agree?'

Rosalia sat down at the writing table and dipped her quill in the ink-well. *Dear Doctor Bolecki*, she wrote.

> Your interest in my person fills my heart with gratitude. You were not mistaken in your belief that your hopes for the future of our beloved country are my hopes too, and so it is with great regrets that I must decline your proposal.
>
> The reason for my refusal is such that I blush to present it to you. I have no other hopes for happiness and no definite prospects for the future. However

everything in me tells me that I am not worthy of the trust you have placed in me and that my character is such that I would only hinder you in your mission. Please don't judge me too harshly.

Wishing you happiness, I remain your true friend,
Rosalia Romanowicz

Outside, in the courtyard she could hear Pietka play his bandura. It was an old tune her father had used to sing, too.

> In this sinful land
> Even the crows over my head
> Wonder at the way I have been orphaned.

Sophie

Men, the couplings of her life, are like shining pebbles in a stream. Lifted from the water they have all turned dull and ordinary. But each of her children are so different. It amazes her still to think of them so independent of her. Once they were all like her grandson. Little bundles of pleasure and fear, hunger and contentment, little mysteries that would unravel. Warm, tiny hands, plump faces, eyes looking at her with such trust.

Small things are important, my child, she could tell her daughter: the gleam of white glistening teeth; the glitter of diamonds; the whiteness of her complexion. Isn't a magpie's nest always filled with bright and shiny objects, a silver spoon, a watch, a golden chain? The words of submission, the fickle promises of love. 'My hope, my angel, my saviour.' The rustle of silk. The folds of her dress being raised, revealing the shape of an ankle. The looks of other men, the spice of jealousy.

She knows a set of tricks as old as the world, tricks

her daughters don't have to know. I've made sure love doesn't fool you, she mutters. There are people whose hearts believe in decency and goodness, who carry this faith in them all their lives, who nurture it and pass it on to others. Blessed but delicate, she thinks, like this daughter of hers. Like her gentle Rosalia too, afraid of anything that is not duty, as if pleasure were a warning, a measurement of pain. These are beautiful souls that have to be protected from things that could disrupt that balance inside them. To such people one cannot reveal too much.

Her daughters are free to love or stop loving as they wish. Her daughters do not have to please anyone. This is all she has ever wanted for them.

Hasn't Napoleon crowned himself Emperor? What has she done that's so very different? Used whatever gifts God has given her and used them well.

The pain is beginning to stir again, awaking from its slumber, its sharp teeth making their incisions in her flesh. Little inroads of pain, of faintness, stirring, growing. But this pain comes too late. She can already see herself lying in this enormous bed, a mere raised shape under the quilt, a mound, like the *kurhany* in the Ukrainian steppes. Her body is of little concern to her now, an empty shell, it is a battlefield of humours, bile, and blood.

You will die without pain, she suddenly remembers hearing.

How funny they all are and how blind. Her stepsons still wanting to poison the last drops of her life. Kisielev trying to make her ashamed of who she has been. The French doctor shielding himself from the love that could save him. Marusya believing her visits to her son's bedroom have gone unobserved.

Why can't they see how life seeps out of the body each moment? Each body, no matter how young and strong.

Each breath, each movement whips up a cloud of energy that floats away and is lost. Does no one really notice it, but her? Don't wait, she is telling them. Don't waste time. Life is fleeing away fast enough.

Thomas

'France,' General Kisielev said, taking a pinch of snuff from a silver box, but not offering any to Thomas, 'I consider a country inhabited by frivolous people.

'What I mean,' he continued, sneezing into his white handkerchief, 'is that the French have given the most eloquent expression to the tendency of the human mind that values can be arbitrary. This is what is wrong with the modern man.'

Punctuating his sentences with wide and elaborate wavings of his arm, General Kisielev was looking Thomas straight in the eye.

'Religion, morality, economy, politics all have become common and accessible to everyone. The new man believes not in experience but inspiration. Instead of faith he embraces individual conviction. He believes himself strong enough to embrace all questions and all facts. Laws do not bind him, for he has not contributed to make them. Power resides in himself, why should he submit himself to anyone's authority? Nothing that had been conceived in the ages of weakness is deemed suitable in this age of reason and universal perfection. Our morality is passé, our laws are obsolete. He wants to be a sole judge of his own actions and his own faith.'

He continued this tirade for another few minutes. Thomas was relieved to see Rosalia come in. He was just about to stand up to greet her when she begged him to hurry.

* * *

'Stop him from putting flowers on me,' the countess ordered him firmly when he came up to her bed. 'I'm not dead, yet.'

She was flailing her thin arms as if fending off a deluge. She was losing consciousness. He had hoped the morphine would keep working.

'Who?'

'Felix,' she said. 'Felix who could never understand anything.'

She was pointing at the shadows on her throw, the glittering of the gold thread. He drew the curtains to keep the shadows away.

'I'll tell him to stop.'

'Don't tell him anything. Just stop him.'

'He'll not come back.'

'So why is he still there?'

He sat down beside her and wiped the sweat off her forehead. The cold of the sponge soaked with ice-water brought her back to clarity.

'How long will it last?' she asked. She was lucid, now, breathing heavily. She too was thinking of the morphine.

'Another few days, perhaps. I don't quite know.'

He measured another dose and gave it to her. He had to lift her up before she would drink it. He hoped she would not vomit it all out.

'I want to be buried in Uman,' she said. 'Don't let them leave me here.'

'No one will leave you here,' he said, holding her hand.

'It's such a silly thing, breathing, Doctor,' she muttered. 'Don't you think?'

'Perhaps.'

'Resisting death. So utterly silly.'

'Yes,' he agreed. 'It is.'

'As silly as to resist a woman who is ready to love you?' She let go of his hand and closed her eyes.

He didn't dare believe what he had heard.
'Leave me now,' she said. 'I want to sleep.'

'It's not hurting any more,' she tells Felix when he comes in again to accuse her.

Death is soft with morphine, lingering like a patient lover. It puts a metallic taste in her mouth, gives a heaviness to the body, which began in her legs. As if she were being erased bit by bit. Toes, feet, calves, knees, first growing thicker, heavier and then disappearing altogether, a memory in the hearts of those who loved or hated her.

'You have betrayed me with my own son. Hell is waiting for you.'

The new medicine is making its divine rounds inside her. Felix is growing dimmer, melting away.

From behind the curtain the pale soprano is singing:

> Whims are bad guests of mine
> Always a light heart
> Dancing on through life . . .

She can see them all, gathered around her body. Her daughters are crying, unsure what to do. Olga is placing two gold coins on her eyelids. She has kept them in her pocket for a long time.

'No one has to know Maman died,' she says. 'We could just say we are taking her back home.'

There is silence in the grand salon. Rosalia lifts her head. Two tears detach themselves from her eyes and roll down her cheeks. Two tears leave two glittering trails in which the flames of the candles dance. 'Be brave, Rosalia,' she whispers. In the will there is a provision of ten thousand ducats for her.

Sophie, her beautiful daughter, is sobbing.

'We can sit her in the carriage and leave in the morning,' Olga says. 'The doctor will know how to fix that.'

Pavel Dimitrievich Kisielev paces the room in anger. Prussian bureaucracy can only be defeated by having someone set fire to all these German books and ledgers. The special permission to take the body to Uman will not be issued before the prescribed period of ten days.

'Surely, my dear General,' Graf von Haefen says with a smirk, 'even in your mighty Russia there must be laws that cannot be broken at anyone's whim?'

Her body is lying on the table in the small room the French doctor had discovered behind the library, a secret Graf von Haefen pretends to know nothing about. Doctor Thomas Lafleur is bending over her, thinking that the tiled floors could be hosed down, and then the gutter around the room would take care of the water.

He has prepared the room already, covered the paintings with white shrouds, removed the collection of whips and the red ottoman. Now the room is bare, except for a tub filled with von Haefen's best brandy and two tables. The long one is for her body, the low, square one is for the instruments he would need: syringe, lancets, tubes, a blunt hook, horsehair and sweet grass.

He has done it before, of course. A military surgeon had to learn to embalm. The illustrious dead have to be preserved for the state funeral, for the long journey back home. They all did it, Larrey, Corvisart. Perfected the procedure, shortened the required time. Her body is lying in front of him, but the French doctor's thoughts drift toward Rosalia. He can't stop thinking of the rustle of her dress, the sounds of her heels on the floor.

There is not enough light in the room. The windows are too narrow and in November the sky is too dark. To offset it, he has ordered candles to be hung from the ceiling on a wooden plank. Now he lights them, one by one, filling the room with the smell of melting wax.

The blood that drained to the bottom of her body has coloured her back and shins purple. Death, the good doctor thinks, is the natural state of all creation. Resisting it, is another victory of hope against reason, for this resistance is the cause of all pain.

A gift for a gift, mon ami.

He is picking up the brass syringe that he has assembled just minutes before. He is checking if the piston, the valves, the barrel are firmly in place. With the syringe and the tube he flushes out her stomach and large intestine. Then he fills them up. As he is doing it, he recalls the ancient belief that while veins carried blood, the arteries transported spirits.

I trust you will know what to do with it.

Only then does he open her belly to excise the tumour. It has grown into her uterus, a mass of hard tissue, rich tawny red. It is entwined, there is no boundary between the tumour and its unwilling host. A growth that has fed itself on what was not meant for it at all. The French doctor is thinking that he was right not to touch it. He is thinking of the body defending itself, fighting for survival. There could be no compromise in this fight, no peace. It is either one or the other. And justice? Well, he is prepared to concede there is some justice in this war of the flesh. Cancer, when it wins, kills its host and destroys itself too.

For a moment he is tempted to make an incision along her chest, to expose the heart, to glance at what he remembers his teacher Corvisart called 'the evidence of life's emotions, the slate on which life engraves all our feelings.'

He doesn't do it.

His eyes cannot help registering the evidence of her illness. The hands so thin that he can see the ligaments through the skin. The body has been wasted by defence, starved. He cleans the cavity that he has just emptied of the tumorous mass. Then he powders it with oxychloride of mercury and stuffs it with horsehair.

This is not the way you will remember me, Doctor.

Her body is so light he can lift it without effort. When it is immersed in the tub filled with brandy, he pinches out the candles. Before she is dressed and made up, he will coat her cheeks and hands with a slightly tinted varnish, to give them some semblance of colour. More horsehair will go into her mouth to lift her sunken cheeks. She will have to be tied with ropes to the carriage seat. A hat will cover her eyes, glued fast.

The maids have prepared the travelling clothes. Olena is crossing herself, again and again. Her fingers when they touch her body are as careful as if this shrunken shell still smelling of brandy were made of gossamer and could be destroyed by one careless touch. The dress was one of her favourites: the dark blue one, with the black fur trim. Over it Marusya throws her favourite pelisse, lined with sable fur. Dressed and seated in the carriage, her face partially hidden behind a fan, Sophie is ready for her last deception.

The air in the Sophievka is frozen. The lake is one plain of snow, and even the cascades have stopped flowing. This garden of hers where orchids grow as if they were never taken away from the wilderness, where the spring will make petunias bloom, the offspring of that very first one she brought from England. This is a place of beauty where the pain, the despair, the ugliness that is spreading like cancer through this world can be forgotten.

For a moment she can still feel the pleasure of knowing that she moves through the snow-covered alleys without leaving a trace. Behind and ahead of her, the snow remains white and undisturbed.

* * *

The hall of Alfred von Haefen's palace is strewn with opened crates, piles of dishes, sacks of linen and clothes. Thomas is there, tripping on a braid of straw, but recovering himself right away.

Rosalia sits in the grand salon, with its now empty bed, staring into the fire. Her auburn hair shines in the glow of the flames.

'What will you do now?' he asks, still unsure of what he already hopes possible. She lifts her eyes slowly.

'I don't know yet,' she says.

Only a few weeks ago this America where he is going to seemed to her like the magnet mountain of her childhood stories, pulling nails out of ships, snatching anchors from the boards and knives from the sailors' pockets. Drawing pails, kettles, and pans from the ships' kitchens, leaving the sailors who resist its power on a wreck of floating wood. Now instead, she imagines the giant trees that remember the beginning of the world and people who do not bend their necks.

To stop the fire from dying, Thomas feeds it with a new log. The log is wet and the wood begins to sizzle when the flames touch it.

Where he saw desert, he now sees gardens. Seeds swell and break, seedlings poke through the earth, drinking up the light and water. They grow, thicken, become lush and vibrant. But then a voice in him warns it might all be an illusion, a wishful thought he should be laughing at. A mirage, the apparition of light, conjured up by a starved brain of a thirsty traveller in the desert.

But his joy will not go away. Like a bird it perches over him, preens itself, oblivious to the voice of doubt.

He stretches his hand over the flames. He covers Rosalia's hand with his, warm from the fire. He can feel it stir. In his mind images appear, possibilities he entertains with delight. The strength of Rosalia's arms around his neck, the sweet pressure of her lips. The persistence of hope still astonishes him, the power with which the past disappointments are blotted away. The foolishness of the human heart, he thinks, is, after all, its greatest strength.

He presses his lips to Rosalia's hand. She doesn't take it away.

'I love you,' he says and then he waits.

Three carriages stop at the Prussian border on a moonless November night, chilly and dripping wet. Two guards come out of the guardhouse, carrying lanterns and a big, black umbrella, slightly frayed on the edge. The heavy drops of rain splash on the tin lantern lids. Inside the first carriage, the guards see a Russian general, beside him a wetnurse who is rocking a baby in her arms. In the second carriage servants are squeezed in between crates, coffers, and shapeless bundles. It is the third carriage, however, that will make the guards talk long after the travellers have gone on their way. A lady, dressed in a heavy pelisse trimmed with fur, her face overshadowed by the trim of her hat, is flanked by two young women. Countess Sophie Potocka and her two daughters are going home, to their palace in Uman.

Countess Potocka, the guards are told in a curt manner, is indisposed. Thankfully, she has just fallen asleep and should not be disturbed.

The guards nod and carefully unfold the passports, making sure that the black umbrella is shielding the paper from the rain. The passports, bearing the signature of Tsar Alexander of Russia, allow the travellers to travel in Prussia and France. The guards salute and wave the carriages through.

It is only when they see the wheels of the last carriages disappearing into the darkness that the younger guard bursts out laughing.

'That,' he says wistfully, 'must have been a very good brandy.'

Historical Note

La belle Phanariote, Countess Sophie Potocka, died in Berlin on November 12, 1822. She was survived by two daughters and four sons.

Sophie's children led the lives of opposing allegiances, illustrating the complexity of the times and the conflicting political options of a country which had been partitioned, subjugated in its interests, and left to desperate measures.

Jan de Witt, Sophie's first-born son from her first (later annulled) marriage to Joseph de Witt, entered into the Tsar's secret service and gained notoriety for his dubious role in destroying the Decembrist movement and spying on the Polish resistance fighters. In 1831, after the Uprising of 1830 failed to liberate Poland from Russian dominance, he headed a Warsaw court that exercised the Tsar's revenge on the Polish patriots. Named the November Uprising, it was the first in a long line of Polish attempts to regain the lost independence of 1795. Jan de Witt died in 1840.

Alexander Potocki, the oldest of Sophie's sons by Felix Potocki, inherited her beloved garden, Sophievka. Influenced by his sister Sophie's patriotic feelings, he resigned his commission with the Tsarist army in spite of his excellent prospects and in 1830, joined the November Uprising. When it fell, and when a period of repressions began, Alexander refused to ask for the Tsar's pardon and chose to live in exile, mostly in Rome. Sophie's garden was confiscated by Tsar Nicolas I who had renamed it, *Tsaritsin Sad*, The Tsar's Orchard. Alexander died, childless, in 1868. He had never married.

Sophie Kisielev was instrumental in her brother Alexander's conversion into a Polish patriot, though she herself led a largely cosmopolitan life of privilege. She left her Russian husband and lived in France most of her life, winning big amounts of money in the casinos of Europe. Volodia died at the age of two. Later, Sophie Kisielev had a natural child, St-Claire, whom she officially 'adopted' and raised, but she never married again.

Olga married General Naryshkin and did not share Alexander's and Sophie's allegiance to the Polish cause. A few years after her mother's death, she had a love affair with Pavel Kisielev, her brother-in-law.

Mieczysław Potocki had left a peculiar trail of betrayals behind him. His first wife, Delphine Potocka née Komar, fled the Tulchin palace and demanded a separation, citing her husband's brutality and deviance as causes of her decision. Mieczysław then married again only to have his second wife accuse him of trying to murder their baby son, and he was then imprisoned for fraud and perjury in St Petersburg. In the end, after his sisters managed to obtain his release, he sold all his Russian assets and moved to France.

Bolesław (called Bobiche or Bob), fathered by Sophie's stepson Felix-George (called Yuri) lived a long and quiet life in Niemirów, in Ukraine, with his wife and daughter.

A Mademoiselle Romanowicz was one of the unknown beneficiaries of Sophie Potocka's last will. Like Ignacy Bolecki and Thomas Lafleur, she is a fictional character.

Acknowledgements

Dancing with Kings is a work of fiction. In writing it, however, I have depended on a number of historical sources, either for the basic facts of the story or the inspiration to disagree with their interpretations.

I have read many 18th and early 19th century memoirs, letters, and monographs that let me absorb the details and the voices of the times. There are too many to list here, but I would like to acknowledge all direct quotes.

My greatest debt goes to two books: Jerzy Łojek's riveting biography of Sophie Potocka (*née* Glavani), published in 1970: *Dzieje pięknej Bitynki (The Story of a Beautiful Bythinienne)*; and to Łojek's Polish translation of Charles Boscamp's manuscript *Mes Amours Intimes avec une Jeune Bythinienne*, presented to the last Polish King, Stanisław August Poniatowski, in 1789.

Jerzy Łojek's biography provided me with the basic facts of Sophie's story and her letters to Charles Boscamp, to Felix Potocki, and to her daughter Sophie Kisielev. Readers familiar with this book will notice that my interpretation of Sophie's character and personality differs significantly from Jerzy Łojek's.

Charles Boscamp's manuscript has lent its voice to the four italicized passages that proceed the four parts of the novel.

The fragment from Trepka's *Liber Chamorum* quoted to Sophie by Boscamp comes from Norman Davis's *God's Playground: A History of Poland.*

The conversation between Sophie and Emperor Joseph of Austria is based on *Secret Memoirs of Princess Lamballe.*

The song Thomas and Ignacy sing in the Berlin tavern comes from *Harriette Wilson's Memoirs Written by Herself.*

The lines of the Polish poem Ignacy recites to Thomas come from Adam Mickiewicz's *Oda do młodości (Ode to Youth).*

The translation of Suvorov's letter to Prince Potemkin comes from Simon Sebag Montefiore's *Prince of Princes: The Life of Potemkin.*

The last stanza of the poem that Count de Lagarde recites for Sophie is his own translation into French of *Sophievka*, a poem by Stanisław Trembecki.

Many people have helped me most generously in the writing of this novel and I would like to thank them all. My research into the history of medicine profited enormously from the generous and selfless help of the members of Listserev Caduceus, especially Eric Luft whose prompt responses to all my queries and help in verifying the accuracy of medical references were priceless. Any mistakes I have made are mine alone.

Shaena Lambert, Barbara Lambert, Janice Kulyk Keefer, Bethany Gibson, and my wonderful agent, Helen Heller, have read this novel in manuscript at its subsequent stages, offering insightful comments and invaluable encouragement. Without them and without the editorial assistance of HarperCollins editors, Susan Watt and Iris Tupholme, this book would not be the same.

I would also like to acknowledge the financial help of the Canada Council in funding the necessary research trips to Polish libraries and archives.

And, as always, for sustaining me over the years I've worked on this novel, to Zbyszek and Szymek Stachniak I owe thanks beyond words.

Lightning Source UK Ltd.
Milton Keynes UK
UKHW01f1148080618
323937UK00001B/10/P

9 780007 180455